HERONSMILL

A Country story of Little England beyond Wales

HERONSMILL
Roscoe Howells

NEW ENGLISH LIBRARY/TIMES MIRROR

For
Eric & Rhoda
My friends

First published in Great Britain in 1979 by
Hutchinson & Co. Ltd
© 1979 by Roscoe Howells

First NEL Paperback edition September 1980

NEL Books are published by
New English Library
Barnard's Inn, Holborn,
London EC1N 2JR.
Printed and bound in Great Britain by
©ollins, Glasgow

45004797 0

Contents

FAMILY TREE

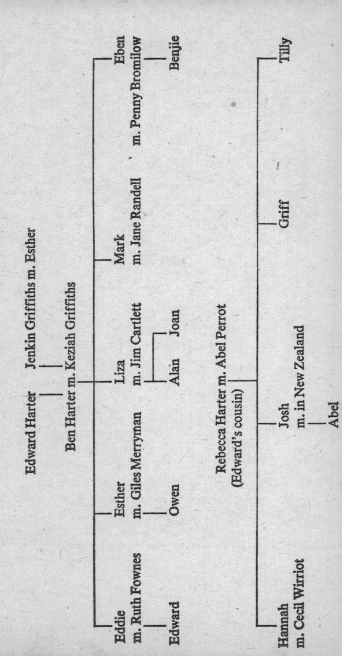

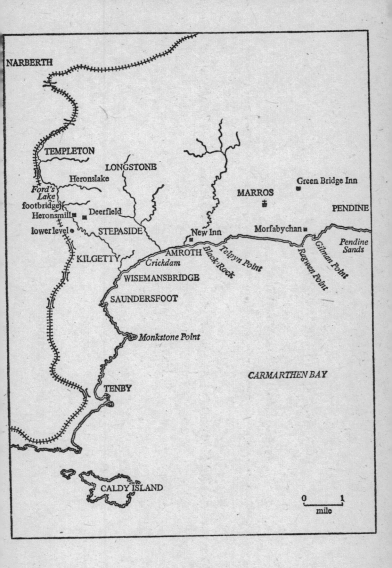

NARBERTH

TEMPLETON

LONGSTONE

Heronslake

Ford's Lake
footbridge
Heronsmill

lower level

STEPASIDE

KILGETTY

MARROS

Green Bridge Inn

PENDINE

Deerfield

New Inn

Morfabychan

Pendine Sands

AMROTH
Crickdam

Black-Rock

Telpyn Point

Ragwen Point

Gilman Point

WISEMANSBRIDGE

SAUNDERSFOOT

Monkstone Point

CARMARTHEN BAY

TENBY

CALDY ISLAND

0   1
mile

1

Heronsmill

You take my house when you do take the prop that doth sustain my house.

SHAKESPEARE,
The Merchant of Venice

There was fear as well as anger in Eben Harter's young heart as he clambered over the stone stile and ran down the lane for home. His tack boots kicked sparks from the cobbled track as he ran and their clatter disturbed the quiet of the Sunday afternoon, and small birds were startled from the hedgerows now thickening with spring growth.

He didn't care whether he would be in trouble for missing Sunday school. He just thought of the look in the eyes of the badger tugging helplessly with its front leg in the steel jaws of the gin-trap.

His brother Mark, a year older, had been ahead of him as they walked to Sunday school and had not heard the rattle of the chain. But Eben had heard it and had squeezed through a gap in the hazel saplings to investigate.

There was mud on the badger's white face and on its small white-tipped ears, and whoever had set the trap had deliberately set it for a fox or badger and not a rabbit, for there was a strong extra peg holding the end of the chain. In a circle around it the growth had been flattened and the soil churned up as the tormented creature had fought to drag itself free. But the steel jaws held firm. The leg bone was showing and there was blood congealed on its sodden paw.

By the time Eben had shouted to Mark he was out of earshot. For a moment he stood in the road wondering what to do. He thought to run after his brother but realized that even the two of them together would be helpless. Instead, he began to run for home, and it was for Gramfer he called as he came running down the lane.

He nearly cried with relief as he found Gramfer Jenkyn leaning on the farmyard gate smoking his pipe before going back to his corner by the big open fireplace for his Sunday afternoon nap.

'Gramfer, Gramfer, come quick. There's a badger in a trap.'

'Lord sowls, boy, I thought the place was on fire the way thou was't comin' hollin' an' shoutin'.' The old man took his short clay pipe from his mouth and spat.

'But Gramfer, he's in a trap an' his leg is broke an' he can't get from there an' he's all to clush.'

'All right, my honey. There be no need to be afeart. Where is he?'

'In the burgage up by Killa Mountain,' sobbed Eben.

11

'Right then,' said his gramfer turning towards the barn, 'we'd better get a pick an' a bit o' Stockholm tar. I don't suppose his leg is proper broke. They be tough chaps them badgers.'

'Ay he is, Gramfer, he's broke,' said Eben.

'How do'st thee know?'

'Thou ca'st see the bone.'

'That don't mean to say he's broke,' said the old man. 'If the bone isn't broke he might be all right.'

Comforted, the boy went with his gramfer as he looked behind the barn door for a pitchfork and reached up on the dusty wall-plate for an old tobacco tin, half-full of the black sticky paste which was always such a stand-by for injuries and wounds in the livestock. Then, close companions that they were, they set off up the lane, with Eben keeping up a steady flow of chatter as to how he had heard the chain rattling and how he had seen the badger and called for Mark and how Mark was gone and how frightened the badger was and so he had run to fetch Gramfer.

When at last they came to the trap, the old man put the tin on the ground and, taking the pitchfork, moved the two prongs quietly towards the back of the animal's bristled head and, with a deft movement, plunged them into the ground, one either side of the neck, to hold the head as in a vice firm to the ground. When he was satisfied that the head was secure, and that there was no danger from the badger's strong jaws, he said to the boy, 'Now then li'l man, catch holt here.' Then, putting Eben with his knees astride the badger's body, he said, 'An' howld hard now, for when I looses his leg he'll try an' go for us.'

Putting his boot on the top of the spring of the trap, and with one hand helping his grandson on the handle of the pitchfork, he pressed downwards with his foot and the badger writhed and struggled in its torment as the jaws of the trap eased open. When at last it was still, the old man took the injured leg in his hand, and with skilled touch gently moved the joint.

'No he haven't broke'n,' he said.

He smeared some of the black ointment on to the wound with a stick and, standing up at last and holding on to the pitchfork, said, 'Now then li'l man. Stand you back an' leave'n to me.'

Pulling the pitchfork quickly out of the ground, but holding it at arm's length, he had to nudge gently with the prongs to show the animal that it was free at last. Then, with a startled grunt, the badger whirled round and, dragging its injured fore-leg, shuffled away heavily into the undergrowth.

As the sound of its retreat died away, Gramfer Jenkyn looked down at the boy, winked and, putting his hand on his head, ran his fingers through the curly hair. Looking up and smiling, Eben said, 'How was he gwain to bite us when we loosed the trap?'

'Aw, boy, the pain. As them owld steel jaws comes open the pain is terrible an' he thinks we're causin' it.'

'Will he be all right?'

'Right?' echoed his gramfer. 'Right? Aye he'll be all right. Them badgers is the toughest buggers thou ca'st meet in a day's march. But don't tell thy mother what I said.'

Laughing at this dark secret, because Eben knew how Mam scolded Gramfer for his language sometimes, he said, 'What about Sunday school though, Gramfer?'

'Never thee mind about Sunday school.'

'But doesn't thee think Mam'll be cross?'

'No, I don't think she'll be cross. But if she is we'll tell her what the Saviour said.'

'An' what did the Saviour say?' enquired the boy.

'The Saviour hisself said, "If a' ass or a' ox falls into the pit on the sabbath day which of you will not straightway pull'n out?" That's what the Saviour said. But thou wou'sn't have to remind thy mother about that. She knows every word he said.'

As they walked back along the road towards the Mill Eben said, 'How do anybody want to catch a badger, Gramfer? Do they do any harm?'

'Why no, boy. Harm, no. 'Tis just as they got to be tor-mentin' an' killin'. There be a heap o' needless sufferin' in the world for animals an' people. Look at all the sufferin' for the sowldiers out fightin' the Kaiser, an' half of em' dyin afore they gets as far as that with the conditions they be livin' in.'

'I wonder what Mam will say.'

Eben loved his mother and nothing could be more important than what she thought. He loved his father too, but it was a love that was touched with fear because his father saw to it that all the children did their share of the work. That was Ben Harter's philosophy and work was his life.

When his trade as a miller had finally succumbed to the increasing tempo of the early twentieth century, Ben Harter had had to look elsewhere for a living and he had turned to farming because it was the only other trade he knew. How long his people had been at Heronsmill nobody could say. Certainly his father, Edward Harter, had been a miller there before him. So had his grandfather, old Walter Harter, who had lived to be over a hundred, which fact was recorded on the old stone in Ebenezer's cemetery.

Ben Harter knew much of the story himself and Eben was always glad when he would talk about it. But Gramfer knew even more and ever since the short time Eben could remember the old man had lived with them. Jenkyn Griffiths, blacksmith, he was, who had come down from the Welsh people in the north of the county and now lived with his daughter Keziah, who was Ben Harter's wife and Eben's mother, in the English-speaking south.

Gramfer Jenkyn had been gone so long from the Welsh parts that he had even lost his native accent. But he had not forgotten his younger days before he came south. In his youth he had ridden with Rebecca in the first Riots, and had even known the great Twm Carnabwth.

'Mind you,' he would say when they were around the fire of a winter's evening and he could be induced to talk about those days, 'Twm was a tidy enough sort of chap an' a lot of what was said about'n wasn't right. An' he packed it up after we'd had the gate down at Efailwen. It was them other buggers was the cause of most of the trouble an' never had no interest in the gates at all.'

'Stop that language now, Father,' Keziah would say. 'You knows I won't have it in front of the children. Sometimes I wonders how Mother ever put up with you.'

Then old Jenkyn would shake his head and wink at her and think back over the years.

Unable to stay at home as a boy on the family's own few acres of poor land near Maenclochog, he had been apprenticed as a blacksmith. When he was just out of his trade he went on the great annual outing to the seaside at Amroth Big Day, next village along the coast to Stepaside. And it was on this summer outing that Jenkyn had met Esther Nash.

Esther's father was already failing in health and Jenkyn moved in to help him in what was still a thriving blacksmith's trade at the Gangrel, standing on the bank within shouting distance of Heronsmill. It was at the Gangrel that Jenkyn and Esther raised their family and when the youngest of them, Keziah, married Ben Harter of Heronsmill she had only a short journey to make to her new home.

At that time the little hamlet was flourishing and most of the people were related. Except Jenkyn Griffiths, of course.

'About time there was a bit of fresh blood mixed with you buggers to improve the strain,' he would say when they gathered near his smithy. But he was liked because he was likeable and bore ill will to nobody, and he was respected because he was a craftsman without equal.

He thought of the community, too, and when he first joined them he was troubled to see the children from Rollin and even the farm at Killa Mountain drag long distances to carry water for their households. Eventually he persuaded old Merryman, the mason from Brandyback, to chip a well out of the rock-face by the side of the road where a spring had forced its way through. Jenkyn kept his tools sharp for him and when eventually the well became a reality it was later called 'Gramfer's Well' by the grateful young water-carriers whose task had been made lighter.

Eben had already begun to absorb something of the story of how the community had lived at that time when there was scarcely a job which needed doing which could not be done by one of their number.

Nearby there was work at Stepaside at the small ironworks and down the Lower Level pit.

From Stepaside the coal was carried in iron drams behind a squat steam engine, along a railway track which ran at the foot of the cliff and through three tunnels, to the harbour at Saundersfoot for shipment round the coast or overseas. Saundersfoot was a busy place with a pit of its own at Bon-villes Court, feeding good coal into the holds of the sailing ships that came into the harbour. So there was no lack of work for the various tradesmen at Heronsmill.

The mill itself was kept busy and the miller, whose fortunes fluctuated with those of the farming community, kept a tithe of the corn which was brought to be ground so that he was never short of flour for his own needs or those of his neighbours, and he always had plenty of oats for his stock.

'I can mind the time,' said Gramfer, 'when owld Watty had twenty donkeys here bringin' the corn back to folks after he'd milled it for 'em. He'd have the panniers slung over their backs an' they was busy all day long. Apart from a cow for the house an' a couple o' pigs he never had no animals about the place apart from the donkeys for fetchin' the corn to grind an' bringin' it back again after.'

The land at the mill was good and ran down to and alongside Ford's Lake. It was referred to as a Lake after the Pembrokeshire custom, although it was flowing water. Scarcely big enough to be a river yet it was something more than a mere stream. The land on the banks above the valley was poorer but the meadows were rich with lush grass. Where the 'lake' curled round them, hurrying beneath the trees and sparkling out again into the sunshine, to swirl here and there in deep, inviting pools, a heron would come in, deceptively fast, on great, silent and slow-moving wings, to stand patiently on one long, thin leg, watching and waiting, with head drawn well back between hunched shoulders, ready to strike at the speckled trout. The place was a favourite haunt of the herons and scarcely a day went by without their harsh call disturbing the stillness of the peaceful valley.

It was with the coming of the railway in the middle of the nineteenth century that the interests of this self-sufficient community had begun to decline. The railway brought with it from distant factories all manner of iron tools, new machinery and ready-made furniture. Jenkyn Griffiths had been too old to adapt himself to the repairing of the new machines for cutting hay and corn. Those who failed to see that they would lighten the toil of the people who remained on the land, thought only of losing their own meagre living as labourers with the scythe and sickle, and were tempted to come to him for iron bars to drive into the ground where they would wreck the machines that came to mow the hay or reap the corn.

'Don't be so damn dull,' he would say to them. 'It's no good grumbling and calling the things. Thou might'st just as well leave 'em be for if thou wou'sn't work with 'em there be plenty of other buggers as will.'

He was content to carry on shoeing horses, which were to survive for some time yet, and he had sufficient work to occupy him in his advancing years.

Ben Harter had taken over at Heronsmill when his father died in the early 1890s and he married Keziah Griffiths from the nearby Gangrel later the same year.

At first Ben Harter ran the mill as it had been run by his ancestors for generations before him. Soon, the arrival of three babies in quick succession meant that life became even more of a struggle. First came Eddie, named after Ben's father, and then the two girls, Esther, after Keziah's mother,

16

and Liza. Mark was born some years later in 1906 and Eben, the youngest of the family, was born in the spring of 1907.

As the Harter family grew, the income from the mill declined. Farming fortunes, however, began to improve almost imperceptibly, and Ben Harter turned more to farming for a living. As the neighbouring smallholdings became vacant on the departure of their tenants to seek their fortunes further afield, he acquired more land. Soon he became more of a farmer and part-time miller and, when Eben arrived, the transition was well-advanced. By the time Eben was ready to walk to school Ben Harter was a farmer and the mill was silent.

One of Eben's earliest memories was of a day in spring when the cold wind had given way to the first warm sunshine and he was coming back from the Gangrel where Aunty Becca had lived since Gramfer Jenkyn had come to live with them at Heronsmill. Coming down the bank he stood and listened and gazed far up into the limitless blue where a lark was pouring out a cascade of song.

Funny that, he thought, for Mam sang a song about the skylark sometimes, and it was a very sad song about a little boy whose mother had died and she was up there with the angels, and he wanted the skylark to carry a message to her, because the skylark was up so high he must be close to the angels where the little boy's mother was.

Eben was sad about the little boy in the song whose mother had died but he was glad it wasn't him and that his own Mam was home there waiting for him. And the lark today was obviously so happy about everything that Eben couldn't help but stand and listen to this exhilarating overture to the days of warmth and sunshine.

Eben never forgot the skylark that day, and the feeling of new life it aroused in him, which was to return on many occasions in future springs. As he ran, he delighted in the feel of his new clogs. From Uncle Tom Harter at Rushyland they'd come and were made from best sycamore.

By right, as his mother told him, he shouldn't have had them before starting school. But Mark had just had his to start school, and Eben would be starting after the summer, so he might as well have them now as long as he was a good boy and looked after them.

That was how it went with Mark and Eben. More often than not Eben had to have passed on to him what Mark had outgrown. It did not occur to Mark that Eben was unlucky only to have the cast-offs, because he was always completely absorbed in his own affairs. This was not really selfishness on his part, because whenever Eben had problems Mark would concern himself deeply although he did not share Eben's love for the creatures of the fields and woodlands. Mark was more interested in pulling things to pieces to see how they worked.

Gramfer Jenkyn was well up in his eighties and his black-smith's shop had long ceased to have any significance in the local pattern. But when there was a small job to be done he would 'make tracks all b'leejurs' for the Gangrel and get the old bellows wheezing away once again.

'Not too boisterous with'n,' he would say to the watching Eben, 'otherwise it'll blow'n out. Take a bit o' time and thee's'll have a tidy flam' in no time.'

That had been his brother Eddie's trouble. 'Pump like hell he would,' grumbled Gramfer, 'till the damn culm was skittin' all over the place.'

Then Eben would laugh with great glee, for Eddie was the hero. Eddie had been a legend before he was barely a youth, especially after the big fight, which had happened when Eben was still a baby.

Fear, to Eddie, was unknown. Not even Massa, as they called Trevor Midgelly, could frighten him, although when he had come to Stepaside school a reign of terror had begun. Mr Twyning was still the headmaster, and he had a deep sympathy for those from the poorer cottage homes. Now, however, he was getting on in years and the young Massa Midgelly was able to inflict brutality every day. Hatred of him had been building up for a long time and it erupted when Mr Twyning had to be away from school all one day to attend a funeral and Massa had the class of older children as well as his own.

Eddie sensed that there was going to be trouble. He didn't mind trouble, and he was not afraid of Massa, but he was determined not to give him the satisfaction of venting his temper on him.

That day Massa's brutality knew no bounds. He even caned poor Johnnie Wee Wee for wetting himself because he was too frightened to put up his hand to leave the room, and everybody knew he had to go a couple of times morning and afternoon – Johnnie Wee Wee, whose mother lived on the parish and was a widow with three small children who came to school when they had the clothes to wear, with their

18

hungry-looking eyes set deep in their pinched and frightened little faces. Their father had been killed by a runaway dram down the Lower Level pit and there was nobody now to fight their battles against the Midgellys of life. And this was the pitiful soul Midgelly had out to thrash in front of the school to make an example of him when Mr Twyning was away.

Eddie bowed his head at his desk in the corner and bit his lip rather than witness the terror in the eyes of the screaming child. 'Dear Jesus,' he whispered to himself, 'give the bastard some of his own back soon!'

Sensing that Eddie was restraining himself, Jimmy Cockles in the next desk started looking for trouble. At dinner time Jimmy went home, but Eddie was one of those who lived further away and came to school with some bread and cheese and a bottle of cold tea. Before they went into school for the afternoon, Eddie was waiting for Jimmy in the playground.

'You stop arsing about this afternoon, Cockles.'

'What's the matter, boy,' sneered Jimmy. 'Ar't thee afeart o' Massa?'

'I'm not afeart o' Massa nor thee, Cockles. An' any more from thee this afternoon an' I'll be waitin' for thee after school.'

'Arsehole,' said Jimmy, as Massa blew the whistle for them to stop playing and line up.

When the afternoon came to an end the whole school assembled for prayers and sang 'Now the day is over'.

Jimmy Cockles did not see Eddie in the playground, and they lived in opposite directions, so he looked surprised when he found Eddie waiting for him on the green.

'Now then, Cockles,' said Eddie, 'let's see who's afeart.'

'Don't be so dull,' said Jimmy. 'Cans't thee take a bit o' fun?' and made as if to edge past Eddie to carry on across the green.

The fight was over almost before it started, and, as Eddie pinned Jimmy to the ground, there was Midgelly standing behind them and saying, 'Get up, you two.'

'The sly sod,' thought Eddie as he got to his feet, wondering from where Massa had sprung.

'Back into school,' Midgelly snapped, and he walked behind them as they made their way across the green.

Eddie's heart was pounding as he said to himself, 'What's it gwain to be?'

So sudden had the action been that there were still children in the playground and these chance idlers were quick to gain suitable vantage points by the open door and on the bank from where they could see right into top class.

Inside the schoolroom, Midgelly went straight to business. Commanding them to stand before Mr Twyning's desk, he went down to the far end of the big room to fetch his own cane. Then he came back and faced them. For one long moment he held the cane in front of him in his right hand, and with his left hand bent it into a bow. He looked down with a smile. But his trim moustache seemed to bristle.

Then, through tightly compressed lips, he almost spat at them, 'You will now be shown who is in charge here.' Fixing his eyes on Jimmy Cockles he rasped, 'You first Gittow,' – for such was Jimmy's name. His grandfather had sold cockles in the area for many years and the old man's donkey and panniers had not long departed from the village scene. 'Step forward.'

Jimmy shuffled forward.

'Hand out!' snarled Midgelly. And then the cane whistled down on to the palm of his outstretched hand.

Jimmy bit his lip and fought back the tears. Six he had. Then his tormentor said, 'Now the other hand.'

As in a dream, insensible with the burning sting of it, Jimmy held out his other hand stiffly and, the caning over, as he turned to go, Eddie winked at him. But Jimmy was so glad to get outside, and wring his hands and blow on them, and comfort himself by putting them under his armpits, that he missed a ringside view of the epic which so suddenly followed upon his exit.

'Now you, Harter.'

Eddie made no move.

'Did you hear me?' said Midgelly.

'Yes, sir.'

'Then hold your hand out.'

'No, sir,' replied Eddie.

'What d'you mean, "No, sir"?'

'You're not going to cane me because I haven't done nothing wrong.'

'Oh indeed,' he nodded. 'We haven't done nothing wrong, have we?'

'No, sir.'

For a moment Midgelly was tempted to hand out an impromptu grammar lesson. Instead, he sneered and, when at last he spoke, he only said, 'What do you call fighting in school?'

'I never fought in school,' said Eddie.

Annoyed at himself for giving the boy the chance to contradict him he said, 'We won't split hairs, Harter. You were fighting. And you will be caned.'

'Not by you,' said Eddie, becoming truculent. 'If I get to be caned I'll have it from Master when he comes back.'

Without warning Midgelly sprang at Eddie to catch him by the arm. But Eddie had expected it. At that time he had just turned fourteen and would be leaving school in a matter of weeks. Long hours he'd spent pumping the bellows for Gramfer Jenkyn and striking with the big hammer. He had started ploughing with the horses and could work alongside some of the men pitching in the hay-fields. And how to swing a blacksmith's hammer was not all that Gramfer Jenkyn had taught him. He was strong beyond his years.

In his younger days, before he 'came down from the Welsh', Jenkyn had been a fighter of the bare-knuckle school and had fought some good fights stripped to the waist on the slopes of the Preseli foothills. 'Nail the buggers,' he would say, 'afore they can move an' then, afore they knows what have hit 'em, on top of 'em an' finish 'em off.'

Eddie could hear the old man's voice even now: 'Watch his eyes an' keep yours open.' And he was ready to throw every punch the way Gramfer had taught him.

As Midgelly sprang, Eddie moved in, left foot forward, and drove his right fist flush into the teacher's mouth.

Midgelly staggered back and the fight was on. He put his hand up to his mouth but before he had time to know that three teeth had been loosened, or even for the blood to come, Eddie tore into him. A hard left to the solar plexus caused the man to drop his guard and Eddie followed it with a right cross that crashed him back against the desk.

Eddie was thankful for the advantage he had thus gained. Midgelly was a man against a boy and, once recovered from the first shock, he came back at Eddie with renewed venom. He made no attempt to strike but closed in a fierce hold that hurled them both back against the door of the open cupboard, tearing it off its hinges and bringing down a cascade of books, chalk and writing slates. As Eddie wrenched himself free, the man came after him and tripped over the pile of slates. Eddie knew from the desperation in the master's attempt to close in with a wrestling hold, that he had the upper hand of him. As Midgelly tripped, Eddie swung a right fist that caught him on the side of the jaw and stretched him in the corner behind the desk, banging his eye on the arm of Mr Twyning's chair as he fell.

Eddie was breathing heavily but he had hardly a mark on him apart from the blood where he had cut his knuckles on Midgelly's teeth. Exultant in the moment of victory he saw again the terror in Johnnie Wee Wee's face that morning, and he picked up the cane which Massa had dropped. As Midgelly struggled to his feet and came at him again, Eddie lashed him a fearful blow with the cane across the side of the face. The man cried out in agony and his hands flew upwards only for Eddie to drop the cane and rain a stream of blows on him until he collapsed in the corner from which he had just risen. But this time he made scarcely a move as he lay there groaning and whimpering.

Eddie spoke for the first time since it had started. Standing over the helpless teacher he said, 'Get up an' fight then.'

But Midgelly had had enough. Spitting blood from his broken teeth, one eye already closing, and an ugly gash across his cheek where the cane had cut him, he looked a wretched sight. On the floor lay an unopened stone jar of ink which had fallen from the wreckage of the cupboard and rolled across to where Eddie now stood. Flushed with excitement, he unscrewed the stopper and poured the entire contents over the prostrate teacher.

'And that's from Johnnie Wee Wee,' said Eddie.

Then he threw the overturned blackboard on top of him and walked out.

Afraid to speak to him in case they should be suspected of some sort of complicity, the witness children ran to spread the news round the village.

It was the custom at Heronsmill for the family to have their meal when the children came from school. Then the children would have their own particular jobs to do, Eddie helping with the milking and the girls feeding the calves and chickens and the pigs or doing something in the house. After that, in the spring and early summer, they would have to go into the garden for an hour or two or even in the fields to hoe swedes or turnips.

That day they were all late, even Esther and Liza. The girls had started for home before the fight with Jimmy Cockles, but news of it had caught up with them and they had run back in time to see Eddie's revenge on the teacher. They had watched from outside the school door, looking very frightened.

Eben, who in those days was just beginning to toddle, was holding on to a broomstick that stood by the back door. When he saw Eddie coming down the lane he took a few uncertain steps towards him and held out his hands to be picked up as usual and thrown high into the air. As Eddie bent to lift him, however, Eben saw blood on his brother's hands, and looking up wide-eyed, saw a new hardness in his face and a smudge of blood on his cheek.

Ben Harter and his wife and Gramfer Jenkyn were already at the table when the children arrived. Before Ben Harter could ask why they were late, Keziah had pushed back her chair and said, 'What have happened?'

'Oh, Mam,' blurted out Liza, 'Eddie been fightin'. He been fightin' Mr Midgelly.'

Ben Harter put down his cup, the big one with a bunch of roses on it, and looked hard at his son. Gramfer Jenkyn got up from the table and went over to his seat in the corner of the open fireplace.

Liza would have begun to pour out the story, but her father silenced her.

'Hisht, girl,' he said.

Their mother took Eben and sat him on her lap. The child sat silent and wide-eyed, gazing at Eddie.

'What happened?' his father said.

Haltingly at first, and then gathering confidence, Eddie told his story.

When he had finished, his father glanced at Gramfer Jenkyn sitting in the breast of the chimney, but the old man's face was inscrutable. All his attention had suddenly become riveted on a fly on the ceiling.

Ben Harter said, 'Why did'st thou bother to fight with Jimmy Cockles?'

Eddie said, 'He was askin' for it.'

'But you ought to have knowed, boy, them Cockles is all the same. Like a' owld moory hen – all wind and water.'

'I know,' said Eddie, 'but fair dos, he never jibbed when Massa gave'n the cane.'

'Why did'st thou fight with the teacher, Eddie?'

Eddie never answered.

'Thee'rt not afeart o' the cane?'

'No, Father. I've never been that.'

'Was it because o' Johnnie Wee Wee?'

'Yes it was.'

'I thought as much,' said his father. 'Thee'rt owld Gramfer Watty all over again.'

Then he walked slowly across the kitchen to where Eddie was standing and said, 'Has't thou ever read what it says on Gramfer Watty's headstone?'

'Yes, Father. It says "Blessed is he that considereth the poor. The Lord will deliver him in time of trouble."'

'All right then,' said Ben, putting his hand on his boy's shoulder, 'but don't go gettin' big ideas into thy head. An' remember there's always somebody who can hit harder than thee. So don't ever look for trouble. I'll go see Mr Twyning in the morning. Now get thy tea down an' out into the cowshed.'

What happened between his father and Mr Twyning was never talked about, but Eddie did not go back to school and at the end of term Midgelly was moved to Saundersfoot.

After the summer's haymaking Eddie went to work down the Lower Level pit. When it closed some of the men managed to get work in the pit at Bonvilles Court. The rest, mostly the younger ones, decided to try their luck 'up off', and Eddie went with them to the pit at Ammanford.

He was lucky. He found good lodgings with a family who had gone from Stepaside some years before, and it was one of their sons who told him of a vacancy for a blacksmith's butty underground.

In the summer Eddie would be coming home for a week's holiday, and Eben was thinking of the joy this would be for them, as Gramfer Jenkyn leaned on the bellows' wooden handle, polished to a smooth shine with generations of effort, and coaxed the coal-dust fire to a glow.

A set of horseshoes he was making that day, although he no longer shod horses for outsiders. But the two horses and the cob at the mill he knew and could trust. He had shod them all round before the spring work began, but it would be as well to be prepared in case any of them cast a shoe while they were busy on the land, or, later on, during haymaking.

As the old man chattered on, the child hung on every word, delighted because he could sense the jesting in it, yet knowing, too, that there must also be wisdom there. For Gramfer was very wise because he was old, and had seen so much.

When the iron was hot, Jenkyn Griffiths moved with easy assurance and said, 'Now, Eben, stand back over there, that's a man.'

Then he took the great tongs and, holding the white-hot iron on the anvil, hammered it round the toe midst many flying sparks to shape the horseshoe, whilst the bulging muscles in his forearms tightened like bunched whipcord. Thus the routine continued from the anvil back to the fire to heat the shoe again, and from the fire back to the anvil, tap-tapping with a ring on the anvil to get the balance, and then more sure blows to bring the completed shape a step nearer. Chewing a plug of twist as he worked, Gramfer occasionally spat a stream of tobacco juice to sizzle on the hot iron to see if it needed reheating. When he did this, the boy was in his seventh heaven of delight. If only he could spit like that.

As Gramfer worked, Eben thought of the day when the shoes would have to be put on. How he loved to see Captain put his great feet on the three-legged iron stand, and smell the burning hoof as Gramfer, with the horse's foot held firmly between his knees and the hot shoe held by a punch driven into one nail-hole, pressed it, smoking fiercely, into position. Then, when the shoes had been cooled, came the hammering, the turning back and closing of the nails where they protruded through the hoof, the rasping of the hoof to bring it in line with the shoe and, last of all, the dab on the hooves with the brush of harness-oil from the old tin, and Captain clip-clopping down the lane with himself perched on his withers and holding on to his mane for dear life.

Now as the craftsman finished each shoe, he plunged it, sizzling, with the tongs – a quick touching little plunge to start with – into the water in the stone trough where boys came to bathe their hands when they had warts to get rid of, and then hung all the shoes on the wall ready for when they would be needed.

The job finished, he took off his worn leather apron, hung it behind the door, put on his jacket, took his pipe from his waistcoat pocket and cut a plug of twist with a worn clasp knife to work between his calloused hands. This ritual completed, he took a piece of stick to the dying embers of his fire and applied himself to lighting his pipe. Then he eased his ancient bones on to a large block of wood that served as a seat outside the smithy door, and turned his attention at last to his small grandson.

The evening before there had been some talk in the house about the Rebecca Riots. Eben had heard Gramfer talk of this before. Now, out of the blue, he said:

'Gramfer. That Rebecca you was saying about last night –

was she anythin' to do with Aunty Becca?'

'No, no,' laughed his gramfer, 'nothin' at all. There wasn't no such person as Rebecca really.'

'Well, how cou'st thee ha' been with her if there wasn't no such person?'

Old Jenkyn looked at the boy, and then shook his head. 'Thee-rt mortal keen to know the how, where, why, when and what for, I'll warrant.' Then he said thoughtfully, 'I suppose thou wousn't give me no peace till I've towld thee, so I might as well tell thee now as best I can.'

For a while he gazed down the sheltered valley, where spring came early. The blackthorn was already in full bloom with a glory of white where it stood near the corner of the old smithy, and the blackbird was nesting there.

At last, almost as if he were talking to himself, Jenkyn Griffiths said, 'An' they blessed Rebecca an' said unto her, let thy seed possess the gates of those which hate them.'

Pressing the tip of his forefinger on the tobacco burning down in the bowl of his pipe, he sighed. 'What it was, the people was poor. They wasn't only poor, they was starvin'. I can mind some o' the childern. Only little bitties they was an' lookin' lear an' cranted. Then they built the workhouse an' poor people was tore from their homes to be starved an' ill-treated. I can mind one young chap with three small childern an' nothin' for 'em to yeat an' he set a gin for a rabbat. But they caught'n an' sent'n to Botany Bay an' took his wife an' childern off to the workhouse.'

Jenkyn paused then and pulled at his pipe which had gone out at last, but he didn't seem to notice, and Eben said, 'Where's Botany Bay, Gramfer?'

'It's over the ocean, son, an' they used to send criminals there.'

'An' did they send'n there just for snarin' a rabbat?'

'Why aye, boy. There was no mercy.'

'What happened then?'

'Oh, he was never heard tell of again. His wife died of a broken heart an' I never knowed what happened to the li'l childern.

'Times was main common after the wars with the Frenchmen. Then they started puttin' up the toll gates on the turnpike roads as they called 'em, an' nobody should go through the gate until he'd paid. Them as claimed the money was supposed to keep up the roads but they was always sayin' as they didn't have enough money. The big trouble came when the farmers had to fetch lime for to put on the land. Every gate they went through they had to pay more money. By the time they got the lime home it was costin' more than the worth of it.'

'Was't thee drivin' lime, Gramfer?' enquired the boy.

'No,' he said. 'I'd just gone to my trade with a' owld blacksmith name of Morris David. Not long after that they put up a gate at Efailwen and it was just when the lime season was startin' about May. The farmers said they was gwain to smash the gate an' that's what they done. They asked Morris David to go with 'em an' they was all customers of his so he didn't have much choice. They was gwain all dressed up in 'oomen's petticoats an' black on their faces so a couple o' us boys decided to go with 'em. Devilment it was more than anythin'. One o' the farmers was a big chap name o' Twm Rees of Carnabwth. A great fighter he was an' he taught me some o' the tricks as that brother o' thine used on Midgelly. He was so big they had a job to find a petticoat to fit'n. In the end they got one from big Rebecca as they called her who lived in Llangolman.

'Any road, we smashed the gate an' set the toll-house afire. They catched Morris David, but he got off because the toffs was gettin' afeart by now. They even sent for the Castlemartin Yeomanry as had fought the French at Fishguard an' here they was now fightin' agin us. After that they put up a chain instead of a gate at Efailwen but we smashed that lot up as well, an' that was the end of it.

'But in one o' the disturbances somebody called the leader Becca and what with that an' Twm Carnabwth wearin' owld Big Rebecca's petticoat or nightdress or whatever 'twas, the name got started. Then everythin' went quiet for a couple o' years till they smashed a gate up along St Clears an' they started a big caper about Rebecca's daughters possessin' the gate an' Lord knows what. But by that time all the scruffs in creation was gwain about threatenin' folks as they didn't like an' burnin' ricks o' corn an' terrorizin' folks in their beds at night.'

Suddenly Gramfer Jenkyn's face looked weary. He rose to his feet and said, 'Well, honey, this'll never make the babby a bonnat, so I reckon we'd better make tracks.'

'See Aunty Becca first.'

'Aye, all right, we'll see Aunty Becca. Better lock the door though.' And he shut first the bottom half of the smithy door and then, forefinger through the well-worn hole in the top half, with the finger crooked upwards, lifted the wooden latch inside, pulled the door to and then let the catch drop into position.

Rebecca Perrot had witnessed the interrogation outside the blacksmith's shop and knew the various stages in the ritual full well. By the time the pair's footsteps were heard coming over the cobbles to the door she had the kettle boiling on the ball fire and some plank cooks ready buttered. The iron baking plank was the one Jenkyn Griffiths had made for her mother not long after he had come to the Gangrel. A cousin of Ben Harter's, her husband had been killed down the Lower Level pit and had left behind four children with their young widowed mother.

She had lost her cottage, and old Jenkyn had given up the Gangrel to her, reckoning it was to be either that or the workhouse for the children.

As always he passed it off with a feigned jest.

'Lord sowls, maid,' he had said. 'What do a' owld man like me want with a house to myself? Cheaper for me to save the rent and go live with Keziah.'

But Becca knew that Keziah was already looking after her father and that he was well cared for. She knew how the old man valued his independence and what a wrench it would be for him to give up his home. She knew, too, how difficult his going to live at Heronsmill would make it for Keziah. But Keziah had said, 'The Lord relieveth the fatherless and widow'd. An' I still got my man, thank God, so isn't it up to me to help?'

By this and other means it was possible to help Rebecca in her struggle to keep a roof over her family. God and she alone knew how she did it but she managed to survive without having to ask for parish relief. A day here and a day there with some sewing when she could get it, and now and then a parcel of second-hand clothes for the children, which somehow she managed to alter so that they looked new, until the children were old enough at last to go out and fend for themselves and send a little home whenever they could.

Hannah was now twenty and working for a good family in Narberth. But Becca was not sure how long it would last, for Hannah had been keeping company with a young man who was working in the railway office there. He was living in lodgings, and came from a smallholding called Morfa Bychan, along the coast from Amroth, towards Pendine. Cecil Wyrriot his name was, and his father had come from near Heronsmill and 'married in' to Morfa Bychan.

The last time she had been home Hannah had been talking about Canada. Cecil, it seemed, was looking for something better, and seeing little future as things were, had written for details about emigration.

Becca did not need telling. Hannah's mind was made up, and now she was trying to break it to her mother as gently as she could.

'What do you think about it, Mam?' she asked eventually.

'What do I think about thee gwain to Canada?'

'I never said that.'

'That's all right, maid. Thou di'sn't have to,' said Becca, 'thou hasn't forgot I was young myself once, has't thee?'

Hannah's heart warmed to her mother as she thought of their years of poverty and struggle.

'I'll still send something,' she said.

Becca gave her a smile and said, 'Don't thee worry about that, maid. Thee's'll want all thy man can earn to set thyselves up. An' things is a good bit better here now with both the boys workin'.'

After a while Hannah said, 'But isn't Canada a long way to go and a long way from home?'

'The time and the place dunnat count, girl. It's the one who's there.'

'I'd follow'n to the ends of the earth,' said Hannah.

'Well, that's how it ought to be. Thy place is with thy man an' my prayers'll always be with thee.'

Then Hannah saw her mother's tears falling and she was in her arms and they were both crying.

'Well, there's a' owld fool I be,' said Becca at last, dabbing her eyes, and Hannah said, 'We'll be back one day.'

Becca gave Jenkyn Griffiths the news of Hannah as he poured his tea in his saucer and then blew on it. Eben was more immediately interested in the fresh-baked and buttered plank cooks.

When he had heard the story, Jenkyn put down the empty saucer and placed the cup back on it and then he said, 'Well, maid, now's the time for 'em to go if they're gwain. There be nothin' in the wide world home here for 'em.'

At last the tone of the conversation reached Eben. Licking the buttered crumbs from his lips, and wiping the back of a chubby hand across his mouth he said, 'Where's Canada, Gramfer?'

'On it's right th'other side of the world, boy.'

'Th'other side of the world?'

'Aye, miles an' miles across th'ocean.'

'How big is the world then?'

'Oh, it's a big owld place altogether, boy,' said the old man.

Eben considered the seriousness of it and, having decided that it was beyond him for the moment, came back to the more immediate problem and asked, 'When'll Hannah be coming back?'

Becca started moving cups and saucers about on the dresser so that the boy could not see her face.

Gramfer said, 'Oh, I 'spects she'll be home afore long.'

Well, that wasn't so bad then, thought Eben. He was fond of Hannah. Most times when she came home she remembered the children at the mill, as well as her own brothers and sisters, and brought them a bag of peppermints with great brown and white stripes. You could go on and on sucking them and they'd last for ever and ever.

Darker than the Harters with her laughing brown eyes, Hannah was a Perrot for sure by her colouring, but she had the Harters' broad forehead and resolute chin. A good-looking girl was Hannah with her wavy hair held back by a ribbon, and good, strong teeth that would flash a smile to match the sparkle of her eyes. Whoever this Cecil Wyrriot might be, he was a lucky man.

She was not without her misgivings about leaving her mother but, as Becca had said, the boys were working now and they were good to her. Joshua was nineteen. He had learned his trade as a mason and now had gone to Cardiff where he was getting on well. Whenever he wrote he sent something for the purse, and at Christmas when he had come home he had put two golden sovereigns into his mother's hand.

Griff was sixteen. For two years he had stayed on the farm at Tregant and hated every minute of it. He didn't mind the work but he hated the people. The only thing in its favour was that he was able to come home at nights. Now he had gone 'up line' to London itself, to work in a London dairy, milking cows. And nobody worried about Griff. If anyone came up smiling he would, and never would his mother want for anything as long as Griff had a shilling.

So that only left Tilly, and she was eleven now, so it would not be long before she could be earning as well. It was a train of thought which made Hannah feel easier in her mind.

Next time she came home Cecil Wyrriot came with her. Rebecca took one look at him and knew that she need never have doubted Hannah's judgement.

The same day there was a letter from Josh to say he was coming home for a few days and he had sounded excited.

When he came, the cause of the excitement was soon evident. In a fortnight's time he was sailing for New Zealand with a carpenter who had landed a wonderful job out there for the pair of them and it was too good a chance to miss. How could Becca do anything else but try to share his excitement for his sake although her heart was breaking? As old Jenkyn had said, there was nothing there for the young people at home any longer.

So Josh sailed for New Zealand and, before the year was out, Hannah and her Cecil Wyrriot were on the seas for Canada.

Hannah looked radiant on her wedding day. Her costume was light blue, with gold and silver brocade down the edges and the lapels and sides of the knee-length coat. Shining black shoes peeped beneath the hem of her new skirt. The white silk blouse had a ruff at the throat and, just below, Hannah wore a brooch of thin gold with two hearts intertwined, which Cecil had given her for the occasion.

Never, thought Eben, had she looked more beautiful. A year previously he had declared his intention of marrying Hannah himself, but if she was set on this business of going to Canada he couldn't see much point in it.

All the men wore high, hard white collars and this had caused some argument on Gramfer Jenkyn's part. He couldn't remember when he had last worn a collar and he thought a muffler over his flannel shirt would be adequate for an old man of his age.

But Keziah had remained quite resolute. 'God drabbit,' the old man said, 'look at us. Like a lot of bloody donkeys lookin' over white-washed walls.'

'Father!' whispered Keziah quickly and firmly as they had gone into chapel, 'that's enough.'

Now, at last, it was all over. Cecil, through his job with the Great Western Railway, had been able to get passages for them on a cargo boat from Fishguard. Hannah had placed her bouquet on her father's grave and now, following a meal, they were ready for the walk to Kilgetty station. Ben Harter had taken their tin trunks on ahead with Dandy, the smart-stepping Welsh cob, in the spring cart.

The day before the wedding Keziah had gone over to the Gangrel with her present for Hannah. It was a new Bible and on the fly-leaf she had written in her slow, round hand, 'I will not fail thee, nor forsake thee.' Hannah knew now that she would want all the faith she could find and there was the best part of half an hour to wait before the train was due. Gramfer Jenkyn, however, had no intention of allowing the time to hang heavy. With the assistance of young Griff, home from London for this great occasion, he soon had things organized and, as 'the only proper Welshman' there, assumed the responsibility as conductor of a hastily-formed station choir. Neither he nor Griff moved far from Becca, who had gone through the day as one in a dream. What it was costing her now to put on a brave face nobody could ever know.

Jenkyn had started the performance with a rendering, in a remarkably firm voice for one of his great age, and of the only couple of verses he could remember in the Welsh of his youth of 'Mochyn Du'. But now they had passed through a happy series of lively tunes until they were on to the familiar Sankey and were suddenly embarked on:

'God be with you 'till we meet again,
By his counsels guide, uphold you . . .'

Here the choir failed somewhat, but, as they harmonized the last chorus, the smoke of the engine was seen pushing up over the fields which hid Saundersfoot station from their view, and then, the train was rounding the distant bend and breasting the gradient up the straight for Kilgetty and all was at once great stir and excitement. Becca and Hannah were in each other's arms and clinging to one another, the last carriage door clanged shut, the blast of the guard's whistle pronounced the finality of the occasion, and there was the train gathering speed around the long bend towards Templeton and Hannah's handkerchief fluttering through the carriage window and the guard's van disappearing from view. At last Becca let out a great sob and her tears could be contained no longer.

Much as Eben loved the spring and summer, with its rich life in field and hedgerow, he loved the winter nights too. This winter it was better than ever, for when Eddie had been home in the summer he had said if some of the colliers he knew could have two pianos then it was a pity if his own family couldn't have one. Esther had been doing some sewing for old Mrs Twyning and, when it had come time to pay, the schoolmaster's wife was surprised when the girl said would she perhaps give her some music lessons instead. The old lady was delighted, but Ben Harter was not so pleased. He couldn't see the call for it, getting ideas about things that wouldn't put anything either in the purse or in the larder. Keziah, however, had seen to it as always and smoothed the path. Now, when Eddie said the girl couldn't expect to learn if she didn't have a chance to practise and he was going to see about getting her a piano, Ben Harter said, 'All right, boy. I'll come with thee.'

So it was that next day, which was Narberth market day, Dandy was harnessed and off she went with the pair of them in the trap and Eben sitting between them.

Ben Harter tied the cob in Market Square and called to a boy he knew to keep an eye on her. He ordered some groceries for Keziah, talked to some of the farmers he knew, and then said to Eddie, 'Now then, boy, let's see what they got to say about it.'

His broad frame and stout, gaitered legs looked somewhat out-of-place amidst the music stands and the stools and a couple of fragile-looking bentwood chairs.

Without any preamble he said to the thin little man who fluttered round him like a moth round the table lamp, 'I wants to buy a piana.'

'Oh yes, sir. And may I say, sir, you couldn't have come to a better place. We do indeed pride ourselves on the quality of our merchandise, supplying the gentry and all the very best musicians in the area.'

'Right, then, well about this piana then.'

Seeing the need for more direct business talk, Mr Theodore Simpson, for such the name over the shop had proclaimed him to be, said, 'Well now, sir, what sort would you like?'

'Well, we wants a good 'un, don't we?' said Ben, turning to Eddie. But, like his father, Eddie didn't reckon to know much about pianos either. So he just said, 'Oh yes, we wants a good 'un.'

'It's for my eldest maid,' said Ben with an air of some pride. 'The schoolmaster's wife says as she've got a good idea of it an' so I should think she better have somethin' tidy.'

'Quite so, sir. Quite so, indeed,' said Mr Simpson.

What he had to show Ben Harter, however, did not measure up to what Ben Harter thought a good piano should be, and Eddie said that some of the colliers he knew were getting some very smart pianos indeed.

At length Ben noticed an instrument in light-coloured wood

inlaid with a nice pattern of climbing roses and with two ornate candle-holders on either side of the music-rack. He could just see Esther's face when it arrived.

'How much is thicky?' he said.

'Well that piano is fifteen pounds, sir,' said Mr Simpson, 'but I'm afraid that is one I've ordered specially for a customer.'

Ben Harter dug deep into his inside pocket and drew out a leather bag with a tape around the neck and counted out fifteen golden sovereigns. Putting them on the counter he said to the agitated Mr Simpson, 'Now thee's ha' better order another one for thy customer for I'll be comin' to fetch thicky tomorrow if 'tis fine. So if thou's'll just be good enough to make me out a bit of a receipt I'll be makin' tracks for home.'

As Dandy slowed down to a walk to take the long hill outside the town, Eddie broached the subject of paying for the piano. His father said, 'Thee'rt not payin' for nothin'. Look after thy money the same as I've always done so that thee ca'st do somethin' for thy own childern when the time comes.'

Eddie was inclined to argue, but, closing one eye, his father said to him, 'Look here, boy, thou hasn't got Midgelly to deal with now, mind.'

After a long and thoughtful silence, Eddie suddenly asked, 'Father, what happened about that?'

'What happened about what, boy?'

'What happened,' said Eddie, 'when you went to see Mr Twyning?'

Ben Harter thought for a while, then he took off his high billycock hat, rising almost to a point at the crown, to wipe his brow with a large red and white handkerchief, and said, 'Well, I suppose I can tell thee, boy, if thee's 'ud really like to know.'

'Of course I'd like to know,' said Eddie.

'All right then,' his father said, 'I'll tell thee. I paid Midgelly ten sovereigns for'n to agree not to summons thee, for if he'd done that, Lord only knows what might ha' happened.'

Eddie looked at his father dumbfounded.

'That's all right, boy,' said his father, 'thou nee'sn't look at me like that. 'Twas money well spent.'

'What d'you mean?' asked Eddie.

'Well,' his father said, 'what sort of life would it ha' been for the girls and young Mark and Eben to go through their schoolin' with a tack like that poundin' an' flakin' 'em?'

'Well by damn!' said his son.

By the time winter came Esther was able to learn tunes

herself and the old house at Heronsmill had never known such gatherings. It was mostly Sankey, for these were the hymns they could sing together. One by one Esther added the well-loved favourites to her repertoire and soon found that she could keep the tune going well enough for them to be able to sing with her.

Saturday became the night for these sessions and then Mark and Eben were able to stay up later. Becca came down from the Gangrel and Tilly came with her. Only Tilly was left at home now that Hannah and Josh were over the ocean and Griff was in London. A nice little voice Tilly had, and Becca was there with her firm alto and always 'right in the middle of the note and no messin' ', as Gramfer Jenkyn said. A keen ear the old man had and was good on the harmony, and Keziah took after him. Ben Harter had a useful bit of bass when he'd let it go, and he enjoyed the singing as much as anybody.

There were always fresh candles in the holders on the piano these evenings and the brackets were swung out on their hinges to throw light on to the music. On the oak table, on a lace mat crocheted by Keziah when she was a girl, stood the best lamp. And a handsome lamp it was, given to her for a wedding present by the Sunday school where she had a young class before she married and which she continued to teach until Eddie was born.

Lighting the lamp was the big event for Eben. Mam would stand by him, as he stood on a chair pulled out from the table, and let him strike the match and put it to the wick in the double burner. Then she would make sure it was turned low enough before, very carefully, putting on the globe followed by the big shade. Then, at last, when the steam had cleared from the glass and she was satisfied it was warm enough, up would go the wick and the whole room would be flooded with light, with a clear beam somehow always seeming to fall just over the mantelpiece where there hung the framed embroidered text, 'I will not fail thee, nor forsake thee', the same as Mam had written in Hannah's Bible. And in the bottom corner was embroidered, in silk of another colour, 'Josh. 1:5', which seemed to give it an air of great authority and authenticity. It also made Eben wonder sometimes how Josh and Hannah were getting on so far away.

They were getting ready for the Harvest Festival once again at Ebenezer Chapel when Gramfer and Eben came with their big surprise. It was a marrow. Not just any old marrow, but the most special marrow that had even been sent to Harvest Thanksgiving. Gramfer said so, and Gramfer knew. The old man was surprised that Eben had been able to keep the secret, especially this last couple of weeks when he'd been bursting to tell. But Gramfer had tried hard to keep a careful guard on his young, prattling tongue, and Mark was about his own devices and knew nothing of the big secret.

It was in the spring that it had all started, when Mark was in school and Eben had been so much with the old man. Jenkyn told Ben Harter what they were doing, so there was no fear of disturbance of the old heap of farmyard manure which stood in the sunny corner behind the calves' cot. They had fetched some soil 'tobegether', as Eben called it, in the wheelbarrow and put it on top of the miskin, as the manure heap was called.

Ben Harter brought a few marrow seeds from Narberth and these the old man and the boy planted together in a small box, with great secrecy, after the manner of all true conspirators. Each day the watch was kept and at last a spike, and then another, forced their way up through the soil towards the light. Then came the leaves, and at last Gramfer said it was time to put the plants off.

The next step was to put some lime round them to stop the slugs, and then some blackthorn bushes round the miskin itself to stop the ducks and the geese.

'That scaddly owld lot,' said Gramfer, 'would put paid to 'em afore a man got time to look about, but I'll warrant they won't be keen to push their heads through thicky bushes.'

And so it proved as the plants grew apace. Then, at last, came the first marrows and, when one of the most promising of them had grown to half a dozen inches or so, Gramfer said, 'Now then li'l man, the time have come.'

He was no great scholar and he didn't intend to take any chances, so, first of all, on a piece of paper he wrote *Ebenezer*.

Then, with Eben holding the paper for him, the old man took a pin and, with infinite care, scratched the letters on the marrow. Wide-eyed with wonder Eben watched until, at last, the job completed to his satisfaction, Gramber straightened up and said, 'There it is, boy. Now all we got to do is wait and watch and by the time it comes Harvest Festival them letters'll be as big as the marrow. But mind you, honey, not a mewk to a soul.'

Next day Eben was out to see how much the letters had

grown and was disappointed to see no difference. Eventually he lost interest and then, at last, he could see the letters growing. All through the summer as the marrow grew, so the letters grew too until, by the time of Harvest Thanksgiving, as Gramfer had said, *Ebenezer* was emblazoned across it like a great banner.

So it was at last, as Keziah busied herself with her final preparations for Harvest Thanksgiving, that Gramfer winked at Eben, and they tip-toed out to their corner behind the calves' cot where the old man opened his great clasp-knife and, watching over him carefully, let the child cut the marrow himself. It was so big that Jenkyn carried it until they came nearly to the door of the house, and then he handed it over to the enfolding little arms. Holding his prize tightly to his body, with his arms in front of him, Eben walked quietly into the kitchen. Keziah saw him, and after a puzzled smile, said, 'What'st thee got there, my pet?'

Saying nothing, Eben let his mother take it from him and watched her as she looked at the marrow with the great letters spelled out across it. Then she said, 'Where di'st thee get this?'

'We grow'd'n for you,' said Eben.

Keziah looked at her father and back to her child, then she put the marrow on the table and swept Eben up into her arms to smother him with kisses and laughter.

'Is it good, Mam?' asked Eben.

'Good! My dear soul, it's the finest marrow I ever seen!'

'Indeed, Mam?'

'My darling,' said Keziah, 'there be no need to say indeed. For the Lord said, "Let your communication be yea, yea; nay, nay for whatsoever be more than these cometh of evil." But it's a lovely marrow, my darlin', so come an' give your mother another big kiss.'

That year Eben really felt he was part of the Harvest Thanksgiving. There *it* was, right at the front of the table under the pulpit, and the chapel had never looked better. The seats and the stained boarding round the pulpit had been polished till they shone and everywhere was evidence of the abundant harvest. Sheaves of oats and wheat were surrounded by dishes of apples and pears, beetroot, carrots and parsnips. And from every house the very best dishes had been sent to hold the offerings of thanks. There was honey and there were pots of home-made jam, and there were butter and eggs in baskets lined with the best white linen cloths, and there were potatoes and swedes and turnips along with two fine hanks of onions, some rhubarb and a few blue bullet-hard pickling cabbages. Everything with which the Lord had blessed the community was acknowledged by its very presence. There was a glass of water and Aunty Becca had offered a lump of coal.

As she said, 'It have cost some of us dear, but that isn't the fault of the good Lord who have gave it to us.'

Either side of the pulpit the great paraffin lamps with their white shades swung out on curved brackets and spilled a cascade of soft light over the polish and shine of the well-cleaned produce. And, in the middle of it all, catching and returning stabs of light from many different angles, was Eben's marrow. This, he felt, was a great occasion.

In May month there had been the turning out of the two calves that had been in the cot since they were born during the winter. Rather a special day it seemed. Eben had a feeling of the grass growing, and of everything astir and quick with life. Then there had been the spectacle of his father not hurrying back to his work in the field, but pausing to lean on the gate and chuckle as the calves sniffed cautiously at every fresh-discovered object. In their new surroundings, and in the unaccustomed daylight, they dug their feet in four-square and then galloped off, heads high and tails outstretched behind them, until Mam, who had also come to watch this annual bit of excitement, put her hand to her mouth and gasped for fear they would do themselves some harm. But they never did, and Ben Harter said, 'A bit o' luck an' they'll make a couple o' good cows by an' by.'

He needed good cows, too. First of all there had been a run of bull calves, so that there were no heifers coming on to take the place of older cows that had to go, and then a cow had 'thrown her calf' so she had been fattened off and sold to the butcher.

'There be no profit in sendin' a cow to the budger,' he said, 'but what's a body to do?'

It was because of the abortion that Ben Harter eventually decided to buy a goat. The first hint of it had been there that spring, when Eben had watched with him as the two calves had been turned out to grass with all their promise for the future. The following year all eight of his cows and two in-calf heifers aborted. Not one of them carried her calf full-time and he knew that the disease had struck.

In their many talks about their misfortune, Gramfer had

spoken of the benefit of running a goat with the cows to prevent abortion, and Keziah, trying hard not to show how desperate she felt, said, 'How doesn't thee try it, Ben? It can't do no harm.'

'Well, aye, aye,' said Ben, 'we can try anythin'.'

So it was that Ben Harter decided to go to see George Wyrriot at Morfa Bychan, and Keziah wrote in her slow but firm round hand to say he would be coming on the Saturday of the following week.

Eben was seven now and walking to school with Mark and the two girls every day. It was early summer and there were birds' nests to be looked for. The girls had already gone on ahead.

'Come on,' said Mark, 'you're like Gramfer says – come day, go day, God send Sunday.'

'There's a' apple-bird's nest up there in the thorn bush.'

'Climb thee up there an' you'll tear th'arse out of your trousers.'

'I only wants to look at the eggs. I don't want to take 'em.'

'You'll still tear th'arse out of thy trousers and Mam got enough trouble already.'

'Gaw, you're talking big. Anybody'd think you was the Kaiser hisself.'

'Kaiser or not,' said Mark, 'if you tears th'arse out of your trousers you won't be able to go with me and Father to Morfa Bychan on Saturday.'

On his way from school on the Friday evening, Eben picked a small bunch of primroses and ran in with them to Keziah saying, 'Here y'are, Mam, I've took thee a bunch of summer blossoms so thou ca'st have somethin' to remember us when we be gone tomorrow.'

With a light in her eyes that had not been much in evidence of late, she bent down and hugged her youngest boy, and then fetched from the old oak dresser a pretty patterned cup in which to place the flowers.

Tea finished, the boys needed no bidding to be out and about and looking for jobs which they might do, so that they could get away early in the morning. Long after they had gone to bed, too excited to sleep for a time, Gramfer Jenkyn was out in the stable grooming Dandy, plaiting her mane and tail, and, with the curry comb, removing the last faint remnants of her winter coat so that once again the gloss of her rich bay colouring proclaimed her fitness; the white blaze on her forehead completed a handsome picture. And, as if this were not enough, he was out betimes in the morning to go over it all again, and comb out her mane and tail to ensure that she looked her sprightly best.

Once out on to the road, Dandy broke into a trot, lifting her forelegs in a smooth, easy action, and was away, past Rollin and Dianah, both now empty and forlorn-looking, before easing to a brisk walk up the sharp pinch round the bend above Gramfer's Well. Then she was away again by Killa Mountain and round by the sweep of the stone wall that hid much of the house at Deerfield from the road, and down the hill by the school to the village.

The road from Stepaside to Wiseman's Bridge ran through Pleasant Valley alongside the courses, as the rush meadows were called, and Ben Harter passed the shell of the old iron-works on the way, to have a quick look at a couple of steers which young Billy Seckerson of Light-a-pipe had offered him. From there he took the road that climbed eastwards up a winding steady pull towards Green Plains and out towards Summerhill above Amroth. As Dandy settled into a walking pace he slackened his hold on the reins and said, 'Now then, men, who wants the lines?'

'I do,' the two boys shouted together.

'Oldest first,' said Ben. 'Mark from here to Summerhill and Eben after we gets out of Amroth up the long hill.'

'How long is the hill out o' Amroth, Father?' enquired Eben.

'About ten times as long as thicky.'

'Ha, ha,' crowed Eben, but Mark was content with the pleasure of the moment as he took the reins very carefully from his father and sat very straight, with his hands held in front of him, and resting the weight of the reins gently on Dandy's quarters.

Along the hedgerows, the orange-tipped butterflies were already on the wing and the dandelions were turning to clocks that could be blown upon to tell what time it was. Where the grass was growing it was beginning to hide the primroses, and the campion and bluebells were now combining to form a patterned carpet of rich beauty. Here and there the fern was bursting in curls out of the ground and Ben Harter said, 'Watch for thicky fern and that'll tell thee when the grass is growin'. Once thou ca'st see that fern curlin' out o' the ground then thou ca'st say that things is movin'.'

When they reached Summerhill Mark passed the reins back

to his father with a satisfied smile and they were soon on the steep descent down into Amroth, with Dandy holding back against the breeching, and the shafts pushing on in front of the collar.

Halfway down the hill they entered an avenue of great trees, which met overhead to form a cool, shady tunnel from which Dandy and her passengers emerged to find themselves looking down on the village sheltering in a deep valley which opened on to a stretch of golden sands. As the boys took in the view before them their father showed them where the sandbanks had been before they were washed away in the great storm, so that now the tide came right up to the boundary of the cottage gardens. But to look at the sea today was to find it difficult to believe that it could ever be lashed into such a fury as the Amroth people had often witnessed. At low water on spring tides, Ben Harter told them, there could still be seen the remains of a forest which had been submerged when the tide had rushed in and swallowed everything in its path. He had himself many times picked up bunches of decaying nuts, and years ago his grandfather had dug up the antlers and skull of a stag at low water between Amroth and Wiseman's Bridge when he had been digging slime for making balls for the fire. Today, however, the tide lapped in long lazy white ribbons that broke their length in places and then finally joined forces again to lay themselves down gently on the firm sand. Out in the bay the tide was running steadily westwards and the sun's rays danced on the water in a thousand glancing patterns as the breeze darted here and there to chase ripples across its surface.

'They reckons down here that it be a good sign to see the tide runnin' down from Telpyn like that,' observed Ben Harter.

'Where's Telpyn?' asked Eben.

'There it be,' said his father, pointing across the sands. 'Telpyn is the second point thou ca's't see. Black Rock be the first an' then Telpyn an' way on after that is Ragwen. An' Morfa Bychan is round the corner behind that, an' that's where we be headin' for.'

'How far is it, Father?' asked Mark now that he had had his first turn at the reins and was anxious for new developments.

'Well, I reckons it be fower or five miles,' said his father.

Through Amroth, Ben Harter gave Dandy her head to go at a smart trot. There was no harm in letting them see how a good cob should move, because they were known not to think over-highly of the Stepaside folks.

Beyond the village green, where the road led out of the village, they had to pass The Hermitage, a smallholding where Dipper Treluggan never missed much of what was going on. His people had come from Cornwall years before in one of the coastal trading vessels. There wasn't a bit of wreck ever came in that he wasn't the first to get to, and a dozen times a day he would be out to the beach to see what was in the offing. He had got his nickname, Dipper, when he went in too far in his excitement for a fine baulk of timber, lost his balance on the pebbles when a wave came in further than he had anticipated, and had a winter's dip for which he had not bargained. Nor did poaching come amiss to him. His trade, in fact, was anything that could avoid an honest day's work.

By the time Dandy had reached The Hermitage gateway, Dipper was standing in the road for all the world as though he was there by the merest chance. And standing in such a way as if the one thing in the world he wanted to do was to exchange greetings.

Ben Harter reined Dandy to a halt, pulled up alongside Treluggan, and said, 'How beest thee gwain here?'

'Aw, middlin',' said Dipper, 'can't complain.'

'Nice bit o' weather we be havin'.'

'Aye, aye, not so bad at all. But I'm thinkin' by the way the tide is runnin' down from Telpyn we're in for a tidy spell of it an' we'll be wantin' rain afore we be done with it.'

'Aye, boy. True enough,' said Ben, 'we canna go long without a drop o' rain this time o' year.'

'No indeed, we canna go long without it.'

There followed a brief pause whilst Dandy fidgeted and Ben Harter peaced her and Dipper switched his ground.

'Thee'rt out early this mornin',' he said.

'Oh, I'd'n'know,' replied Ben cautiously, 'I wouldn' say it was early like that.'

'No, boy, so it ben't, but thou must ha' made a' early start.'

'No, not like that,' persisted Ben, 'we got a useful cob here and she can pick 'em up a bit.'

'Aye, boy,' admitted Dipper, 'I seen her comin' along. A smart li'l mare she be.' And then, as a sweetener, he added, 'I reckon she be as smart a li'l mare as a body might see anywhere in the rounds.'

'Aye, boy, I think she be,' agreed Ben, without being fooled.

'Aye,' echoed Dipper, 'she be a smart li'l mare.' And then, more directly, 'You be gwain far then?'

'No, not far. Not like that.'

'Aw, an' how be the cows milkin' with thee?' asked Dipper with a side glance on his sly face.

'Aw, middlin',' said Ben, 'we canna complain.'

'Ha'st thee saw anythin' o' Morfa Bychan folks lately?' said Treluggan.

'No,' said Ben. 'I was only sayin' in the house th'other day I hav'n't set eyes on 'em since last Big Day.'

'Go thee on now,' said Dipper. 'Bad job about that maid o' theirs gone and got a bun in th'oven.'

This was news to Ben and he was momentarily taken aback, although it was no surprise to him from what he had ever seen of Bridget.

He said, 'Who was tellin' thee that then?'

'Oh, 'tis right enough,' gloated Dipper. 'Somebody have filled her by all account. She be tryin' to put the fault on a bloke from Laugharne, but he swears it isn't him an' he reckons she've been with so many she dunnat know who the father be.'

'Aw, well, that be a bad job altogether then.'

'Maybe thou's'll be gwain along that way today,' said Dipper.

'Aye, boy, maybe I might,' said Ben, and, with bright inspiration, added, 'I was thinkin' o' buyin' a donkey for the cruts here, an' owld George Wyrriot generally got a few owld donkeys about the place, so maybe I'll call in there.'

And before Treluggan could pursue the subject Ben said, 'But this'll never pay th'owld 'ooman her ninepence, so we must be makin' tracks.' And, with a gentle flick of the reins with one hand, said, 'Gee up then, Dandy,' and, holding his pipe in his other hand raised it in salutation and said, ' Mornin' now,' and once again they were on their way.

Dandy, who had been champing at the bit, rejoiced to be into her stride again and only eased when they came to the lake that crossed the road at this point. There was a footbridge for those who walked, and there was talk now, from some of the gentry in the area who had gone in for the new motor cars, of the need for a proper bridge to take wheeled traffic. But as yet it was only talk, and horse-drawn vehicles, as they had done through the centuries, went right through the water.

Immediely beyond the ford stood the white-washed, unpretentious public house called the New Inn. For the couple who kept it, Will and Annie Short Measure, it provided little enough of a living. It had twenty acres or so of land so that they kept a few cows, a sow, half a dozen geese and some ducks which now disported themselves upstream above the ford, curled tails twitching disdainfully, as they left a widening path of ripples in their wake and their heads turned sideways for their beady eyes to keep a careful and curious watch upon the travellers. The geese retreated with a waddle, which eventually became a studied walk of great dignity, towards the inn door, whilst the gander came boldly towards the wheel of the trap with neck extended and hissing his defiance. A few hens powdered themselves in the dust and a dull-eyed sheepdog, lying in the warmth of the morning sun on top of the old horse-mounting step, raised his head but did not otherwise disturb himself. Nothing else stirred and there was no human to be seen.

Dandy hardly had time to break into a trot again before they were facing the long hill out of Amroth and she once more slowed to her walk as Eben took over the reins. 'Ar't thee really gwain to buy us a donkey?' Mark asked.

'Why, no, boy,' he laughed, 'I only said that to put'n off the scent, the damn owld tack.'

'Thou di's'n't like'n.'

'No, I've never liked'n. Like Gramfer Jenkyn would say, "They only reared'n to spite the neighbours." He be no mortal good to man, God, beast nor the devil.'

'How did'st thee tell'n though that thou wa'st gwain to buy a donkey?'

Ben Harter once more took his tobacco box out of his pocket and began to refill his pipe with shag. At last he said, 'I'll tell thee, for 'tis a lesson thou's'll hatta learn for thyself one day. He was only wantin' to hawse us an' if I'd towld'n we was gwain to get a goat he'd have knowed straight away what that meant. An' when thou ha'st abortion in thy cows it isn't the sort o' thing to go tellin' everybody, certainly not the likes o' thicky with his owld lab about the place. If there be a bigger owld labbican anywhere in the rounds than thicky Treluggan I've never heard tell of'n.'

This much having been said he began to light his pipe. When the match had almost burned itself down to his finger, he took a few puffs before taking the pipe from his mouth. Then he said, 'But I wouldn't be surprised if he knowed about it by the way he was askin' how the cows was milkin' an' had we saw anythin' o' Morfa Bychan folks. Still, he never had the satisfaction o' me tellin'n.'

' 'Twould be all right to have a donkey though, wouldn't it?' said Mark.

'Why no,' said his father, 'what do we want with a donkey?'

'I wouldn't mind havin' one,' persisted Mark.

His father looked at him and said, 'What would'st thee do with'n, boy?'

'Aw, I'd'n'know,' said Mark, frowning and gazing into the distance, 'I could drive balls for people in the village an' give childern rides on the beach in the summer an' things like that.'

'Aw, aye,' laughed his father, 'I suppose thou cou'st do that all right,' whereupon Mark lapsed into silence.

The climb from the bridge to the top of Telpyn Hill was a long one, relieved only by the flat of Hannah's Plain halfway up, and here Dandy again broke into a steady trot. The road here was straight and Eben's father watched him carefully but made no move to take the reins off him. As Dandy eased again to a walk where the hill resumed its gradient, Ben Harter smiled indulgently to himself.

Now, however, the fields gave way to woodland which on their left hand stretched inland as far as the eye could see along the sides of a deep valley, then the road entered the wood and they discovered the labyrinth, of which they suddenly became a part, to be a delightfully cool place of sun-dappled shadows and all-enveloping secrecy. Time was, in the long forgotten past, when some prodigal landlord, in time of national need and consequently higher prices, had plundered this woodland of its great wealth and abandoned the ground that had been laid waste for the trees to regenerate themselves. This, at last, if not with their former greatness, they had done. Now they hid behind each other as they marched into the darkening distance, and beneath their shade a green carpet, patterned with a wealth of bluebells, stretched away into mysteriousness and was lost in the sound of birds, whose song was at first stilled by this sudden clip-clopping intrusion, before swelling again in a burst of trills and fluted cadences. Immediately, almost as if this had been regarded as a signal that all was well, two red squirrels, which had frozen into immobility, now resumed their sport and raced round the trunk of a young oak before taking to the branches again, with no apparent effort, via the trunk of the tree, and disappearing into the rich tracery of green leaves that canopied the world beneath.

At the top of the hill the road emerged into open country

and now, feeling the call of nature after their half-dozen miles or more of travel, Ben Harter said to Eben, 'Now then, driver, howld hard here a bit an' we'll have a sweet-pea or else we'll all be burstin'.'

This accomplished with due solemnity by the roadside, the three of them climbed back into the trap and, with their father once more taking the reins, the boys settled to their first sight of country which was wilder than their native valley, whilst Dandy again resumed her steady trot on the last long lap of their journey.

Hereabouts the land rose on their right-hand side away from the road to obscure any view of the sea beyond. On their left the wood gave way to rough land where acres of furze blazed in a glory of yellow, seeming to capture the very life of the morning sun, which was by now approaching its meridian, and impregnating the whole world about them with its fragrant scent. Elsewhere heather predominated and here and there amongst it some scattered sheep foraged hopefully for the odd green shoot. Overhead, where the few white clouds rode high, three buzzards wheeled and circled gracefully in great, sweeping glides, their rounded wings upturned at the tips, as they soared effortlessly on their ever-watchful patrol.

The road led them by the small, lonely church at Marros, standing four-square to the Atlantic gales, to where the great stretch of Pendine sands lay before them until they came at last, at the bottom of a long hill, to a field through which a lane turned off into a woodland glade to follow down another small valley in the direction of the sea. On one side of the road at this point a stream bounced and splashed in its hurry down the slope. When they turned off the road, however, beneath which the stream seemed to run, and took to the lane, they found there was now no sign of the stream and Ben Harter explained to them that it really ran into a kind of tunnel.

'At one time,' he said, 'they reckons as it was used by smugglers as a hidey-hole. But by all account it must be a big owld hole for there was a man went down there one time to have a look an' brought his dog with'n an' only the dog came back.'

Here, all of a sudden, was real adventure to spark the imagination on a journey which was an adventure in itself.

With the boys excited and their father in good spirits, they advanced upon the last stage of their journey to Morfa

Bychan. Overhead a wood pigeon, seemingly untroubled by their presence, called to its mate with its familiar *coo-coo coo coo-coo*. Raising his head, Ben Harter said, 'There be the owld woodgush, an' do'st thee know what she be sayin'? Well, I'll tell thee. Years ago she built her nest in the long grass an' laid her two white eggs there. But th'owld brown cow come an' trod on 'em an' smashed 'em, so she went over th'other side o' the field an' laid two more eggs but th'owld cow come grazin' over there an' trod on 'em an' smashed 'em again. So then the woodgush got fed up an' went an' built a nest in the tree out o' the way. An' now she's sayin' "come-now owld brown cow".'

And this he said with a cooing noise like the pigeon's and it sounded so good that Eben said, 'Is it true, Father?' But his father laughed and said, 'No, honey, it b'aint true, but it be a good owld story.' And as they went Eben and Mark went *coo-coo coo coo-coo*, just like the pigeon calling to the old brown cow.

At last, after passing a cottage which was inhabited and well-cared for, but where there was obviously nobody home, they found the valley opening out before them and they came in sight of the sea. Hereabouts the trees were stunted in their growth and bent over by the strong salt-laden winds that blew in from the sea throughout the winter.

Where the wood came to an end there was marshy ground which suggested that the lost stream might again be coming to the surface, and lower down it did indeed concentrate itself into a clear and sparkling rill which danced by the small stone house before disappearing into a bank of pebbles to emerge once more on to the sandy beach below. The house stood with door and windows open and a skein of smoke rising lazily into the clear air from its broad chimney. A few small fields ran down to the pebbles above the beach and the whole scene was hemmed in and overshadowed by towering rocky escarpments that were topped with a mat of gorse in full bloom. Beneath them the land fell away to a carpet of bluebells where the strong green fern was already pushing its way through and where, lower still, on rough ground, George Wyrriot's goats looked for their meagre living.

Here, too, long centuries ago, the Romans had landed, and there still remained the rough foundations of their fortifications which had no doubt witnessed, could they but have told of them, the stealthy comings and goings of the smugglers in a much later age.

But now there was neither Roman nor smuggler to be seen as George Wyrriot advanced to meet them looking genuinely pleased to see them.

A man of slingy build he came towards them, in his fustian trousers and jacket, wearing clogs and with a round cap well back on his head, to reveal a face of rural honesty and simplicity.

The greetings over, the boys ran down the pebbles, which cascaded after them as they went, to romp on the sands, whilst their father unhitched Dandy from the shafts of the trap and then took off her harness, bridle and collar.

'That's it,' said George Wyrriot, 'leave her in here for a hour to cool off, then she can go out an' graze a bit,' and he indicated a small shed which seemed to have been made from an assortment of timber and planks. Outside, stacked against a low wall, was a great pile of such timber with not a few masts and spars amongst it.

'Lord ha' mercy,' said Ben, 'what do'st thou want with that lot?'

'Why, fella,' replied George, 'I can nearly reckon to pay the rent with wreck. Of course, there b'aint the stuff comin' in now as there was when the sailin' ships was in full swing. In them days there used to be sailin' ships bound for Llanelly an' Burry Port an' they'd be drove afore a sou' wester up on to the Cefn Sidan sands an' once they got drove over the sandbar up there they'd never come from there. But there was a power of 'em never got as far as that but was drove in here and all along this coast from Amroth along past Pendine right up to Ginst. I can mind Nelly's father tell how the wreck used to come in here an' it was days o' drivin' from here at a time.'

'Who buys it?'

'Lord ha' mercy, fella,' said George, 'they reckons as most o' the houses in Pendine was built from wreck. 'Tis cheaper than payin' for new stuff.'

As they talked they began to walk towards the pebbles to look down on the beach where the boys had begun drawing patterns with their clogs in the sand.

'Well how be things gwain with thee?' ventured Ben at last. 'How be Nelly and young Bridget?'

George shot a quick glance at him and said, 'Hasn't thou heard?'

'Heard what?' said Ben.

'Well, I may as well tell thee,' said George, 'for 'tis beginnin' to show. Bridget have been put in the family way.'

'Well, that wunnat be so bad as long as the bloke'll marry her.'

'That be the trouble,' said the girl's father, 'the bloke she says 'tis wunnat own to it. But I'm not sure that's a bad thing for he's a proper waster.'

'How did she pick up with'n then?'

'Why!' said George in a tone of disgust, 'at these damn owld dances doin' this owld tango as they all be at nowadays.'

'Zounds,' said Ben, 'I always did reckon as no good would come out o' that damn owld business.'

'But there it be,' said George, ' 'tis no good for me to say nothin'. Her mother can't see no wrong in none of it, so I just shuts up.'

Eventually they talked of Ben's problems.

'Lord ha' mercy, aye. I'll let thee have a goat,' said George, 'but why do'sn't thou have a donkey?'

Ben looked at him and laughed as he said, 'What would I want with a donkey?'

'Well,' said George, 'they reckons as a donkey runnin' with the cows will stop th'owld abortion quicker than anythin'.'

At this point Nelly called from the doorway of the house and waved to them. 'Come on then, boy,' said George, 'an let's see what there is to yeat.'

Ben shouted to the boys and beckoned to them to come up from the beach and he and George walked through the field towards the house.

'What's thicky cow thou's ha' got there?' asked Ben looking with great interest towards a fine, deep-bodied, black cow which raised her head as they approached and showed herself to be bright of eye and with a good broad muzzle capable of biting off a wad of grass. Black all over, apart from a white spot or two in front of her capacious udder, her coat shone and her wide-spread white horns swept upwards to their sharp, black tips.

'By gaw, boy, she's a fine cow,' said Ben admiringly as he walked round her. 'Where's't thee get her from?'

'Well, I'll tell thee. I bought her back in the spring with a bloke where I was catchin' rabbats. She was dry at the time an' she was a fair owld skymer. He could do nothin' with her, fella. As soon as he'd have her back she was out again. In the end he got danted an' he very nigh gave her to me only fetch her from there.'

'An' be she any good?'

'She be calved three weeks, an' last week Nelly made fourteen pounds of butter from her an' she be feedin' a calf as well.'

'What sort o' calf have she got?'

'Heifer calf, by a Castlemartin bull.'

'How much do'st thee want for'n?' enquired Ben.

'Do'st thee want to buy a calf?'

'Well, aye, boy. There be nothin' else for it. 'Tis not a mortal bit o' good for me to think about buyin' cows. All I can do now they reckons is to rear some calves an' let 'em get pickled to it.'

'Thou's ha' better have a look at'n then,' said George.

By now the boys had come panting up to join them, and, at talk of buying a calf, Eben was all agog. They found it in another of George's wooden buildings, penned off in a corner. It rose enquiringly to its feet as they came in through the open door, stretching its sleek black body, and pushing its hind legs down into its bed of dried fern, and thrust its velvety muzzle over the wooden rail towards them.

Ben Harter came straight to the point and said, 'I don't want to try and banter thee down, George. How much do'st thee want for'n?'

'Let's have a bit o' grub first,' said George, 'then we can talk about it after.'

Fair dos to Nelly, thought Ben afterwards, whatever Keziah might say about her and however foolish she might be in the way she had spoiled Bridget, she had not been a bad wife to old George. She kept the house clean, and had a good meal for them and she had her flower border looking nice in the courtyard in front of the house. In her time she had probably been pretty enough, but there was no real character there and Bridget took after her. Whoever else might be worrying themselves about her condition Bridget certainly was not and she made a big fuss of the boys, who responded to her.

Over dinner the talk again turned to the donkey, and Mark was quick to remind his father what he could do to earn money with one.

'Well,' said Ben, 'we got a li'l donkey's cart there an' a harness from the time the mill was workin'.'

'Look here,' said George, 'I got a li'l donkey out there would suit'n a masterpiece. Two years owld an' no mischief with her at all.'

'Is she broke in?' asked Ben.

'Why aye,' said George, 'came from Laugharne she did. One o' the cocklers there died an' his missus persuaded Arse an'

Pockets to take her in payment o' the bit of a bill they owed. Well, o' course, Arse an' Pockets didn' want her so he gave her to me for a bit o' wreck he had his eye on.'

'Thou's'll have the calf though, wou'sn't thee, Father?' exclaimed Eben, who feared from the turn in the conversation that the question of the calf might be overlooked in favour of a deal over the donkey.

'Aye, aye, boy, do'sn't thee worrit thy li'l head now. We'll have the calf an' the donkey. That'll be one-a-piece for thee an' I'll have the goat for meself.'

Dinner finished, Eben said, 'Can I go and see the calf?'

'Where's the donkey?' demanded Mark.

'All right,' said Bridget, there being apparently no thought of her helping her mother to clear the table, 'I'll show thee the donkey.' And she took them, one by each hand, and proved herself to be a cheerful companion, telling them the names of the few animals they had.

Meanwhile, whilst Nelly cleared the table and set about washing the dinner things, the two men enjoyed a pipe together and talked of the old times, when they had been boys in the fields and woods around Heronsmill, and of the way things were going in farming and the rabbit trade and the latest news about the Kaiser. Then, when it was time to make a move, George looked at the old clock standing in the corner alongside the dresser and said, 'How wou'st thee like to go look for a couple o' prawns?'

'Aye, aye,' replied Ben, 'how's the tide answerin'?'

'Well, I was just thinkin',' said George, looking at the clock again, ' 'tisn' low water till three o'clock, so we got a couple o' hours yet an' that'll give us time to bale a pound.'

First of all, however, Ben Harter turned Dandy out into the field behind the house where she snorted, lay down on her side, then rolled over on her back and finally came to her feet again. Then she shook herself, raised her head and pricked up her ears and had a good look round at her strange surroundings before walking off and then, at last, sniffing the ground, found a spot to her liking and began cropping the young grass. George Wyrriot emerged from a shed behind the house and the five of them set off down the pebbles on to the sands and made for the rocks running out into the sea at the point itself at Ragwen. They had two buckets and a couple of old saucepans, a prawning net, a small sack and a stout hazel stick, and George also carried a long, thin iron with a crook on the end.

'What's thicky iron for?' enquired Eben.

George Wyrriot looked at him with a smile and said, 'Well, now, we may not want'n for all, so what say if we wait an' see an' then if we wants'n there'll be a bit o' surprise for us.'

Once out across the sands they found that they could now see round the point and right across the bay to Caldey Island, rising out of the water in a shimmering haze, whilst on the mainland the church spire at Tenby, on its rocky promontory, reached like a spike towards the sky. Standing off the land towards Worms Head, a three-masted schooner, crowding on as much white canvas as ever she could carry, made no more than leisurely way towards the open sea, whilst two more three-masters lay in Caldey Roads waiting for the next tide so that they could run in for their cargo of coal to the harbour at Saundersfoot. In the distance smoke rose from the funnel of a steamer heading for the Bristol Channel.

As they approached the rocks there was a flurry of black and white as a small party of oyster-catchers, disturbed at their business of searching for mussels and limpets now exposed by the receding tide, rose into the air with their warning call ringing out in a staccato *bleep, bleep, bleep* and swept low over the sea with a busy wing action, orange bills conspicuous, to resume their search further along the shore. Then, as the party came to the pond, the prawning operation began, and, young though he was, Eben somehow sensed the efficiency and the well-drilled approach to the task.

First of all the men took off their footwear, Ben Harter his tack boots and George Wyrriot his clogs, then they took off their woollen socks and rolled up their trousers. Treading carefully with his bare feet on the barnacle-covered rocks, George bent down and worked his hazel stick carefully along through the water under the rock, probing and poking as he went. At last he winked at Ben and said, 'They be here all right.' Beckoning to the boys he said, 'See their owld whiskers there.' And the boys looked closely and at last their eyes caught a movement of the prawns' whiskers down in the water protruding under the edge of the rock.

Handing his stick to Ben, George said, 'Pass the bucket then, boy.' Then he went to the task of baling out the pond.

The boys looked on in wonder and eventually their father said, 'What we be gwain to do is empty all the water from the pond, then as it gets lower, the prawns'll follow the water out an' we'll just pick 'em up.'

After a while, as George threw each bucketful of water well

clear of the nearest rock so that there was no danger of it seeping back into the pond, Ben said, 'Now then, partner, let's give thee a spell.'

By this means, turn-and-turn-about, they could see the water going down and, at last, looking where each bucketful landed as it was thrown, George called, 'Howld hard, Ben.' On the rock two fair-sized prawns jumped like fire-crackers. Fetching the prawn net he said to Mark, 'Now then, man, howld thee by the handle with the net down like this,' and he placed the straight front of the metal frame flush to the surface of the rock with the handle held upwards and the net draped away so that each bucketful of water could now be thrown through it. Then he placed Eben alongside him and said, 'Thou ca'st watch the net an' every time thou see'st a prawn pick'n up and put'n in the bag.'

Soon, however, the water in the pond was so low that they had to have recourse to the saucepans, filling the buckets with them, and straining each bucketful through the net away from the pond and picking out the prawns that were left behind. And then, almost as if their quarry had been flushed from cover, the water, which now did little more than cover the bottom of the pond, seemed to come to life with such a splashing and jumping that the boys shouted in their excitement and began to scoop up the prawns with their eager little hands, grabbing them by the whiskers or by the tails as they tried to escape. But there was no bolt-hole for them. No dark recess to which to retreat. As the water level had been lowered so they had followed unsuspectingly in its receding path and now, in the open, their ability to dart backwards availed them nothing. In no more than minutes the sweeping massacre was complete, with anything between four and five hundred prawns to show for it.

George took the long iron with the crook on the end of it and, getting down on his knees, pushed it far into the dark recess beneath the rock from which the prawns had been enticed. Suddenly his face lit with excitement, there was a sound as of furious scuffling within and, with a dexterous turn of his strong wrist, he said, 'Got'n!' Then he drew the iron rod towards him and with it, firmly held by the crook, came a great dark blue, almost black, lobster, more than a foot in length. It moved its huge claws in front of it in an effort to find some tangible enemy but it was helpless now in George's expert hands.

'Now then, honey,' said George as he held it up in front of

a wide-eyed Eben, 'thou know'st what we wanted thicky iron for.'

'What do he weigh?' said Ben.

'I reckon he's seven pounds if he's a' ounce,' declared George and then gave the one claw a quick twist to break it in the joint and render the lobster harmless.

Later that afternoon, when they had returned to the house, George fetched a three-legged iron stand from the back shed, along with the iron pot which stood on it, and this he filled with sea water they had carried up from the beach in buckets. Then he lit a fire of driftwood beneath it and before long the water was boiling. Whilst he was waiting he had two old iron pokers in the fire and now he tipped prawns into the boiling water until it nearly came up to the rim of the pot and then, taking the red-hot pokers out of the fire, plunged them sizzling into the pot to bring it back quickly to the boil. Soon the prawns turned from their original pale transparency to a white, that deepened as they watched to a rich and appetizing pink. More wood was piled on to the fire and the operation repeated until their entire catch had been cooked. This task completed, George stoked his fire and plied it with more wood and, when the water was again boiling, he took the lobster, still moving its claw and legs helplessly, and eased it into the boiling water to its sudden death.

Bridget, with her hands to the side of her head, made a grimace of horror at having to be present at a scene which she must have witnessed many times before and said, 'Oh, Dadda! How can you be so cruel!'

Undeterred, George once more plunged his red-hot pokers into the water with a furious hissing of steam and said, 'There we are, then. We can leave'n out whilst we have our tea an' by the time we've finished he'll be done fit for a king.'

On this day of untold happiness, not least of the highlights for Eben was having the prawns for tea that afternoon in the kitchen at Morfa Bychan, with its flagstone floor and the dark oak beams that seemed to weigh down low above their heads. He and Mark sat at the table alongside Bridget on the oak settle and she showed them how to squeeze a prawn's head and tail together before pulling them apart to expose the tasty flesh, which they ate, and, whilst they struggled with their small unskilled fingers to perform this task, she shelled a basinful for them so that they could continue with their feast unhindered. Fresh-baked, wholemeal bread spread with butter made from the black cow's milk completed a meal which, as

George Wyrriot had said, was 'fit for a king'. Eben could not know how long it would be before, in other company, he would visit the place again.

Tea over, Ben declared himself as being anxious not to leave it too late before setting off, since, with a donkey tied behind the trap, their pace would be considerably slower on their homeward journey. The deal was a formality. For the donkey, calf and goat the price asked and immediately agreed on was a moderate three sovereigns.

Turning round to look at their newly acquired livestock as they went, the boys saw Bridget still standing by the house and she waved to them.

Once on the road and over the top of the hill they found themselves on the flat heading for Marros church and Ben Harter allowed Dandy to extend herself a little into the gentlest of trots. This was something which was strange to her, but she soon realized what was required, and the donkey coming behind had no trouble keeping pace with her. Turning to reassure himself that all was well, Ben said, 'Keep thee a' eye on Arse an' Pockets back there now.'

'Is that her name?' said Mark.

'I'd'know,' laughed his father, 'but that's who she came from. But thy mother mightn' like the name so thou ca'st call her Pockets for short unless thou ca'st think of somethin' better.'

When it came to Eben's turn to name his calf he said with finality, 'Her name is Blackie.'

By the time Keziah heard them coming down the lane for Heronsmill, dusk had fallen and was fast turning to night.

Tired though they were when they reached home, the boys stayed with their father whilst he saw the new arrivals bedded down for the night.

Keziah had warmed some milk for the goat, which she needed little persuasion to take from a bottle with a teat on it, and, as she did so, the twitching of her stump of a tail left no doubt as to her approval. Blackie, however, was deemed to have had sufficient off her mother before leaving Morfa Bychan to see her through the night.

'She was full her skin when we left,' said Ben Harter, 'so she wunnat take much hurt till mornin'. An' there's gwain to be a scuffle tryin' to get her on to the bucket so it b'aint no good takin' on a contract like that this time o' night.'

Pockets, in the morning, was ready to be turned out from the shed where it had been thought it would be safer to leave her for her first night, in case she roamed, and she now bent her head straight to the task of cropping the lush grass, which was better than anything she had ever known either at Laugharne or Morfa Bychan.

Blackie's setting in and feeding, however, presented an entirely different problem. Whereas Martha Jane, as the goat had been named, had taken readily to the teat on the bottle, which was not too unlike feeding from her mother, Blackie was expected to make the transition from her mother's udder to drinking from a bucket.

Keziah had mixed some fresh milk with warm water and now her clogs rattled on the cobbled yard as she and Eben set forth with the bucket to find out what sort of reception Blackie would give them. First of all, holding the bucket in one hand, she offered the fingers of her other hand to Blackie, and these the calf sucked obligingly. Next, Keziah lowered her hand towards the bucket, and the calf's head came with it. But only so far. Once it came down near the milk she pulled her head away. By way of getting the taste to her, Keziah dipped her hand in the milk and once more gave her fingers into Blackie's eager and very willing mouth, only for the attempt to coax her down into the milk to prove just as fruitless.

'All right then,' said Keziah at last, 'howld the buckat for me, pet, an' let's try again.'

So, with Eben holding the bucket, his mother again gave the fingers of one hand to the calf, and, with the other, pushed her head down gently into the milk until her mouth and nostrils were submerged. Blackie, however, regarded this as a challenge, dug her feet in and backed into the corner. After a much great struggle, Keziah once more managed to force the defiant black head down into the milk, but to hold it there was more than she could do. Shaking her head and hitting the bucket sideways, so that some of the milk was spilled, the calf pressed back into the corner and remained obdurate. So the battle continued until the milk had gone cold and Ben Harter came to the door of the calves' cot.

'How be things shapin' here then?' he enquired.

'Aw, no shape at all,' said his wife, a wisp of her greying hair falling over her flushed face, 'the blessed tack wunnat aim to drink.'

'Leave her be then, Kizzy,' he said, 'she'll take to it when she be real hungry.'

There had been a time when Keziah would have refused to

heed such advice. Her natural instinct was to take the milk back to the house to warm, and then come back to try again. But she knew from experience that her husband was right and she said to Eben, 'All right then, pet. Let's leave her an' see what she'll be like this afternoon.'

In the afternoon, however, in spite of her pitiful calling throughout the day, Blackie was as stubborn as ever and the battle even more furious than it had been in the morning. In the end, flushed and frustrated, Keziah said, 'We'll try her again after chapel.'

But after chapel, when she had changed out of her best clothes and warmed the milk, she made no better progress and the calf remained defiant.

Eben could have cried for his mother as she became more and more upset at the calf's struggling and point-blank refusal to drink. In the end, she stood up to ease her aching back, drew her forearm across the sweat on her brow and said, ' 'Tis no use, we'll have to call thy father.'

Ben Harter, when he came, took the calf between his legs, backed her into the corner and pushed her head down into the milk with one great hand, whilst giving her the fingers of the other hand to suck. Yet, even held in his powerful grip, she found the strength to struggle. Eventually he took his fingers from her mouth and used both hands to hold her muzzle down in the milk. She blew into it, as the bubbles confirmed, but drink she would not, and only when her frantic struggles showed that she was short of breath, and in danger of smothering or drowning, did he finally release her and say, 'All right, then, she've had her chance. But I warrant she'll be ready for it in the mornin'.'

All through the night the calf called without ceasing. Early the next morning Eben looked into the cot. Blackie looked at him with her ears forward and called even louder. When, at last, Keziah came with some milk she seemed to have a different outlook on the bucket altogether. No sooner had Keziah coaxed the calf's muzzle into the bucket than she discarded the fingers she had been so ravenously trying to chew, blew once into the milk, shook her milk-covered face and then plunged it deep into the milk and drank and drank until the bucket was empty. Then she swished her tail and bumped the bucket as she had always bumped her mother's udder when trying to draw more milk down into the teat. At last Keziah managed to get the empty bucket away from her and, laughing, said to Eben, who was crowing with delight,

'Mark thee my words, honey, she'll be a real owld gorral guts. An' she'll do well on it.'

In the afternoon she was jumping round the cot, ready for her food, and, as from the following morning, Eben was able to feed her himself.

Outside, in a far away and harsher world, a dark shadow was falling. By August, when Blackie was still on the bucket and not yet on dry feed, German troops had marched into Belgium and the war of 1914–18 had been declared. With this news came three hammer blows for the Harters.

The first realization of what the war meant to them, as a family, came to Eben when Eddie came home in his soldier's uniform, with his brass buttons and the badge on his cap shining and his puttees wound round his legs above his strong black boots. It was so sudden they were hardly able to understand it, especially as with him came a young wife who was, as Esther and Liza said, the most beautiful girl they had ever seen. More to Keziah's joy she was as gentle as she was beautiful. Quiet at first, she won every heart at Heronsmill within twenty-four hours.

Her name was Ruth Fownes and her people had gone to Ammanford from Saundersfoot. Eddie had been walking out with her for some little time when the war came and, with the impetuosity which had prompted him to pitch into Midgelly, he now enlisted to go marching off to see what he could do with the Kaiser. With his embarkation leave coming to him he had asked Ruth to marry him.

It was a sudden decision, leaving no time for any plans, other than to write home to say they would be at Kilgetty station on the six o'clock train the following Saturday evening. There was no room for them at Heronsmill, but Becca prepared a bed at the Gangrel and there, for a few brief days and nights of happiness, they spent the only married life they were ever to know.

Before the leaves on the trees had started to turn colour Eddie had sent a card from France with a picture of the Union Jack and the verses of one of the songs of the day, 'Just before the battle, Mother'. It was followed scarcely a week later by a letter from Ruth saying that she had heard Eddie had been killed in the battle for the Marne River.

The carnage had been such that no one ever came to know any details, and it did little to improve things when some pictures arrived from Eddie's young widow which they had

had taken on their wedding day. Keziah sent them to Narberth to be framed and, with an aching heart, hung them on the walls of the parlour.

Much as he tried not to show it as the miserable winter dragged on, Ben Harter, too, was stricken with grief. Eddie, his firstborn, had somehow always had a special place in his heart, with his devil-may-care courage and his generous nature. And now he was gone. For young Ruth there was perhaps some small measure of balm for a wound which she, too, knew would never heal. It was not possible to lose someone as full of life as Eddie and not know that a part of you had died forever. But at Christmas she wrote to the Harters and, in a letter in which she tried to sound so brave, said, 'I'm thinking you will be glad to know that my dear Eddie left me with a child. The doctor said it will be in June that the baby will come so that will be the haymaking time which Eddie did love so much, so it isn't as if he is all dead, but oh it's breaking my heart I am to know that it's a joy we will never share together.'

Something of the grief over Eddie had got through to Eben's young mind, but losing Mam was altogether different. She had been a part of his life during every day since he had been born.

It happened suddenly, and with scarcely any warning, that Sunday afternoon in spring, when once again the countryside was emerging from its winter sojourn and when Gramfer and Eben had released the badger from a trap.

In the morning, Keziah had persuaded him to go to chapel with her and the two boys, whilst the girls stayed home to get the mid-day meal. Afterwards, having said at the table she did not feel like much to eat, she said she would 'have a lie-down on the bed'.

'You do that, Mam,' said Esther, 'and I'll bring you up a cup of tea.'

Shortly afterwards, when she went upstairs, Esther could see that her mother looked faint. Frightened, she called to her father, who hurried up to the bedroom. His wife smiled at him and he sat on the bed and held her hand.

'What's the matter, Kizzy?' he asked and then, urgently, 'shall I send for the doctor?'

For a few quiet minutes she lay there as her husband and daughter watched over her. And then, very slowly, she folded her hands on her bosom and whispered, 'Heavenly Father, receive my soul,' and she was gone.

The silence in the low-ceilinged kitchen with its oak beams

was broken only by the sobbing of Esther and Liza. The tick of the grandfather clock was loud and the sound of every trickle of ash from the fire echoed through the stillness of the house. The song of the big black kettle seemed to mock at their misery.

Ben Harter sat at the end of the kitchen table and raised unseeing eyes to his father-in-law as he and Eben came into the room.

'What be the matter here, then?' asked Gramfer.

'It's Keziah.'

'What be the matter with her, Ben?'

'She's dead.'

'Dead?' He gazed with his mouth open but saying nothing. Esther and Liza once more began to sob.

The last thing Eben had heard his mother say was that she was going to have a lie-down.

Before anybody knew what he was doing he was pounding up the stairs to her bedroom. Raising the door latch he looked in, seeing the big, familiar, secure-looking bedstead with its brass knobs. Only the patchwork quilt covered his mother and he thought she was sleeping.

'Mam!' he said.

Going to her bedside he gently touched her face and, at eight years old, he knew about death.

The third loss, for all its sadness, was more natural.

As the days lengthened, and the birds sang through the eventide, until darkness had enfolded the valley and all but the nearest trees in its mysterious embrace, and in the weeks when the cuckoo could be heard calling far oftener than it could be seen, the old man began to fail. Gramfer Jenkyn had now passed his ninetieth birthday, and the loss of his daughter, who was not yet fifty, seemed to paralyse his mind. At first he began to mumble odd words in Welsh, the language of his boyhood which he had virtually lost. Not long before the end he had one of his brighter moments, and with a flash of his old wit, said, 'The young may die, but the owld must.'

Somehow Becca managed to persuade him to move back to the Gangrel where she could the better care for him, and somehow, leaning on her arm on one side and on Ben Harter's on the other, he managed to walk very slowly up across the field from the mill to the house which for so long had been his home, and where the blacksmith's shop, now draped in cobwebs and already in an advanced stage of decay, had been the very hub of his life. And there, where the great pine tree stood like a sentinel looking down the valley, with the golden chain and the lilac in full bloom, before the first rattle of the mower was heard as harbinger of yet another haymaking season, and before word came that Ruth in Ammanford had given birth to Eddie's son, he breathed his last.

Until this time, Eben's had been a happy, carefree childhood in a home full of love, across which outside fears cast few shadows. But now, all this had been snatched away. Ben Harter grieved after his son, he was broken-hearted at the loss of his wife, and he sorely missed the company and support of old Gramfer Jenkyn. Small wonder that he could do little to sustain his young family in their loss. From now on it looked as though they would be fighting their own battles, and Eben's young heart was so heavy with his troubles that it was to be a long time before he could think back with gratitude to all that his happy and peaceful childhood, slow-moving like the age in which it had been lived, had meant to him.

It was Rebecca who rose to the occasion. A Harter by birth, she had always been very close to the family at Heronsmill. Nobody could have shown her more Christian kindness than Keziah. Gramfer Jenkyn had given up his home for her when her man had been killed underground. She knew what it was to suffer and to need a friend. It was unthinkable to her that either Esther or Liza should give up their jobs to stay at home. Tilly was just leaving school and could help, and so, almost unnoticed, Becca took over the housekeeping at the mill. With haymaking close upon them she had her hands full, but Esther and Liza did what they could in the evenings and at the week-ends.

Before the last of the hay had been gathered in, a long letter full of news came from Hannah in Canada. The most joyful part of it to Becca was where Hannah told her she would be a grandmother before the year was out.

When Becca finally sat down to write to her daughter she had much sad news to tell her but her heart was lighter than it had been for some time. And Becca hoped it would be a boy, 'like my Eben. He's like my own now,' she wrote, 'and I loves him.'

The worst part about it for Eben was the way in which his father became first morose and then tyrannical. 'Sharp back from school this afternoon, now,' Ben Harter would say, and then it would be hoeing swedes until sunset. Sometimes, when the work had fallen behind, he would even keep the boys home from school for the day.

It was an anxious time, this hoeing. As the sun scorched down on the young plants there was always the danger of their being taken by the flea-beetle. Hour after hour Eben dragged sacks soaked in paraffin along the tops of the rows for the smell to discourage this destructive pest. Often, unless the plants could be singled in time for the crop to be well-established before the fly could strike, all the effort was in vain and then, in June, when haymaking was upon them, another crop would have to be sown in the hope that it would still come to something in time for the winter.

Haymaking, too, was hard, but it provided company at work. Mowing was done early in the morning, and the horses rested in the heat of the day. The workers, thought Eben, had to put up with it. Hour after hour the men, women and boys toiled with wooden hay-rakes or with pitchforks, turning the sweet-smelling grass as it dried, until at last it was ready to be put into tumps from which it was eventually carted to the rick-yard. Hard though it was, there was something satisfying about it. The distant fields never looked so peaceful, and the cattle never so lazily contented, as they did in the heat haze of haymaking time. Dinner was brought to the field by Becca and Tilly and perhaps a woman or two from Stepaside who had come to help. It was nice when the cold meat and potatoes had been washed down with a drink of tea, to lie there, amongst the rows of hay, when the honey scent of the clover mingled with the primeval smell of the damp earth, and gaze way up into the endless depth of blue, blue sky, where chance white clouds like balls of cotton wool drifted idly by and gave rise to all sorts of pleasant daydreams.

Such respite, however, was short-lived, and then it was back to the grind, with boys doing men's work, leading the horses with their loads of hay to the rick-yard, where another horse, at the end of a long line, pulled the grabbler up the pitcher pole to swing it over the rick where the men shook out the hay and trampled it underfoot as the rick pushed higher and higher. There was no shortage of horses because, looking for other ways to make a living when he had been so plagued by his abortion troubles, Ben Harter had bought some cobs from the Preseli mountains. Sturdy, willing animals they were, and now he was making a good thing of breaking them in and selling them to the army authorities.

So it was, from the field to the rick-yard with a full load, then back to the field to start all over again. Back and forth, to and fro, mile after weary mile, until the heavy boots felt like lumps of lead, and legs and arms seemed not to belong to the body. At last, as darkness fell, the horses were turned out with the shape of the harness still visible in their sweat-soaked coats. Then there was supper, swallowed gratefully in a kind of daze, and just enough energy left to stumble upstairs and fall into bed oblivious to everything except the dull aching of weary feet and the throbbing of blistered hands before the mind lost consciousness and had respite from driving the weary flesh.

'That's a smart cap,' said Eben when Mark went to the County School at Narberth. 'I'd like if I could go there and have a cap like that.'

Dark blue it was, with yellow stripes from back to front and side to side. 'Like a hot cross bun,' said Mark. 'What d'you want with an old cap like this?'

'It must be good to go to school there.'

'I can't see nothing good about it. I wants to leave. The only thing is it's better than having to hoe swedes and everything.'

'Well I hopes I can pass the scholarship next week for I wants to go there.'

'You'll pass all right. You been top of the class all the time and Mr Magrath been giving you extra help.'

'The idea of the exam,' Mr Magrath had said, 'is to find out what you know. So when the questions are placed before you, read them through carefully and do the ones you know you can answer first of all.'

'And another thing,' said Mark, 'don't take no notice of old Foghorn in his black gown. I've knowed cruts do a trousers-full at the very sight of'n afore now.'

Eben stood in some awe of the master that day when he went to Narberth to take the exam. It was the first time he had seen anyone wear a scholar's gown and was glad Mark had warned him. The questions he found easy enough. Ever since Hannah had gone to Canada he had read much of that great country and about America and Alaska, and about the gold rush and the lakes, and how long it took steamers to cross the Atlantic. And because of Josh he had read much about New Zealand, too.

Yet his brightest memory afterwards, as he told Aunty Becca all about it, was of the interval in the morning when he had looked at the football field. There was nothing like that at Stepaside school, where they played football in the playground, or else on the green with coats on the ground to mark the goals. Of course, there had always been a football field at Kilgetty, and now the war was over they had started up the village team again, and Eben went to watch them when he could and played behind one goal with the Stepaside and Kilgetty boys once the match was under way. But such Saturday afternoons were all too rare because his father so often insisted on him staying home to work. Once he went to Narberth it would be different.

Why he should have had this longing was more than he could have explained, because he liked farming. He liked the country things about which Gramfer Jenkyn had taught him so much, he liked being with the animals and he liked to watch things growing after he had planted them. He could not have admitted even to himself that he wanted to get away from his father. The bond which came from having to cling together in times of poverty had gone because now, with the prosperity which came to the land in time of war, there was no shortage of money. Worse still, his father had now taken to going to the pub regularly for the first time in his life, and his temper had deteriorated with it. He became subject now, after heavy drinking bouts, to moods of brooding taciturnity.

Esther and Liza, thought Eben, were well out of it. Within six months of each other they had both married and set up homes of their own, Esther in Saundersfoot and Liza 'up off' in the Rhondda Valley. Esther had married Giles, a descendant of old Merryman of Brandyback, who at Gramfer Jenkyn's prompting had fashioned Gramfer's Well, and who was himself a mason and setting up on his own. Liza's husband was young Jim Cartlett, who also came from Saundersfoot. He had worked down the pit there but decided that there would be a better future in the Rhondda. So Heronsmill now seemed to be going the way of the other holdings with only Mark and Eben left at home.

All these thoughts were in Eben's head as he pictured himself at Narberth school and waited for the results of the exam. As the days went by he began to have doubts. Just as he had abandoned all hope, Mr Magrath opened class after morning prayers by saying he had the results of the exam for the County school. Looking very pleased, he said, 'I want to congratulate every one of you for you have all passed and have brought great credit to this little school. Well done all of you.'

Eben was hardly aware of the other children in the class. All he knew was that there were great waves of relief and happiness sweeping over him and engulfing him, and he felt he wanted to jump up on the desk and shout to the top of his voice. Yet he remained rooted to his bench until he was conscious of Mr Magrath's voice speaking to them again.

He was starting to give them their marks and their placings. 'The top mark from this school,' he said, 'was three hundred and sixty-eight out of four hundred, and that was Eben Harter.'

All eyes were turned to Eben and he knew that he was blushing furiously. Vaguely he heard the master's voice drone on. Top of the class was one thing. But top of the whole district!

At last Eben brought his mind back to the schoolroom and to Mr Magrath, still smiling and looking very pleased and saying, 'And now, in honour of this achievement, today we shall have a half-holiday.'

So now there was excitement in which the whole school could join. Eben thought he might take Drifter and Boogles out to look for a rabbit, then he realized there were too many young ones about for them to bolt properly, so he thought that maybe he would go up the banks to Ford's Lake to where the herons nested. They would have their young now, high up in their nests in the tree-tops, and he loved to watch these great birds glide in and ease themselves on to the slenderest branch of a tall pine and sit there swaying gently. It would be nice to lie there in the sun and watch them and think about going to Narberth County school. Wait till he told Mark. Yes, he would go to see the herons, and then come back in time to meet Mark and tell him all about it.

His plan, however, did not work out as he intended. He had rushed home and Aunty Becca, who was at the Mill cleaning and doing some baking, hugged him close to her as he told his news. His father, however, said little, and showed no interest in the form which Mr Magrath had sent to be filled in without delay.

'Thou ca'st get thy clothes changed now then,' he said, 'an' come an' help me lime the cowshed an' calves' cot.'

Stupefied, Eben said, 'But 'tis a half-holiday an' I'm gwain up to see the herons.'

'Thou'rt not gwain to see no herons – thou'rt gwain to help me lime the cowshed an' calves' cot, so thou ca'st get any other ideas out o' thy head an' go an' change an' look sharp about it.'

'But I've passed the exam,' Eben sobbed yet again, as he stood with the long-handled lime-brush dripping over the bucket of lime.

'There's more than enough work home here for thee an' one of thee wastin' his time there is plenty. So thou ca'st tell Mr Magrath that there'll be no form filled in an' let that be the end of it.'

Even Aunty Becca could make no impression when she came down from the Gangrel to make some supper for them. Eben had never seen her look or sound so angry.

'What the hell's the matter with thee,' she demanded, 'an' God forgive me for usin' such language, but what's a body to do?'

'I've told thee,' he said, 'there's work to do here.'

Mark and Eben sat at the table not daring to speak.

Finally, Becca turned to pleading and put her hand on Ben Harter's shoulder.

'Look, Ben,' she begged, 'think what Keziah would ha' said if she'd been here. Thou know'st she'd ha' done anything for the childern to get on an' she'd ha' been so proud of 'n.'

'God drabbit, 'ooman,' he fumed as he pushed back his chair on the stone floor, 'leave it be'. And he put on his billy-cock hat and stamped out.

Eben felt the tears welling up again and Becca, in the silence broken only by the ticking of the clock as the flames from the ball fire danced into the darkening shadows of the kitchen, said quietly, 'Perhaps thou's ha' better go to bed both o' thee out o' the way,' and she turned away and lifted her apron to wipe her eyes. Whereupon Eben left the table and put his arm round her, all manly protection, and said, 'Don't cry, Aunty Becca, perhaps Mr Magrath can put it right.'

Magrath came next day, a tall, dignified figure, very quiet and gentlemanly, and the whole question was thrashed out again without any of the harsh words that had been spoken the previous evening.

'Look here, Mr Magrath,' Ben Harter said, 'I appreciates thy interest in the boy an' I knows he's bright enough but there's plenty for'n to do home here an' times is better with us now than they've been for years.'

The schoolmaster, in his gentle voice, said, 'Mr Harter, history tells us that wars have to be paid for, and you know as well as I do what will happen to farming before very long.'

'Not this time,' said Ben Harter. 'Not this time. Lloyd George will see to that.'

'Mr Harter,' came the sad reply, 'I fear you may soon be disillusioned, but far be it from me to start an argument on politics. I'm more concerned about Eben's future.'

'Aye, aye, that's quite right. An' there be a future here for'n with me. But if I changes my mind I'll let thee know.'

Whether it was born in him, or whether it was something he had assimilated through teaching and example, Eben was a realist. Somehow, he managed to settle to the routine which he already knew only too well. Before he left school he was milking in the morning and then hurrying home to milk again in the evening. It was a job which he did not mind, and Blackie was his pride. Grown now to a fine, deep-bodied cow, every bit as good a looker as her mother the day he remembered her when they had been on that trip to Morfa Bychan, she was milking with her third calf and, at morning milking, now that the cows were out on the rich meadow grazing of high summer, she was giving more than a bucketful of milk. As Eben sat under her on the three-legged stool, the bucket held expertly between his knees and his head pressed against the black silk of her flank, and as he changed hands diagonally from hind and fore teats to the other two hind and fore, and the milk frothed up as he squeezed its warm flow into the steadily filling pail, so would his mind wander to the day his father had bought her for him at Morfa Bychan and he would think what a wonderful and cheerful father he had been that day, so different from what he had now become.

Pockets, too, was still with them, and Mark had kept her busy driving coal dust from the tip at Lower Level to various householders in and around Stepaside, and, in the summer, giving children penny rides on the sands at Amroth. His sharp mind, however, did not see this as his future niche in life.

'That's going to be the thing, boy,' he said to Eben, 'these motor cars. Get to know about them and there'll be something in it.'

Going to Narberth to school did not excite him, and as he grew older he would often take a day or two off to further some particular money-making scheme he happened to have in mind at the moment. Nobody was surprised when he announced that he proposed to leave school in the summer and go to work with Arter Wogan who had opened a garage at Kilgetty.

Thus it was that life had once more settled into a steady

pattern again and, although Eben had never forgotten his sorrow and the bitterness of his feelings against his father over the question of County school, he worked with him as harmoniously as he could.

Eben met the postman that morning by the stone stile at the top of the lane.

'Ar't thee gwain straight back, boy?' said Billy Thank-you Ta, stooping more these days with his canvas post-bag slung over his shoulder and leaning a little more heavily on his gnarled staff.

For forty years he had carried the post on the same round and nobody could ever remember when he had missed a day or been more than a minute or two late.

'Aye,' said Eben, 'I'm gwain straight back. I only came up to see the gate wasn't open not for the cows to go through into the hayfield.'

'Well there thee ar't then. 'Twill save my poor owld legs a bit. There be two letters here today for thy Aunty Becca if thee's'll be good enough to bring 'em down to her for me.'

'Aye, aye,' said Eben, 'I'll bring 'em down to her.'

'Well thank you then, boy. Thank you now – Ta. 'Twill save my poor owld legs a bit.' And he said, 'Thank you now – Ta' once again as he handed the letters over.

'There be one from Hannah out in Canada an' one from that young Griff up in London. 'Tis about time for'n to get married now I shouldn't be surprised. That was a nice li'l maid he had with'n last time he come home. I 'specs they'll fix the day afore long. An' I hopes Hannah's all right for all. Nice li'l maid. Well that'll save my poor owld legs a bit. Thank you now – Ta.'

And off he went down the road in the direction of Templeton to the last farm where his round ended.

Becca was as excited as any schoolgirl to have the two letters by the same post.

'Let's open Griff's first,' she laughed, 'for there'll be more news with Hannah an' he'll take longer to read.'

She was happy about Griff's news because he had been a good son and looked after himself. And he had always made sure his mother did not want for anything as far as it was possible.

'He've been a good boy,' she said, 'an' I hopes he'll be happy. But Lord ha' marcy I canna go all the way to London for a wedding. I'd be afeart.'

'Don't be dull, Aunty Becca,' said Eben, who was full of enthusiasm, 'thou's ha' gotta go. Griff'll meet thee at the station an' he'll look after thee an' he said he'll send thee the money for the fare so that's that an' all about it.'

'Oh Lord sowls,' said Becca, 'there's gwain to be a fandango.'

There was more in the letter about how he had taken charge of one big milk round for his firm now that they had given up milking cows in the city, and when he married he was to have a job in the dairy which would mean better hours and more money.

At last, however, Eben said, 'Let's see what Hannah got to say then.'

He had happy memories of Hannah and was always glad to see a letter coming in her round, clear hand, so much like his own mother's writing had been, and with the Canadian stamp on the envelope.

What Hannah had to say, however, drained the blood from her mother's face as the writing slowly began to make itself understood to her and, putting a hand to her breast, she groaned at last, 'Oh my Godfathers.'

'My dearest Mam,' Hannah wrote:

This is a sad letter and I haven't been able to write to you before this but my dear Cecil have passed away and I am still in a dream because it have been so sudden. He never complained much but I seen he was bad and begged him to go to the doctor. On the Monday morning he complained of a pain in the stomach but said he had to go to work but he would go to the doctor if he didn't feel better when he come home. He collapsed just after he got to work and they rushed him to hospital to operate for apendisitus – but it had gone too far and was burst. I was with him when he died and I closed his dear eyes with my own hands. Oh Mam I am breaking my heart he was such a good man. I turns to the Bible Aunty Kizzy gave me when we come out here and there's her writing in it – I will not fail thee nor forsake thee – but its hard at times like this. He loved his little Rebecca so much and was such a wonderful father to her. She is seven years old now and got my colouring and dark hair and brown eyes and everybody say she is like me but she have her fathers lovely gentle ways and kindness. I know she is breaking her little heart for him but she creeps into my bed at night and puts her arms round me and tells me that she will always be with me. I knows now how little Eben must have been when dear Aunty Kizzy died so sudden because she loved him so much but of course he isn't little now. I don't

69

know what is going to happen now. The company have been very good and Cecil was paying into a society they haves so I will get a very small pension but it won't be much. I been thinking about coming home but I got Rebecca to think about now as well and if I was to come home there wouldn't be nothing much for us. So I will try for a job here if I can get one and write to you again when I knows more. It have been bitter cold here and nobody knows what it is like unless they been in it. It have made me think of the summer days back home and how I would like to live them days again with the smell of the hay and the honeysuckle in the hedges. Is the big pine tree still there by the Gangrel and the sicamore growing alongside Heronsmill? I don't like the cold. It was something we never thought about until we came out here and we was never used to it before because the weather was so mild and Heronsmill and the Gangrel was so sheltered. Still we got to learn to put up with it when it comes and it is very healthy and it is lovely here sometimes. Give my love to Eben and Uncle Ben and Mark and the girls. I forgot to say I had a letter from Josh in New Zealand to say he is getting married to a girl who's parents went out there from Saundersfoot but I expect you heard from him yourself by now. Give my best love to my dear sister Tilly. It is wonderful the way she have stuck by you and Uncle Ben. I hope she is lucky to have a good man one day like my dear Cecil was to me. My little Rebecca sends a big kiss to the grandma she have never seen but I tell her all about you. Write to me soon Mam.

    Your loving daughter Hannah.

The day after Hannah's letter came, Becca went with Ben Harter in the trap to Morfa Bychan to see the Wyrriots.

When at last they reached Morfa Bychan it was evident that George Wyrriot had heard from Hannah. The meeting was too much for him and he just broke down and cried.

A child's wheelbarrow lay on its side outside the garden gate and there was a pair of small clogs by the door. They reminded Ben of Bridget's condition that day and he thought that George, too, had had his share of trouble.

'Aw aye,' said George as they pulled up to the table for the snack that Nelly had rustled up for them, 'we kept the li'l boy an' he's the toptest li'l crut thou cou'st ever clap thy eyes on.'

Bridget had gone away and married a soldier during the war and left her child behind her.

'How's she gettin' on?' asked Becca.

'Oh, fine,' said Nelly. 'The chap she married had a good

job afore the war an' he's only waitin' to get fixed up again now, an' then they'll move into a new place.'

George looked at her. Normally he took no notice of her empty chatter and her obsession with Bridget. Now, the grief which was upon him had taken its toll of his patience.

'For Gawd's sake, 'ooman,' he said, 'don't talk so damn dull. She've married the biggest waster as God ever put breath in an' thou know'st it.'

Nelly bridled. She said, 'He's a smart, good-lookin' chap.'

George ignored her.

'Becca,' he said, 'he was stationed down here in the war an' all dolled up in uniform an' he filled poor Bridget's empty li'l head with some rammas about his family, an' Lord knows what else an' after she'd married'n she went home with'n for the first time an' his family was no better than gypos.'

It had not been the happiest of visits and Becca was glad when it was over.

The letter from Josh came two days later and Becca's moods alternated between gladness for the boys, despair for Hannah and fluster at the thought of going to London.

Tilly, as Hannah had said in her letter, had been wonderful to her mother. Indeed she had been wonderful to everybody and was always the quiet helper without ever being much in the limelight. Like Hannah she had the Perrots' colouring and her mother's features, yet her dark hair wasn't the rich wavy hair that Hannah had and her brown eyes didn't have the sparkle and dancing mischief of her older sister. She was quieter and more retiring altogether.

'How wou'st thee manage if I goes to London?' said Becca.

'How doesn't thee think I'll manage, Mam?' smiled Tilly.

'Wou'st thou be all right, maid? Or shall I write an' tell Griff straight off I canna do it?'

'Thou's'll do no such thing,' said Tilly. 'An' how does't thee think I managed when I had thee in bed with flu for a week in the winter an' feed 'em at the mill as well?'

'But it seems a lot to leave a li'l maid on her own.'

'Mam, I'm twenty-one this year, or ha'st thee forgot?'

'Lord sowls! It'll be thy turn to get married next.'

'If I gets married who'll look after thee, Mam? An' how can I get married when I haven't got a chap?'

'Never mind,' smiled her mother, 'perhaps there'll be some smart young chap with new folks comin' into Deerfield.'

'We'll cross that bridge when we comes to 'n,' said Tilly.

It was Eben who was the fount of all knowledge on Deerfield as far as the family was concerned.

In the winter Mr Magrath had started evening classes for young men in the area and, remembering Eben's bitter disappointment at not being able to go to Narberth to school, and knowing his ability, he asked him if he would like to join.

Mrs Magrath had a big interest in drama and was producing three one-act plays. She wanted a boy of Eben's age for a play called *The Squire's Son*, and she thought he would be just right.

Out of affection for Mr Magrath, Eben had agreed to take part.

'Now, Eben,' said Mrs Magrath in her sitting-room at his first practice, 'you mustn't slouch back in the chair like that. Sit up straight and fold your hands in your lap.'

'Lord sowls, Mrs Magrath, I feels as if I'm all hands and feet.'

'Now don't say "Lord Souls". Say "Good gracious". And you must keep the vowel open and make sure you pronounce the vowels clearly. Like this.'

So the lessons had gone on, and that winter Eben would stand in the kitchen at the mill, or sometimes at the Gangrel, and speak in his posh voice and have Becca and Tilly laughing, and Mark, too, sometimes, although he was not often home. Off first thing in the morning for the garage, and late coming home in the evening, they did not see much of him. And Ben Harter was not often there in the evenings either. It was the pub for him still.

Liz Whithow, whose hard-working mother had made the effort for her to go to the County school at the same time as Eben was being denied, was also in the play as a parlour-maid. Eben had to steal a kiss off her behind the door, and, whatever the parlour-maid was supposed to think of it, Liz Whithow liked it. There was something about Liz that stirred Eben physically. He had not bothered about girls before, but he had spent the whole of his life close to living things and he knew every phase in the cycle of procreation from mating, through advancing pregnancy, to birth and life and death.

Liz had warmth and hair that was golden, and eyes that were violet blue. Mr Magrath had been talking about poetry to them one evening in night school. He did that sometimes to give them a wide knowledge, he said. And they had had a poem by Rossetti about the Blessed Damouzel. Eben could not understand it all and it sounded mysterious and sad, but it made him think of Liz.

> Her eyes knew more of rest and shade
> Than waters stilled at even;
> She had three lilies in her hand
> And the stars in her hair were seven
> And her hair lying down her back
> Was yellow like ripe corn.

Except that Liz did not have her hair lying down her back any more. She had piled it up on top now and very grown-up it made her look.

'They'll be moving in before the end of the month,' said Liz as they talked over a cup of tea after practice. 'Mam has nearly finished cleaning, and there was a letter from Mr Bromilow this morning saying that they've made arrangements about moving the furniture.'

'It will be nice to see the house lived in again,' said Mr Magrath, 'and a help to the village.'

'The land is gone in a bad state,' someone offered. And another added, 'The way things are going now they'll have a job to get anybody to take it off 'em.'

So the talk had gone concerning Deerfield, the old country house between Heronsmill and Stepaside, sat there on top of the hill looking down Pleasant Valley to the sea at Wiseman's Bridge. When the iron works had been in full swing, and the pits still working, the agent had lived there in some style but it had been empty since before the war. Now some 'toff' had bought it and was coming to live there.

'No,' said Eben, as Becca and Tilly mentioned Deerfield, 'I haven't heard tell of any young man comin' there. Liz Whithow reckons it is just this toff an' his wife who's delicate an' a young maid with 'em still in school.'

'How owld is she, boy?' said Tilly.

'Who, Liz Whithow?'

'Never mind about Liz Whithow,' said Tilly, 'how owld is the li'l maid these new people got?'

'I don't know how owld she is,' replied Eben, 'but Liz reckons she's a spoilt brat. Her mother was there last time they came down to see how the work was gettin' on an' it was all Penny this an' Penny that an' what colour did she want the doors painted an' Lord only knows what else.'

'Maybe she'll have a brother,' said Becca.

'No, there's no brother,' said Eben, 'just this li'l maid.'

'And her name is Penny,' said Tilly.

'That's what Liz Whithow said.'

Eben was soon to find out for himself.

It was one of those springs when the fields were still bare.

'We got plenty o' grass,' Ben Harter would say, 'but 'tis very short. Better put the cows in the long meadow for a' hour or two.' And so Eben had taken them up the road where the grass grew in the hedges long before the many mouths of cows, horses and sheep would give it a chance to start growing in the fields.

On the tops of the hedgerows there were clumps of double daffodils, and here and there the slender little 'Tenby daffs'. There were pink primroses, too, 'escaped' from the gardens of the cottages and houses which, one by one, had fallen into ruin. There were celandines and daisies which opened to the sun by day and closed by night. There were trees in bud, the birds sang, and everywhere there was that renewed feeling of well-being of which Eben had first been conscious as a small boy, on that day in spring when he had run shouting across the meadow from the Gangrel to the Mill.

In the ditches the flags threw up their first spikes, and the cows breathed on them, and smelt them, and then returned to the grass on the verges and the banks where the violets grew. Steadily they wrapped their tongues round the long grass, tore it out, munched and passed along. Now and again Blackie would prod some of the others on, or hold them back according to her whim.

Today she had gone on ahead. As Eben made a move to go after her he noticed an odd primrose or two lying in the road.

As he rounded the bend at Rushyland, where Uncle Tom the clog-maker had once lived, he came in sight of the lake where it crossed the road. Carts and traps went through the water, but for those on foot there was a stone bridge. Gramfer had told him that Merryman the mason had built it. A fine bridge it was too. The walls left a pathway wide enough for one person to walk in comfort, and beneath it three culverts carried the water through to the road where, like all fords, it spread out before collecting again to travel on towards the sea.

Blackie stood now, blocking the exit from the bridge and gazing, with ears forward and head held high, at a girl standing in the middle of the bridge. About twelve, Eben judged her to be. She had nondescript dark hair, light blue eyes, a sharp nose almost hooked, a small mouth and pointed chin. She had a bunch of primroses in one hand.

Ignoring Eben, she said in a loud voice, 'Go away, you horrible brute.'

Blackie continued to gaze at her.

'Go away I tell you.'

Eben took no more notice than Blackie who suddenly regurgitated and began to chew her cud.

At last, the girl said, 'I say, is this your cow?'

Eben decided he did not like her.

'Are you talking to me?' he said, in his best Mrs Magrath voice.

'Who else would you suppose I was talking to, you oaf?'

He looked at her. Then he said, 'Your manners leave something to be desired.'

That was a line he had had to say in the play as the Squire's Son and he thought it sounded good. It made her mad anyway.

'Do you know who you're talking to?' she demanded.

'Not for sure, but I wouldn't be surprised if it isn't little Penny from Deerfield.'

'Miss Penelope to you.'

'Honey, dear God!' laughed Eben, 'hark at that!'

'Now will you move that cow so that I may pass?'

'Aw you can pass. She won't bush you.'

'What do you mean by "bush you"?'

'What I said, and she won't.'

'She won't what?'

'She won't bush you.'

Getting red in the face, the girl said, 'You are an insufferable lout.'

'And you are a horrible little child because you pick flowers and then throw them over the road.'

'How dare you speak to me like that! I'll tell my father what you said and I'll do what I like with the flowers because I picked them.'

'Will you now?' said Eben.

'Yes I will.'

'And what will you do with 'em?'

At a loss for words, and with her temper rising, she glared at Eben. Then she blurted out, 'I'll do *that*!' and she flung the primroses over the wall of the bridge down into the water.

Eben watched as they floated away. Then he said, 'You're

a little bitch. And you can tell your father that as well.'

Then he put his hand on Blackie's neck and said, 'Come on then, maid.'

Blackie lowered her head, turned and set off for home.

The next day, as Eben turned the cows into the roadway, the girl was standing in the road close to the gate. As the cows settled to their grazing along the two hedgerows she smiled a half-hearted smile and Eben said, 'Good morning.'

That was something his mother had always taught him. Never say 'hello'. Always 'good morning' or 'good afternoon' or 'good day'. Be dignified. And he was very dignified now as he said 'good morning'.

The girl said, 'Good morning. You may call me Penny if you wish. What's your name?'

'Eben Harter.'

'I thought you wouldn't speak to me this morning.'

'I'll speak to anybody as long as they know how to behave themselves,' said Eben.

'You made me very angry,' said the girl.

Eben thought for a moment. Then he said, 'Do you always get angry if you can't have your own way?'

'I was frightened.'

'What of?'

'Of that big black horrible cow.'

'She's not horrible and I told you she wouldn't bush.'

'What do you mean by bush?'

Eben looked at the girl. She was serious. It was his first encounter with anyone from outside the community in which he had always lived. Slowly he began to realize that there were words which these people really did not understand, just as there were things of the country of which they knew nothing. He said, 'When I said she wouldn't bush I meant she wouldn't gore you with her horns.'

'Oh! I see.'

The girl seemed to think about this. Then she said, 'What did you think when I threw the primroses into the water?'

'You know what I thought.'

'It was silly of me. I like flowers very much. I'm terribly fond of them.'

'Then why did you throw them into the water?'

'Because you made me cross.'

'So it was my fault according to that.'

'Of course it was,' the girl smiled. 'I'm so glad you see it that way.'

'But I don't,' said Eben.

'You're horrid and I can't think why I bothered to come and explain to you.'

'Neither can I,' said Eben, 'so now you can go on home again.'

But she did not go. Eben sat in the hedge and the girl stood in the road. The sun was getting warmer and it was sheltered from the wind. It was pleasant and very peaceful.

Suddenly there was a harsh quick call, *kraak, kraak*, and a flash of colour and blue and white as a bird darted between the trees and disappeared from view again with only time for a glimpse of it to be had.

'Oh, what was that?' said the girl.

'A jay.'

'How do you know?'

Eben looked at her. He said, 'If you didn't want to know, why did you ask me? Unless you just want to start an argument.'

The girl ignored this. 'It's a beautiful bird,' she said.

'Only to look at,' said Eben. 'But it's horrible really, and very destructive.' Then he added, 'Like little girls who pick flowers and then shed them all over the road.'

'I'm not a little girl. I'm twelve.'

'Then you're old enough to know better.'

'How old are you?'

'I'm fifteen,' said Eben.

'Do you know all about the birds and flowers and wild animals?'

'Not everything,' said Eben, 'I don't know everything. But I know what Gramfer taught me. And I've seen things.'

'What things have you seen?'

'I've seen a stoat killing a rabbit, and a buzzard flying up with a rabbit in its claws, and a heron catching a trout, and a fox going off with a hen, and I've seen a badger in a trap.'

'Oh, how horrid you are,' said the girl, making a face which reminded Eben of Bridget's silliness when George Wyrriot had put the lobster to boil at Morfa Bychan. Blackie was a calf then and she had had six calves herself now. Martha Jane had gone, but Pockets was still with them. The girl broke in on his thoughts. 'What does a heron look like and which way does it catch a trout?'

Eben told her. And he told her much besides to open for her the pages of a book which she hardly knew existed. She had come from the town and knew little of country things.

There was hardly a question she could ask him about the ways of the wild creatures that he could not answer.

Next winter, he said, he would show her how to set a rabbit snare and take her ferreting, but he didn't want any of her old nonsense.

When she had gone, Eben thought about this odd girl who had so suddenly come into his life, and he realized that all the time he had been with her he had been careful how he spoke. With what he had learned at night school, and the lessons Mrs Magrath had been giving him on diction, he would show her whether he was an oaf or not.

In the course of the next week or so, during which the cows took a daily bellyful from the roadside hedges, she came every day, and if the friendship did not exactly blossom, at least some sort of understanding was reached. Several times the girl had been on the verge of flying into a temper, but had soon realized that it would neither upset Eben nor impress him, and she soon came to understand that she was much more anxious to be in his company than he was to be with her.

Algernon Berrington Dankworth Bromilow had been 'something in the army' before he retired to live at Deerfield. Before that he had been for less than a decade in the family cotton business in Lancashire. At Oxford University he had played rugby and cricket with some distinction but had failed to get a degree. The world knew him as Algie.

After the war, he decided that he could not face again a humdrum life of commerce. His own share in the family cotton business was more than sufficient to keep him in comfort for the rest of his days, and with that prospect he was content. He had a wife whom he loved and a twelve-year-old daughter who was without fault in his eyes.

He came to Heronsmill with his daughter one morning some weeks after his arrival at Deerfield. A tall, dark man, with curly hair going grey at the temples, and a face that had known wind and sun, he wore plus-fours and strong, brown brogues. He smoked a cigar and had a stout walking-stick with a silver band on it.

Eben was just coming out of the stable, leading Dandy, older now and survivor of a period at the Mill when so many horses had come and gone. He let go of her as he saw the visitors and she walked off down the lane for the bottom meadows.

'Good morning, young man,' said the newcomer, 'I suppose

you'll be young Harter.'

Eben searched the man's face, weighing him up. Then he said, 'That's right, Eben Harter. Good morning.'

The man looked at Eben more carefully.

'My name is Bromilow,' he said, 'and I've come to live at Deerfield.'

Eben noticed that he had not said Major Bromilow nor even Mister. Just Bromilow. And he had not said he had bought Deerfield. Just that he had come to live there.

'I'm pleased to meet you, sir,' he said, and held out his hand.

Algie Bromilow shook hands with the youth and was surprised by the strength and firmness of his grip. No wonder his daughter had been so impressed that she had scarcely stopped talking about him.

'Is your father about?'

'He's down in the meadow looking at a cow close to calving.'

'How long will he be?'

'I can call him if you want him,' said Eben.

'I'd be glad if you would. I'd like to buy a pony for my daughter.'

'I didn't know you could ride,' said Eben, turning now for the first time to Penny who had not so far spoken.

'I can't yet,' she said, 'but it's terribly easy to learn and I thought that now we've come to live in the country I might as well take it up.'

Eben looked at her father and said, 'She'd better have something quiet to start with. I'll call my father,' and he went to the gate and gave a shrill double-whistle. His father, walking across the lower meadows, stopped, looked up, and raised his hand in acknowledgement.

'He'll be here now in a minute,' said Eben.

Bromilow said, 'Thank you very much.'

By way of conversation he said to Eben, 'How do you like living here?'

'I've never lived anywhere else.'

'Then you mean you're happy here.'

'Very.'

'Then that's because you've a happy nature,' said Bromilow. 'Good thing that, happy nature. Jolly good, I'm all for it. Lot of people about today not a bit happy. Wanting something for nothing all the time. Never be happy that way. Lot to be said for the old days. Everybody very happy then. Glad you're happy. Jolly good.'

Those who knew him would have said that Algie Bromilow had made a speech.

'Play any football?' he asked.

'Soccer sometimes up at Kilgetty,' said Eben, 'but there's no boys' team there.'

'Try rugby. Better game altogether. Any rugby teams round here?'

'There's a good team in Tenby but I've never seen them.'

'Pity about that. Next winter we'll go and see them together.'

'Thank you very much, sir,' said Eben, 'I'd like that.'

'Jolly good,' said Bromilow, and added, 'What about cricket now? Play any cricket?'

'Only a bit now and again in the evenings. It's awkward in the summer with haymaking and one thing and another. If you can't be sure to play they won't pick you, and you can't be sure on a farm.'

'Good game, cricket. Come on up and we'll fix up a net on the lawn. See what you're like.'

Eben thought he was going to be busy. But there was more to come.

'Any shooting round here?'

'Not a lot,' said Eben. 'There's nobody breeding and the rabbit trappers don't give 'em much peace.'

'Trappers be damned. Setting in the open I suppose?'

'I'm afraid so, sir. You go into Tenby and see the pheasants hanging up with one leg missing.'

'Do you let your rabbits or catch them yourselves?'

'Oh no,' said Eben, 'my father catches them himself. He won't have a trap on the place. He reckons they only swarm the rabbits.'

'Very wise. Very wise. What d'you use?'

'Mostly ferrets and nets, or the bitch with a lamp at night.'

'Do you use a gun?'

'Not very much, unless it's for pigeons on the corn or the green crops. And maybe look for a woodcock in the hard weather.'

'I should think this is a good place for a woodcock?'

'Oh yes, a topping place all along these bottoms.'

'Jolly good,' enthused Bromilow, 'we must see what we can do about it.'

They had been talking with such interest that they had quite forgotten the girl when Ben Harter's arrival was announced by the slamming of the gate.

'Good morning, Mr Harter,' said Bromilow as he advanced towards Ben Harter with his hand out, 'my name's Bromilow. I've come to live at Deerfield.'

'Good mornin', maister,' said Ben Harter touching the brim of his old billycock hat and then extending his hand to receive the newcomer's handshake. 'I hopes you'll be main happy there. 'Tis nice to see th'owld place bein' lived in again.'

'And this is my daughter.'

Ben Harter raised his hat and said, 'Good mornin', missy,' and Penny smiled back at him.

'I've just been talking to your son here,' continued Bromilow. 'Most knowledgeable young chap. We'll have to get together.'

'Now then, Daddy,' said Penny, 'shall we see about the pony?'

'Ah, yes, the pony. That's quite right. Do you have a pony to sell, Mr Harter? I'm told you do a bit with horses and my daughter's very keen to learn to ride.'

'Well, now, I'm not doin' so much with 'em as when the war was on but I still keeps a few for the trade to Bonville's Court. An' I got one li'l pony here as would suit her a master-piece if she can ride.'

'Oh, I'll soon learn,' put in Penny, 'it's terribly easy.'

'Better start on somethin' steady, missy. Come you over tomorrow afternoon an' we'll put a saddle on Dandy an' see how you shapes for all.'

The following afternoon Penny presented herself in a new pair of riding breeches for her first lesson.

Dandy, who had a mouth like velvet, responded to the slightest touch of the reins so that the first few minutes were spent in turning in circles, first in one direction and then in another. When a forward direction had finally been embarked upon, the girl pulled on the reins, having nothing else to hold on to. Dandy stopped, and the girl fell forward on to Dandy's neck and slid gently, but nevertheless undignifiedly, to the ground, where she sat, with Dandy looking down at her.

By the end of a month she had improved slightly and Ben Harter let her try the pony he had in mind from the bunch intended for the colliery. The pony was not too lively and the girl managed fairly well. Mr Bromilow expressed himself well-satisfied and bought it. By that time Eben had been accepted as a reliable young friend and Bromilow had recognized him as a natural ball-player.

'If you haven't got time to play cricket,' Bromilow said, 'think about rugby for the winter.'

'But I've never played rugby,' said Eben.

'Never mind. The best way to learn a game is to watch people who play it. We can go and see Tenby in the winter and maybe we can see an international match. Good idea that. Good rugger players these Welshmen.'

Eben was not sure how he would fare at rugby.

'No trouble,' said Bromilow. 'Go on kicking your soccer ball about. Play all you can. But watch a bit of rugby. Then when you're a bit older have a go. Just the build for it.'

Eben had all of the Harters' width of shoulder, but, if he kept on growing, he was going to be more than their average height. Already he topped his father by a couple of inches and was even stronger than Eddie had been at the same age.

He did keep on growing. The hard work strengthened him, and the cricket practice and occasional game of football at Kilgetty both helped to develop him further, but it amounted to little compared with the influence which the new company had on his bearing and on his speech.

In short, Eben was trying to improve himself. He continued to attend Mr Magrath's evening classes and to take books home to read in the evenings. Sometimes he would read by the light of the lamp at the kitchen table and sometimes by the flickering light of the candle on the chair by the side of the bed, until the wick burned low and finally guttered itself into darkness in a pool of grease.

Reading on until late into the night often caused him to oversleep, and his father usually had to call him at least twice before he would get out of bed in the morning. Sometimes his father would grumble about this. Eben tried not to be rude to him, but he was not going to be brow-beaten. On one occasion there had been an argument.

'Pay thee better to get thy sleep at night an' get up ready for a day's work,' said Ben Harter.

'I like reading.'

'What good will it do thee now?'

'If by now you mean since you stopped me going to County school, then it might help me to get a better job one day.'

'Look, boy, don't go gettin' big ideas into thy head becos of the Bromilows.'

Eben bridled.

'What's wrong with the Bromilows?'

'I'm not sayin' there's anythin' wrong with 'em, but don't

let 'em put big ideas into thy head.'

'What big ideas?'

'Like gettin' better jobs an' that.'

'They've never said anything about it. I just want to read and get on for myself the same as I wanted to go to the County school.'

'Never mind about County school now. I've said afore there's plenty of work home here for thee.'

'Oh, aye,' said Eben, 'plenty of it. And that's about all.'

'What else do'st thee want?'

'I wouldn't mind being paid half of what I'm worth instead of having to catch rabbits for the only bit of money I get.'

'Money's tight.'

'Not too tight for you to go to the pub.'

Ben Harter blazed. 'What the hell have it got to do with thee how I spends my time and my money!'

'Nothing, Father, but that wasn't what you used to tell Eddie. "Look after it," you used to say. "There's always the good and the bad so make sure you try to be one of the good ones." That's what you used to say, wasn't it?'

Mention of Eddie was like a douche of cold water. And Eben, as he grew older, was beginning to understand how his father must have been shattered by the loss of his eldest boy and his wife in such quick succession. He knew now what was meant by drowning your sorrows.

Nothing more was said about the reading and Eben started to receive a few shillings every week.

Mark had his own money. He and Arter Wogan were getting on well together. Wogan had bought a charabanc and they planned to get another as soon as Mark was old enough to drive. It would not be long now. The future looked good.

'Can't go wrong, boy,' Mark said to Eben. 'It'll be years before people can afford cars. Only the toffs. And the charabancs'll go where the railways don't.'

'Good boy,' said Eben, 'keep at it.' Then he laughed, and, imitating Bromilow, said, 'Jolly good.'

'You wait and see,' said Mark. 'You'll live to see the day when the railways'll be a thing of the past. People want to go where they like and see a bit of the country.'

'Don't thee start gwain too fast in them owld tacks,' said Becca, 'or everybody's gwain to get kilt.'

'No, no, Aunty Becca. We won't get killed,' said Mark. 'The roads are too rough for that, cutting the tyres to pieces. The roads'll all have to be tarred.'

'Lord sowls, boy, there've been enough trouble with that already with the horses scuttin' and sliderin' all over the place.'

'Never mind about the horses. Another ten years and they'll be finished. They'll go before the railways.'

'Hisht, boy,' said Becca, 'afore thy father hears thee.'

'Do'n good to hear a few home truths,' said Mark. 'Help'n to move with the times a bit.'

'Don't be too hard on him,' said Eben. 'Something died in him when he lost Eddie and Mam.'

'Aye indeed,' said Becca, 'life can be mortal hard sometimes.'

And life indeed was getting harder. Mr Magrath's prophecy on the likely future for farming, when Ben Harter had been so determined on Eben leaving school, had already come true. Shortly afterwards it had been followed by a worsening of conditions in the towns, and nowhere was it worse than in the mining valleys.

Liza was home for a week from the Rhondda with Jim Cartlett and their baby, and there was another one on the way. They were staying with Esther in Saundersfoot and came out on a Sunday in summer with Ruth who had come back to Saundersfoot to live. Her boy, Edward, was nine years old. He had Eddie's features but none of his father's boisterous ways. None of his devil-may-care bravado. Books he liked, and drawing.

Esther and her husband, Giles Merryman, came with them and the gathering of his family around him again cheered Ben Harter beyond recognition.

They had walked along the dram-road, through the tunnels from Saundersfoot, and followed it up past the old iron works in Pleasant Valley. When they reached Heronsmill Liza said, 'The first thing I'm gwain to do is go an' pile a stone down Lower Level pit.'

It was a ritual with the children from the Mill and the Gangrel. Often when he wrote home Griff would say, 'Don't forget to chuck a stone down the Lower Level pit for me.'

How deep the pit was nobody knew. Old wooden posts surrounded the mouth of it, and thick wire rope going rusty had been used as fencing. Where the ground sloped away from the fence to the mouth of the pit, brambles grew thickly, and the choicest fruit each year went unpicked. The terror of the place had been so ingrained from an early age that no child would have dreamed of venturing inside the fence. It was enough to stand outside and throw a stone into the mouth which gaped darkly where the brambles did not quite meet.

As Liza threw her stone Eben remembered the dread which he had felt when he was very small and Gramfer had initiated him into this awesome practice.

Taking a stone the size of his first, Gramfer had thrown it. 'Hark now,' he had said.

Eben heard the stone hit the side of the pit high up. As it began to fall it clattered from side to side and then came an echo. As Eben stood there the clatter and the echo merged into one and then became a distant intermittent booming.

He was suddenly afraid as seconds passed and there came another boom from the dark depths. And then, after an eternity, came the final thundering reverberation as the stone at last hit the water lying stagnant so far below the face of the earth and the echo rolled away through the still, silent woodland. A frightening place was the Lower Level.

'Come on then, boy,' Gramfer had said, 'let's go from here.' And Eben had been glad to catch hold of his hand. He had never needed any more warning about keeping away from the pit.

The previous winter, Eben had gone with some of the boys to a political meeting in Kilgetty, where there was always the chance of some noise and nonsense, so that he knew something of what his father and Jim Cartlett were arguing about later that afternoon.

At the meeting the speaker had been Willie Jenkins, the Labour candidate for Pembrokeshire. A small man, with bushy eyebrows and piercing eyes under a high forehead, he radiated vitality and good humour. Words flowed from him in a rich and powerful voice as he covered a vast range of subjects from armaments to world trade, and from social conditions and the dignity of labour to the slump in the price of cattle. He held his packed audience spellbound until, at last, the torrent of words ceased. Then, old man Wier of Tregant, in his loud nasal grunt, demanded, 'What did ya do in the war?'

There were a few scattered cries of 'Hear, hear.'

Willie Jenkins folded his arms and, screwing up his jaw in a characteristic mannerism, glared at the speaker.

At last Bob Wier lowered his eyes.

'Unfortunately, it would seem,' said Willie Jenkins, 'I was troubled by a fundamental belief in the sanctity of human life. I was a conscientious objector and sewed mail-bags in a number of His Majesty's prisons. That's what I did.'

There was just an odd shout of protest and then, still glaring

85

at Wier, he rasped out scornfully, 'And what did you do? Stand up and tell the people.'

Wier was a dealer as well as a farmer. Nothing had been too hot or too heavy for him during the war years when the money had flowed freely. He was not a likeable man, and many in the audience, as well as Ben Harter, warmed to the pocket-sized giant on the platform.

'I'll tell you what you did,' said Willie Jenkins, 'I'll tell you what you did. You stayed home and made money while the blood of the nation's manhood flowed in rivers from Flanders to the Dardanelles. And what is there to show for it? We've got their comrades tramping the roads begging for a crust, and that's nothing to the poverty and degradation we're going to see before long unless we have a radical change in government policy. Is this what Lloyd George was talking about when he promised you a land fit for heroes to live in?' Then he was off again on a tirade against the social evils of the day.

Now, in the old kitchen at Heronsmill, Ben Harter was saying, 'I'll tell thee what'll happen. If there be no money in farmin' it wunnat be long afore there's no money in nothin' else. So just remember that when thee'rt standin' on the street corners up there in the valley an' not a crust to put in thy bellies.'

Baldwin's government gave way to Ramsay MacDonald. Then, after a year struggling on without a clear majority, Labour gave way again to the Tories. In opposition the politicians knew what needed to be done. In power they failed to do it. At an impressionable age, Eben decided he wanted nothing to do with politics. Ben Harter's prophecy came true sooner than anyone could have expected, and times became as hard for some as anything Gramfer Jenkyn had ever talked about.

Esther, down in Saundersfoot, gave birth to a boy, and Liza, in the poverty-stricken Rhondda, had her second baby, a girl. Now and again Becca would send her a pair of rabbits which Eben had caught, and there would always be a warm and pathetic letter of thanks as soon as they arrived. When they came down in the summer they went back with half a ham and as many potatoes as they could carry.

As spring changed to summer, and autumn turned to winter, conditions seemed to grow steadily worse. The Farmers' Dairy Society, for which Willie Jenkins had worked so hard, went into liquidation, and the farmers who had supported it lost still more money. But at least, said Becca, they were not going hungry.

It was in the early spring, at the end of a long hard winter, that the flames of bickering between Eben and his father blazed into an open confrontation. And Blackie was the cause of it.

Eben had played a few games of soccer for Kilgetty and had also joined the Tenby Rugby Club. Just coming up to his eighteenth birthday he was marked down as a player with a future at either code. Whatever hopes he may have entertained, however, he knew that he would always have to contend with opposition from his father.

'I've towld thee often enough,' said Ben Harter on the Saturday morning, 'as there be work to be done home here without wastin' time trapesin' about the country to chase a blessed football.'

'And I've told you often enough,' said Eben, 'that as long as I'm working home here I'm going to play football on a Saturday and nobody's going to stop me.'

'Well, I'll stop thee.'

'Which way will you stop me?'

'I won't give thee no money.'

'Then I'll go and work somewhere else.'

'Where wou'st thee go? There be no work to be had.'

'Don't be too sure about that,' said Eben. 'Times aren't that bad that I couldn't find something somewhere for as much as the bit I get here. It's only for what I make on the rabbits that I can work here for what I do.'

That evening Blackie was sickening to calve. It was her ninth calf. Every year she had calved regularly in the spring and looked like going on for ever.

Eben, back early after a 'home' game, looked at her now as she fidgeted in the loose-box at the end of the cowshed. She lowed gently as he raised the hurricane lamp above his head and a mouse scuttled through the straw and into a crack in the stone wall where the shadows fell away to darkness.

'How's it going here then, maid?' said Eben as he ran his hand over her back.

Earlier, the water-bag had been hanging and it had now burst. Blackie swished her tail and was ill at ease. Her udder was hard and hot. It would be a relief when she had calved.

'I don't like the look of her,' said Eben as he went back to the house.

His father, who was shaving before going to the pub, said, 'How not?'

'Her bones have gone this good time and the water-bag is burst with her.'

'There ought to be a calf there soon then.'

'All the same,' said Eben, 'I'd like to see her calve before you go.'

'She'll be all right. She never have gave no trouble. Thou ca'st keep thy eye on her.'

An hour later Eben went out to the farmyard again and he felt sure that Blackie was in trouble. As it happened, both Aunty Becca and Tilly were out and Mark was seldom home anyway.

He had never calved a cow himself but he had often helped his father. So he fetched a bucket of warm water and a bar of soap and took off his shirt. When he had put a halter on Blackie's head and tied the end to a ring in the wall he soaped his arm well and then gently put his hand inside her. At last, exploring carefully, he could feel the calf's feet, but there was no sign of its head. For a long time he tried. His arm was in right up to the shoulder and he began to sweat. Then he found what he was looking for and knew the task would be more than he could manage. The calf was upside down and the head was back.

At first he thought he would go to Tregant for help. Bad neighbours or not, they were still neighbours, and would help in an emergency. They would no doubt be pleased to come so that the Harters would feel obligated to them. And this was something Eben wanted to avoid. Putting his shirt and jacket back on he set off for Deerfield. A few months previously the Bromilows had had the telephone installed. It was still the only one round Stepaside.

Mrs Bromilow came to the door. Her pleasure at seeing Eben was evident. A slightly built dark-haired woman, she had none of her husband's joviality but her kind nature showed in her face. Eben wondered again how Penny had come by her nasty streak.

'I'm sorry to trouble you, Mrs Bromilow,' said Eben, 'but I wonder could you telephone for me?'

'Of course, Eben. It's no trouble at all. Come in. Is anything wrong?'

'I'm afraid there's a cow with us can't calve and I'm on my own there.' He did not want to say his father was at the pub, and Mrs Bromilow, whatever she was thinking, was too much of a lady to say anything.

'Well come on in then. I'll tell my husband you're here.'

Bromilow, however, had heard Eben's voice and came out now, wearing slippers, into the hall from the lounge.

'What's the trouble?' he asked.

'Blackie can't calve and I'm on my own.'

Bromilow darted a quick look at him. 'I see. Who d'you want to phone?'

'Well I don't know. I was wondering if we could get a vet?'

'Good idea. Who'd you usually have?'

'We've never had a proper vet before. Old Klondyke Skeel used to come whenever there was any trouble, but he died just before Christmas and we haven't had anybody since.'

'There must be a vet about somewhere.'

'There's one come to live in Narberth. When Klondyke died I remember we were talking about it and Father said we'd have to go to the Narberth man next time we wanted somebody, but we haven't needed anybody this long time.'

'What's his name?'

'I don't know.'

'Never mind,' said Bromilow, going to the telephone which was fixed to the wall and picking up the earpiece cradled in a hook on the side. 'We'll ask Narberth post office. They'll know.'

They did know. His name was Mr Bannerman and he was home. Bromilow spoke to him and he said he would come straightaway. 'Jolly good,' said Bromilow.

'Well, thank you very much,' said Eben.

'Not at all. No trouble at all. Now then, let me get something on my feet and I'll be with you.'

'Oh, no indeed,' protested Eben, 'there's no need. I'll be all right with the vet.'

'Nonsense. Might need a bit of help. Always worth having a spare man. Good idea.'

And so Algie Bromilow put on the boots he wore when he went shooting, reached for his hat and top-coat, and the two of them set off together for the Mill.

On the way they spoke little. Penny, it seemed, was not home from her boarding school for the week-end.

'Some play or something they're getting ready for the end of term. Says she wants to be an actress now and become a film star. Good God, what'll she think of next? Like some female Charlie Chaplin. Funny chap that. But Penny couldn't do it. Change her mind again next week.'

Like the pony, thought Eben. The riding business had not lasted very long.

As they arrived at the gate at the top of the lane they heard the sound of a motor in the distance and saw a stab of light away through the trees. A barn owl screeched somewhere in the direction of Tregant and the small feet of some nocturnal creature scurried through the dead leaves beneath the undergrowth.

Eben felt less alone now and the thought of the vet gave him confidence. They heard the car crawl carefully through Ford's Lake, and then come grinding up the slope round the bend by Rushyland, to chug to a halt where they waited.

One of the new high-backed Fords with brass lamps it was, Eben noted. Mark would have been interested in that. But Eben was more concerned about Blackie.

The vet was a young man of heavy build and looked competent and self-assured.

'How many of the neighbours have had a go at her?'

The question was direct but without sarcasm and Eben did not resent it.

'Nobody. I felt inside her myself but the head seemed to be back as far as I could tell and the calf upside down so I didn't try any more.'

'Well, thank God for that. I've only been here six months and most of the calving cases I've been called to so far have been those where some ignorant bugger has balled it up first.'

Ready at last, the vet said, 'Now then, old girl, let's see if you can get up,' and gave Blackie a push and a slap on the back. She gave a grunt and a half-roll, then heaved herself on to her hind legs and raised herself by her front legs to a standing position.

Bannerman looked at her appraisingly. He said, 'She's a fine cow. How many calves has she had?'

'This is her ninth.'

'Is it indeed! She's worn well.'

'Aye, she's been a grand cow.'

'What's she in-calf to?'

'A Welsh Black.'

'Are there many of them round here?'

'No, not many,' said Eben, 'but they bought a black bull at Merry Vale last year and they let us take her there. It's the first time for her to have a black bull at all.'

'Good job it's not a Hereford with a damn big white head. They can be sods to calve sometimes.'

Eben thought Gramfer Jenkyn would have liked this character, as he poured some disinfectant into the water and said, 'Now then, can you hold her tail for me, please?'

Eben took Blackie's tail and held it along her side, and Bannerman, his hand and arm well soaped, set to work.

'How long since the water-bag burst?' he said.

'About five o'clock or maybe a bit before that.' Now it was nearer ten o'clock.

'Pity. Things have gone dry now.'

'How does that affect it?' asked Eben.

'Well it makes it more difficult for me and for the cow.' At last he said, 'Which way do you reckon the calf is?'

Eben hesitated, 'Well I thought it seemed to be upside down with the head back.'

'Then you thought right and I wish you hadn't.'

'Is that bad?'

'Not normally, but the trouble is she's forced the calf right out into the passage so we've got to push him back into the womb to turn him.'

For maybe a quarter of an hour Bannerman worked. He spoke no word as he pushed and struggled and Algie Bromilow watched anxiously. Then he withdrew his arm to resoap it and started again. His jaw clenched and beads of sweat stood out on his forehead and began to trickle down into his eyes. He wiped them away with the back of his free hand.

'This is a bad one,' he said at last.

'Can you do anything?' Eben asked.

'Well, we can do something. We can get the calf. But with all this forcing there could be damage to the cow.'

'Like what?'

'Like an internal haemorrhage – in which case she'll be dead before morning. Or peritonitis – in which case she'd last two or three days. At the best there's always the chance you won't get her in-calf again.'

Eben was silent. His mind went back to Morfa Bychan and the father he had that day, and he thought with bitterness of the father he had become. What the hell was the matter with him to let a thing like this happen? He said, 'Is the calf dead?'

'I wouldn't like to say. But we'll know before long, I hope.'

The vet took three slight ropes from his bag, dipped them in the bucket and soaped them. Then, one at a time, he looped them and put them gently inside Blackie's vagina to fasten one round the calf's head and one round each front leg. Each of the three ends he looped with a half-hitch around short, strong sticks like chair legs.

'Now, sir,' he addressed himself to Bromilow, 'I take it you're willing to help.'

'By Jove, yes. Anything you say. Don't know much about it mind, but I helped an army chap pull a foal from a mare once. Same sort of thing I suppose.'

'You'll do. But I suggest you take that nice overcoat off first.'

'Good idea.'

With one on each rope, and each holding on to a stick with his two hands to give more leverage, they began to pull.

'Steady now, men. As she strains, pull downwards. That's it. Hold the strain. Now then – as she strains. Pull now.'

It was slow work. Blackie groaned and was distressed.

'Poor old bugger's lost heart a bit,' said Bannerman. 'She isn't straining as she should. Still, keep at it. Now then – again! Pull now!'

At last, as the two front feet parted the vulva and came into sight, Blackie went down.

'Let her go down,' said Bannerman. 'That's it. She'll have a better chance now!'

They loosened the halter and then resumed pulling until Bannerman was able to work the calf's head through. Encased in its prenatal covering it lolled foolishly. Then, with a heave, the shoulders came and, with one more pull, the body came sliding out followed by the hindquarters, and Bannerman was slapping the calf's sides, cleaning the slime from its nostrils and down on his knees blowing into its mouth. The calf gulped and kicked drunkenly.

'He'll be all right,' said Bannerman.

Eben saw that it was a heifer calf and was glad.

'A hell of a big calf,' said the vet.

Blackie was lying helplessly with her neck extended and her head on one side.

Eben noticed blood and slime on Bromilow's shirt sleeves and down his trousers.

'I'm afraid you've got yourself in a bit of a mess, Mr Bromilow,' he said.

'Nothing at all. All in a day's work. D'you think the cow's going to be all right?'

Bannerman looked at her.

'She's had a rough time,' he said, 'and her age doesn't help her.'

He rinsed his hands and arms and slopped water down the

front of his overall.

After a while they lifted her head by the horns and pulled her up into a more natural lying position. Eben dragged the calf to Blackie's head. She immediately pricked up her ears and lowed but made no attempt to get up.

'That's a bad sign,' said Bannerman. 'Still, we've done all we can for her, so all you can do now is wait and see. I'll leave you a drench that might help her a bit.'

When he was ready to go, Eben said, 'How much do I owe you?'

'That's all right. We'll send a bill.'

'No, I'd rather pay you now.' He hesitated. 'It was I sent for you and she's sort of my cow anyway.'

'All right then, if that's how you feel. As you wish.'

'How much?'

'Make it half a sovereign.'

When they had gone Eben stood in the road listening to the sound of the car dying away in the distance. The wind sighed in the leafless branches and it began to spot with rain. All of a sudden he felt alone again.

There was a light showing in the bedroom window up at the Gangrel and this was a comfort.

Eben mixed the drench for Blackie, but when he went in to give it to her, she seemed weaker. He hung the lamp on the beam and rubbed the calf with straw. It was shivering slightly. There was no immediate hope of getting Blackie to her feet so he fetched a small bottle and tediously squirted into it some of the rich glutinous colostrum from her teats, and somehow dosed the calf with it, half-pouring it into its mouth. He repeated the process several times and at last, weary and dispirited, said, 'Well, there y'are little'n, that's the best I can do for you. You're in with a chance now.'

Blackie was stretched out on her side again. Eben felt her horns and ears and they were cold. He fetched two sacks, filled them with straw, and, pushing the cow back up into her lying position, pressed the sacks in pillow-wise behind her shoulder. He fetched water for her and she drank a little, but showed no interest in the hay he put in front of her. There was no more he could do.

He stood looking at the cow his father had bought for him so long ago, when she was only a calf scarcely bigger than the one curled up now where a stray beam from the hurricane lamp caught the softness of its black coat that was just beginning to dry. How well he knew her and her idiosyncracies, and how the memories came flooding back. He saw again the wisps of grey hair falling across his mother's forehead as she had battled to get her to take to the bucket, and he recalled something of the excitement and the fullness of the day they had fetched her. Was it possible that so much could have happened since, and life become so sour? Eddie, his hero, gone, the mother he had loved and the Gramfer who had been his constant companion following so soon. And the father he had loved, worse than dead. Where he had once respected him, at times like these he came nearer to despising him.

The sound of Mark's motor-bike cut in on these thoughts and Eben came out of the loose-box as Mark came slowly into the yard astride the bike and, with either foot held close to the ground, paddled the machine to a halt. Eben told him about Blackie. 'We'll have a quick cup of tea and you go to bed out of the way. There could be all hell let loose here when Father comes back.'

'Would you rather I did?' said Mark.

'Yes, much.'

'All right then, boy. Whatever you say.'

Worried and unsettled, Eben went outside again. His dog Drifter came quickly to him, tail wagging, to nuzzle his cold nose and velvety head into Eben's hand.

'What's up with you then, boy?' he said. 'There's no work for you tonight.'

Drifter whined and stayed close.

Eben was surprised. Drifter was not normally the affectionate type. He was a worker. In spite of the deep affinity between them he never looked to follow Eben unless they were going after rabbits, and he had an uncanny sense of knowing what was afoot. He was not a true lurcher, having a slight preponderance of greyhound blood which had been picked up somewhere along the line, and he was deadly in the chase. He rarely barked and he remained independent and uninterested in everything except his trade. His pale yellow coat still shone like silk but there were grey hairs now around his muzzle. Eben thought it would be hard to reckon up what money he had earned from Drifter in his time, who could sweep up rabbits, moving by night smoothly from the darkness on to them as they ran uncertainly, bewildered by the dazzle of the lamp's beam, or accounting for any which missed the nets when they were ferreting by day. This was his life, yet tonight he seemed to know that he was needed as a friend to give comfort.

Eben was still with Blackie when he heard his father's heavy footsteps come down the lane. He must have seen the light because the footsteps stopped, then came towards the loose-box.

A thick finger came through the hole in the door and lifted the latch. The door was pushed open and Ben Harter stood there, his eyes glazed, and none too steady on his feet. He blinked at the light and then looked at Blackie.

'How is she?' he said.

Eben spoke no word. Blackie was evidently sinking.

'I said how is she?'

'How do you think she is?'

'How the hell should I know when I haven't been here?'

'Then you should have been here and then you'd know.'

'Couldn't you look after her?'

'I couldn't calve her myself so I sent for the vet.'

'The vet be damned. What vet?'

'The new man from Narberth.'

Ben Harter blinked. This took time to sink in. 'How di'sn't thou come for me?'

Eben sensed there was a row coming and he had no mind to avert it.

'You knew how she was before you left. If you'd had any interest you could have stayed home from the pub for once.'

'I'll please myself what I does and where I goes.'

'You've said that before.'

'An' I'm sayin' it again.'

'Well keep on going there then but don't grumble to me when things go wrong. Just go and tell the story to Betsy Carter.'

'What the hell d'ya mean?'

'Well she was at the Prince, wasn't she? And what do most of the men go there for?'

Ben Harter glared at him. 'I'll flog the hide off thy bloody back,' he roared, and came for Eben.

'You dare lay your hands on me!' he said quietly.

His father stopped.

'Would you raise your hand against me?' he said.

'Just lay a finger on me if you want to find out.'

'I thought thou was't supposed to know somethin' about the Bible. It says, "Honour thy father an' thy mother." '

'Yes, I did honour my mother and there was a time when I honoured you. Now you're welcome to as much honour as you think is due to any other drunkard.'

'Damn you!' roared Ben Harter, and struck at Eben.

Eben topped his father by about four inches. He merely gripped him by the throat and pushed him away.

What happened afterwards Eben would have found it diffi- cut to describe. He only saw his father being spun round and Mark's face a mask of rage as he hit him. Mark wasn't as tall as Eben, but he was strong, and their father, for all his physique, was now sixty and drink had taken its toll.

In one movement the fight was outside the door and Mark landed a quick savage punch that up-ended his father into the clinging softness round the perimeter of the winter's muck- heap.

Then there was silence.

'Good God,' said Eben at last, 'what did you want to do that for?'

'Serve the drunken bugger right. Better for me to do it than you, for you got to live with'n but I'm not bound to.'

'I thought you'd gone to bed.'

'You didn't think I'd go to bed and leave you to face'n on your own?' said Mark.

'But you could have killed him.'

Mark looked at his father where he lay.

'We'll see about that,' he said, and, picking up the bucket from the cowshed door, he dipped it in the water-butt, filled it with water and poured the whole lot over his father's head and chest.

Ben Harter stirred and spluttered. At last he glared at Mark but said no word.

'Last drinks, please,' said Mark.

Eben slept the healthy sleep of the young but he was first up the next morning and went straight out to see Blackie before making the usual cup of tea. The rain which had threatened was now falling steadily. It was a dark, depressing morning.

Blackie lay with her nose buried in the straw. The sacks propping her up had prevented her from rolling on to her side and death had come to her quietly as she lay.

Eben felt her ear and it was the coldness of death he had felt on his mother's face so long ago. That was how long Blackie had been with them. Since just before his mother had died so suddenly. And now this other link was broken.

The calf was on its legs, swaying uncertainly and looking for something it could not find.

'All right,' said Eben, 'we'll get you something now in a minute.'

There was still a Blackie on the place. Life would still go on.

That summer Penny Bromilow came a great deal to Herons-mill on various pretexts, and she was often around when Eben went to have some cricket practice with her father, but he gave her no encouragement. She had matured suddenly and was prettier now than when he had first seen her that day on the bridge.

Becca could see what was happening.

'That li'l maid be nearly gwain mad over thee,' she said.

'Don't talk so dull, Aunty Becca. She's only a child.'

'How owld is she?'

'About fifteen, I suppose.'

Becca waited for the significance of this to sink in. Then she said, 'Ha'sn't thee seen the way she looks at thee?'

'All I know is what I've always known, that she's a spoilt little brat.'

Nothing more was said, but from then on Eben became even more off-hand with her. If he ever thought of girls it was of Liz Whithow.

He was working as hard as ever at home, but he was also enjoying what little spare time he had. During the latter part of the previous winter he had played the odd game of rugby for Tenby's second Fifteen and he had enjoyed himself. Now he did an occasional stint of training in the hope that he might be more involved in the game in the coming season. Algie Bromilow ran an experienced eye over him from time to time, giving him some useful hints on kicking, and impressing on him the need to be able to kick with both feet. Out on the lawn he fixed up a frame with a swinging sack filled with sawdust at which Eben could practise hurling himself in a dive, as in a flying tackle. Whatever opportunities he may have missed in life it would be through no fault of Algie Bromilow's if he failed to make a sportsman.

But, if girls were not part of the pattern of Eben's life, on the odd occasions when he saw Liz he could not help being attracted and oddly disturbed by her. Tantalizing she was. Her enjoyment at being kissed behind the door in Mrs Magrath's play had developed along predictable lines.

'A proper hot 'un, by all account,' said Mark.

It was talk which made Eben sad. He did not like the

thought of her being fair game for anybody who fancied her, but that was how it seemed to be. She rarely missed a dance in the area or going to Tenby on a Saturday night, and she was never at a loss for some young hopeful to see her home.

Eben felt drawn to her whenever he met her, but there had been no sign of it going further. Until the incident when he and Penny Bromilow had been caught in the rain.

It was in the autumn and Eben had gone ferreting to Deerfield. He had Drifter with him and a young ferret he had only recently bought. Penny was there, too.

'Haven't you gone back to school, then?' said Eben.

'No, I'm staying home for a few days. I'm fed up with school. It's terribly boring.'

'What does your father think about it?'

'I please myself about these things.'

'Then go and put a coat on if you're coming with me because we'll have rain before we're finished.'

'Oh no, I'll be all right as I am. This jacket's terribly warm.'

'Please yourself and then you'll be sure to please somebody.'

And so they set off, Penny in her tweed costume and Eben with a greatcoat tied round the waist with twine, and some nets and a sack with the ferret in it slung over his shoulder. Drifter, nosing here and there, trotted amongst the patches of fern and the mole-heaps long grassed-over.

They had caught a dozen rabbits when the rain began to fall and, when it came, it came quickly. The wind, too, began to blow harder and drove the rain stinging into their faces. Eben had just hurled himself on to a rabbit as it bundled into a net and the ferret came nosing out of the hole after it. Eben picked it up and put it into the bag.

Penny was shivering slightly and began to whimper. 'Oh, dear, what can I do?'

'What you could do,' said Eben, 'is to get a bit of sense into your head and listen to somebody who knows better. Let's get in here.'

They were near a blackthorn tree that grew out over the field, and the bracken, now brown and dead, ran right up to it. There was shelter from the driving rain, but, wherever they stood, the drips increased.

Eben took off his coat and, holding it over his head, said, 'You'd better come under here.'

Penny smiled at him and cuddled up close.

To hold the coat over both of them Eben had to put his

arm round her shoulder. Very gently she pressed against him and Aunty Becca's words came back to him as he became conscious of the womanly shape of her.

For a while they just stood there and neither of them spoke. At last Penny said, 'You're never very nice to me, are you? Some boys would very much like to be here with me like this.'

'Perhaps they would.'

'They might even want to kiss me.'

Eben could see a situation developing which for once he had no idea how to handle. And then he heard someone calling. It was Jimmy Cockles and, if Eben had not called back to him, he would have passed by, so well concealed were they.

'Aw, here y'are,' he said, 'the boss sent me with this mack for you miss. The missus was worried as ya'd get drenched. It have been emtin' down but I can see you been all right.'

She took the mackintosh with ill-concealed humour. But Eben said, ' 'Tis easing a bit now. We'd better make a dash for it when we've got the chance.'

There was nothing more to the incident than that, but a few days later Eben met Liz as he came out of the post office.

'What's this I hear about you then?' she laughed, and there was a merry, seductive tinkle in her voice.

'I don't know,' said Eben, 'what have you heard about me?'

'Don't look the old innocent, boy.'

'What are you talking about, Liz?'

'About you having a bit with young Penny Bromilow up in the ferns. Don't think I don't know.'

Eben's temper flared. 'I'll thrash that snivelling little bastard Jimmy Cockles till he won't move for a month – is that what he told you?'

'Oh no. There's no need to get worked up about it. It's thinking I am.'

'Then you shouldn't think the wrong things.'

'Come on, boy, own up. Did you give it to her?'

Eben coloured.

'Well you're a fool, whether you gave it to her or whether you didn't.'

'What d'you mean?' said Eben.

'Well you're a fool if you did because she's only fifteen.'

'I know she is.'

'And you're a fool if you didn't because I bet she was asking for it.'

Without malice, but rising to the challenge in her voice, Eben said, 'You mustn't judge everybody by yourself, Liz.'

'What d'you know about me?'

'Only what I've heard.'

'Then isn't it about time you found out for yourself?'

'I'd like the chance,' Eben laughed, still a little uncertainly, but emboldened by the course the conversation was taking.

'Then why don't you ask me?' she said.

'I'm asking you now.'

'Where shall I meet you?'

'How about the Lower Level wood?' said Eben.

Liz rolled her eyes.

'That sounds interesting,' she said.

'When?' said Eben.

'How about Saturday afternoon?'

'All right,' he said. 'I'll meet you by the stile.'

Liz vamped her eyes at him again. Then she laughed and said, 'Perhaps I'd better make sure I've got a mack with me.'

Eben's pulse beat quicker at the prospect. It was Thursday tea-time.

He thought a good deal about it on Friday, and had been thinking about it again on Saturday morning when Penny came running down the lane into the farmyard. She had left her bicycle up by the road gate.

'Oh, Eben,' she called, 'I've got wonderful news for you. Daddy's just had a phone message for you to play for Tenby this afternoon. Can you come straight up to phone and tell them?'

Eben had dashed on his own bicycle to phone at Deerfield. One of the regular centres, it seemed, had an injury which had failed to respond to treatment and the reserve three-quarter had gone down with flu. Would Eben play and could he get there in time? He needed no second bidding, but it was going to be a rush to finish his work and catch the train. Algie Bromilow, too, had had the flu and was not well enough to go out, so he could not offer to take him.

It was as he was about to get on his bike that Eben suddenly remembered Liz. There was no time now to let her know. He paused and frowned.

Penny was still with him. 'What's the matter?' she asked. 'Have you forgotten something?'

'No, not forgotten anything. Just remembered.'

'What have you remembered then?'

Without thinking, Eben said, 'I'm supposed to meet somebody.'

'Who is she?'

'Liz Whithow.'

So there it was. It was out.

Eben had certainly had no intention of telling anybody, and Penny, perhaps, least of all.

'I didn't know you were going with her.'

'I'm not,' said Eben.

'Then why are you meeting her?'

Eben thought for a moment. Now it had gone so far the solution seemed obvious. 'D'you know where she lives?' he said.

'Yes, of course I know.'

'Well could you go and tell her what's happened?'

'Why should I?'

'There's no reason at all why you should except that I'm asking you.'

Penny did not answer.

'Will you do that for me?' said Eben.

Suddenly her face lit up. 'Yes, of course,' she said. 'Now you'd better go or you'll miss your train. And the best of luck.'

'Thank you very much,' he said, and then he was gone.

It was a home game, and he could be back in time to feed the stock and finish up the work about the buildings. Most of the cows were calving in the spring so there was not much milking to be done at the moment. A few of them were dry already.

He had finished work, and was washing in the tin pan on the low wall by the back door, when he heard the sound of Mark's motor-bike coming down the lane. It was a new AJS and it was Mark's great pride with a pillion seat, and a fine gold line round the sides of its petrol tank.

When Eben had changed and come downstairs he said to Mark, 'Before you go off this afternoon perhaps you could do me a favour.' Then, with half a smile, he added, 'I'm supposed to meet Liz Whithow this afternoon.'

Mark almost jumped. 'Jesus,' he said, 'now look at that for a sly bugger.'

'It's not what you think.'

'How do you know what I think, and how the hell does anybody know what to think round here? How long have this been goin' on, boy?'

'I've never met her before.'

'Where you supposed to meet her?'

'By the Lower Level stile about half past two.'

'And what do you want me to do?'

Eben thought for a while. He decided against telling Mark about Penny Bromilow. He was none too sure that she would give the message. But, then again, she might. So he said, 'I'm not sure whether she'll turn up or not. But in case she does, if you could nip down and tell her what's happened, it won't look so bad.'

'Aye, well, if she does turn up I'll give her a rattle myself.'

'You wouldn't do that!' said Eben.

'Why not?'

Eben did not answer. Then his mind turned back to the rugby and he never gave Liz another thought.

The game was against Llangwm and a tough crowd they were. Cocklepickers most of them were, and as hard as nails. But Eben was not worried about that. He could take care of himself. He was more concerned in case he did not play well. Tenby were a good side and he would hate to let them down. As the train came in over the viaduct, he looked down and saw the first supporters making their way towards Heywood Lane for the rugby ground, and he felt the butterflies in his stomach. He was not well known in Tenby, and few people had watched the games in which he had played for the seconds. Still, the committee must have thought something of him to have asked him to play.

The players, some of them still strangers to him, all gave him a cheerful word of greeting. Almost before he realized, he had pulled on the jersey with its red and black hoops and they were running out on to the field to a great welcome from the town supporters.

He stood now, rubbing his hands and jigging nervously, waiting for the referee's whistle to start, and many of the crowd asked each other who was the new centre. If looks meant anything he had the makings. He was only a fraction under six feet tall and weighed all of thirteen stone. He had the Harters' barrel chest and width of shoulder, and he had thighs like seasoned oak. His crisp hair had lost some of its fairness and his boyhood curls had become waves which would yet jump back into curls in the rough and tumble. And his face, with a firm set of the jaw, had become that of a determined man.

Tenby had won the toss and were playing down the slope to where the ground looked out over the marshes away to Penally and the sea. Then there was a blast on the whistle and the ball was in the air and coming straight towards where he stood, back near the 'twenty-five' and twenty yards from the touchline. As in a dream he caught it cleanly, and, with the Llangwm forwards bearing down on him, banged it back into touch with a long raking kick that took play inside the Llangwm half. There was a round of applause and encouragement. The tenseness left him and he felt better. Then, from the line-out, there was a loose-maul, the Llangwm forwards heeled and their backs were away, only for Eben to flatten his opposite man with a tackle that would have knocked even the sawdust from Bromilow's sack. He was in the game.

These were the only two incidents Eben could ever remember about that first game. Apart from his try, of course. And he would never forget the thrill of that.

The first half had been a dour battle, and, although both sides had tried to run with the ball, the tackling had been deadly. There were fewer than five minutes to go for half-time when the Tenby forwards heeled from a scrum well inside the Llangwm half. The stand-off made a half-break, and, missing out Eben, threw a long pass to the outside centre. The Llangwm backs stood flat-footed and the wing was away with only the full-back to beat. The wing failed to round him, but the forwards were up, and only a knock-on right on the line prevented a score. The crowd began to shout as the scrum was formed five yards out. Back came the ball and right along the Tenby line until there was only Eben left to handle with his wing outside him. From the corner of his eye he saw the Llangwm wing close in on his own partner, but he had left the semblance of a gap in doing it. As Eben gathered the ball he threw back his shoulders and, with his near hand free for a hand-off, burst through and round his opponent. He was only yards from the line as the Llangwm full-back came across for the tackle, but Eben had dived first and nothing short of a battering ram could have stopped him as he hurled himself at the line.

The full-back's kick from nearly out on the touchline hit the upright and bounced back so that, when almost immediately afterwards, the half-time whistle sounded, Tenby led by three points to nil. But that was a great morale booster to start the second-half against the slope, and as it turned out, it was the only score of the game. The Tenby defence hung on for a hard-earned victory.

As Eben sat in the changing-room afterwards a committee man came in and said, 'Well played.'

'Thank you very much,' said Eben.

Then the man said, 'Will you be all right for next week?'

'Well yes, of course, if you want me.'

'We'd certainly like you to travel as first reserve, even if you're not picked to play.'

By the end of the season he had established himself as a regular member of the side.

When Mark came home that night Eben had just gone to bed. Mark went into his bedroom. 'How'd you get on?' he said.

'We won three nil.'

'Good boy.'

'Did Liz turn up?'

'Oh, aye, she turned up all right.'

'Did she now!' So that little bitch had not given his message. 'And what happened?' Eben asked him.

'Oh, she was very disappointed you weren't there, but she seemed pleased to see me, mind.'

'Did she now?'

'Yes she did now.'

'And what then?'

'Well, then, I didn't think it would be proper for me to be seen hanging about the wood with her, so I asked her if she'd like to come for a spin on the back of my motor-bike.'

'And did she?'

'Can a duck swim!'

'Which way did you go?'

'Walked up through the wood to pick up the bike first.'

'Up here?'

'Well, where else, what the hell d'you think?'

'Did Father see you?'

'No, he wasn't here, but what the hell odds if he had been? What difference would that make?'

'Where did you take her?'

'Oh, I took her up to Narberth and back down to Amroth and she enjoyed it. And so did I.'

'I'll bet you did.'

'But all above board mind.'

'Was it?'

'Yes, it was. I couldn't take liberties with my brother's girl now could I?'

'She isn't my girl.'

'You should have told me that in the first place.'

'I did.'

Mark laughed. 'I think she was wondering why I didn't

give her a tumble. And I don't think a chap would have any trouble with her at all. But you find out for yourself next time.'

Next time, however, was to be a long time. The following week Liz went to Haverfordwest to keep house for her uncle whose wife had just died, and, for the time being, passed out of Eben's mind.

It was a year now since Blackie had died. From that night onwards, Ben Harter had seemed to go less to the pub and to take hold of himself. Eben was not dissatisfied with his life. He had been able to play rugby regularly throughout the winter, and, far from grumbling, his father had even shown a certain amount of interest. Eben still caught rabbits on his own account part of his time, and his father did a little dealing. Sometimes his dealing was done by way of obliging a smallholder, and at these times Eben saw in him again something of the character he had known as a boy. It was probably because of this that Billy Seckerson came to see him to ask if he would buy his two bullocks.

A small, rather inoffensive man, he had a buxom wife and a steadily increasing retinue of children, all with their mother's good looks. There was another one on the way and the last one just toddling. Working down Bonville's Court pit the money was tight, and, like so many of the men who worked there, he was glad of his few acres of land and the fact that he could keep a cow for the house. But when it came to selling stock he was up against all the difficulties of the times. And times were bad.

'How much you wantin' for 'em, Billy?' said Ben Harter.

'I was hopin' to get about thirteen pound apiece for 'em.'

'An' how much did owld Wier offer?'

Billy looked as if he was about to cry.

'Seven apiece.'

'Seven! Name of God!'

'I knows, Mr Harter, but what's a body to do with rent day comin' up?'

Ben Harter knew Wier's tricks well. He would drive round the country in his high trap, and, over the hedges, he could see which smallholders had stock they would be wanting to sell by rent day. And he knew when rent day was due, too.

'Last year,' said Billy, 'he bought 'em with me an' then left 'em here for six weeks afore he fetched 'em.'

'All right, Billy. I'll come down tomorrow evenin'.'

When he went, Eben went with him to help drive the two bullocks back. The swallows with their long forked tails, the martins with their white rumps and the swifts with their short tails and long scything wings were once again around the buildings and clinging to the walls beneath the eaves. Eben knew them all because Gramfer had taught him when he was very young.

Already the air was full of the renewed promise of another spring. A blackbird on the top bough of a young ash tree told the world that this was his. Buds everywhere were lending new shades of green to the cloak the countryside was once again assuming and there were signs of early growth. As yet, however, the grass was slow, and Billy Seckerson, like many others, having kept his cow and a couple of young cattle over the winter, had precious little hay left. It was all too easy to browbeat such people into give-away prices.

As it turned out Billy was not home. His wife said, 'He sent a message with one o' th'others to say as he'd been gave the chance of an extra shift an' he couldn't afford to leave it go. But you shall see the steers, Mr Harter. They be round the corner here.'

The smallest child was toddling by the door and dragging a rag doll by the leg. She had dark brown eyes and brown curly hair and a face which was also brown as if from the summer's sun.

She smiled at Eben. He bent down to her and held out his hands and she came to him.

'What's your name?' he said.

'That's Rachel,' said her mother. 'She haven't said much yet but she be into everythin'.'

'Moo,' said Rachel and pointed to the cow grazing beyond the garden hedge. 'Moo.'

'Yes, that's the moo cow,' said Eben. He was attracted by her and she did not want to be put down.

'Moo,' she said.

'All right then. We'll go see the moo cow.'

The two bullocks were in the same field.

'I'll give'n twenty-five pound for the pair of 'em an' pay you now an' drive 'em straight home.'

'Oh, I'm sure he'd be pleased with that, Mr Harter. We're gettin' main low on hay.'

'Open the gate then.'

Eben held Rachel up high. 'What about you then? How much for this one?'

She gurgled.

Before handing her back to her mother he held her to him and she put her arms round his neck and pressed her cheek against his. 'She's going to break a few hearts one day, I'll warrant,' said Eben.

Billy Seckerson had serious problems. Scarcely had he paid his rent when the colliers came out on strike and the pits closed, to be followed a few days later by a general strike. And, in spite of rumour and counter-rumour, it had also been announced at first that the shipyard at Pembroke Dock was to close. Poverty in the area was acute and every day, men, looking for work that was not to be had, were turned away from Heronsmill as from elsewhere. The general strike did not last long but the coal strike was to drag on until the autumn.

It seemed to Eben somewhat out of keeping with the times when, late in the summer, Algie Bromilow invited him to dinner one Saturday evening.

'My sister's coming down for a long week-end,' he said. 'On her way to Ireland. Her husband's a keen rugby man. Good type. You'd like him.'

Eben felt inclined to refuse, but he did not want to appear churlish. 'That's very kind of you,' he said.

'Not at all. It'll be nice to have you.'

Then he began to worry about the right things to do on such occasions. To have improved his speech and his mind by practice and reading was one thing. To acquire new habits was another. But he had joined the Bromilows for an occasional informal meal before now and he was careful to observe. He reckoned he would know which knife and which fork to use. Give them a few seconds' start and keep his wits about him and he hoped he might manage.

Fortunately, back in the spring, he had bought himself the first proper suit he had ever had. It had good wide trouser bottoms and one of the new-fashioned waistcoats. Aunty Becca pressed and aired it for him and made sure his shirt was right and that he had a tie-pin.

The invitation was for 'about half past seven'. He timed it nicely and was there about two minutes early.

Penny met him at the door. No word had ever been spoken between them on her failure to give his message to Liz Whithow, and this piqued her more than if she could have known what had happened. Now he treated her with even more indifference. But he thought she looked very well in a frock of some kind of orange-coloured material. Her dark hair had been well brushed and he caught a faint whiff of perfume. Her father came close behind her.

'Come in, Eben. You're right on time. Come on in and meet my family.'

Algie Bromilow's sister had his features and dark wavy hair but her eyes were hazel. She had a kind mouth and face and was a striking woman. Once again Eben found himself wondering how Penny had come by her nastiness. But tonight she was on her best behaviour. She always was in company.

'Now then, Tricia,' said Bromilow, 'where's that husband of yours?'

'He's just gone upstairs, Algie. He'd forgotten his cigarettes. End of the world, poor dear.'

'I thought I heard you say you wanted one, my lady,' came a voice from the hall. There was just a trace of a Lancashire accent about it.

When Jerry Forsdyke came into the room, he went straight up to Eben and shook his hand without waiting for any sort of introduction. 'So you're the future Welsh international I've been told so much about.'

He was a fair-complexioned man, gone very thin on top but radiating cheerfulness. Not as tall as Eben, he was powerfully built, and looked as if he might have been an athlete at one time.

'No, no,' laughed Eben, 'you've got it all wrong. I've had a few games for our local team, that's all, and the luck's been with me so far.'

'But they tell me your local team is quite something. Didn't Ned Stanbury play for them?'

'Yes, he learned his rugby in Tenby before he played for Plymouth Albion.'

'Great forward. If you can turn out English internationals like that there's nothing wrong with your local team.'

'Yes,' said Eben, 'fancy England having to come down here to find players.'

At this point Mrs Bromilow, who had always struck Eben as gentle and perhaps a little timid, said rather diffidently, 'Algie, what are you doing about drinks?'

'Everything under control, old girl. Coming up now.'

Eben settled for a glass of sherry.

It was not long before they were back on rugby.

'No,' said Eben, 'I've never been to an international. But I'm hoping to go this winter.'

'Who are you going to see?' asked Forsdyke.

'If it comes off, it'll be Wales and Scotland at Cardiff in February.'

'That's looking ahead.'

'Well, my brother and his partner have bought another charabanc. They had a good season with the Sunday school outings – lucky with the weather too.'

'Marvellous summer,' said Bromilow, 'couldn't go wrong.'

'But now they're planning for the winter with some football trips and the Scotland match is one of them,' said Eben.

Forsdyke offered a cigarette, which Eben declined. 'Quite right. They're killers really. Centre you play, isn't it? Well, watch McPherson for Scotland. Tremendous player. Everybody talks about Ian Smith and he's a great wing, of course, but I reckon if a man can't play outside a chap like McPherson, he'll never play.'

Then they started talking about outside halves.

'What do you think of Windsor Lewis?' said Eben.

'Marvellous player,' said Forsdyke. 'The only chap I know who could take Powell's passes. Fine strong player, Powell. But erratic with his service.'

Bromilow took Eben's glass and refilled it. Eben hardly noticed.

'Now that's an end to it,' his wife interrupted. 'If there's one more word about rugby I'll . . . I'll . . .'

'What'll you do?' laughed her husband. 'You won't leave me, will you?'

'I don't know. But I'll do something.'

The dinner gong sounded in the hall.

'No side,' said her sister-in-law. 'Saved by the whistle.'

Eben noticed that their glasses were all empty, and, with a quick gulp, he drained his own. His face was beginning to burn a little and he thought that perhaps sherry was stronger than he had supposed. Then he remembered that he had not eaten anything since a hurried meal at midday. He would have to watch his step, but it was a good feeling.

Inside the dining-room, Dolly Gittow was standing very correctly in her black frock with a white apron and the little white cap of the servant-maid. She had been in the Bromilows' employ since leaving school and had graduated from the kitchen where her young sister Bessie was now learning under Cari's eagle eye.

Eben smiled and said, 'Good evening, Dolly.' They had been in the same class at school.

She returned his smile without familiarity and said, 'Good

evening, Mr Harter.'

'You sit here, will you, Eben.' Bromilow motioned to the chair on his left, where he stood at the head of the oblong table, so that Eben found himself next to Penny.

There had been a break in the good weather and, now that the nights were drawing in, the curtains had been drawn. The oak table had been set with mats, and silver and cut glass threw back diamond points from the red candles that burned in silver candlesticks. A fire of ash logs sent flames dancing up the wide chimney and their reflection was mirrored in the polish of the solid oak furniture. Melon quarters were already set at each of the six places at the long table.

Cari, who had rejoiced in this opportunity to prepare something special, had mushroom soup to follow the melon and she ladled this herself from a steaming tureen on the oak server whilst Dolly waited at table.

Bromilow carved the sirloin of beef when it came. Then, from the server, he produced a bottle of wine which had already been uncorked. It was wrapped in a spotless white table-napkin. Eben saw the dark red of it through his glass as he held it up to sip it speculatively, and found himself thinking it was darker than the red in his Tenby jersey. Then he thought that was a damn silly idea to come into his head at such a time. The sherry must have been strong. Thank goodness the wine tasted harmless enough.

Penny was talking about her summer holidays. She had spent much of her time with friends at Saundersfoot who had a sailing boat.

'It's been absolutely wizard,' she said, 'really super.' 'Terribly' was no longer her pet word. 'We sailed right round to Tenby one day. It was absolutely wizard. And last week we sailed to the beach above Amroth and landed there and had a super picnic with a fire on the stones.'

'You want to be careful going up there,' said Eben. 'I've always heard the locals say it's a bad place to take a boat.'

'Not really,' said Penny. 'Not if you know what you're doing, and Tommy's a wizard sailor.'

So Eben made polite conversation with her, and the talk was of general things which were of small moment.

'Now then, Eben, a drop more.'

'No, indeed. I'm doing fine, thanks, Mr Bromilow.'

'Don't be silly. Never heard such talk in all my life. The season hasn't started yet. Plenty of time to get into training. Drink up.'

Eben drank what was left in his glass. Bromilow refilled it and topped up the other glasses and then went back to the server for a second bottle.

'You're doing us proud, Algie,' said his brother-in-law.

'Not a bit of it. Don't often get the chance to entertain the family since I abandoned ship and let you chaps carry on.'

The beef was followed by a superb meringue pie, which was one of Cari's specials. When the cheese came, Eben said he had had enough.

Forsdyke had taken Bromilow's remark about abandoning ship as an opportunity to start talking about the cotton industry. At first the talk meant nothing to Eben. The candles seemed to be moving away from him on the table and it took him a little time to get them back into focus. A cup of strong coffee revived his balance and then the ladies withdrew.

Forsdyke started talking about the cotton industry again. 'I tell you, Algie,' he said, 'I don't like it.'

'But last year's dividends were up again.'

'I know, and that's part of the trouble.'

'Well, what's wrong with that?'

'I'll tell you what's wrong with it. There are too many of our people taking too much out and not putting enough back in. We ought to be ploughing money back into modern machinery and getting geared up to meet world competition. I keep telling our board but I'm on my own.'

'Are the workers happy?'

'If there's trouble ahead at all it'll be worse for the workers than anybody. They'll catch it on both sides because they've nearly all got money in the industry and it will hurt 'em. I hope I'm wrong mind, but I tell you, I don't like it.'

'Well I don't pretend to know much about it,' said Bromilow, 'and I expect you know even less, Eben.'

'No, Mr Bromilow, I don't know anything about cotton, but I know about the workers' side of things. And they don't often come out on the right one.'

'Good God. Don't tell me you're one of these damned socialists.'

'No, indeed I'm not. I'm not anything. I think Willie Jenkins in this county is a good man, but I don't suppose he'll ever be elected. I haven't much time for what little I've seen of politicians as a breed. What I do know is something of the workers' problems and they have all my sympathy. Especially the miners.'

'Sympathy! But damn it all, did you sympathize with the

rest of 'em over the strike?'

'Who's to say what were the rights of it? Baldwin reckoned that it was a question of near revolution. Citrine said the TUC were in control and would never have allowed the Reds to take over. So who are you going to believe? But the rest of the country went back and they've left the miners on their own, standing against a reduction in wages and an increase in their working hours.'

'What's your interest in the miners?'

'My brother who was killed in the war was underground as a blacksmith and would have gone back to it. My sister's husband is a miner. She and their two children are hungry up in the Rhondda whilst he sticks out for what he believes to be right. He's a rabid socialist I grant you. But he's an honest man and a good husband.'

Bromilow looked at him. The wine had loosened Eben's tongue.

'But look around you, Mr Bromilow. Ask Dolly Gittow how things are going with her family. Take the men all round this area with the pits idle all the summer. The only good to come out of it is that the poor sods have had a wonderful summer in the sun. How long has it been since any of them last saw any summer? And at what sort of price have they bought it this time?'

'You're not suggesting the strike should have been allowed to continue, are you?'

'I'm not suggesting anything.'

'Dammit all, I had to turn out to drive a lorry myself.'

'Did you have to?'

'Well I did it.'

'And I bet you enjoyed every minute of it.'

'You bet I did.'

'Mr Bromilow, it isn't for me to tell you what you should do. Perhaps it was necessary for the strike to be broken. But the miners won't thank you for it. And whatever may be the rights and wrongs of it, Lord Birkenhead is supposed to have said that he always thought the miners were the most stupid men in the country until he met the owners.'

'Where did you hear that?'

'Willie Jenkins said it at a public meeting after the strike was over.'

'Well what shall we do this winter if there's no coal?'

'We'll just have to manage with logs, won't we?'

'Won't you dig coal?'

'What d'you mean? For ourselves or to sell?'

'Why not to sell? Some farmers are doing it.'

Eben thought for a moment. 'Yes,' he said, 'some farmers who have coal on their land are digging it and selling it. And things are so bad I don't blame them. But I wouldn't do it, and I can't see my father doing it.'

'Why not?'

'Because we've been too near the colliers for too long not to understand their troubles too. My Auntie Becca has been wonderful to us as you know. Her husband was killed underground right here at the Lower Level. I know the struggle she had to bring up her family until they were old enough to scatter to the four corners of the earth. Don't misunderstand me, Mr Bromilow. You're a well-to-do man living in comfort, and I don't begrudge it to you. But neither do I deny poor people the right to do what they can for themselves.'

'Do you agree with all this talk about wealth being shared then?'

'No, I don't. I don't think it would work. There'll always be the haves and the have-nots. You can see that round here with those who can make do and those who can never have enough. But there'll have to be an improvement in working conditions for a lot of people. I tell you honestly. I've had a conscience about eating the wonderful sort of meal we've had tonight when I know how many children have already gone to bed hungry.'

And as if to add point to his argument, the beautifully carved clock on the mantelpiece, with its deep Westminster chime, sounded the hour. It was ten o'clock. As the chimes died away there was silence again and Eben said, 'Mr Forsdyke. You were talking about the need for new machinery in the cotton industry. I don't know anything about that, but I know that the machinery in the pits around here is so antiquated it could have come out of the Ark.'

Forsdyke had remained silent throughout Eben's tirade. Now he said, 'I know how you feel, young man, and your sentiments do you credit. There's a lot of bad feeling about.'

'Well can you wonder, with all the strike-breaking and the poverty we've seen with everybody at almost everybody else's throats?'

'That's just about it. The other workers have let the miners down, haven't they? And I'm afraid that's what it's always going to be. There's going to be a swing right over with the workers running the show. But you'll still have the strong

113

looking for the lion's share and the weak going to the wall.'

'What we shall have to have,' said Eben, 'is a change in men's hearts, whether they be rich or poor.'

'That's talking a bit like our damned parson,' said Bromilow.

'Isn't that what religion ought to be about?'

'Good God, boy, what's religion got to do with rates of pay?'

'My mother was a good woman, Mr Bromilow. I was too young when she died for me to remember much about her, but she always taught us that Christianity was about how we lived.'

'But that's religion you're talking now.'

'No, not religion. Christianity.'

'I know what you mean,' said Jerry Forsdyke. 'At least I think I do. But I doubt whether we'll ever see that Utopia. What we're going to see are some awful changes, with men doing so little work for so much money that we'll price ourselves out of the world's markets. Whether I live to see it or not it'll come, you mark my words.'

'Cheer up, old sport,' said his brother-in-law, 'you're getting morbid. That always happens once you get on to religion. Have a drop more port.'

'No, thanks, Algie. Not for me.'

'What about you, Eben? Sure you won't change your mind?'

Eben had declined to take any port in the first place. 'No, thanks,' he said. 'I've talked too much on what I've had.'

The two men laughed.

'We'll make a politician out of you yet,' said Bromilow.

Forsdyke said, 'Get that international cap first.'

It was Eben's turn to laugh. 'I'd better think about to-morrow's milking first,' he said. 'Morning will soon be here.'

Eben was having a good season in the Tenby side and enjoying his rugby. He was also looking forward to the outing to Cardiff to see the match with Scotland. Over the years he had gone with Bromilow a few times to see club games at Stradey Park in Llanelly, and once to St Helen's at Swansea, but he had never seen an international match and he had never been to Cardiff. Mark's charabanc trip was fully booked.

A fortnight before the game, which was to be played early in February, Eben was rabbiting at Deerfield. Bromilow came out to him.

'How are things going with your outing?' he asked.

'Oh, first class. Mark's as happy as a lamb with two mothers.'

Bromilow laughed. 'Well you can't be much happier than that. Have you got tickets?'

It was Eben's turn to laugh. 'Oh no. We don't run to that sort of thing.'

'Then how will you manage?'

'Oh, we'll just crush in the best we can.'

'They're expecting a record crowd there.'

'So they say. Especially with the Prince of Wales going to be there.'

'Indeed. Popular chap. Grand young fellow.'

'And a big sympathizer with the miners!' laughed Eben.

Bromilow laughed with him. They occasionally made a joke about Eben's oratory when 'the drink was talking'.

'Well I've got a bit of news for you,' said Bromilow. 'I heard from that brother-in-law of mine this morning and he's sent a couple of stand tickets with his compliments. One for you and one for me. Damned fellow knows everybody.'

'You don't mean that!' said Eben. 'Not a stand ticket!'

'Why not? Might as well go in comfort.'

Eben laughed and shook his head in disbelief. 'You must let me have his address for me to write and thank him.'

They talked then about the ground capacity and the size of the crowd expected, and a good deal about the merits of the two teams. Windsor Lewis, the experts said, would be the key man for Wales, and Ian Smith the danger man for Scotland. Eben felt the excitement of it already. Then he said, 'Will you go by car?'

'Yes, we're all going. We'll go up on the Friday and stay the week-end in Cardiff. My wife wants to go round the shops. Can't stand that sort of thing myself. And Penny says we can go to the theatre. Says since we came down here we've become like cabbages. Good God, what an expression.'

Eben laughed. He was so excited he could laugh at anything.

Mark's charabanc set off early on the Saturday morning and he could have filled it three times over. There looked to be a future in the business. He parked near the station and it was agreed that they should be back at the charabanc by eleven o'clock.

There had been something of a seasonal flu epidemic and the great Windsor Lewis had been declared unfit to play. And so had Ian Smith. So that took a lot of the glamour out of it. Having to replace Windsor Lewis the selectors had also

– for the sake of understanding, they said – dropped his partner, 'Wick' Powell, and brought in the Cardiff pair of half-backs, Gwyn Richards and Billy Delahay. Still, it was an international and could still be a good game. Perhaps it would have been had it not been for the weather.

It had rained all the morning in Cardiff in a steady downpour. Eben had a meal with Mark in a crowded café, steaming with a damp and noisy crowd, and then went off to locate the Angel Hotel, where the Bromilows were staying.

In spite of the rain the crowd outside the ground was already a large one and they were in surprisingly good spirits. A group of kilted Scots were the subject of some good-natured ribaldry from a happy Welsh crowd. The Scotsmen all sported large blue and white rosettes.

A policeman directed Eben to the Angel.

Arriving at the hotel, Eben found more of a crowd on the pavement outside the entrance. The Scottish team, it seemed, were staying there and had just left for the ground opposite. The hotel foyer was crowded but, above the talk, a voice called, 'Ah, there you are, Eben.'

Bromilow came over to greet him. 'Come and meet some old friends of mine,' he said.

Eben shook hands with a few men whose names he scarcely heard. Then some more people came up to their own little crowd and Algie Bromilow said, 'Come on then, let's go.'

Their seats were good ones, mid-way between the half-way line and the twenty-five. The bank opposite was already crowded, and the singing was something which Eben could never have believed possible. Wave after wave of glorious harmony came floating through the driving rain, with tenors soaring way above the rich bass that rolled across the field like thunder coming over the mountains. He knew many of the hymns they sang and, although he was no singer, he joined in with them. But when he first tried he found his voice choked with emotion.

Then the teams came on to the field to a great roar from the waiting crowd. Forty thousand it was reckoned there were there. The teams lined up facing each other along the half-way line. They slapped their arms across their chests, rubbed their hands, jumped up and down and held their heads down sideways against the rain. Eben knew the feeling. Then the crowd were on their feet, almost delirious with joy, as the Prince of Wales, the darling of the Welsh miners, came out on to the field, the first royalty to tread the hallowed turf of

Cardiff Arms Park. Caps were in the air. They sang 'God Bless the Prince of Wales' and 'For He's a Jolly Good Fellow'. He shook hands with the players. With him was a florid-looking man in a big overcoat, a programme in his hand. He was one of the men to whom Bromilow had introduced him at the hotel.

'Who's the man in the big overcoat?' said Eben.

'That's Walter Rees. Big shot of Welsh rugby.'

So Bromilow knew people too, as well as Jerry Forsdyke.

And then, before the crowd realized, as they still cheered the Prince returning to his place in the stand, the game was on. And that was as much as Eben remembered. Players slipped and slithered and, although the rain stopped before the end of the game, so much had already fallen that within the first five minutes it was a mud-bath. Long before half-time, red jerseys were indecipherable from blue. In spite of the conditions, the Welsh forwards seemed determined to heel the ball and Ifor Jones, a giant amongst the Welsh pack, was left unsupported as time and time again he broke away in powerful dribbles. Scotland won by five points to nil, and to Eben it was merely an item for the records after a disappointing afternoon in which the Scottish pack had been magnificent.

After the game they met Mrs Bromilow and Penny for a meal. Then they went to the New Theatre to see *Robinson Crusoe*. There was variety at the Empire which Eben thought he would have liked. But the pantomime turned out to be far better than anything he had expected. They all joined in the singing of a daft song with actions. Penny sat next to him and it would have been difficult not to share her enthusiasm as she forgot that, at nearly seventeen, she now regarded herself as a young lady.

They walked back from the theatre amongst the crowds who jostled in Queen Street, and past Cardiff's great castle until they came to the Angel. Eben thanked the Bromilows for their kindness, and they parted.

Westgate Street was now littered with the debris of the afternoon's confrontation. Discarded programmes and newspapers lay trodden underfoot on the wet pavements. Bits of ribbon, some red and some blue, trailed bedraggled in the gutter. Eben crossed the street before a tram clanked by, and sparks flashed above it where the overhead arm swung round at the junction as the tram turned off for the bridge. A lighted panel on the front said 'Cathedral Road'. The scene of the battle was almost deserted. The Angel was lit up and there was the sound of singing. Eben walked on down Westgate Street.

If he was thinking of anything he was thinking of how you can plan things in life and be very disappointed. He had anticipated nothing of the pantomime, but had enjoyed it and loved the glittering atmosphere of the theatre. Yet the match, to which he had been looking forward so eagerly, had been a complete let-down. Still, that was life, he thought.

Then he saw her. On the other side of the road a woman was standing at the corner of a dark side-street. As Eben looked she moved along the pavement under the street light and he knew it was Bridget Wyrriot from Morfa Bychan. It was thirteen years since he had last seen her but there was no mistaking her. And then he remembered that she had married and gone to live in Cardiff. So now Aunty Becca would have another bit of news for Hannah when she wrote. What a small place the world was after all.

As Eben went to cross the road to greet her a tram came clanging down from the direction of the castle. He waited for it to pass and then found that there was another tram coming in the opposite direction. He waited for that, too.

By the time he reached the other side Bridget was talking to somebody. The light shone full on her painted face and her hair had been peroxided. Her companion was a middle-aged man. He was looking up and down the street furtively.

Eben hesitated. He heard the man say, 'How much?'

'Ten shillings,' Bridget said.

The man looked up and down the street again but seemed not to see Eben. 'All right,' he said, and he and Bridget walked away down the side-street.

Eben stood there. How long, he hardly knew. But he pulled himself together as a woman spoke to him.

'Are you looking for anybody, dearie?' she asked.

Eben turned towards her. 'Yes,' he said foolishly. 'I just saw somebody I know.'

'You wanted Bridget, did you?'

'You know her, do you?'

The woman looked at him. Her face was heavily painted and there was a smell of cheap perfume about her.

'Of course I know her, darling. She's one of the regulars, the same as me.'

'Oh, I see,' said Eben.

The woman moved closer to him and he could smell her

stale powder. 'Do you want to do business, darling?'

'No. No, thank you,' said Eben.

'Just a short time. I've got a nice clean room and it's the same price as Bridget.'

'You don't seem to understand,' he said.

'Do you want it or not?' she said, her manner changing suddenly.

'I told you, no.'

'Then piss off,' she said, 'wasting our bleeding time.'

Eben tried again. He said, 'But I . . .'

'Bollocks,' she said, and disappeared down the side-street.

Eben looked up and saw two policemen walking along the pavement. They eyed him carefully and passed on as he stood there unable to collect his wits.

The lights from the saloon-bar windows of a hotel fell across the pavement. A noisy band of erstwhile spectators came barging along. There was the sound of drunken singing, maudlin over a Welsh hymn. But Eben heard and saw none of these things. He saw only a forlorn girl waving to them from outside a little house above a lonely beach. He saw her as she had taken him and Mark to see their few animals and topped-and-tailed the prawns for them at tea-time.

But, dear God, what had reduced her to this? Had she been driven to it by some wastrel husband or was it something of her own choosing? He did not suppose he would ever know the answer to these things. But one thing he knew for sure. No word of this must ever be made known.

He walked on towards the place where they had left the charabanc.

Before the end of his first season with Cardiff, Eben found himself being singled out for mention in the national press.

> Turning to the future, one sees a number of young players with considerable potential. Of those not yet tempted to go north there are few more promising than the young Cardiff centre, Eben Harter. Of powerful build he has a fine burst of speed and is a deadly tackler. A two-footed player and a reliable place-kicker, he is equally at home in the full-back position and it can hardly be long before the Welsh selectors will have to give him serious consideration.

He was not yet twenty-three and, if not exactly a young player by general standards, he had come later to the game than the varsity and ex-public schoolboys who were not only prominent but were from the sort of background which made it unlikely that they would be tempted by the money to go north in these depressed times.

He had had two more full and highly successful seasons with Tenby and then, near the end of his second season, he had had an approach from Llanelly.

'Jolly good,' said Bromilow when Eben told him. 'You'll jump at it, of course.'

'I couldn't afford it,' Eben said.

'That's no problem, boy. They'll pay all your fares. Good chance. You take it.'

'No, there are other problems. It would mean being from home a lot and I'd be earning nothing.'

Bromilow thought for a while. Then he said, 'Leave it to me.'

Eben scarcely gave it another thought. He had learned his lesson the hard way over Narberth County school. It would be a wonderful thing to play for the famous Scarlets, but he would just have to go on working and enjoy what rugby he could play locally.

A few weeks later the letter came from Cardiff. Exactly what the job was which he was being offered he could not be sure, but it was as a salesman on a part-time basis at a wage of five pounds a week. He could start in August. It would also be possible for him to have time off to play rugby.

'Di's't thee apply for a job then?' said his father.

'No, I never applied for a job.'

'How have this come about then?'

Eben read the letter yet again and told him what Bromilow had said over the Llanelly offer.

'Then thou's ha' better go up an' see'n an' see what he says.'

Bromilow, it seemed, had acted to some purpose. 'Nothing in writing you understand. There never is. But the job is nothing at all. As long as you make the grade you'll be almost your own boss.'

Eben could hardly believe it. He tried to thank him.

'Nonsense,' said Bromilow. 'No good playing down here when there's a better chance to be had.'

As Eben walked down the lane for the Mill there was a lark soaring upwards, singing as it went, and his hopes were as buoyant as the lark's flight. Everywhere he sensed that new hope which spring always brought.

Becca and Tilly were both at the Mill, Becca getting a meal and Tilly making butter. Selling milk was again unprofitable. Not that making butter was any better. One week last year they had buried in the garden nearly a hundredweight of butter which they had failed to sell. Ben Harter was just coming into the house as Eben came back, and Tilly was 'having a spell' whilst the butter drained.

Eben told them of his talk with Bromilow and was prepared for opposition from his father.

To Eben's surprise, he said, 'Well, if there's a job goes with it, 'tis a chance for thee. Better than thou ca's't do home here the way things be now for all.'

Eben looked at his father. He was sixty-five and looked his age. Eben said, 'How will you manage on your own?'

'Don't thee worry about that,' put in Tilly. 'I'll help with the milkin'.'

'An' do'sn't thee worry neither, maid,' said Ben Harter. 'I've come to the conclusion we'd be a sight better off without th'owld milk at all. A body may so well be a' idle fool as a busy fool.'

Eben knew it to be true. The better a man farmed the more money he lost.

'What will you do?' he said.

His father looked at him. 'What I should ha' done afore if I'd had any sense. Sell some o' the cows and rear calves on the rest. Things aren't gwain very well down Bonville's Court so there wunnat be nothin' much with the ponies, but I can buy an' sell a few cattle an' hope as things'll improve by an' by.'

Eben had never worked with more zest than he did that summer and he relished every moment of the fragrance of haymaking time. At least there would be plenty of hay there for them for the winter. And then the time had come and he was in Cardiff. Lodgings had been found for him in a quiet street off Cathedral Road which was no more than a sharp walk from the Arms Park. That seemed to be the main consideration. His employment for a firm somewhere down in the area of the docks was evidently of secondary importance. Perhaps after the season was over something would be sorted out. For the whole of that winter he was so engrossed with rugby, and thrilled at his good fortune, that he was not disposed to let conscience concerning the job trouble him.

His lodgings were comfortable and Mrs Lewis, his landlady, looked after him well.

Whenever he walked down Westgate Street, especially at night, he wondered about Bridget and whether, if he came face to face with her, he should speak to her or take no notice.

121

She would hardly know him, because she had not seen him since he was eight years old. But suppose she saw his name in the paper and came to ask for him at the ground. The thought appalled him. He always kept his eyes open, but never did he see her. And he knew better than to loiter.

It was the first time he had ever slept away from home, and for the first time in his life he bathed in a proper bath. He had used the flush toilets downstairs at Deerfield, and he had seen the bathroom there. At the Mill, bath night was a performance in the zinc bath in front of the fire, carrying water and boiling kettles and 'get it over and done with'. There was no stretching out and thinking of the luxury, with more hot water just by leaning forward and turning a tap.

He had been in Cardiff a couple of months when a letter came from his sister Liza in Treorchy. She thought he might be lonely on his own, and if he would like to come out one Sunday there was a bus all the way. He went a fortnight before Christmas.

When he had talked to Bromilow and Jerry Forsdyke about his sister and her family being hungry up in the Rhondda he had only read and heard about the place. Now, as the bus wound into the heart of the mountains, the misery of it all oppressed him, and he found himself suddenly understanding Jim Cartlett's fierce socialism. Once, this land must have been beautiful, but now it had become a place of unspeakable squalor and misery. Today, even on Sunday, odd little groups of men stood at street corners, waiting for they knew not what. One had a couple of whippets on a string lead. Here and there, loose-wooled, coal-begrimed, unthrifty-looking sheep walked hopefully across the road in front of the bus to explore the garbage on the opposite pavement. Rows of cold stone houses, small and miserable as they huddled together, rose steeply, back-to-back, from the main street to where the over-shadowing coal-tips weighed down upon them. Rusting zinc and rotting timber added nothing except more dejection to the overall picture of forlorn poverty. Some shop windows were boarded up, and those that were open had little in them. For miles, it seemed, the scene was unchanging except that occasionally there would be a shorter row of houses, with a low wall in front with iron railings and an iron gate, where the foremen lived in better style. And here and there, away from it all, was the still greater affluence of the managers' houses.

Eben found Liza's house in the middle of the row and she

answered the door excitedly herself almost as soon as he had knocked. She was ten years older than Eben. Already her face was drawn and her hair turning a premature grey. She put her arms round him and hugged him. There were tears in her eyes.

'There's nice it is to see you,' she said, 'and there's well you're looking.'

'Come on in then, boyo,' said Jim Cartlett from behind her in the narrow passage. He took Eben's hand in a warm, firm grip and ushered him through to the kitchen. The children were shy at first, but were soon at home with him for they remembered him from the last time they had been down to Heronsmill.

'Now then, Jim, pack this lot away,' said Liza.

Jim Cartlett picked up the federation books on which he had been working. 'Aye, put 'em away with pleasure,' he said. ' 'Tis hard trying to get the pennies out of them that haven't got 'em.'

The house was spotlessly clean, and the warmth of the welcome had been there, but so had evidence of the poverty. Eben had seen poverty at home, when the pits had closed during the strike and men were out of work. But there was always the odd rabbit to be had, and men had their gardens and a few hens, and could have a row of potatoes in the field in return for seasonal help. And they could keep a pig. Here, there was nothing. Only empty purses and empty bellies.

In the evening they had gone to chapel.

'How often do you go, Liza?' Eben had said.

'Every Sunday, the same as Mam. What about you?'

'Hardly ever these days.' Eben felt a little guilty.

'Well, that's how it's getting up here now. When we first came here it was full to the door the chapel was. But it's falling away they are now.'

Even so, the singing was glorious. Eben had never heard anything like it and was content just to listen to the beautiful harmony as it swelled out and then died away pianissimo way up in the varnished oak rafters.

> Lead, kindly Light, amid the encircling gloom
> Lead Thou me on!
> The night is dark and I am far from home —
> Lead Thou me on!

There was a depth of feeling in singing such as this that no words of his could have described. Perhaps it was the encircling gloom all about them in the hemmed-in valley, dark and far from home as many of them were. He wondered whether Liza was yearning for the meadows by the Mill, and whether Jim was thinking of the harbour at Saundersfoot. Or was this really home to them now after so many years?

The visit disturbed the peace of mind which he had found in his first months in Cardiff, in the excitement of his own life and the success he was already achieving. There were others beside himself in life and they were less fortunate. Before he left he gave Liza two pounds. Jim saw him do it and said, 'Now put that back, boyo.'

'No, indeed I won't,' said Eben.

'I'm tellin' you now. Put it back.'

'And I'm telling you I won't.'

'Look now, boyo, you've got yourself to think about.'

'Aye, well, that's all right. But it's only myself. You've got Liza and the children as well.'

Jim frowned. 'It isn't good enough, see.'

'You're not offended, are you?'

'Diawl, no. When you've been through what we've been through you don't waste time with false pride.'

'Then have it for the children for Christmas.'

Liza put her arms round him and kissed him and there were tears in her eyes again.

As he saw the lights in the dark sky ahead and the bus neared Cardiff he felt some of the despondency lifting.

At the end of the season he would have to find out more about what his job was supposed to be. He knew the rugby could not last forever, but it could lead to the right contacts in life and the chance of a decent job. The thrill of playing at the historic Arms Park was one thing, but there was also the future to be thought of sometimes. Seeing the struggle which Jim and Liza were having he also remembered how things had been at home, and it made him appreciate his own good fortune all the more.

It made him even more determined to succeed both on and off the field. Although he had played most of his rugby in the centre, he now found himself converted in an emergency to full-back when the regular full-back broke his arm. His name was 'Clapper' Williams, and in the irksome period when he was waiting to be able to play again he spent hours with Eben practising kicking and fielding until they became close friends.

However, Eben's own first set-back came with an injury to

his knee in the dying seconds of a game. He was tackled hard and awkwardly and found himself under the opposing pack of forwards. It felt as if someone was trying to push a red-hot poker through his twisted knee-joint. When the referee blew his whistle to break up the loose scrummage he blew for no-side as well so that, although Eben had to be half-carried from the field, the incident escaped any particular notice and made no headlines. His knee was bandaged and the pain eventually abated, but the joint remained stiff over the week-end.

The club doctor saw him on the Monday and examined it carefully. 'There's one thing certain,' he said, 'you're out for the rest of the season.'

'Is it as bad as that?'

'Yes, my boy, it's as bad as that.'

The doctor sensed his disappointment. 'The most important thing now is to decide what's best for the future.'

'Is it really cartilage?' Eben almost choked on the word.

'Yes, it's cartilage all right. But if you're careful it needn't be the end of the world.'

'I thought cartilage usually meant you were finished.'

'Not always. Personally, I'm not keen on operating. If you can rest it properly, and I really mean rest it, you can come back next season as good as new. Have some heat treatment and massage from now till the end of the season and then go home for a few months. If the worst comes to the worst, and you get any more trouble, we can still try operating if we really have to.'

Having arranged with Mrs Lewis to return in August, Eben found himself in May back for the summer months at Herons-mill. And his wage as a part-time salesman still came through every month.

Eben had to be home for the beginning of May to be best man at Mark's wedding. Once home, he stayed.

'I thought I'd better come and give you a bit of support,' he laughed, when Mark met him at Kilgetty station.

'When your turn comes I'll do the same for you,' said Mark.

'That won't be for a spell. I haven't found anybody yet.'

'Couldn't you find something up there in Cardiff?'

'No time, boy. Too busy.'

'Busy doing what?'

'Didn't you know I was a salesman?'

'What d'you sell then, boy?'

Eben laughed. 'Nobody's told me yet.'

'That sounds like a hell of a good job. You'd better look after it.'

'I'm going to.'

Mark had a new Austin Swallow.

'This is quite a little motor car,' said Eben.

'Do you like her?'

'She'd suit me down to the ground.'

'I'll see if I can find one second-hand for you.'

As they came down the hill for Stepaside, Eben looked back up the valley towards Heronsmill and, for the first time in his life, knew the thrill of coming home. Eventually he said, 'How's Father and Aunty Becca?'

'Aunty Becca's like a two-year-old, but the old man isn't so good.'

'What's the matter with him?'

'Nothing the matter with'n. Just going to look old.'

'Is he drinking now?'

'Hardly touches it.'

After a while Eben said, 'Who's the girl you're marrying? I've never heard of her as far as I can remember.'

'Jane Randall? Don't you know Jane?'

'No, I don't know her.'

'Her father's got a garage and a couple of buses in Tenby.'

'Oh, that's the family. Like Gramfer used to say, "If you can spell, I'll read".'

Mark laughed. 'Well, Arter Wogan and I have two charabancs now and two buses and I'm buying them off him. He's more interested in the garage side of it. So I'm going in with Jane's old man and we'll run a damn good bus service as well as the summer trips.'

By one of those odd twists of fate, Penny was also at the wedding. She had been in school for a short time in Tenby with Jane Randall, and they met one day in Tenby when Jane was preparing for her wedding.

'I'm sure you'll look awfully nice,' said Penny. 'How many bridesmaids are you having?'

'Only one.'

'Only one?'

'Yes, I don't like a lot of fuss. In fact, I'll be glad when it's over.'

'You ought to be marrying Eben instead of Mark. He doesn't like much fuss either.'

'Do you know him well, then?'

126

'Oh yes, awfully well, and Daddy's awfully fond of him.'

'Well, good gracious, you must come to the wedding. I'll put you on the list.'

Penny bought her a present and delivered it the following week to make sure she would not forget.

From the early days when he had started tinkering with motor-bikes and second-hand cars, Mark had seen to it that Eben could drive, so that, with Penny going to the wedding, Bromilow said to Eben, 'You take my car.'

'Do you think I'll be safe?'

'Safer than that young Penny on her own. Wild as a hawk sometimes. You take charge.'

Bromilow's car was a Crossley with real power under the bonnet, and Eben could imagine Penny being let loose with it. It was hardly her fault that she had been so thoroughly spoiled.

The wedding was in the afternoon. After the reception, some of them went back to the Randalls', and Eben drove his family home. Penny, however, was enjoying herself with friends who had also turned up at the Randalls', and wanted to stay. Eben came back for her later in the evening. A few of his old Tenby team-mates were there and talked rugby. Then they started to sing. Penny had been drinking gin and she began to sing too. Eventually they had sandwiches and sausage rolls and coffee. It was nearly midnight and time to go home.

In the car Penny moved up close to Eben and put her head on his shoulder. Then she brushed her lips against his cheek.

'Do you still hate me?' she said.

'I've never hated you.'

'You called me a little bitch once.'

'That was a long time ago.'

'You know I'm in love with you. Why don't you do something about it?'

She was slightly drunk. Eben said nothing. Soon she was breathing heavily and he knew she was asleep. He drove steadily and carefully in order not to wake her. When they reached Deerfield the gates were open and so were the garage doors. He stopped the engine and turned off the lights. Penny sighed and cuddled closer to him. Eben put his arm round her to wake her. She slipped down and put her arms round his neck. Then she pulled his head down and kissed him passionately. He felt her firm breasts against him and his hold on her tightened.

Penny pulled her mouth away from his and kissed the side of his neck. 'You're actually human,' she sighed.

Then she kissed him again, and pressed herself close to him.

The blood was pounding in Eben's head, but he said, 'If you're still of the same mind another time, we'll have a play-off on a neutral ground.'

A week later Eben was in Tenby and he met Liz Whithow. She was smiling as always.

'Well, well, my handsome, I haven't set eyes on you since you stood me up in the Lower Level wood.'

'I didn't stand you up, Liz.'

'No, quite right. You sent me a very well-behaved substitute.'

'And now he's gone and got married.'

'So now he knows what's what.'

'I reckon he knew that without getting married.'

'So they say, but he was quite the gentleman with me.'

Her face was harder these days and her hair had been bobbed, but she still stirred him physically.

She smiled and gave him her old enticing look. 'So what about dating me up again?'

'What have you got in mind?'

'There's a dance in here tomorrow night.'

'Which way would I get home at that time of night?'

'Don't you know anything, and your brother in the business? They're running a late bus now after the big dance. But don't worry your head about that – I've got my own room if you'd rather go home in the morning – and nobody bothers me, as long as I'm very discreet.'

'I'm not much for dancing,' he said, 'but you make it sound very interesting.'

'Then think about it.'

Things were well under way by the time Eben arrived and the place was crowded. Eventually he saw Liz. She was dancing, but she winked at him as she went round. In the interval he went over to her and asked her for the next dance. They had the next three dances together and then stayed together until a gents' 'excuse me'. They had only been on the floor a few minutes when a pleasant young man tapped Eben on the shoulder and, with a big smile, said, 'Excuse me.' Eben shook his head sadly and said, 'There's no justice in this life.' Then he smiled and handed Liz over.

'See you after,' he said.

He left the floor with his mind far away and walked straight into Penny.

'What's the matter, lover boy? Somebody cut you out?'

He looked at her in surprise.

She smiled at him. 'Will I do as second best?'

'What are you doing here?' was all he could say.

'Doing? Why, what would you think I'm doing? Dancing, of course.'

'You're not on your own, are you?'

'Oh no, I'm with you.'

'What d'you mean, with me?'

'I told Daddy I was coming with you and he let me have the car.'

Eben thought for a moment. Then he said, 'But how did you know I was coming?'

'I met your cousin Tilly at tea-time. It's surprising what one can find out if one is interested.'

So that was the way the wind was blowing.

'But tell me if I'm not wanted,' she said.

He looked at her. 'Of course not.'

'Of course not what?'

'Of course you're not not wanted.'

He laughed and she said, 'There's funny they talk in Cardiff. Do you mean by that that I'm wanted?'

'Well, yes, of course.'

'Then don't be afraid to say so sometimes.'

She held up her arms and they began to dance. Eben was no great dancer, but Penny was as light as a feather and, whatever his shortcomings, she covered them up. In the next dance she held herself very close to him.

In the interval, looking over Penny's shoulder, he saw Liz. She was the centre of attraction in a little knot, mostly of young men, and he knew that was the end of Liz for the evening.

Penny looked at him. She said, 'Well, who's it to be? Liz or me?'

Eben smiled at her. 'You're here with me, aren't you?'

'If you say so.'

'And you said so, too, so that's two of us.'

'Let's go then, shall we?'

'So soon?' Eben was surprised. He knew how she enjoyed dancing.

Penny looked at her watch. She said, 'It's half-past ten.'

'All right then. Let's get your coat.'

The moon was high over the sea towards Worm's Head across Carmarthen Bay. Near the edge of the tide, which was lapping the shore in gentle ripples, a young couple walked hand-in-hand. Goscar Rock stood out clear in the moonlight. Somewhere in the stillness a pair of oyster-catchers called and then hurried across the path which the moon swathed along the water's edge on the damp sand. Contrary to her father's opinion, on this occasion at any rate, Penny drove carefully. Eventually she turned off the main road and drove until she came to a wide part where the Council sometimes tipped chippings for tarring the road. Tonight, the space was clear and she pulled in and switched off the lights.

Eben saw her face in the moonlight. Then she smiled at him.

'All right,' she said, 'we're on a neutral ground.'

There was a warm rug on the wide back seat and a couple of cushions. It was one o'clock before they left. Eben thought of Algie Bromilow on the way home. This girl was the eyes in his head, but he did not feel too badly about what had happened. When he had finally taken her he knew he was not the first.

Penny came the back road for Heronsmill so that she could drop Eben at his own gate. She drove carefully through the lake and said, 'Remember that bridge?'

'Yes, and the primroses.'

She laughed. Eben could see she was very happy.

When she stopped at the gate at the top of the Mill Lane she said, 'I'll see you again at the week-end.'

'What's on?'

'Daddy has to go to Bolton.'

'To Bolton?'

'Yes, there's a special emergency meeting of the board of his company.'

'I thought he'd finished with all that?'

'He has really, but apparently there's some sort of crisis in the cotton business and Uncle Jerry says Daddy simply must go.'

'Where do I come into it?'

'I'll persuade Mummy to go with him for company, so I'll be on my own for a few nights.'

Cari had died the previous winter and Burridge had gone back to England. So their house was empty, and Penny sent the Gittow girls home each evening.

Eben felt a little guilty the first evening when she took him to her bedroom, but soon forgot it in the sensuousness of her embrace. They had three such evenings of reckless passion, and then Penny's parents returned and they had to settle again to their normal routine.

For a week Eben stayed home. The garden had been neglected, and he had the excuse to clean it up. Eventually, Penny appeared. She was very self-assured.

'And why haven't you been to see me?' she said.

'I suppose it sounds stupid but I just haven't been able to think of an excuse.'

'Do you need an excuse?'

'Not really, but you know how it is.'

'You're a fool. Daddy will only be suspicious if you don't call.'

'I'll call tomorrow.'

'Tomorrow we're going sailing.'

'Who's we?'

'You and I.'

'Good God! Or, as your father would say, "What will she think of next?"'

'What's odd about that?'

'Well, I can row a boat, but I've never sailed one.'

'I have. Hundreds of times.'

'On your own?'

'Well, sort of.'

'Whose boat are you having?'

Penny had it all worked out. Old Jubilee Barlow at Saundersfoot knew her well and she and some of her friends had hired a boat from him before. She had already made the arrangements.

It was not a very smart boat, but it was a serviceable fourteen-footer. Penny had arranged a picnic and the weather was good.

Jubilee Barlow said, 'Thou's'll be all right today, miss. Sail you back and fore from Monkstone to Wiseman's Bridge and thou's'll come to no harm. But I shouldn't go much further than that if I was you. Can the young gentleman sail a boat?'

'No indeed,' said Eben, 'no sailor at all.'

'Never mind then, there bain't much harm in it. Keep you inside Monkstone and thou's'll be all right.'

Eben rowed the boat out of the harbour round the pier-head without feeling too awkward and then, under Penny's directions, hoisted the main-sail and then the jib. Then he put down the heavy centre-plate. The tide was on the ebb. There was a gentle but steady breeze coming off the sea, and the boat heeled slightly under it as she hissed through the clear blue water and the prow slapped rhythmically into the very slight swell. It was an exhilarating sensation, and Penny, at the tiller, seemed to be quite competent.

The sand-banks and wooded cliffs slid past them and, in a surprisingly short time, they were off Wiseman's Bridge.

'We'll go about then,' said Penny. 'Keep you head down.'

She pushed the tiller hard over to port, the bow of the boat came up into the wind, the sails flapped drunkenly and the boom swung across just above their heads.

'I see what you mean,' said Eben.

Penny shifted her position and hauled in the mainsheet, to sail close to the wind, and headed for Monkstone. The ebb tide was running with them.

The bay lay before them with Worm's Head away to the south. Sitting amidships, and looking back beyond Penny, Eben could see a couple of small red-sailed boats well up the bay towards Amroth. There were no coal boats anywhere to be seen. Bonville's Court colliery was closing down and, since it was too early in the season for there to be many visitors about, they seemed to have the whole ocean to themselves. Eben found it a strangely satisfying feeling. He had no wish to talk. He just wanted to sit there and drink in the complete peace as the salt tang came in with the breeze. An empty cigarette packet drifted past and a bright-eyed gull circled it speculatively. Penny was engrossed and, as Eben looked at her slim figure, he wondered where it was going to end.

Presently, through the gap between Monkstone and the mainland, he saw the big sea-front houses of Tenby on their rocky eminence with the church spire pushing itself towards the sky above the town. Then Monkstone itself hid the town from view. A dozen cormorants lined the rocks above the water and stood statue-like and somewhat foolishly, with their drying wings extended in the warmth of the mid-morning sun and long necks held high like eagles in some elaborate heraldic design.

'What do they do that for?' asked Penny.

'They've been fishing and now they're digesting it and drying out.'

Soon they were out beyond Monkstone, and Tenby again came into view. Outside the harbour several sailing boats lent an air of contentment to a lazy scene and Caldey Island rose

132

clearly to the south-west.

'Time to go about again,' said Penny.

Once again they settled themselves for a steady sail across the bay, running before the breeze. The pebble ridge above the beach at Wiseman's Bridge was becoming more distinct when Penny said, 'Look at those boats way up beyond Amroth.'

'What about them?'

'Let's go up there.'

'What's wrong with this as we are?'

'It's super up there.'

Eben was a little perturbed. He said, 'Old man Barlow back there said not to go too far.'

'Oh, I've been there lots of times.'

He had to admit that the other boats were there.

'We can land on the beach there for a picnic.'

'Land?'

'Oh, yes, I've often done it.'

The locals reckoned it was a bad place to keep a boat. That was the sum total of his knowledge.

'It's low water about three o'clock this afternoon. So we can beach the boat when we get there and then she'll refloat about six o'clock this evening. And by that time there'll be enough water for us to get back into the harbour.'

Penny seemed to have it all worked out again and it sounded feasible. She pushed the tiller over, took in the mainsheet half-way, and they began the long reach for Amroth. They left Wiseman's Bridge behind them and sailed on past the cliffs and the old iron-ore workings at Crickdam. They saw the cottage gardens which ran down to the beach at Amroth, and then the long ridge of pebbles which sheltered the New Inn from the fury of the sea in south-westerly gales in winter. Then they were leaving the point at Black Rock behind, and at last they found themselves coming up for Telpyn. The high cliffs gave way to woods running down to pebbles, and then there was hard sand glinting like gold in the midday sun. It was in weather such as this, and at this time of year, that they had gone to Morfa Bychan when they bought Blackie. In a wild moment he almost said to Penny that they could sail right on past Ragwen to Morfa Bychan. It would have appealed to her immensely, but he checked himself in time.

Penny had let out the sail and the boat was running for the beach.

'Oh, my God,' she said suddenly, 'lift the centre-plate.'

Eben heaved it out of its narrow box and laid it in the bottom of the boat.

'Now lower the sail,' she said.

The boat began to lose way and slid gently in to the shallow water and came to rest with her keel in the sand.

Eben had taken off his sandshoes. Rolling up his trousers, he went to the bow of the boat and, jumping down, pulled it a little way towards the water's edge where the small waves lapped harmlessly on the sand and round the gently rocking boat. It was noon, and, according to Penny's reckoning, it would be about six hours before the boat refloated. The two red-sailed boats were tacking far out to sea. There was not a living soul in sight.

Penny took off her shoes and paddled along the edge of the water. She let the wet sand squeeze between her toes and then splashed her feet to rinse them in the clear water. The sea was blue and there was hardly a cloud in the sky.

Eben fetched the picnic basket, and Penny said, 'Bring the rug as well to put on the pebbles.'

The tide was receding and the boat had already been left firmly on the sand.

Penny took the rug, and Eben carried the picnic basket up to the pebbles. It was warm and the sea looked inviting.

He said, 'Wouldn't it be a lovely day for a bathe!'

'Super!'

'A pity we didn't think to bring bathing costumes.'

'What does it matter about costumes?'

Penny had already started to undress.

They ran naked down the sands and plunged into the water. It was cold and they gasped for breath. Eben thrilled as Penny slipped into his arms.

They walked up the beach holding hands and lay on the rug to dry in the sun. At last Eben sat up. He said, 'We're going to have company.'

A figure was clambering round the rocks under Black Rock point in the distance.

'Probably somebody going prawning,' said Penny.

He said, 'Maybe we'd better dress for lunch.'

He pulled on his trousers, and Penny put on only her frock. Then she opened the picnic basket.

When Eben saw the food he realized how hungry he was. There were melon slices and chicken legs with salad and new garden potatoes and butter. There were crisp bread rolls and strawberries and cream. Wrapped in a snow-white table napkin

134

was a bottle of hock. Eben pulled the cork and passed the glasses for Penny to hold whilst he poured the sparkling wine.

Replete after the meal, they finished the bottle. Eben felt pleasantly merry. Penny got up and said, 'Come on, shift yourself.'

Eben got up too, and she picked up the rug.

'Up there beyond those trees,' she said, 'there's a bank with deep ferns and a green carpet beneath them where the blue-bells have been.'

She walked up over the stones towards the wood. Eben knew what was in her mind and he went with her readily.

By the time they stirred, the sun had lost its brightness and the wind had gone round to the south-west. It was getting colder. Eben was no sailor, but he could see that to make Saundersfoot they would have to sail against the wind. And he also knew that the tide ran up across the bay when it was on the flow, so that they would have the tide against them as well. He could see, too, that, whereas the sea had been calm when they landed, it was now beginning to get choppy. He was worried. The two red-sailed boats were out towards Monk-stone and running before the wind for Saundersfoot harbour.

'What happens now?'

'What do you mean what happens? We've just got to manage, of course.'

'Well, come on,' he said, 'we'd better get dressed and pack the things up.'

They went down through the wind-stunted oak trees in the wood and on to the pebbles. As they hurried down, with the pebbles sliding and rolling beneath their feet, Eben's knee gave way. He felt a searing stab of pain and his leg folded beneath him. As he held his hands to his knee and gasped for breath, Penny said, 'What's the matter now?'

'My knee's gone.'

'Oh, my God! Did you have to pick a time like this!'

Gradually the pain became bearable and he hobbled the rest of the way down the stones. They dressed sullenly and packed the picnic basket. Penny, it seemed, had miscalculated. Low water had been considerably later than three o'clock and it would be more like seven before the boat would refloat. It was now half-past five.

As they waited, with the tension growing between them, the sea seemed to be getting steadily more choppy. It was intolerable waiting, with conditions deteriorating every minute, and being helpless to get the boat into the water. Once, Eben tried to drag it across the sand. With his strength he could probably have done it, but not with his knee as it was. It was as much as he could do now to bear his weight on it.

By the time the boat was afloat the sea was quite rough. Eben had put Penny in the boat and told her to take the oars. In agony with his knee, and with the boat being buffeted and almost swamped by every wave, he somehow managed to turn the bow to face the incoming sea. He said to Penny, 'Now then, row,' and began pushing at the stern. He was up to his chest in water and then, at last, he heaved himself into the boat. Somehow, he managed to take over from Penny and rowed away from the beach. When they were far enough out he shipped the oars, hoisted the sails and lowered the centre-plate. Then they beat out towards the open sea and Eben baled out the water they had shipped in the process of getting launched.

After a quarter of an hour's sailing they came about. On the return tack Eben could see that they were making no progress but coming back in for the beach from which they had started. If anything, they were nearer to Telpyn Point to the east, which was somewhat useless, he thought, for anybody trying to go to the west. They made for the open sea again. Eben thought about it and came to the conclusion that the swiftly running tide with the wind behind it was probably taking the centre-plate broadside on and dragging the boat with it. He took the centre-plate out, but when they tried to come about next time the boat simply refused to answer to the helm.

'Of course,' said Penny at last, 'we could run with this wind and tide all the way up to the Laugharne estuary. It would be awfully simple and we'd be safe there for the night.'

Eben rarely swore, but he looked at her now in his exasperation and said, 'Will you stop being so bloody stupid! There are sand-banks up there that even the locals who know them are afraid of.' Then he began to lower the sail.

'What are you doing that for?'

'I'm going to row the damn thing.'

'You can't row to Saundersfoot.'

'And we can't sail there either, so let's try something where I know what I'm trying to do.'

His knee was in agony as the rowlocks creaked and he took the strain of the oars. After half an hour he turned his head and thought he had made some progress. After another half-hour he looked again and his heart almost sang with joy as he realized he could see a little further round the corner of Black Rock than the last time he had looked. At least they were heading in the right direction. Out of sheer relief and to try to ease the tension he sang:

> *Pull for the shore, sailor, pull for the shore,*
> *Heed not the rolling waves but bend to the oar.*

Penny was not amused. She sat grim-faced in the stern. Then he began to recite:

> *Blue were her eyes as the fairy-flax,*
> *Her cheeks like the dawn of day,*
> *And her bosom white as the hawthorn buds*
> *That ope in the month of May.*
>
> *The skipper he stood beside the helm,*
> *His pipe was in his mouth,*
> *And he watched how the veering flaw did blow*
> *The smoke now West, now South.*
>
> *Then up and spake an old Sailor,*
> *Had sailed the Spanish Main,*
> *'I pray thee put into yonder port,*
> *For I fear a hurricane.*
>
> *Last night the moon had a golden ring,*
> *and tonight no moon we see!'*
> *The skipper he blew a whiff from his pipe,*
> *And a scornful laugh laughed he.*

Eben gasped with the agony of his knee and rowed on. Penny would never know what effort it had cost to try and put this face on things. He could feel his hands beginning to blister. But all she did was sit there sulking in a foul temper. Damn it, he thought, it was her doing, and he was doing his best to get them out of it.

'All right,' said Eben. 'If you don't like my company you can always get out and walk.'

The light was beginning to fade the next time he looked round. They were very nearly level with Amroth village. His knee was throbbing and he felt utterly weary. He doubted whether he could go on much longer. And then, as he stared, he caught a glimpse of white spray that was more than the tip of a wave. It was a motor-boat and it was coming towards them. Joyfully he turned again to his task and rowed on.

137

It was old Jubilee Barlow. Eben was ready to placate him, but the old salt was chuckling delightedly. He turned and came alongside to leeward of them. He shouted, 'Ah, well, miss. I see you was determined to learn the hard way.'

The humiliation for her, thought Eben, must have been unbearable.

To his amazement she laughed at him and even contrived to look coy.

'You've done well, young sir. Thou must be main strong I reckon. But I was never more glad than when I seen you pull th'owld sail down.'

Barlow threw them a line and Eben made fast at the bow. As the motor-boat took up the slack and roared away Eben put his head wearily in his aching hands and said, 'Now let's face up to being the laughing stock of everybody on the harbour.'

Earlier in the afternoon he had wondered where it would all end. Well, it was ending here. And he did not mind. Penny had made the running and there had been others before him. He felt no shame and no obligations.

Eben's knee remained swollen for some days and it continued to pain him. When it showed no improvement he went to see the young locum standing in for the local doctor who was on holiday. Eben told him the whole story.

'I would say rest it,' said the doctor, 'or maybe an operation. But it's too important to you to take any chances, so what I'd advise you to do is go up to Cardiff and see the club doctor and maybe a specialist.'

Eben went back to Cardiff a week later. The doctor was not optimistic. The specialist, he said, was away on holiday and would not be back for another week. In the meantime he suggested heat-treatment and massage.

It was a fortnight before Eben saw the specialist. His rooms were along the Newport Road and Eben boarded the tram with a feeling of anxiety and doubt.

'Do you want the truth?' said the specialist.

'You don't make it sound too hopeful.'

'It's not hopeful.'

'Then what is the truth?'

'I don't think you'll ever play rugby again.'

Eben had been only half expecting it. 'Never play again!'

'I'm afraid not. You can't play as it is, for it will let you down and maybe get worse every time you go on the field.'

'How about an operation?'

'Forget it. We can operate if you like, but you've seen enough of that without me having to tell you. And in your case I wouldn't even give you a fifty-fifty chance of it being successful. And even if it were successful enough for you to play again you'd never be sure of yourself. You'd lose a lot of confidence and you'd never be as good a player as you were before it happened.'

Eben said nothing.

'Is that what you would want?'

'No,' said Eben, 'I wouldn't want that.'

'I thought not.'

Eben went back on the top of an open tram. The sun rode high in a blue sky and the world should have been a good place in which to live. Yet here were his dreams all shattered again, and in a mood of black despair he fought back the tears.

The tram swayed along Newport Road, down into the dip under the bridge, and then ground its way up the slope into Queen Street. He liked Cardiff and would be sorry to leave it. He would either have to look for a job or go back to Heronsmill where the prospect was not encouraging.

The time had come to see what his present job was supposed to be and to talk to somebody about it in earnest. As the thought came to him the tram was just stopping opposite the castle at the top of High Street. Eben alighted and waited for a tram for the Docks.

Bute Street was not the most attractive part of Cardiff but, by day, it was busy with the comings and goings of people of commerce. Eben was lucky. The manager was in and was free to see him. Eben came straight to the point and told him of his position. The manager was a slight man, in late middle age, with a keen look in his close-set eyes. He had spent all his working years in the Docks area.

'So I suppose the long and short of it is you're wanting a job,' he said.

Eben tried to sound cheerful. 'I thought I had a job. What I want to do now is find out what it's supposed to be.'

The manager gave him a wry smile. 'Once your football is finished you'll soon find out what your job is.'

'I was afraid of that,' said Eben.

The manager took a file of papers from the shelf and thumbed through them.

'Well, I'll give you full credit for one thing. Ever since

139

you've been on our books you've always offered to do something and tried to show a bit of interest, which is more than I can say for most of the ones they've sent me.'

'Can you do anything for me?'

'Times are bad.'

He looked at the file again. After a while he said, 'I think I can find you something at the beginning of September, but not before. Is that any good to you?'

'Well, yes indeed, and I'm grateful to you. What will the job be?'

'I'm not sure yet. We'll talk about it when the time comes, but it will be in the selling line.' He put the file back on the shelf. 'How will you manage till then?'

'Well, so far they've gone on paying my salary every month.'

'Yes, of course. I'd forgotten.' The manager looked out through the high window and gave his wry smile again. 'Ah, well,' he said, 'I suppose we've all got to live. You've been honest with me, so we'll say nothing about this at the moment. Keep your own counsel. Go home until I send for you and no doubt your cheque will still come through every month.'

Eben left the office with a lightened heart.

He came by train to Templeton and walked home. He had already begun to accept the disappointment, bitter though it had been at first, of a wrecked football career and begun to feel thankful for the possibility of a decent job with some prospects. As he walked, the air hung heavy with the scent of the honeysuckle and wild roses that enriched the high hedgerows flanking the dusty road. The bees moved industriously amongst their bloom, for day was not yet done. Deep in the woodland a pigeon cooed its familiar call. The sounds of nature were all that disturbed the tranquillity of the warm summer evening. It was so still that he heard the silvery tinkle and the murmuring of Ford's Lake in the distance. When at last he came to the narrow stone bridge, he saw Penny leaning over the wall looking down into the cool, sparkling water. She wore a summer dress, and her straw bonnet swung idly from her fingers.

Eben checked. 'Oh my God!' he said to himself, 'here it is again!' She had not changed since the day years ago when she had flung down the primroses in her temper, and turned up the following day as though nothing had happened. Well, there was to be no reconciliation this time.

As he came to the bridge on which there was hardly room for two people to pass, Penny looked up, turned to meet him and smiled. She held out her hands and said, 'So you've come back.'

He ignored her outstretched hands. 'Yes, I've come back, but only for a short while.'

'And you never even wrote to me.'

'There was nothing to write about.'

'Don't be silly. Everybody quarrels, but they make it up.'

'Well, let's be different then. It was fun whilst it lasted, and now let's leave it at that.'

'Oh, fun was it?'

'What else was it for you?'

'Are you in the habit of seducing girls and then dropping them just like that?'

'If you want to know, you're the first.'

'I guessed as much. I had so hoped it would have been different.'

'What made you think it would be?'

'I had just hoped, that's all.' She lowered her head. Looking at the ground she said quietly, 'I'm pregnant.'

Eben seemed not to grasp what she said, 'You're *what*!'

'I'm pregnant. I'm going to have a baby.' She paused – 'Your baby.'

'Good God!' was all he could say. Then he said hopefully, 'How do you know?'

'Don't be such a fool. Women know these things.'

'Are you sure?'

'Of course I'm sure!'

'Good God!' he said again. He began to sweat.

'Well, maybe it's been a shock for you, but how d'you think I've felt these last weeks with nobody to turn to?'

'I'm sorry. I had no idea.'

'And you didn't care either.'

'I just didn't know, that's all.'

'Well, you know now, so what are we going to do?'

'What can we do?'

'Well, girls take things to get rid of babies, but I don't know what they are or where to get them. And anyway I'd be frightened.'

'No, you can't do that. We'll have to think of something else.'

'There's nothing else to think of, unless you marry me.'

'We can't get married.'

'Why not?'

'We're not suited.'

141

'We were suited enough to make a baby.'

'My God, we've made a mess of it!'

'If you don't marry me you can imagine what it will be like.'

Eben said nothing. The stream was loud in its rippling as it hurried away beneath them. He could imagine all right.

'Look,' he said at last, 'this has knocked the stuffing out of me. Does anyone else know about it?'

'Good God, of course not!'

'Then let's sleep on it and I'll meet you tomorrow afternoon by the Lower Level stile.'

'All right,' she said. They walked as far as the Mill gate together, but made no attempt to hold hands, and they went in silence, oblivious to the scents and the gentle sounds around them.

Eben spent a night of fitful and troubled sleep. For long periods he would lie awake thinking of the awful predicament.

Worst of all was the shame which Aunty Becca would feel, and he almost groaned as he thought how he had betrayed his mother's memory. God only knew how he was going to face Bromilow or what his attitude was likely to be. Even Penny would not expect to get round him this time. Always he would come back to the same conclusion. Like it or not, he would have to marry her. When dawn was breaking, he slept.

Sick at heart he went that afternoon to the Lower Level wood. He was leaning against the stile, deep in thought, when he saw Penny coming. She came up to him and put her head on his shoulder. Then she began to sob. 'What are we going to do?' she said.

'There's only one thing we can do.'

'What's that?'

'Get married.'

'Do you mean it?'

'Of course I mean it.'

She put her arms round his neck and clung to him. He returned her embrace and then loosed her hands and held her away from him. 'Now let's consider what else we've got to do. First of all I've got to go and see your father.'

'Oh, no! You mustn't do that.'

'Why not?'

'Leave it to me.'

'All right, for the time being.'

'We'll have to get married soon.'

'Yes, I suppose so.'

'As soon as we can make arrangements and get the invitations out.'

'What invitations?'

'To the people we invite to the wedding, of course.'

Eben looked at her horrified. 'You can't have that sort of wedding!'

'Why not?'

'Because once the reason for the haste becomes obvious we'd be the laughing stock of the district.'

She argued, but Eben remained adamant.

They talked then of the financial position. Eben told her of the decision concerning the end of his rugby career and of the promise of a job. She was not enthusiastic at the prospect of living in rooms in Cardiff.

'Let me break the news to Daddy first,' she said, 'then we can decide what we're going to do.'

When they met by the stile the following afternoon Penny seemed not to have a care in the world. She flung her arms round Eben's neck and said:

'Oh, darling, isn't it exciting! Daddy's quite willing for us to get married and he said we can have the farm and he'll give us some help to get started.'

The farm at Deerfield had not been farmed since the war, but the grazing had been let over the summer each year and the place had possibilities. Times were bad but they could always improve.

'I'll have to go and talk to your father about it first,' he said.

'Oh, it's all right. Everything's arranged.'

'But I'll still have to talk to him.'

'All right, but when can we get married?'

'As soon as we can slip away quietly, and the sooner the better. Then there'll be less gossip when the reason becomes obvious.'

So here he was, back where he had started. Rugby finished, job gone, he felt again something of what he had felt when his father had refused to let him go to the County school. He had studied in the evenings with Mr Magrath and could have done all right in a job. He felt sure of that. Instead, he was back to the farm, and a hard life, and it was nobody's fault but his own.

Before Eben and Penny set up house in the cottage where the Burridges had lived, and before ever they took over the farm, Eben was to understand the Bromilows' attitude towards their marriage. But, at the time when the news was broken to them, it puzzled him. He had gone to face them with all sorts of pretty speeches of apology and contrition in his mind, but none of them had been needed. Mrs Bromilow even planted a kiss on his cheek. Eben found it difficult to say anything about Penny's condition, and since they appeared to have decided to say nothing, he thought it best to leave the matter for the moment. And Bromilow was on his side about quiet weddings.

'Never could understand the need for all this damned fuss.'

Little had been said about his financial affairs, except that the cotton crisis had been a severe blow, but he had suggested going to the bank and also drawing up a partnership so that Eben and Penny would be farming the place together and could have a joint account.

Things now seemed to be happening so quickly that Eben felt he would like to confide in somebody. His father was out of the question, and he did not feel as yet that he could tell Aunty Becca. Mark seemed the obvious choice. He and Jane had moved to a detached house near Kilgetty and it was there that Eben went to see him.

'You're looking prosperous,' said Eben.

'I'm not complaining.'

They were sitting in a comfortable room looking out across the moor, and the sounds of a warm summer evening drifted through the open window. In the distance a young gipsy was leading a skewbald pony by the forelock to tether it near his rickety caravan. Alongside was a rough tent of sacking and, through a hole in the roof, a wisp of smoke rose lazily.

'What's the news, then?' asked Mark.

Eben looked at him with a smile before replying. Then he said, 'I'm getting married.'

'Well I'm glad to hear that.'

'Why?'

'To know you're making an honest woman of her. I wouldn't like to think of my brother giving the family a bad name.'

Mark was smiling and seemed to be enjoying the joke as Eben frowned.

'What the hell are you talking about?'

Mark said, 'It is Penny Bromilow you're going to marry, I suppose?'

'Well, yes, it is. But how did you guess?'

'Guess? Good God, boy, I only keep my ears open.'

'What have you heard then?'

'I've heard a good many things altogether, but the best bit was about the pair of you chasing about on the beach bare-arse naked.'

Eben blushed. 'What the hell, there wasn't a soul in sight.'

'I suppose you wouldn't have the sense to look up at the cliffs, and how d'you think Dipper Treluggan passes his time?'

'What else have you heard?'

'Parking down a side-road, and the week-end her parents went away and left the pair of you alone. But tell me if there's some more I haven't heard about because it looks as if you've been pretty busy.'

Eben was embarrassed, and Mark laughed at his discomfiture, until Eben had to laugh with him.

'The sooner I get married the better, I can see.'

'That's about the size of it,' said Mark. 'I suppose now you want me to give you away.'

Eben laughed again. 'I should think I've done that myself. Good God, how daft can anybody be!'

'Oh, well, there it is,' said Mark, 'they say that love is blind.'

'I'm not sure that it is love though.'

Mark looked at him, 'Then why the rush to get married?'

'We've got to.'

'Oh, dear God, you haven't half made a bloody mess of it!'

Eben told him then of his talk with the specialist in Cardiff and the offer from the manager of the firm by whom he had been nominally employed. Then he told him of Bromilow's offer of the farm with a certain amount of backing to start them.

'And what did he say when he knew what you'd done to his daughter?'

'Well, that's the funny part about it. He never said a word. Just welcomed me into the family and his wife even kissed me.'

'Then she hasn't told them.'

'D'you think not?'

'I'm sure of it – it's obvious.'

'So what had I better do now then?'

'Go to Narberth registry office and get a licence and go off quietly before anybody knows.'

'What about the Bromilows?'

'Please yourself, but that's what I'd do in your place.'

Eben thought about it on his way home. The next morning he called to see Penny and they went to look at the cottage together. When they were alone, he said, 'Have you told your father and mother why we're getting married?'

She was disconcerted by the directness of the question and coloured a little.

'No, I haven't,' she said.

'Why not?'

'Because Daddy would have been so mad he might have stopped me marrying you. After we're married it won't matter. In fact he mightn't even know if we get married soon enough, and I can say it's a honeymoon child premature.'

It sounded reasonable. Penny could always handle her father.

2

Deerfield

Though the mills of God grind slowly,
yet they grind exceeding small;
Though with patience he stands waiting,
with exactness grinds he all.

LONGFELLOW,
Retribution. From the *Sinngedichte*
of Friedrich von Logan

Before they moved into their new home, Eben discovered that Penny was not pregnant after all. As Mark said when Eben told him, 'Oh well, there 'tis, boy. She isn't the first woman to lead a chap to the altar with a pillow under her frock.'

It was the final irony. There he was, married to a girl with whom he was not in love. He doubted very much whether he could ever be happy with her. For some reason she had seemed determined to get him. Presumably, as with other things, the novelty would wear off.

Penny settled to her new role better than might have been expected, her parents no doubt being a steadying influence. She and Eben were in partnership on the farm, and, having no rent to pay, were able to manage well enough with a slow start. Eben was working so hard that there was little occasion for them to have more than the odd quarrel.

There was no thought of being able to make money. To pay his way was as much as Eben could hope to do. His father helped him with a moderate start, giving him a small bunch of young cattle and also a fresh-calved cow with a calf at heel. It was the young Blackie, born the night when Ben Harter had come home drunk and he and Mark had come to blows. She was milking now with her second calf, and was every bit as fine a cow as her mother, who had frightened Penny that first day on the bridge, and as her grandmother as he remembered her when he had gone as a small boy to Morfa Bychan. But Eben had no thought of doing anything with the milk other than feeding calves, and this was what took him one evening to Light-a-Pipe. Billy Seckerson's cow had just calved with twins.

'They're a nice pair of calves,' said Eben.

'Ay, they be that, an' one's a heifer.'

'But the other's a bull,' said Eben, 'so the heifer won't breed.'

'Does't thou reckon there be anythin' in that?' said Billy Seckerson.

'Father reared a heifer once that was twin to a bull but it was no good.'

They were interrupted by Rachel who came round the corner of the house holding a patient bundle of fluff and squeezing it to her.

'And what's this?' said Eben.

Rachel said nothing but smiled up at him with her bewitching little smile. She was five now.

'What's your little dog's name?' No answer.

'Well, what's your name?'

'Rachel.'

'And do you go to school?' Rachel shook her head.

'When are you going to school?'

'Next year.'

'Have you got a kiss for me today?'

Rachel reached her little face towards him and Eben picked ner up, puppy and all.

'I'd like a puppy like that. Would you give him to me?'

To his surprise the child smiled and pushed the puppy towards him. He put her down and she ran off. Then she appeared round the corner of the house again holding another puppy.

'Oh, I see,' laughed Eben, 'there's more where this one came from.'

'Does't thee want a good puppy?' said Billy Seckerson.

'Aye, I could do with a good one. My old Drifter died last year when I went to Cardiff.'

'Well, thicky's mother is the toptest bitch I ever clapped eyes on.'

'What'll this one be?'

'He'll be a bit more greyhound than lurcher. The Cockles boys reckons as they're the same strain as thy owld lurcher.'

'Well, they should know.'

'So there thee ar't if thou wants'n. But leave'n be for a couple o' weeks till he be fit to leave the bitch.'

'Right then. Let me know when he's ready.'

'Ar't thee gwain to try and plough?'

'No indeed I'm not. I'll keep cutting the fern and see what happens, but I'm not going to waste money ploughing and growing corn. I'm just going to try and hang on and hope for things to improve. But I could do with a good cob or pony.'

Eben had seen the pony in Billy Seckerson's paddock.

'Do you want to sell your pony?' he said.

'No. He was with me ten years underground in Bonville's Court an' they gave'n to me when the pit closed. He've gone a bit in the wind anyhow.'

Eben did not press the point. Even men as hard pushed as Billy Seckerson had their feelings and their pride, even when they faced the inquisition of the means test and were told to sell their furniture and live on the proceeds.

Algernon Benjamin Harter was born a year after Eben and Penny married. It was haymaking time, and the hedgerows were resplendent with a wealth of growth and wild flowers. But, for Eben, the excitement attendant upon young Benjie's arrival was tempered by the death of Ben Harter the day after his grandson was born.

At sixty-six he could not have been considered old, especially compared with ancient Gramfer Jenkyn who had remained active until he was ninety. Whatever it was from which Ben Harter had died, and the doctor had never told them exactly, he had faded rapidly in the last week or two before the end came. And he had been breaking for a long time before that. Yet, as Eben looked at the resolute face, peaceful in death as his father lay in the coffin, it seemed to have assumed again the strength and understanding which Eben had known as a boy. Eben was sure he could remember his compassion when Eddie had come home after thrashing Midgely. Or was it that he imagined it? How far he could remember back he could never say. But he could remember well the many little manifestations of love between his father and mother.

Ruth came to the funeral with Esther and Giles Merryman, and Liza came down from the Rhondda. When she arrived Eben wondered whether he should have sent the money for Jim Cartlett to come as well. How they must be suffering there now.

It was in the evening after the funeral that Liza spoke of her own trouble. Her own boy, Alan, was now twelve.

'But, oh, he's ill, poor little soul. Break your heart it would to hear him coughing. The doctor said to get him into the fresh air, but what can we do where we are?'

So it was, at the suggestion of Aunty Becca, that Alan came, with his thin hands and deep-set, dark circled eyes, to walk a little in the warm sunshine.

'Have a cherry, Uncle Eben,' he said one day as Eben sat for a while by the side of the bed.

Consumption was a dread word that carried with it a horror of possible infection. 'I'll take a couple,' said Eben, not to hurt the boy's feelings, 'but I won't eat them now. I'll eat them on the way home.'

Eben decided to keep the land on at Heronsmill following the death of his father. Becca was living a day at a time and

Tilly was talking in terms of looking for a job. She had stayed at home in the interests of others for so long that now, at thirty years of age, it was doubtful what sort of job she could expect to find. Such was the scene when Billy Thank-you-Ta, ancient now and dragging his bent figure along in a slow plod, called at the Mill. Becca and Tilly spent more time there than they did at the Gangrel, for there were still some animals to be cared for. The letter he brought was in a strange hand and bore the familiar Canadian stamp. No letter was expected from Hannah because they had heard from her a few weeks previously. Apart from saying that she had been suffering from some rather bad headaches and having tablets from the doctor she had seemed her usual cheerful self.

Tilly opened the letter and looked at the signature. It was signed Rebecca. She had never written before except for Hannah to enclose a note with her own letter. Tilly glanced through the letter and then, all the colour having drained from her face, read it to her mother in a dull, flat whisper.

As a result of the letter Becca went through the rest of the day in a daze and died in her sleep that night. The shock of Hannah's own sudden death had been too much for her.

So it was that Tilly was left on her own. And so it was that Mark, who had a remarkable ability for being able to fix things, came one afternoon when Eben was down at Herons-mill looking at a few young cattle and generally wondering what was now to be done. Tilly had just called him in for a cup of tea when Mark arrived.

'Now then, my dear cousin,' said Mark eventually, 'what are you going to do about a job?'

'Where do they grow, on trees?'

'Yes, if you know the right trees.'

'What have you got?' said Eben.

'There's a lady living on her own in Tenby, a relation of the Randalls, and she's looking for a sort of companion house-keeper. And don't thank me, because she will be very grateful to me for finding her such a gem as our cousin Tilly.'

'But it would mean leaving here,' said Tilly.

'Jesus,' said Mark, 'what a bloody sacrifice!'

'Mark! Your language!' But Tilly was smiling as she remonstrated with him. Then, suddenly, she put her arms round his neck and kissed him.

'Well, what about me, then!' Eben laughed. 'I've been much closer to you all these years than he has.'

'Yes, you too.' And, as Tilly kissed him, Eben saw there

were tears in her eyes.

She fixed up the move and wrote to Griff within a week. Griff, continuing to prosper in the dairy trade, had been down for their mother's funeral and had pressed Tilly to come away and make her home with him and his wife. Tilly had cared little for the idea and was happy to have been able to remain independent. And so, just as all those years ago the passing of Eddie and Gramfer Jenkyn and Keziah seemed to tear the heart out of life at Heronsmill, these more recent deaths seemed to bring another chapter to its close.

Mark, who was making progress, insisted that Eben should take whatever stock was at the Mill, on the grounds that times were so bad it was not worth anything to sell, and the household effects they divided amongst themselves and the two girls. Mark and Eben also insisted that what little money their father left was to be divided equally between Esther and Liza. Eben took the grandfather's clock, and some lustre jugs which his mother had cherished as having belonged to her own mother.

The weeds had long since taken hold of both gardens, and now the houses, for so many generations quick with life, began to degenerate as they became hung with cobwebs and the damp crept in with never a fire to drive it out. The links with the past seemed to have been broken beyond repair, and by the time news came later in the winter that young Alan had been called away to play his games on greener fields than ever he had known near the coal-tips of his home, the signs of neglect were already far advanced.

When Eben began to collect himself after all the troubles of the summer months it was to the realization that he was now on his own. Of his relationship with his father-in-law he was not too sure. Algie Bromilow had undoubtedly suffered financially but still had enough to get along quietly. He and Eben still talked sport and they went out with the gun for the odd day of rough shooting, and even talked of putting down some pheasants and taking whatever shooting there might be' on a few neighbouring farms along the valley. But Bromilow was still blind to his daughter's faults, and when she and Eben had their differences she would slam the door and march off to her father and mother for long hours at a time, leaving Eben either without a meal or to get one for himself.

Benjie was often left at Deerfield. Penny owned him, and his grandparents worshipped him. Eben wondered ruefully sometimes what sort of a spoiled brat they would make of him.

153

But of one thing he was certain. No son of his was going to be as thoroughly ruined as the mother had been who had borne him. In the meantime, the best thing to do was to keep the peace and get on with the job of trying to make a living, which was no easy matter with things as they were.

The country was in the throes of a financial crisis, with every prospect of things getting worse rather than better. Willie Jenkins, enthusiastically adopted to carry the Labour flag in the county once more, was addressing a meeting in Kilgetty. Few places were feeling the bite of unemployment more keenly, and support for him was whole-hearted now.

Talking of the differences within the Labour party, he said that Ramsay MacDonald and Philip Snowden had got cold feet but still saw their task as one of leading the children of Israel out of the land of bondage. Then, at last, he came to the current topic.

'They tell me there is a rumour that Labour will not fight the election in Pembrokeshire but line up behind Gwilym Lloyd George. I challenge him to deny that as a member of the National Government he was partly responsible for the cuts in wages and dole which they effected. Do you expect us to line up behind such a candidate?'

He glared at his audience from beneath his bushy eyebrows, and then he rasped, 'Let me tell you now that if I'm the last man in Pembrokeshire I'll stand.'

Eben knew something of the sufferings of the families of the unemployed in the area, as well as the despair of the farmers, and he said so to Bromilow when they talked about the meeting the following day.

'You sound as if you're going to vote Labour,' said Bromilow.

'Yes, I am.'

'Damn it all, you're a self-employed man now. You're in business.'

'Well, I'm trying to farm, if that's what you mean, and the Tories have betrayed us once already. Willie Jenkins is a farmer, too, and he knows something about the problem. What's more, he isn't the sort to sell you down the river the same as a lot of these politicians.'

'I wouldn't trust these damned Labour crowd at all. Cut your throat as quick as look at you. This Jenkins chap now. You reckon he's honest?'

'I'm sure he is.'

'Then he'd better watch out or they'll cut his throat as well.'

A fortnight later it was announced that Willie Jenkins had been obliged to withdraw as Labour candidate for the county.

'There you are,' said Bromilow, 'you'll have to vote for Gwilym Lloyd George now.'

'Gwilym Lloyd George be damned,' said Eben. 'I don't know what he's supposed to be like in Parliament, but he's got no more interest in Pembrokeshire than a pig's got in a holiday.'

'In that case then, you'll have to vote Tory.'

Eben was sick of the whole business. In the event, Gwilym Lloyd George was returned for the county with a big majority in spite of a huge landslide towards the Tories nationally. Eben never again evinced the slightest interest in politics, and vowed in future to think his own thoughts and to keep his own counsel.

On the farming side there was no attempt at interference. Eben said, 'There's only one thing to do, and my father knew it. Cut your expenses and spend nothing unless you really have to.'

Bromilow knew something of the truth of this because Jimmy Cockles, like so many of the young people of the area, had gone away to look for work in the towns and had not been replaced. The only work in the garden now was done occasionally by unemployed miners, who were thankful to have a day here and there.

Yet somehow, like others at the time, Eben managed to hang on and, when times were at their worst, the setting up of the Milk Marketing Board brought fresh hope. If a firm of wholesalers failed to pay one farmer, they could no longer buy milk from another. The regular guaranteed milk-cheque every month became the one thing in which the farmers put their faith.

'I'm going to start selling milk,' said Eben.

It was no use talking to Penny. Her only contribution on such matters was to say, 'Why not talk to Daddy about it?'

'You'll need money,' said Bromilow.

'Yes, we will,' said Eben.

'Well, you'll have to get it from the bank. They've got the deeds of this place against what you owe them now, so there won't be any trouble.'

'We'll have to build a new cowshed to start with.'

'Never mind, it'll put value on the place, and it'll be your own when I'm gone.'

There were one or two useful tradesmen in the area who

were willing to help him in the evenings and who would indeed be glad of the work. By day he could do some work himself, and Billy Seckerson came as a labourer on a shift basis.

'The buggers stopped my dole in the end last time,' said Billy, 'but things is improvin' again.'

Loveston colliery had reopened and Billy was working there.

'Mind thee, 'tisn't up to much but 'tis a help. None of us can go full time yet.'

'Why, Billy?'

'Well, what we does, see, boy, is go for a fortnight an' then stop home a week for somebody else to take a turn. Then we're all right for our benefit. After twenty-six weeks' dole, see, the buggers cuts us down and puts us on the means test. 'Tis a hell of a thing that is, mind.'

'I know it is.'

'But that be it, see. There be no work to be had. Not down the pit, any road.'

'Isn't there anything else to be had?'

Billy Seckerson already had the rattle of coal-dust in his lungs.

'Why, fellah,' he said, 'digging coal is all I knows, apart from a bit on the farm and there's nothing to be had there neither.'

'You like the pit, I suppose.'

'Likes it? Good God, no! I bloody well hates it. And half the pits round here isn't safe. Th'owld men have worked out a lot of 'em hunderds of years ago an' never left no plans of where they went nor nothin'. Half the seams is worked out an' full o' water an' you never knows what you might strike on. No. Like it, no. But we got to do it to feed the childern an' keep gwain.'

They were digging out the ground, level for the foundations, as they talked of these things and Billy was due back in the pit the following week. The next day, however, he said to Eben, 'I wonder, cou's't thee keep me on for next week?'

'What's happened then?'

'Nothing have happened, only I seen Banter Knox last night an' he wants one more week for his twenty-six. I wants a week as well so I said I'd ask you an' then we could work it for'n to have my week at Loveston.'

'Well, there won't be much next week, Billy. I'd reckoned to start getting some sand and cement and one thing and another.'

'I could drive the gravel for thee from Wiseman's Bridge.'

'What with?'

'With Zulu in the cart.'

'Your pony?'

'Why aye, fellah. Come all beleejurs, an' I'll do it by the load so't won't cost thee no more.'

Eben sensed his anxiety.

'All right,' he said, 'we'll fix something.'

It was late in May. Once again the promise of spring had passed into the fuller growth of another season, warm rain had quickened the countryside to a new awareness, and birds sang until it was nearly dark.

Billy Seckerson had tipped his last load of gravel for the day, and Zulu stood quietly in the shafts, when the news spread through the stillness of the late afternoon that disaster had struck at Loveston colliery.

Eben loosed the pony out of the shafts and took his harness off, whilst Billy Seckerson set off for home in a running walk to fetch his bike and pedal as fast as he could for Loveston. Late that evening he called at Deerfield. There was no definite news but seven men had been drowned for sure and their bodies had not yet been recovered. Banter Knox was all right and told how the survivors had saved themselves by holding on to the wire rope as the water swept them up the road underground. Without question, what all the miners had feared had happened at last – someone had tapped an old working with its millions of gallons of water which roared down upon them in the darkness. Billy Seckerson was shaken.

'The poor bugger who was gave my length was one of 'em,' he said.

'So you can reckon yourself lucky,' said Eben.

'Aye, fellah. An' there won't be no more. I'll find somethin', but I'm buggered if I'll go back.'

Eben's misgivings about Benjie had proved to be without any great foundation. Home life, on Benjie's account at any rate, had not been unduly difficult. Dark, like his mother, he was a quiet child and never at any time showed the slightest sign of his father's interest either in animals or in any form of ball game. With toy aeroplanes, however, he would play all day long. Now that the time had come when the question of his schooling could no longer be avoided, it was decided that he should go to a private school in Tenby as a weekly boarder, coming home only for week-ends.

To Eben, thinking back to the security and family love of

his own childhood, the thought was intolerable, but it would take the boy out of the atmosphere of such acrimonious bickering as there was from time to time, and his character could perhaps be moulded that much better than would be the case at home, with too many people having a say in how he should or should not behave, and not infrequently disagreeing amongst themselves. How much the opportunities which now presented themselves might have influenced Penny's thinking in the decision Eben did not know, but now that Benjie was not at home during the week she once again wanted to go dancing. He had no grounds for saying that she had been unfaithful to him, but he was beginning to entertain his suspicions.

That winter he began selling milk. Although it brought a regular income, the work became harder and more of a tie.

The following summer Penny's cousins invited themselves to stay at Deerfield. Eben disliked the man on sight, and loathed his fifteen-year-old son.

The man, who answered to the name of Pugsy, was sufficiently under medium height to be called short. If there was a neck anywhere between his shoulders and his chin there was no outward evidence of it. The son, Clarence, was like his father only more so, with the additional attraction of a pair of heavy horn-rimmed spectacles.

'I can't understand you yokels,' was Pugsy's first sally. 'The whole area round here is ripe for development. Absolutely crying out for it.'

'Oh, I don't know,' said Eben, 'we like it as it is.'

'You types are quite pathetic,' said Pugsy. It was not the most propitious of starts.

The following morning, on his way to fetch the cows, Eben was startled by the sound of a high-powered air-rifle being fired, and the ping and whine as the pellet struck the roof of the hayshed and ricocheted up into the trees. Clarence came round the corner with his air-rifle at the ready.

'And what do you reckon you're doing, young man?' said Eben.

'Shooting, of course.'

'And what are you trying to shoot?'

'Anything I see.'

'Then you'd better change your ideas. To start with I don't want you to shoot anywhere round these buildings, and I don't want you to shoot at the birds. But you can go down to those bottom fields and you'll see some rabbits down there.

And you can shoot as many of those as you like.'

The boy looked at him and said, 'Stuff and nonsense.' As he said it, he turned and walked away.

Eben had tied the cows ready for milking and was on his way to the dairy for the milking buckets and stool. A blackthorn tree grew in the hedge and most mornings the blackbird sang there. Eben wondered sometimes if it might have been a descendant of the bird he had come to know when it sang in the blackthorn near Gramfer Jenkyn's blacksmith's shop at the Gangrel when he was a small boy. The blackbird was singing now, its yellow beak opening as it poured out its full-throated song. And, as Eben raised his head to look at him, there was the kick of the air-rifle, the lovely song was cut short and, with a pathetic little shower of feathers, the bird dropped into the bush.

In one bound, Eben was on to the bank, over the hedge, and on top of Clarence before he knew it. Eben pulled the gun from him and said, 'You little sod.'

'And what do you propose to do with that?' said the boy quite unabashed.

'I'm putting it out of your way and you can have it back the day you go home and not before. Now get out of my sight.'

'My dear man, I'll see my father about you. He'll settle your hash for you.' And with that he stalked off towards Deerfield.

Eben went into his own house and put the air-rifle on top of the dresser.

'What have you got there?' said Penny.

'That damn boy's air-gun.'

'Why put it there?'

Eben looked at her, trying to control his temper.

'Because he isn't safe and he's just shot the blackbird that's been with us all winter.'

'I can't see anything not safe about shooting a blackbird.'

'I'm not concerned with what you think, and I haven't got time to argue. He's humbugged me enough already this morning and I haven't milked yet. But it's staying there for the rest of the time they're here and he can have it back to take home.'

Eben had simmered down by the time he had finished milking. He had put the milk to cool in the dairy and was about to turn the cows out. From somewhere outside came the plop of the air-rifle, a pellet screamed in through the open door of the cowshed and Blackie jumped in fright. Eben spoke to her and soothed her and then, silently and swiftly, moved out through the adjoining barn and out through the door at the back. Before Clarence knew what was happening his neck was held and the air-rifle was wrenched out of his grasp. Eben pushed the boy from him, fired the gun into the air and then, holding it by the muzzle, with the stock on the ground, put his foot on the joint, heaved with all his strength and bent the thing almost double.

As he threw it from him into the bushes the boy shouted with rage and jumped at Eben to kick him. As his foot came up, Eben caught it and upended him into a clump of nettles. Screaming now with the pain of the nettle stings, as well as with temper, he got up and hurled himself at Eben. With the flat of his open hand Eben hit him across the side of the head back into the nettles. As he fell, his spectacles came off and shattered on the concrete. Choking with great sobs, he got up more slowly and said, 'My father will see you about this.' Then once more he marched off for the house, but not, Eben was pleased to note, with quite such self-assurance.

Eben had turned the cows out, and was just seeing them off the yard when Pugsy came blustering out, with Clarence peering short-sightedly behind him. Eben could just imagine the pleasure with which Penny would have handed him down the air-rifle from off the top of the dresser. Much of the anger now seething within Eben was directed against his wife, and it was Pugsy's misfortune to have been in any way associated with her.

'Damn your eyes,' said Pugsy, without preamble. 'What the bloody hell do you think you're doing?'

'Doing?' said Eben quietly. 'Ah, yes. Now what would I be doing?'

'I understand,' said Pugsy, 'that you've broken my son's air-rifle.'

'Oh, yes, I've done that.'

'And you've also broken his spectacles.'

'That's quite right, accident though it was. And if he sets foot near these buildings again I'll break his neck as well.'

'Well now then, you bloody bumpkin, you've got me to answer to.'

Eben laughed in the man's face.

'Well look at that then, and what sort of questions are you going to ask? But before you ask them, let me tell you one thing. I'll stand for many things in this life, but one thing I won't stand for is being threatened on my own farmyard.'

'Your own farmyard my arse. You're getting ideas above your bloody station in life. This place no more belongs to you than . . .'

He did not get any further.

Eben took a swift step towards him and, with one powerful hand, gripped him by the shirt-front, lifted him up, and carried him to the concrete water-trough outside the cowshed door where he pushed him under on his back. He held him down for some seconds until he began to kick, and then allowed him the further indignity of climbing out unaided, spluttering and sodden. Then he said, 'Now get to hell out of it, and if you or your brat set foot here again I won't be held responsible for my actions.'

He need not have uttered the warning. Pugsy and his wife and son left within the hour. Eben had scarcely spoken to Pugsy's wife who seemed quiet enough. It was she, so it transpired, who was Penny's cousin.

Whilst Eben ate his breakfast, Penny knew nothing of the impending departure of Pugsy, and, Eben choosing to say nothing, she contented herself by slamming the frying pan and crockery about, moving chairs with considerable violence, and generally making it clear that she was in ill humour. Eben had cleared his plate and was enjoying his second cup of tea when there was a courteous knock on the open door and Bromilow said, 'Can I come in?'

'Aye, aye, come on in,' said Eben.

Bromilow smiled and said, 'What a splendid chap you are. They've gone.'

'Oh, my godfathers,' said Eben.

'Impossible fellow. Damned outsider.'

'Who's gone?' said Penny.

'That Pugwash character.'

'Where's he gone?'

'Never mind. Just cleared out bag and baggage.'

'Why has he gone?'

'Sensitive, I should think. Must have guessed he wasn't welcome. Damn it all, my dear, what would you think if somebody dumped you in a tank full of water?'

'You insufferable brute,' Penny snapped, turning on Eben. 'And I suppose you think you're such a he-man. My God, how breeding will out. Just imagine me being fool enough to think I could make a silk purse out of a sow's ear.'

Her father looked at her horrified.

'My dear girl . . .'

'Oh, I know you think he's marvellous, but you ought to have to live with him.'

Bromilow looked at his son-in-law who remained silent.

'What's it all about?'

'Ask Penny.'

Bromilow turned to his daughter.

'Well, he thinks he can order everybody about. He thinks that just because he . . .'

'Never mind what I think or what I'm supposed to think. Just tell your father what happened.'

'How do I know what happened? I wasn't there.'

'Then I'll tell him. This little lout came out with his air-rifle and I told him to go down to the meadow to shoot at rabbits and to stay away from the buildings and not shoot at the birds. Next thing I knew, he'd shot the blackbird that's been with us all winter. So I took the gun off him and put it on top of the dresser.'

'And I gave it back to him. I've got just as much right here – and more for that matter – to do . . .'

'Nobody's talking about your right to do anything.'

'Well, I am, and you should have thought about it before you married me.'

'Why did I marry you then? Do you want to tell your father that? Or do you want me to tell him?'

'Please yourself what you tell him. He won't believe you.'

'Well maybe it's time he knew that I only married you because you persuaded me you were pregnant.'

'And I couldn't have done that unless you'd seduced me first.'

Bromilow was staring at his daughter in utter disbelief. Eben said quietly, 'I always thought it was you seduced me. And whilst we're at it, do you want to say anything about how many seduced you before I did?'

'Is this true, Penny?' said Bromilow.

'Of course it isn't true. You wouldn't take his word before mine, would you?'

'Do you want me to name some of them?' said Eben.

'What lies are you going to make up now?' She was looking frightened.

'I didn't know before I married you who they were, but I know some of them now. People haven't been slow to laugh behind my back.'

'You can get out from here as soon as you like,' she shouted. 'Get back to the ill-bred lot you came from.'

Eben had already pushed back his chair and risen to his feet as she raved.

'Here! This is what I think of you and all your damned family.' And as she said it she grabbed one of his mother's lustre jugs from the dresser and smashed it on to the floor. Then she ran from the house.

Bromilow gazed, white-faced, at the shattered pieces.

'My dear boy,' he said at last, in a strained voice Eben had never heard before, 'I can't tell you how sorry I am.'

'That's all right. I've learned to live with it, but it's time you knew one or two things, and I'm glad you've seen it for yourself.'

'That jug.'

'It was my mother's. And her mother's before that.'

'It was like some fish-wife, not my own daughter.'

'Oh, she'll get over it.'

But she did not get over it quickly. Eben got his own rough meal at midday. In the evening Penny was back in the house, but she was still in a vile temper. For once in a way, it seemed, she had not found her father quite so pliable.

'I suppose you think you're smart to try and turn my own father and mother against me.'

'We've had enough rows for one day,' said Eben, 'and I don't propose to let you start another.'

With that he walked out and she slammed the door behind him.

He had had a long, trying day, and would have been glad to sit down. Yet he found solace working in the fields, with the sweet smell of the newly gathered hay, and the peace of the summer's evening. It was getting dark by the time he came home.

When he reached the farmhouse door, he saw something scattered about on the ground outside. The first thing he picked up was his new jacket. Then his overcoat. Shoes, books, shirts and seemingly everything he possessed had been hurled outside. He tried the door. It was locked. So was the back door, and every window was shut. He knew it was no use shouting and he preferred not to disturb them at Deerfield. For the same reason he decided against breaking a window.

Slowly he sorted out the confusion and put his things away in the barn. Boyser whined when he came in. Billy Seckerson had done him a good turn when he gave him the pup. Like Drifter, before him, he was usually only interested in work, yet seemed to sense when a friend was needed. He put his cold nose and smooth head into Eben's hand, and then walked close to him as he set off across the fields. There was a new moon and the stars were bright in a clear sky. In the direction of Heronsmill a barn owl screeched and, as he came nearer, he could see the tall pine by the Gangrel silhouetted against the velvet backdrop of infinity. All mixed up together the memories came crowding in. He was glad he was still here where his forebears had lived and died for generations. A sudden peace came over him.

He went into the barn alongside the old cowshed where he still fed a few cattle in winter and where he had some hay. Boyser seemed not to understand it, but lay down in the corner. Eben stretched out in the hay and slid immediately into a deep sleep.

The following morning, after milking, Eben went in and had a straight talk with Penny. Amongst other things, he told her that if he had any more of her nonsense he would have her every movement watched with a view to divorce proceedings. From the effect this threat had on her he became even more certain that his suspicions had some foundation.

The affair with Pugsy had no immediate repercussions, but he was subsequently reported to have taken an interest in Saundersfoot. Mark, who knew most of what was going on in the area, told Eben as much.

'You surely knew about it?' said Mark.

'Not a word. How should I know what he's doing?'

'Well damn it all, man – your own wife called on 'em twice last week to my certain knowledge.'

'Penny did?'

'Didn't she tell you?'

'She doesn't tell me anything. She'd only tell me if she wanted to aggravate me, and she'd enjoy calling on anybody she knew I disliked.'

'Well there it is,' said Mark, 'he's bought a house in Saundersfoot and a few odd fields.'

'Is he going to live there?'

'It doesn't look like it. Just for the summer they say.'

'And what's he going to do with the fields?'

'Nobody seems to know, except that he says he's going to develop them, whatever that's supposed to be.'

'Perhaps he can sell Griff a plot to build his house.'

'Griff? What's he going to build?'

'That's all he ever talks about, coming back here to retire

and build a house.'

'Well, he can afford it,' said Mark.

'Aye, indeed. He's done well. Started milking cows for 'em and now he's manager. Tilly said last time he was home he reckoned he would probably finish up as general manager of the whole company.'

'Good God.'

'Well, that's what he said.'

'When is he coming down again?'

'Some time in August,' said Eben.

Esther's husband, Giles Merryman, died that August, when Griff was down on holiday, but it was not the only thing that cast a shadow on the occasion. Like thousands of others, Griff cut his holiday short and made for home as Hitler's war-machine rolled into Poland.

The building business which Giles Merryman had built up disintegrated. Esther sold what there was to sell, and her only boy, Owen, left school. He was sixteen and, always having shown more interest in farming than in building, went to work with Eben who was glad to have him. It doubled the number he employed, for Billy Seckerson had already been taken on full-time. Like his pony, Zulu, Billy wheezed and coughed, but they both seemed indestructible.

Scarcely had Griff returned to London when the war made its first impact on Eben personally, with the coming of the army to Deerfield. The Bromilows were away at the time and, before they had a chance to return, a requisitioning order had been served upon them and Deerfield had become an officers' mess.

The demands made upon Eben by wartime farming presented no immediate problems. The great difference was that, with the prosperity which comes to the land in wartime, there was never any question of not being able to market what he produced.

Before long, Eben was sworn in as a part-time special constable. The sergeant came out on his bicycle from Saunders-foot and asked Eben if he would take on the job.

'I've got to make some recommendations for the inspector to put before the chief,' said Sergeant Nelson, 'and I wants to have somebody I can rely on.'

'What makes you think I'd be any good?'

'Your brother suggested you, and I agreed with'n.'

Eben laughed. Trust Mark to have a finger in the pie.

Penny decided that she, too, must do something for the war effort.

'I would think,' said Eben, 'there's enough for you to do here.'

There had been an argument and Eben had made the point that somebody had to cook a meal and run the house, and nobody was asking her to do anything outside. He had a sneaking idea that she was not averse to being near some of the army officers, although it probably irked her that, right on the spot as they were, he was able to keep an eye on her.

Before hostilities had even commenced, Eben's young nephew Edward had gone off like Eddie, his father, before him, and Ruth had a horror of what war might do to her a second time. Edward, quiet and studious, had struggled through university by means of a scholarship and his mother's encouragement and self-denial. With conscription in the offing, Edward and some of his equally unwarlike friends had joined the Territorial Army on the advice of a lecturer who assured them that six weeks at a summer camp would interfere less with their careers than being conscripted into the armed forces. When the time came, their names were first in the book, and before the epic of Dunkirk had been completed the following year, Edward Harter's name had been entered in the lists of the glorious dead. Heartbroken, Ruth was unimpressed with the glory. Three weeks later, her body was cast up by the sea on the rocks near Monkstone.

The war moved into its third year.

One evening when Mark called, Penny was at Deerfield, having a cup of coffee with the officers. Eben had already put the kettle on and now reached for the teapot.

'How about a cup of tea?'

'Will the rations run to it?'

'We're not so bad for tea. That's one of the advantages of having the next-door neighbours we have.'

Mark looked at him keenly.

'Ah, well, it's all the same to me,' said Eben. 'And I can't be watching her all the time. I've got as much as I can do outside.'

'I know all about it, old son. I've got troubles of my own.'

'Oh, what's your trouble?'

'Well, Jane isn't up to much these days. And the hell of it is you can't get anybody in the house. I can get exemption, but I can't find anyone.'

'You can get exemption for a girl?'

'Yes, easy.'

Mark had several buses running on contract to the government and driving men to and from army camps and depots all over the county. Committees could help, too, and he was on most of those which seemed to matter.

'You don't know of anybody, do you?'

'How old a person do you want?'

'I don't care how old she is. Anything from fifteen to seventy-five. As long as she can stand up and do a bit about the house.'

'Well, I don't know whether she'd be any good to you, even if she'd come, but Billy Seckerson's girl is home. Young Rachel. She's been home since she left school because her mother hasn't been too good.'

'Is she any good in the house?' said Mark.

'Bound to be. They've all been brought up to work and clean as a new pin.'

'She sounds all right. What had I best do?'

'Leave it to me and I'll ask Billy when he comes back.'

After Mark had gone, Eben thought about him. Most of what he knew of Mark's affairs lately was what he heard from others and what odd mentions he saw in the local paper. Certainly he had prospered in business and was an influential figure in public life. He had his critics, of course, and even enemies, as did most men in similar position, but Eben also knew that he had done a great deal of good for many people. When Edward had been killed in the early days of the war Ruth had surprised him by telling him that Mark had helped her substantially to see him through university. There were many who thought highly of him. Billy Seckerson was one of them, and it was possibly this which influenced him in telling Eben that he would see what his wife thought about Rachel going to work for Mark and Jane.

'Mind thee now,' he said, 'she've set her mind on bein' a nurse but I 'specs she'll go if I asks her to.'

'Well, she can still go nursing later on, but what about your wife? Is she well enough to manage without her?'

'Why aye, she's a sight better now for all. And the youngest maid be leavin' school now at Christmas.'

Although in later years Eben was to say one of the best things he had ever done was to bring about the move, long before that, and for a time, he was to regret it bitterly. When Rachel had been at Mark's little more than a year and it became known she was to have a child, the news itself, and then the gossip that went with it, made Eben feel sick at heart.

Around this time, Eben was called away for the morning, in his capacity as a special constable, to attend a funeral. On his return, he went straight to the house but, as he turned the knob, the door held firm.

They had had a new mortice lock fitted, for which there were three keys. One was kept in the house, Penny had one in her hand-bag and there was one on the ring with the car keys. Eben felt in his pocket and realized that he had left the keys in the car. They were always warning you about it, and he was usually quite careful, but this morning he had been so preoccupied with other thoughts that he had forgotten. He went back to the car, and removed the rotor arm as well, which was something else you were always being told to do.

As he opened the door and went in he thought he heard the click of the back door being shut. He listened, but there was no sound. Then he called out, 'Penny.'

'Yes,' her voice came from upstairs.

'Where are you, then?'

'I'm coming now.'

As he reached the top of the stairs Penny came through the bedroom door and they met on the landing.

'Did you want me?'

'No, I've come up to change. But why was the front door locked?'

'Locked?'

'Yes, locked.'

'I didn't know it was locked.'

'Well if you didn't lock it, who did?'

'Perhaps the latch slipped.'

Eben looked at her. She was flustered and somewhat dishevelled. He went past her into the bedroom. The bed was crumpled. And he remembered it had been made when he changed earlier to go to the funeral.

Penny said, 'I was just making the bed.'

'It was made before I went out this morning.'

'Yes, but I was changing the sheets.'

Eben turned to look at her.

'Always an answer for everything.'

'What d'you mean?'

Half under the bed he saw a khaki tie. He bent to pick it up, and as he straightened he saw Penny's face in the mirror, and her eyes were wide with fright. He turned the tie over in his fingers and looked at the red-lettered name tab.

'*C. R. Smith-Gilmour.* So that's who it is. The little ginger squirt.'

Penny suddenly hung her head and began to cry. Then she flung herself on the bed and sobbed. Eben put the tie in his pocket and went downstairs.

His first thought was to go straight into Deerfield for a confrontation. But he decided against it and said to himself, 'Let the little sod stew for a bit.'

When Penny came downstairs her mood had changed completely and she held her arms out to Eben. He pushed her away.

He said, 'Just get one thing into your head. I'm going to divorce you.'

'On what grounds?'

Eben looked at her unbelievingly.

'On what grounds!'

'Yes, on what grounds?'

'You little tramp! Have you got the nerve to stand there and ask on what grounds after being caught in the act?'

'In the act? What act?'

Eben was speechless.

'Be sensible, darling. What evidence do you have?'

'Good God, woman, do you really think you can bluster and lie your way out of this one? And if I haven't got enough evidence already, how long do you think it will take to get it once I start asking a few questions?'

Eben went upstairs to change and left the tie in his pocket. When he went for it in the evening it was no longer there.

'You retrieved the tie, of course?' he said.

'Of course.' Penny was off-hand and self-confident again.

They had eaten supper in an unusually heavy silence.

'What have you done with it?'

'Given it back. Roland is coming in here this evening to talk it over.'

'Coming here? To talk what over?'

'Oh, let's be sensible, darling. We'll have to come to some sort of understanding.'

'There will be no understanding, and if you've suggested him coming here you're even more stupid than I thought you were.'

Before Penny could reply there was a tentative knock on the door and she moved quickly to open it. There was the briefest of whispers, and then she came in with the man behind her. He had close-cut sandy hair and a neatly trimmed moustache, but his pale blue eyes were shifty. There were three pips on the shoulder of his uniform, and he was little taller than Penny.

Eben had moved to the fireplace and stood with his back to it with his elbow resting on the mantelpiece.

'Now look here, old chap,' said Smith-Gilmour.

Eben interrupted him, 'Harter's the name, and I understand from your droppings that you're Smith-Gilmour.'

'Captain Smith-Gilmour.'

'And a great credit to King and country. I hope they're proud of you.'

Penny was plainly ill at ease. Smith-Gilmour took a cigarette from a thin case, lit it with a flourish with a small lighter and sat down. He took a deep pull and blew the smoke slowly through his nostrils.

Eben looked at him and, in a voice which Penny hardly recognized, said, 'You do not have my permission to smoke and I did not invite you to sit down.'

Almost insolently, Smith-Gilmour stubbed out his cigarette and stood up. He said, 'I see you're choosing to be aggressive.'

'I'm in my own home.'

'You're also in the presence of a lady.'

'Not a lady – a common whore. Only cheaper. Groundsheets, I believe you call them.'

Penny went white and bit her lip.

'And if you want chapter and verse I can name you a dozen she had before I married her, and perhaps as many as that since. But you're the one I'm divorcing her on.'

'That's what I want to talk to you about. You can't be serious.'

'You think not?'

'Well, damn it all, you haven't got any real proof.'

'Not a lot, I'll admit.'

'You haven't any.'

'You mean because you've had your tie back?'

'You could put it that way.'

Eben put his hand in his pocket and took out a handkerchief. 'You left this under the pillow. I don't think it's important though, although it has your name on it. You see, you also dropped your diary and a letter from your wife.'

Long afterwards, Eben would laugh about the incident as he remembered the look on the other man's face as he made

170

a futile grab for his inside pocket. But now he threw the handkerchief across the table and said, 'Here, you'd better have this. You might need it. The diary and letter will be enough for me, and I reckon any reasonable judge will take my word for the tie and handkerchief.'

With a look of disbelief, Penny turned on Smith-Gilmour and snapped, 'What's this about a letter from your wife?'

'Oh, it's nothing. I can explain to you later.'

'What d'you mean, explain? You said you weren't married.'

'I'm getting a divorce, but let me explain to you afterwards. It's all quite straightforward.'

'This letter doesn't read as if your wife knows about the divorce,' commented Eben. 'Or haven't you told her yet?' It was a good feeling to get the knife in and twist it.

Penny was shaking in her temper. 'You hateful beast, I loathe you.'

Smith-Gilmour tried once more to bluster. 'If you don't return my personal documents to me before I leave this house I'll have you arrested.'

'That sounds exciting. Who'll do it and on what grounds?'

'Under emergency regulations for the defence of the realm. I'm accusing you of stealing documents belonging to one of His Majesty's officers and I'll have you searched.'

'That's good. Very good. But you haven't told me yet who's going to do it, and you haven't told me who's going to authorize it.'

'The army will do it and I have my own authority.'

Eben shook his head and laughed. 'Oh, dear, dear. You'll have to do better than that. You're talking like a child.'

Only the previous day he had received a letter delivered by army messenger. It was from 'Clapper' Williams, his old rugby friend from his brief time in Cardiff. Now he was stationed at Tenby and had asked Eben to come and see him.

'Your commanding officer is, I believe, Colonel C. L. P. Williams. I'll give him a ring now and you can have a word with him afterwards – if you really want to.'

The phone was in the corner alongside the window. Eben picked it up and, after only a short pause, asked for a Tenby number.

Smith-Gilmour looked startled. He said, 'Who gave you that number?'

'I guessed it.'

'It's a private line to brigade headquarters.'

'You be careful what you're saying. Careless talk costs lives.'

Before there was time to say more the number had answered.

Eben said, 'Could I speak to Colonel Williams, please? A personal call. My name is Eben Harter.'

There was a click and a brief pause. Then a hearty laugh and cheerful voice could be heard.

'Is that you, Clapper?' said Eben.

Smith-Gilmour stared in disbelief and the blood drained from his face. After a few pleasantries, Eben said, 'I'll take you up on your offer and come and have a meal with you tomorrow evening. What's that? No, my wife won't come. She doesn't care for that sort of thing.'

There was some more muffled talk.

'Yes, I'm all right for petrol – oh well, if you can send a car for me, that will be great. Many thanks. Hold the line a minute, will you?'

Eben put his hand over the mouthpiece and turned to Smith-Gilmour.

He said, 'Do you want a word with Colonel Williams before I ring off?'

The man stared at Eben, unseeing and speechless.

'Sorry about that, Clapper. I'll explain to you tomorrow. All the best then. Goodbye.'

Then he went back to his original position, leaning on the mantelpiece, and looked at Smith-Gilmour.

'All right, rat-face,' he said, 'now you listen to me. If I don't take divorce proceedings it will be for the sake of my little boy and my father-in-law and his wife. But I don't think it will help you very much because I shall be handing over your diary and letter to your commanding officer tomorrow evening, so I reckon that will be about your last night here. And in case you think the coast will be clear for another little gallop whilst I'm away I'd advise against it. You'd probably catch your tart in bed with your batman. She's not at all particular. So now you can get out of here, and don't attempt to answer back or I'll split you down the middle.'

Smith-Gilmour went within forty-eight hours. Whether or not Penny saw him again before he left, Eben did not know and no longer cared. He had long suspected what had been going on and he had no illusions about the possibility of Penny changing her ways. But he gave her to understand that she would not be doing her whoring in *his* home.

Some time later, without any official explanation, Deerfield was suddenly de-requisitioned.

It was almost as if he had been expecting Tilly when she walked in one day, saying, 'If the muntain won't come to Mahomet, then Mahomet must go to the muntain.'

'Bless my soul,' said Eben, and he put his arms round Tilly and kissed her. 'Did any man ever have a nicer surprise?'

He had just cleared away his own lunch things, after the quick snack he had made for himself. Owen, who came from Saundersfoot every day, and Billy Seckerson both brought their own sandwiches and had a meal when they went home in the evening. Italian prisoners-of-war would soon be coming to help with the thrashing, and there would be neighbours too. Eben was conscious of the shortcomings there would be.

'You seem glad to see me,' said Tilly.

'Glad?' said Eben. 'Lord sowls, maid, I'm like thicky dog with a pair of lamp-posts,' and laughed heartily as he lapsed into his local tongue. 'The kettle's nearly boiling. Have a cup of tea.'

'I won't say no. It's a sharp pull up th'owld hill.'

'What did you come on – the one o'clock bus?'

'Aye, that's right, and I'm going back on the half-past four.'

Tilly was looking well, Eben thought. There was a fleck of grey in her dark hair but her brown eyes were bright and she was as cheerful as ever.

'Are you still on your own in there?'

'So far. I haven't sorted things out aright since poor old Miss Randall died.'

'How long were you with her, Tilly?'

'Eleven years.'

'Good God! How the time goes by. And it only seems like yesterday.'

'She was very good to me.'

'You were good to her, too.'

'Well, it suited me. But she needn't have left me her house like she did. And all her money.'

'How much money did she leave?'

'Just over four thousand.'

'Good for you, girl. The only thing is now you'll have to watch you don't find some chap trying to marry you for your money.'

'Marry? Don't talk to me about marry.'

'Why not? They don't all work out as badly as mine.'

'How badly have yours worked out?'

173

Eben thought for a while. Then he said, 'How much have you heard?'

'Mark's told me a bit. And I know Penny's on about taking a job up at the aerodrome.'

'Damn it, girl,' he said, 'we're milking thirty cows here and I have to wash the milking machine and the cooler and everything myself, otherwise it would only be half done. And the thrashing machine is supposed to be pulling in this afternoon ready to start in the morning, and there's nobody here to make the men as much as a cup of tea.'

Tilly raised her eyes to the ceiling with a look of mock resignation.

'There was I going to be Mary for a change, and start doing some nice sewing and try and read some books. How is it I've always got to be Martha?'

Eben looked at her. It took him a little time to grasp what she was saying.

'Tilly – you don't mean . . .? You wouldn't be willing, would you?'

'Well, my boy, somebody've got to. And if I don't do it I don't know of nobody else as will.'

There were plank cooks and fresh-cut bread and butter on the table, which had been laid with a clean tablecloth. Eben could hardly believe it. The place had been transformed. Before the thrashing machine left at the end of the week Tilly had become a permanent fixture, almost as if she had never been away or as if Aunty Becca had come back again. It was a great feeling to know that she was in the house, and that there need be no sense of having to apologize for household shortcomings, or for not being able to offer even the most meagre hospitality. Not for a long time had Eben known such contentment.

There was something substantial about the slap of the pulley belt, and the great power of the engine, as Billy Seckerson cut the strings of the sheaves where they were thrown to him on the table of the thrasher, and fed the heads skilfully across the face of the drum. The smell of the corn-dust mingled with the smell of the coal, and the steam. Almost as fast as the sacks were crooked on to the spouts of the thrasher, and the plates lifted for the golden corn to come flooding down, they seemed to be full and had to be tugged off and replaced. Two strong Italians cheerfully carried the full sacks on their shoulders up the stone steps to tip the corn on the loft, where the great heap was growing steadily and spreading and rising up the wall. It was all more satisfying than anything Eben could have found words to describe, especially when Tilly would appear at odd times to shout near his ear, above the thud of the engine and the din and rattle of the thrasher, that she was making a trolley for supper or that there would be a can of tea or ginger beer in about ten minutes.

The Bromilows had returned to Bolton some time before, and Algie had gone back into the cotton industry. In the autumn his wife died, and he came to Deerfield for Christmas. Benjie was due home at the week-end after his first term away at public school. Algie had been keen for him to go to an English school, but distance and travelling in wartime had been factors to take into consideration, and eventually he had gone to Llandovery. Eben was more than happy at the idea, and as Bromilow said, 'Jolly good school for rugby. If he'll learn the game anywhere, he'll learn it there. First-class chaps.'

On that score, however, Eben was not too certain. He felt that enthusiasm for the game and a measure of natural ability also mattered. Not that Eben cared in the least. He wanted the boy to do what he had an interest in, remembering only too well the distress and bitter disappointment at the stifling of his own young ambitions. He hoped the old chap would not be too disappointed.

'It's an awful fag, really, Grandpa,' said Benjie, when Bromilow asked him how he was coming on at rugby, 'but I think I've got out of it.'

'How d'you manage that? I thought you had to play rugby?'

Benjie's studious look had become more evident and he now wore glasses which tended to slip down on his nose and give him an owlish expression. He was still dark, like his mother, but he looked as if he was beginning to fill out, and he was certainly no weakling.

'Well, you see, Grandpa, I just applied a little common or garden intelligence.'

'And what form did that take.'

'In the first place I decided that they were all so very keen on the game that they wouldn't want some fool to keep spoiling it for them.'

'So you spoiled it for them?'

'I suppose I did in a way.'

'And how did you manage that?'

'Well, first of all, they put me in the scrum. A most fearful confusion I thought it was, with no sense or reason in it. So I established what mustn't be done and then did it. I just dived

175

in to grab the ball with my hands and, of course, every time I did it the whistle blew and it was a penalty. But I suppose you knew that?'

'Yes, I knew that, Benjie.'

'In the end they got fed up and said if I was so keen to handle the ball they'd put me in the backs.'

'And what did you do then?' asked Eben. 'Drop it, I suppose?'

'Oh, no. The first time some fool threw it to me I threw it back to him. So Pythagoras said I mustn't do that. I must either throw it to someone else or run with it. So the next time I threw it to one of the other side. But that didn't seem very popular either.'

'And what did Pythagoras have to say?' said Bromilow.

'He insulted me, Grandpa. Became offensive.'

'Did he indeed?'

'Yes, he did. He called me to him and said, "Harter, I suppose you know your father played this game with some distinction?" I said, "Yes, sir. So I understand, sir." Then he said, "Does he know of your complete ineptitude at it?" I said, "I believe he has some misgivings, sir." Then he said, "Do you happen to know whether he has any deep-rooted grudge against this seat of learning?" So, of course, I said, "Oh, no, indeed, sir. I'm sure he hasn't." You haven't, Father, have you?'

'Oh, no, Benjie, none at all,' said Eben, 'absolutely none. Nor does your grandpa. But what did Pythagoras say to that?'

'He looked up to heaven, put his hands to his head and, as Thunderguts said afterwards, wailed like a Banshee. Then he shouted, "Then why in the name of God didn't he send you to Brecon where they don't know any better?"'

Bromilow said, 'I can see, Benjie, you're a man of some ingenuity and initiative. Jolly good.'

Eben was surprised to see how mature and self-assured he had become – which, after all, when he thought about it, was not so surprising when it was remembered that he had been away at school from such an early age. He hoped other people would not think him precocious. For his own part he would dearly have loved to have been able to spend more time with him. But he was glad to see how much he was with his grandfather. The pair of them held interminable discussions and were close companions for the whole of the holiday, which reminded him so much of his own marvellously happy relationship with Gramfer Jenkyn. It was almost as if they found in each other a comfort for the loss they had sustained, for, although Benjie showed little, Eben knew better than to imagine he did not feel the death of his grandmother.

The day after Benjie returned to school, however, Algie Bromilow collapsed. The doctor was adamant. It would mean complete rest and it would certainly be several months, even if things went well, before there could be any question of a return to Bolton. He said, 'Your father-in-law has had a slight heart attack, Mr Harter, and is completely run down. I think it would help him considerably if your wife were able to devote some time to nursing him.'

Penny by this time, taking advantage of all the talk of helping with the war effort, had enrolled as a driver at the aerodrome at Templeton. Eben was not convinced now of any possibility of help from her. He said, 'I don't know what commitments there are with the job she's doing.'

'I would support her with a medical certificate, of course.'

Eben looked at him. He said, 'It's no wish of mine, Doctor, that she should be doing the job.'

'All right then. Leave it to me. I'll have a word with her.'

When the doctor had gone, Penny, with all the changeability Eben had known since she was a girl, announced, 'I've decided to give up my job to look after Daddy. I can arrange to be released and Doctor Sutcliffe will give me a medical certificate anyway.'

If any one person was responsible for the impending reconciliation between Eben and Penny, it was Tilly. For some odd reason, which Eben could never quite understand, Tilly and Penny got on well together from the very day that Tilly moved in to help him by keeping house for him. If Penny threw one of her tantrums, Tilly was of such a disposition as to be able to ignore it and not allow it to bother her. And, whenever there was any occasion for them to talk about Penny, Tilly would make excuses for her.

'It isn't all her fault,' she would say, 'she've been spoilt.' Or, on other occasions, 'Don't be too hard on her, Eben, she've never been brought up to work.' And, of course, as often as not, Tilly would herself go and do whatever job it was that Penny had not done, which would infuriate Eben even further. With his own hard upbringing, it was something he could not accept. Tilly had never found life easy either, but she could still make allowances for others.

Eben would talk of his bitterness and the way in which

Penny had wronged him. Tilly would come back at him, if not by quoting the Bible, then at least by quoting what she believed to be the spirit of the Bible. And, of course, to drive home her point, she would say, 'I knows what Aunty Keziah would have said.' Tilly made no pretence at knowing the Bible from cover to cover as Eben's mother had done, but she reckoned on 'trying to come somewhere near the mark', as she put it.

Apart from something special like Harvest Festival, or other very rare occasions, Eben's only contact with chapel was to contribute as a member. If anyone had pressed him for his views on the subject he would have said that the chapel was perhaps a useful sort of institution to be supported rather than a body to which people belonged. It was a building, and functional, rather than a fellowship and spiritual. He knew well enough what his mother would have said, because he remembered her saying once (it could hardly have been very long before she died) that, even if the chapel were knocked down that very night, it would still be standing because it was the members in fellowship who constituted the chapel. He could not understand what she meant then, because he had only been a boy, but he thought he knew now, and he would have a vague feeling of uneasiness when he thought how far he had drifted from his mother's close familiarity with the 'word of the Lord'. So it was, after his fruitless arguments with Tilly, that he would think a little more deeply, and each time find himself giving way, a little here and a little there.

Tilly would remind him he had taken Penny for better or worse and he would say, yes, and it had turned out to be very much for the worse. Then she would have something to say on the question of forgiveness. Always it was forgiveness and understanding, and compassion and love and forgiveness. Always forgiveness. Until Eben almost came to believe in it himself, except that he always had reservations. On one occasion he had said, 'It's all very well to talk, Tilly, but 'tisn't easy.'

'Nobody said 'twas easy. 'Tis hard to forgive. Them that says 'tis easy don't care.'

'How d'you mean, girl?'

'Well, them that don't think somethin' is a sin can forgive easy enough. It's just like sayin' it don't matter. An' that's different to forgiveness altogether. It's when you sees somethin' you knows to be a terrible sin an' it hurts you, then it's forgiveness.'

Eben was not sure he had ever looked at it like that. There was a lot of sense with Tilly. Even so, he could hardly explain to her that his marriage to Penny had never been based on love, or how it had all come about, or that the foundations had been wrong from the start. It was no good trying to talk to her about that sort of thing when she talked about the bond of holy matrimony and taking solemn vows, and the forgiveness side of it and the hurt. It was not only the hurt, but the shame, because everybody knew how Penny had been behaving and he felt the awful humiliation of it. True, he was now financially secure. In spite of all his early disappointments, he had made good. He was respected as a farmer because he farmed well, and he believed he was respected as a man because he lived straight. If only Tilly wouldn't keep on so about forgiveness. It made him think of Arthur and Guinevere.

That night, before he went to bed, he took down his copy of Tennyson's poems to read the familiar story again. There was little time for reading poetry these days, what with work, and reading about farming, and keeping abreast of changing techniques.

It was a great story, how Guinevere had betrayed King Arthur's love, and how it had brought down his kingdom and laid his life's work and dreams in ruins. There were some beautifully expressive passages about Arthur's love for his queen. With his high ideals, he must have thought her sin was great. And certainly the hurt had been deep. Yet, as she threw herself prostrate before him on the convent floor, there was that marvellous passage:

Yet think not that I come to urge thy crimes,
I did not come to curse thee, Guinevere,
I, whose vast pity almost makes me die
To see thee, laying there thy golden head,
My pride in happier summers, at my feet.
The wrath which forced my thoughts on that fierce law,
The doom of treason and the flaming death,
(When first I learnt thee hidden here) is past.
The pang — which while I weighed thy heart with one
Too wholly true to dream untruth in thee,
Made my tears burn — is also past, in part.
And all is past, the sin is sinn'd, and I,
Lo! I forgive thee, as Eternal God
Forgives: do thou for thine own soul the rest.

Well, yes, that was forgiveness all right, on the grand scale.

Eben read to the end of the poem and put the book back on the shelf. Tilly had probably never read a word of Tennyson, but she certainly had the guts of the thing. And Eben's little kingdom, unlike King Arthur's, was not in ruins. The thing with Tilly, she was just like Aunty Becca and his own mother in their belief that Christianity was something to be lived and all about people. It came as something of a shock when the memory suddenly came back to him that it was here at Deerfield, how long ago, when he had come to dinner as a young man, that the wine had loosened his tongue and he had quoted his mother and what she had said about Christianity being about people. Look at it like that and you could say that Penny was people. Look at it which way he liked he could find no answer to Tilly's arguments.

Before this, Eben had been talking to Tilly of the many problems of labour shortage, whilst all the time the war was making more demands upon the land, with stock numbers increasing and a much bigger acreage under the plough. Finally, after a particularly heavy and hectic few weeks, it was Tilly who had said, 'How don't you try an' get a couple o' land girls?'

'D'you think they'd be any good?'

'You won't find out unless you try.'

Eben was not enthusiastic. He had said, 'Where could they live?'

Tilly had had to admit there were problems and difficulties. Now, however, Eben moved into Deerfield and Tilly said she could have two girls in the Lodge. Eben put in an application and was told he could have two girls in the spring. There was nothing more to be done now, only wait.

It was during this period, when Tilly was living at the Lodge on her own, although spending much of her time at Deerfield, that she whispered to Eben one morning, 'Come in an' see me first chance you gets today. I wants to talk to you.'

Her news, when it came, was more disturbing than anything he had expected. Tilly said, 'Have you heard anything lately about young Rachel Seckerson?'

Eben nodded his head and said, 'Yes, it's a bad job.'

'What have you heard?'

'She's pregnant, you mean?'

'Is that all you've heard?'

Eben looked at her. 'What else is there to hear?'

Tilly thought for a while. Then she said, 'Who told you about her?'

'Billy told me a couple of days ago.'

'Did he say who the father was?'

'Said he didn't know. Rachel won't tell them. But I didn't say much about it. I could see he was a bit upset.'

'Well, d'you know who's gettin' the fault of it?'

'No, I don't know. I haven't heard anything else about it or tried to find out. I'm sorry for poor old Billy and his wife and for the little girl. But it's none of my business.'

'I wish you was right.'

Eben looked at her puzzled. Tilly was looking very distressed.

'It's all our business,' she said.

'How d'you mean?'

'Well all the talk is that it's Mark.'

Eben stared at her incredulously. He could see the tears in her eyes.

'Good God, Tilly, what are you saying?'

'It's right enough.'

'Who told you?'

'I heard it at WI last night.'

'That doesn't mean that it's right.'

'Well that's what everybody is sayin'.'

'I'll never believe it.'

'How not?'

'Because he's my brother for one thing.'

'That only means you don't want to believe it.'

Eben had to admit the truth of it. Mark had ever been one for the girls. Rumour had it that he was paying for more than one child. But, even if it were true, no case had ever been brought against him, so at least he had never tried to run away from his responsibilities. And, whatever else he may or may not be, he was as staunch a friend as any man could ever wish to have.

Tilly cut in on his thoughts. She said, 'How old is the girl?'

'About eighteen now.'

'What sort is she?'

'I've never seen anything wrong with her or heard anything about her before now. And you'll always find the ones with plenty to say when something like this happens.'

'Some of 'em didn't blame Mark a bit, an' said you couldn't expect nothing else with the wife he got.'

'By all account she seems to have become a bit of a misery.'

'They say she drinks like a fish.'

Eben was thinking of the times he had called on Mark and he had explained Jane's absence by saying she had a headache or some such excuse.

He said, 'You wouldn't know from Mark, though. He's so loyal.'

When Eben eventually had the opportunity to ask Mark whether the rumours were true, he refused to be drawn. Rachel came home to her mother and, in the spring, gave birth to a baby boy. She still refused to name the father but, within a week or two, Mark had called at Light-a-Pipe and had offered to support Rachel and the child.

When Billy Seckerson told Eben of this he said also that Rachel had refused to accept the offer.

'She's a determined li'l maid. She said if we'd keep the babbie she'd manage to help bring'n up somehow. An' once the missus clapped eyes on'n that was th'end of it.'

'What d'you think now?' said Eben. 'Who do you reckon the father is?'

'I don't know.'

Eben sounded him, trying to lead him. He said, 'D'you think a chap would make an offer like that unless he knew he was responsible?'

'It dunnat mean nothin'. She haven't named'n, an' the babbie dunnat look like'n. He's a funny tack, thy brother, an' I knows as he've helped plenty.'

The catkins were hanging from the hazel trees and the primroses had begun to proclaim their fragrant presence in banks and hedgerows. Perhaps it was this seasonal re-awakening which helped to dispel some of the gloom that had been cast on Eben by Rachel's misfortune and Mark's seeming involvement. Perhaps it was the frantic activity of trying to keep abreast of work on the land. And perhaps it was the coming of Megan Jenkins. Or it could have been something of all three. But most certainly Megan Jenkins, Women's Land Army, played her part as she descended upon Deerfield, all five feet of bouncing energy, like some pocket whirlwind.

From the valleys of South Wales she came, auburn hair curling round her ears and as unruly as the fiery temper which such colouring was reputed to signify. But the only fire in Megan was her effervescent happiness and constant aggression. Her tip-tilted nose was covered with freckles, and her green eyes were bright with the pure joy of living. Her companion, help-mate, protégée, ward and confidante was the most un-likely partner anyone could ever have imagined to run in double-harness with such a character, for Merrial Singleton was very definitely right out of the top drawer. She was not big and she was not thin, and her light-brown hair was pinned in a bun at the back. Although she looked quite smart, even in her Land Army uniform, the immediately obvious incongruity lay in the fact that she topped her self-appointed guardian by a good eight inches. Their green jumpers, corduroy breeches, woollen stockings and heavy brown shoes only emphasized the contrast.

'The trouble with Merry, d'you see,' said Megan, 'is that people do put on her.'

Eben had joined them for tea with Tilly on the afternoon they arrived. Megan was putting the record straight right from the start.

'That's why we did pack up from the hostel. Some farms they did send us to was all right but some of the farmers was proper buggers. Rob Jesus Christ of his shoelaces some of 'em would and then come back for the laceholes. We don't mind work mind, Miss Perrot, but nobody that's any good do like to be put on. The last old bugger we went to used to line us up in the field at the end of the rows setting potatoes and he'd say, "Now then. Heads down, arses up and keep going." Bloody slave-driving I do call that. So I said to Merry, "Let's put in to live on a farm." The thing is, d'you see, Miss Perrot, they did know that Merry had been educated, so they did think she wouldn't know no better than to put up with it all. And she got proper education too. Not just this county school business. It's like Howell's School, Llandaff, only better. I didn't believe her first going off because she said she'd been to Roedean. I said don't be so daft will you that's where they do make the rat poison. Do you use that rat poison here, Mr Harter, dangerous old stuff mind?'

Eben, by this time, was too convulsed to attempt to reply.

'Bloody boy on one farm we was on put a spoonful in a jar of honey and mixed it up. *Iesu mawr*, they was bad for days some of 'em was. Thank God I'd only had the bit of jam myself and Merry don't eat much sweet stuff like, good job as well. The joke was they only kept the bees to get the sugar ration. And another thing is you got some rough types on some of these farms with bad language and all that, and Merry don't like a lot of old bad language for she haven't been used to it like, have you, Merry?'

Thus-deferred-to Merry exchanged a knowing smile with Tilly. Eben noticed her even, white teeth and the freshness of her complexion. She had a fine nose and a kind of sensitive mouth. Before she had the chance to say anything, Megan was into her stride again.

'Better times for the future is what we got to have though, so buggers like that can't put on us. Fair shares for all is what it got to be.'

'Like this Beveridge Plan,' said Eben.

Megan looked at him as if he had just dropped the best piece of china.

'Good God, Mr Harter, you don't believe that do you? The bloody Tories have took all the guts out of that.'

'What d'you mean, the Tories? We've got a Coalition government and they've accepted the Beveridge Report.'

'Well, *Iesu mawr*, and you a man with education! Merry did tell me it's mostly Tories they are and the report was all right when it came out only they've spoiled it, and Merry do know about these things. And my Ivor, last letter he wrote, said when this is all over and he do come home we'll vote Labour and chuck the buggers out.'

'Who is your Ivor?'

'He's my sweetheart, out in the East, God knows where. Wanted to get married before he left but I said no I'd wait for him but if I find out he's been messing about with a bit of black stuff out there I'll chop his legs off. How many cows you got here then and pigs and sheep and that? I won't have to feed the bull will I? They got a bull on one farm I was on and I had to throw the hay over the top of the manger and he was blowing smoke down his nose at me like the dragon the college boys did have during Rag Week in Cardiff. Frightened! *Duw*, you could hear my knees knocking like a skeleton on a tin roof, aye.'

'What can you do on the farm?'

'Well nothing have beat me yet.'

Eben looked at her diminutive form. He smiled at Tilly and said to Megan, 'Do you reckon you could put the collar on the big cart-horse?'

'Of course I can do that. One of the nice farms I was on, oh lovely man he was, like Thomas Big Seat in chapel, proper angel, he did show me how to do it. The men was making fun of me because I'm a bit shorter than Merry like and the farmer put a couple of boxes for me to stand on. And *duw* he was a lovely horse, nose like velvet but big teeth. *Iesu mawr*, like tombstones they was. But when he seen me struggling with this great big collar d'you know what he done? He put his head down for to help me and then they do say animals haven't got no brains. I reckon they got more brains than all them bloody Tories. Like Merry said only asking to be chucked out they are when we do get the chance, didn't you, Merry, that's right isn't it?'

'Now then, Merry,' said Eben, 'let's hear what you have to say about the Tories.'

'That's right, Merry, you say it now like you do explain it to me sometimes.'

When Merry spoke, her voice was gentle and well-modulated. Her grey-blue eyes were serious and Megan hung on her every word.

'It isn't so much what I think of the Tories,' she said, 'it's simply a question of new concepts all round. Just as the time has gone when we merely think of Socialists as people who wear cloth caps and mufflers.'

'So you're a bit of a politician.'

'Only because I think everybody should take an intelligent interest in something which affects us all.'

'And what do you think are the big issues that will be facing us?'

'Whenever the next election comes I believe the ordinary people will vote on the straightforward issue of social security and a better life. All the arguments will be about nationalization and public ownership, but the real issue will be the sort of future people want.'

'You think so?'

'Yes, I do. And I also think a lot of people will be surprised at the result. Some of the press barons like Kemsley and Camrose are bitterly opposed to the new ideals and, of course, you have a hard core of reactionary Tory MPs of the old school. Obviously we can't hope for any sort of progress until they're rooted out, and the younger generation will be determined on doing it.'

Megan said nothing but was bursting with pride and admiration. Remembering his own earlier disenchantment with politicians, Eben said, 'Are you a Socialist?'

'I'm not quite sure. There are so many things involved.'

'I'm glad to hear you say that.'

Merry smiled mischievously. She said, 'Why? Are you a Tory?'

'No indeed I'm not. When I was your age I was full of high-minded ideals about these great moral issues. But long ago I decided that all politicians were highly suspect, to say the least. As a matter of interest, what were you doing before you decided to lend a hand on the land?'

'I was reading economics. Philosophy, politics and economics.'

'Where?'

'Oxford.'

Eben raised his eyebrows. 'I can see we're going to have some weighty discussions.'

He was thinking how much more expressive she was than Penny had ever been. His instinct told him that Penny would be quite certain to react badly to this new personality. He fancied she would not be unduly concerned at the presence of the mercurial Megan, but she might not be so kindly disposed towards a younger woman of Merry's intelligence.

His thoughts were interrupted by Megan, who could contain herself no longer.

'I can see Merry have shook you, Mr Harter, but then she is like that you see in her quiet way. That's what I did tell you. She do know about these things. But what I do want to ask you is what was that you was saying about morals?'

'It wasn't morals,' Merry cut in. 'Mr Harter was talking about moral issues, Megan, which is a different thing altogether.'

'Well, that's all right then because I was thinking you was on about the bulls they been talking about.'

Merry looked at Eben and Tilly with a quizzical smile and then raised her eyes to the ceiling as if to say, 'I did my best.'

'I don't hold with it,' said Megan. 'I know I do hate to see a bull breathing fire at you but they do have feelings, the same as anybody else, funny if they didn't. But there are them who do say it is most immoral what they're going to do now. What they do call artificial something and I don't believe in nothing artificial and they do reckon there won't be no bulls on the farms no more only men coming round with the old artificial stuff in tubes and bottles *ych-a-fi*, disgusting I do call it and proper immoral. Don't you think it's immoral, Miss Perrot, and what do the poor cows think about it I'd like to know.'

'Well, of course,' said Eben, 'it's no good trying to stand in the way of progress.'

Megan bounced up from the table saying, 'There's no bloody progress sitting here and the tea things not washed,' and she was into the kitchen and buzzing around before anybody else could move.

Tilly followed her saying, 'That's all right, honey, don't you worry about them few things now.'

'Don't be daft will you. Why should you be put on? You go back and sit down, Miss Perrot. Merry and me will see you don't get put on. We don't want to put on nobody.'

Eben and Merry were still sitting at the table. Merry smiled at him. She said, 'Quite obviously Miss Perrot has made a big hit. If Megan has declared that she will see to it she won't be put on then that is the highest accolade it is possible to confer. In case you hadn't guessed, she has a heart of gold and is the most honest little soul I've ever met.'

'Yes, I thought she might be.'

'You'll find that you've been very lucky to have her.'

As they rose from the table, Eben said, 'I think I've been very lucky to have both of you.'

Merry said, 'Thank you, kind sir,' and made a mock curtsey. But she dropped her eyes and coloured slightly.

As Eben anticipated, it was not long before the presence of Merry sparked off a reaction from Penny. But it was not the reaction he expected.

With the coming of summer, Algie Bromilow's health improved greatly and he returned to Bolton. Much of the war news seemed remote and, once more, people started coming to the area for summer holidays. Megan remained very much the Megan of her arrival on the scene, but Merry developed a keen interest in farming, which she would discuss with Eben with an understanding he found remarkable in one who had not been born and brought up on the land. She also showed a genuine concern for Eben's own problems and plans for the future. Which was possibly why Penny took the line she did, if, as Eben thought likely, her aim was to establish for Merry's benefit exactly whose place it was, and, for good measure, belittle him at the same time. Reconciliation was one thing, but compatibility and affection were, he knew, different altogether.

Autumn was already tinting the trees, and a hard slog had seen the harvest safely gathered. Tilly had prepared a meal at Deerfield, which she did sometimes, and she and the two girls had joined Eben and Penny at the big kitchen table.

Addressing the girls, rather than Eben, Penny said, 'I've

decided to turn this place into a guest house.'

Having addressed herself to the girls, Penny could have no complaints that Megan now evinced some interest in the project.

'Guest house? What the hell is that then?'

'Well, a guest house is where one has guests who pay one to look after them.'

'Good God, like the workhouse you mean only a bit better. They got a place like that up by us home, aye. Poor old buggers they are some of 'em and nobody wants 'em.'

'Oh no, not that sort of place at all. A guest house is more like a hotel, but smaller, of course, and much more private.'

'Hotel? *Iesu mawr*, that's worse. Buggers coming in all hours of the day and night and ringing bells and fetch this and fetch that. It's all right for them as is ringing the bells but what about the ones being put on? No hotel work for me I can tell you that before you start, not on your bloody life. Give me the cows any day, they don't tell you fetch this and fetch that.'

Penny coloured slightly.

'No, no, Megan,' said Eben, 'it won't be anything to do with the farm. Just a bit of a sideline.'

It was the first he had heard of it but thought it as well to keep the peace.

'Well, hardly a sideline exactly,' said Penny. 'It will be a proper business more suited to a house like this. After all, this was never really a farm.'

Merry looked up quickly. She said, 'You surprise me. I would have thought from the buildings there had always been substantial farming here.'

'Oh no. When Daddy bought it there was just nothing at all here.'

Merry nodded. 'Yes, of course. During the Depression. But many farms were allowed to run down at that time. I mean before that.'

'Of course, but you're talking about the old days when it was a gentleman's farm.'

'Well look at that,' said Megan. 'Gentleman's place you do say. Fetch this and fetch that. And now it's going to be the same again but with the other buggers doing all the fetching just like my Ivor said it's going to be. There's a come down if you like.'

As far as creating effect went, Penny's announcement had been disastrous, but the plan went ahead nevertheless. She had obviously spoken to Tilly before saying anything to Eben and he raised no objection. If it would hold her interest and act as an anchor, then that was all to the good, and with Tilly to lean on, competent cook and housekeeper that she was, there was no reason why such a venture should not be a success. To a certain extent, therefore, and certainly on the face of it, Eben was supporting what looked like a joint endeavour. In any case, there was much work to be done redecorating the house and tidying up generally. Labour was scarce and materials, too, were difficult to come by, and these were problems which Eben would have to solve, as well as the question of obtaining a catering licence.

The last of the autumn leaves had fallen and some cold weather had brought the small birds nearer to the buildings. Already there were redwings amongst them and the wood-pigeons were flighting early. The weather was dry, however, and the cows were still out by night. As long as everything went all right, Merry and Megan were able to manage the cows almost on their own. Owen, a strong young man of twenty now, and developing in the Harters' physical mould, was mostly on the land and with the tractor. He and Billy Seckerson cut and carried the hay which the girls fed to the cows, and helped with heavier work of cleaning out when the cows were in by night, but the animals themselves were now very much in the care of the two girls.

At milking time that evening Merry had asked Eben to have a look at one of the dry cows. These winter calvers were important and came in with the milking cows for their share of whatever feed was going.

Eben ran his hand along the cow's back and felt for the bones either side of her tail-head. Her udder was full, but Eben did not think there was that hard 'nature' in it to suggest that she was on the point of calving. Even so, Merry had done well to recognize the symptoms of her changing condition and he told her so.

'Put it down to woman's instinct,' she said.

'Well, whatever it is, you're not far off the mark.'

'Shall I keep her in tonight?'

Eben felt round the cow's tail-head again and looked at her chewing her cud contentedly.

'No,' he said, 'you might as well turn her out. I don't think she'll calve before morning.'

'Are you sure?'

'No, I'm not sure. There's nothing sure in this life – apart from death. But you can turn her out, and I'll go and have a look at her last thing before I turn in for the night.'

'How will you find her in the dark?'

'There's a bit of moon. And I expect she'll be near some shelter down by the wood.'

Merry did not seem quite satisfied but turned the cow out. Eben sensed her concern and was not surprised when he found her waiting for him when he went to look at the cow before going to bed.

'You're taking your duties too seriously,' he said. 'Or did you think you couldn't rely on me?'

Merry laughed. She said, 'I hope you don't mind me coming with you.'

'My dear young lady, I'm honoured and delighted. But are you warm enough?'

'Oh yes, I'm well wrapped up.'

She wore a muffler and woolen gloves, and the collar of her Land Army coat was turned up around her ears.

'It's you talking about death that started me worrying,' she said.

'Me? Death? What did I say about death?'

'You said there was nothing sure in life apart from death.'

It was Eben's turn to laugh.

'Dear me, Merry. You mustn't take any notice of my nonsense. But I can see I'll have to be more careful what I say.'

What moon there was gave a good light. The sky was clear and a myriad stars twinkled above the great canopy of silence which enveloped them, and the ground was white and crisp as they walked. From somewhere in the distance came the staccato bark of a dog fox and the silence became more pronounced. In the soft light, Eben thought, Merry looked quite beautiful with a peach-bloom complexion and sparkling eyes.

'You look like the maid in the moonlight,' he said.

'What maid in what moonlight?'

'Isn't there a song in some opera about the maid in the moonlight?'

'Ah, you mean Mimi.' Merry began to sing quietly, ' "Lovely, maid in the moonlight! Your face entrancing like radiant seraph from on high appears!" But that's your part. It's a duet from *La Bohème*. Do you know it?'

'No, I don't know much about opera.'

'Well, Mimi, poor soul, is dying from consumption.'

'Don't most of the women in opera die from consumption?'

190

'Not all of them. Some take poison. Usually when they're crossed in love or when the man they love is married to another woman.'

She turned her head away as she spoke, and Eben sensed they were treading on dangerous ground. There had been little passages like this recently on odd occasions when they were alone together. They walked on down the field in silence for a while until Eben said, 'There they are.'

Merry stared in the direction in which he was looking.

'Where?'

'There in the corner, by the wood.'

'Heavens, you must have good eyes.'

They walked towards where Eben said the cows were, and presently Merry said, 'Ah, yes. I can see the white patches on some of them. Now then, where's Blackbird?'

'There she is, next to the old Shorthorn.'

The cow got up as they approached, stretched and walked quietly away.

'Nothing wrong with her,' said Eben.

'You always talk about the Blackie family as if they were something special, and you say she's one of them?' said Merry.

'Yes, they are special. They're all descended from a cow my father gave me when I started on my own. Mostly by Friesian bulls now, of course, but originally they were the real Castlemartin Welsh Blacks. And the first one of all came from a place called Morfa Bychan when I was just a small boy. But that's a long story.'

'I'm a good listener.'

'It's a job to know where to start.'

'Then try starting at the beginning.'

Eben was surprised afterwards at how much he had told Merry about his boyhood, and about meeting Penny on the bridge when Blackie frightened her, and about the night of the row with his father when Blackie died.

Over the winter one of the principal diversions, amidst work and redecorations on the house, was to listen to Megan holding forth on the subject of 'that bloody Ivor'.

For more than six months she had received no word from him.

'I know it,' she would say, 'I do have the feeling in my bones. It's some bit of black stuff he have picked up with, *ych-a-fi.* Do you ever get a feeling in your bones, Miss Perrot?'

'No, indeed, Megan, only th'owld rheumatic I gets sometimes.'

'No, no, this is nothing like rheumatics. Just a feeling. And I been faithful to him I have, never looked at nobody. Faithful to him I've been and him messing about with a bit of black stuff. I bloody knew that's what it would be.'

'You mustn't say that, Megan,' said Tilly, 'perhaps he's somewhere where he can't write. Or maybe he've wrote and the letters haven't arrived.'

'You don't believe that, do you? That's only stories they do make up for the sake of buggers who do go off with a bit of black stuff.'

'No, no, Megan. It happens all the time during the war. You mark my words. You'll be hearing from him by-and-by and then you'll be sorry for all the things you've said.'

'Sorry! And him with a bit of black stuff with eyes sticking out like organ stops, haven't you never seen pictures of 'em, and I wouldn't feel it in my bones if it wasn't right.'

As it turned out, Megan was only half right. It was an Italian girl. And the news came in a letter from a girl at home, whose brother was in the same unit as Megan's Ivor, and who had said in his letter home about Ivor putting this girl in the family way. An Italian girl she was, working in the canteen, and he had married her. A week later a letter came from Ivor telling Megan what she already knew and saying how sorry he was and that she would be better off without him.

'As if I didn't know that without the bugger having to tell me. And what I think I'll do when this lot is over I'll be a nun that's what I'll be. Men is all the same if you ask me. If he'd found a bit of black stuff it wouldn't have been so bad. You seen pictures of them Italians haven't you, Miss Perrot, dangerous-looking buggers like Mr Harter's polecat ferret. What the hell was he thinking about?'

The ploughing had gone well, the land had been dressed and most of the corn had been sown. Owen was working on the root ground, and Eben had gone down to the field in the van with a new type of ridging body they had decided to try. He was anxious to get back to the house, for there was still much to be done and some bookings had already been received, although no visitors were due until Whitsun.

Eben was about to get into the van, when Megan shot through the gateway into the field.

'Mr Harter, Mr Harter, you got to come quick. Miss Perrot said you mustn't stop a minute, you got to come now straight.'

'What's the matter, Megan? What's wrong?'

'*Duw, duw*, there's nothing wrong. A surprise it is, but Miss Perrot said I mustn't tell or I don't know what she'll do to me, hell she looked strict when she said it. Only to tell you there's somebody to see you and it's a soldier and you got to come straight back to the house.'

'Come on then, jump in the van.'

As they bounced across the field Eben wondered whoever it could be.

'Who is it, Megan?'

'I mustn't tell. It's a surprise. But *Iesu mawr* he's good-looking. I tell you now he's only been there about ten minutes and I've changed my mind already about them nuns. I don't think that's natural do you, stuck behind walls like that?'

'Well who is he then?'

'*Duw, duw*, Mr Harter, I've told you I mustn't say but by damn he's a bobby dazzler. I only took one look at him and my knees went like jelly, aye. Dark wavy hair and to hell with the nuns, I wonder how long he's going to stop. And there's tall he is too, head up against the ceiling they must have put something in his boots to make him grow I shouldn't wonder. And Miss Perrot crying her eyes out and laughing all the same time and her arms round him hugging him I never saw nobody so excited.'

As Megan prattled on Eben thought of all the people from his younger days, particularly when he had been playing rugby. But then, it must be somebody closer than that because Tilly was so excited about it and that narrowed the possibilities considerably. All those who had gone away from the Mill and the Gangrel flashed through his mind. Hannah had only had one daughter. Griff had no children. Josh. That was it. There couldn't be anybody else. But Josh had been gone for more than thirty years and Eben was only five when he went. But he remembered him. Or he thought he did.

'Now then,' said Tilly proprietorially, 'guess who this is.'

Eben looked at the boy, tall and broad-shouldered, and there was no mistaking the dark features and brown eyes. He was a Perrot for sure.

Eben smiled. 'Josh,' he said.

'I never said, Miss Perrot, drop dead, I didn't did I, Mr Harter?' But nobody seemed to hear Megan. Eben had taken the boy's firm grip in his hand and Tilly once more flung her arms round him and started crying again.

'Well it's Joshua's son, for sure, but they called me Abel after Dad's old man.'

'Don't he talk lovely!' said Tilly, intrigued at the way he flattened his vowels in the middle of a word.

Abel's smile showed a row of strong white teeth.

'Well, Aunt Tilly, I always thought Dad and Mother talked just a little bit old-fashioned until today but I figure you can beat 'em right along the line. Can you teach me to talk like you do and when I get back home I'll really show 'em a thing or two.'

So excited was Tilly that, for once, the teapot was not her immediate reaction and Megan, unobtrusively, set about laying the table.

'How long are you going to stay with us?' said Eben.

'Well, sure, I haven't figured anything out, but I thought maybe I'd get a bed for the night and a bit of tucker, and then move on and look up a few folks.'

'How much leave have you got?'

'Oh, I've got ten days, but . . .'

'Ten days,' said Tilly, 'isn't that wonderful! And Griff is comin' down next week so you'll be able to see him.'

'Well, sure, Aunt Tilly, I hadn't reckoned to be a nuisance . . .'

'Nuisance indeed! Oh, this is wonderful.'

'There you are, Miss Perrot,' offered Megan, 'he don't like putting on people and that's what do count.'

Abel looked at Megan, 'Nobody's told me yet who this young lady is.'

'Oh, this is our Megan and we all loves her.'

Abel extended his hand and Megan took it and went very red and said, 'Pleased to meet you I'm sure.'

'That's a pretty name,' said Abel. 'Are you one of the land girls I've read about? Is it Women's Land Army you call yourselves?'

'Don't you take no notice of what you read. Anybody'd think we was like some secret weapon but we do get as fed up as everybody else, that's why we left the hostel to come here only we been lucky, me and Merry, that's my friend, I better go and call her for a cup of tea . . .' and she was gone through the door without even pausing for breath.

When she came back Merry was with her. Megan had made some attempt to bring order to her hair, powdered her nose and used a touch of lipstick. Penny came downstairs at the same time. She, too, had been taking some trouble with her make-up.

Tea was more a rapid sequence of questions and answers than a meal. Eventually, Merry said, 'If you'll excuse us now, we'll go and fetch the cows and start milking.'

She rose from the table as she spoke and Megan got up with her. Abel rose, too, and said, 'Well, if you're going to feed me for ten days I reckon I'd better do something to earn it. I'll come and help you.'

'Can you milk?' said Eben.

'Sure, I worked on a farm for three years before I decided to go into the bank. It'll be a nice change for me to get my hand back in.'

'How about clothes?'

'I've got some old clobber in my kit bag.'

'Come on then, and I'll show you where you're sleeping. Where shall we put him?' Eben asked Penny.

'The bed is made up in Benjie's room.' She turned to Abel and smiled. 'Facing the sea, and the sun will wake you up in the morning.'

'That's jake,' said Abel.

'What do that mean?' said Megan.

Abel laughed. 'That means it's fine, it's all right. Like the minute I set eyes on you I said to myself, "She's jake".'

'Don't you jake me.'

Abel roared with laughter and winked at Eben. It had taken them very little time to understand each other.

'All right, Megan,' he said. 'Give me five minutes and I'll be out there with you.'

Tilly was still living in the Lodge and the girls lived with her, but that evening they all had supper in the big kitchen at Deerfield. They were talking of the day's happenings when Merry looked at Eben and said, 'I wonder if anybody'd like to use the tickets for the dance tonight.'

Taking his cue, Eben asked, 'What dance is that?'

'The Land Army dance. We have two tickets, but I simply can't go although I know I should. I really must stay home and write some letters. With all this good weather and the work on the land I haven't had a minute to myself and I had a letter from home this morning and they're wondering whatever's happened. I haven't written to them for nearly three weeks.'

Eben said, 'Yes, I know we've been working you pretty hard lately. But what about you, Megan? You're not such a big letter-writer. You could go to the dance, couldn't you?'

Megan looked blank. 'What's all this about dancing all of a sudden then?'

'Well,' said Eben, 'we just thought we'd like to give Abel as good a time as we can whilst he's here, and we thought maybe you could take him to the dance, seeing that it's a Land Army affair.'

'Well, that's jake,' said Abel. 'I'm no great dancing joker but I reckon I wouldn't want to miss a Land Army dance if I could help it. And if you'd take me, Megan, well, you heard what I said. That's jake with me.'

Megan looked from Merry to Eben and back to Merry. Then she looked at Abel. 'All right,' she said, 'that will be lovely. But only platonic, mind, no messing about. I don't hold with this messing about do I, Miss Perrot, haven't I told you what I do think of this messing about?'

Penny said, 'But which way can you get to Tenby and especially get home afterwards?'

'They can have my car,' said Eben.

Penny looked at him, almost visibly remembering the times he had told her some of her plans would have to be cancelled because of petrol restrictions.

It was evident that the dance had been a success, because the following day the relationship between Abel and Megan was one of easy understanding and happy companionship. They seemed to have eyes only for each other and Eben decided that Merry was not the only one who could play Cupid. When the opportunity arose he said, 'Megan, I wonder could you do me a favour this afternoon? Would you be willing to take Abel and show him Heronsmill and the Gangrel? He wants to take some pictures, so it would be a good chance to go now whilst the weather's good. I can't go myself, I've got to go into Narberth. Could you do that for me?'

Megan's green eyes danced with excitement but, honest as ever, she said, '*Diawl*, Mr Harter, I don't know which is which.'

'Yes, you do,' said Eben. 'You only have to follow the stream up from the Lower Level stile then turn off by the pompren – that's the little footbridge – and the lane takes you straight up past the old mill right to the house. Then the Gangrel is up across the field, right there by the big pine tree.'

Eben turned to Abel, 'Do you know the rhyme about them?'

'Sure, I've heard Dad say it – Heronsmill, Underfoot Hill, Devil's Den and the Gangrel: Brandyback, Pen-y-cwm Slack, Rushyland and Rollin'.'

'Well done,' said Eben, 'and to think that only the Den is now being lived in. That's the one on the other side of the valley. Right up on the top of the hill looking down on Heronsmill.'

'What sort of state are they in now?'

'Oh, very bad. The roof is off the Gangrel and the windows are all broken, and Heronsmill isn't much better. To think that there was a whole community there once – a village almost – and all getting a good living. And now there's nothing there, not a soul.'

'That's a fair cow,' said Megan.

'That's what?' said Eben.

'That's a fair cow.'

Eben looked blankly at her. Abel saw the bewilderment on the faces of the others and laughed his infectious laugh. 'Good on you, little ginger pommie,' he said.

'What's a fair cow?' Eben asked.

Megan looked at Abel. 'That's what they do say in New Zealand about something really terrible and a real calamity. That's right, isn't it, Abe?'

'You sure said it. She's right you know. She's dead right.'

Much later that afternoon, when the shadows were lengthening, Eben, who had helped Merry with the milking, called to her, 'Come and have a look at this a minute.'

Merry came to where he was looking down across the meadows.

'Don't show yourself,' he said. 'I think I'd better call Tilly as well.'

When Tilly came, she and Eben joined Merry who turned and smiled at them. Tilly stood looking for a while, then she said, 'God love her little heart.'

Abel and Megan, for whom the world held no one else, were strolling up across the meadow hand-in-hand. Megan carried a bunch of daffodils. Abel was looking down at her as he talked and every now and again she smiled up at him. Once she leaned her head lovingly against his arm.

'What d'you reckon that is then?' said Eben.

'D'you think that looks like only platonic mind or a lot of old messing about?'

Merry said wistfully, 'If you ask me it isn't either. I reckon it's the real thing.'

'God love her little heart,' said Tilly.

Eben said, 'Well that's jake then.'

Long after Abel had taken Megan back home to New Zealand, Eben would smile to himself as he remembered their whirlwind courtship. For Merry had been right. It was the real thing.

The following week Griff was home for a short holiday and he and his wife stayed in Saundersfoot. They had a couple of marvellous reunions at Deerfield and only Penny seemed like an outsider. Griff was now General Manager of the large dairy company with which he had started and which had now absorbed a number of smaller companies. He was also heavily involved with voluntary committee work with the Ministry of Food. His dark hair had turned grey as he had passed into middle age, and it was much thinner, but he was as cheerful as ever and had been hugely excited to find his brother's son waiting for him when the train arrived at Saundersfoot station. He had been determined that Abel should spend some time with him in London, and this came about when Abel had a long week-end leave in May. Megan was included in the invitation. When she returned she ran in and hugged Tilly and kissed her, then, suddenly very shy, held up her hand to show Tilly her engagement ring and embarked on a long and rapidly-told story as to how they had thought should they wait until the war was over but what was the difference and Abel had actually proposed to her by the big pine tree at the Gangrel, and his father would love that and they saw this ring in a window and it looked just jake somehow so Abel had said, 'We better not miss a chance like this, Megan.'

'So there it is, Miss Perrot, and do you think it would be all right if I started to call you Aunty Tilly now straightaway to get used to it like, for you won't mind will you with me working here, it isn't as if I'd be trying to put on you.'

Tilly kissed her again. 'No, my honey, I loves you like my own, indeed I do.'

Megan sat down suddenly as if exhausted and said, 'Oh Miss Perrot, Aunty Tilly, I can't tell you what sort of time I had in London. I've never seen nothing like it and Uncle Griff is lovely. Wouldn't let us pay for nothing and taxis everywhere and there's a lovely home they got, beautiful house and all thick carpets everywhere. And on Sunday he took us to chapel and him one of the head ones there and the place nearly full, but Uncle Griff said once this war is over they wouldn't see half of 'em again and funny he is with it. And there's loves it down here he do. Once the war is over he said he's going to retire and come down here to live.'

The war was more in Megan's mind now than it had ever been before and Eben wondered how deeply she thought of things beneath her cheerful appearance. Just as she was wondering when she might be seeing Abel again, all leave was cancelled and it was D-Day.

The invasion of Normandy was on, and those in the area who had seen the massive invasion manoeuvres on local beaches the year before, thought they might have some idea as to what it must be like. In the glorious weather of June the wireless had constant news flashes and bulletins of the bitter fighting. The broad flag on the winter wheat rustled in the warm June breezes, the air was joyful with the smell of new-mown hay, but Eben was sick at heart. Surely not Abel. Always he remembered Eddie going off to the front so cheerfully so long ago in that other war, and then Edward, whom Eddie had left behind as no more than the seed he had planted to take his place to care for Ruth. Was Abel's to be just such another young life thrown away? He was celebrating his twenty-first birthday in the thick of it. What a way to come of age.

Penny was full of her catering, for there were people who had come to snatch a desperately needed rest, usually for no more than a week, and it was a great distraction for them all at Deerfield. Merry was deeply concerned for Megan, and Tilly was on edge. The only confident one was Megan. 'Aunty Tilly,' she said, 'Abe will be all right because I got a feeling in my bones so I do know he'll be all right.'

Well, thought Eben later, the feeling in her bones had proved to be right. At long last the war was over, and Abel had come back. He and Megan were married quietly in Ebenezer with Merry as her bridesmaid and Eben giving her away and Owen acting as Abel's best man. And now there they were in New Zealand, and Megan's letters to Tilly were a wonderful new link for her with Josh and his family.

The election, following straight after the war, had gone very much as Merry had forecast when she came to Deerfield, with a huge Labour victory.

'Next thing,' she said, 'is that everybody will be blaming the Government for the shortages which will be inevitable. They will forget that wars have to be paid for.'

'What will you do?' asked Eben.

'I think I'll see about going back to Oxford and taking my degree.'

'We'll miss you very much, you know.'

'We?'

'Well, I shall, and Tilly will, I know.'

Merry said, 'I'll miss you too.'

'Well, you haven't gone yet.'

'No, but I'll be going.'

The season was well advanced when Penny had a letter from her father, in Bolton. He had had a couple of weeks' rest on the advice of the doctor. A few days later she announced that she felt she should go to see him.

'There's no reason why you shouldn't,' said Eben, 'as soon as the holiday people have all gone.'

Penny seemed restless. 'Well I really don't think I ought to wait too long.'

'It needn't be long. Another three or four weeks. Benjie goes back on Friday week and then about a fortnight after that the place will be empty.'

Penny, for the next day or two, however, continued to seem unsettled. Eben recognized that she had perhaps worked harder than usual, although Tilly had been the mainstay, but he wondered whether the symptoms might, after all, be more than the old story of the novelty having worn off. It was the third season of catering.

Eben was not surprised when Penny again referred to the possibility of going fairly soon to visit her father.

'Well, I don't know,' he said, 'it's going to make it a heavy hand for Tilly.'

'I've spoken to Tilly and she says she can manage.'

Eben did not doubt that. Tilly would always sacrifice herself.

Merry was due to leave in six weeks' time. She would, Eben knew, help Tilly all she could, but it was not her work and there was plenty for her to do outside. He said nothing of this to Penny to make her going any the easier or more excusable. At last, after more protestations from her as to her father's need for her, it was agreed that Penny should go the day after Benjie returned to school, which would be the Friday, so that Penny would be going on the Saturday, when, Eben had to admit, most of the guests would also be leaving. Thereafter there would only be a family of three to be looked after, and Tilly repeated her willingness to cope.

On the Thursday evening Benjie developed a cold, and by Friday morning he was found to be suffering from a heavy chill. It was not thought to be anything which a day or two in bed would not cure, but his return to school would need to be delayed. However, the decision finally having been made for Penny to go away for a few days, Eben, to her evident relief, said there was no reason why Benjie's cold should make any difference and, on the Saturday morning, drove her to Kilgetty station to catch the early train as planned.

By the afternoon, contrary to their expectations, Benjie was rather worse, with severe pains in his head and eyes, and, by the evening, both Eben and Tilly were sufficiently worried to think they should send for the doctor.

He examined Benjie thoroughly, and finally said, 'It's sinusitis. Very painful, but it will clear up and if it recurs we'll have to have a more thorough look at him. I'll give you a prescription which you can get on Monday morning and I'll leave you enough tablets to last him over the week-end. Give them to him every six hours and be sure you give him all of them.' He counted some capsules into his hand and said, 'One of the few good things to come out of the war!'

When the doctor had gone Tilly said, 'I'm worried about'n poor li'l sowl. Had you better phone Penny?'

'What good would that do?'

'It wouldn't do no good but she's his mother after all and she'd want to know.'

'If she was that worried about him she wouldn't have left him in the first place.'

'Don't be bitter, Eben. Suppose anything happened to'n and you'd never towld her.'

Eben looked at the clock. 'All right,' he said, 'I *will* phone. She should be there by now but we'll give it another hour in case the train was late.'

More than an hour had gone by when Tilly said, 'How about phoning?'

'All right,' said Eben, but Tilly could see that his heart was not in it.

Algie Bromilow answered the phone himself and sounded cheerful.

'And how are you feeling now?' said Eben.

'Feeling? Top of the world. Been watching some cricket at Old Trafford this summer when it wasn't raining. Never seen such crowds in all my life. Almost makes me think I ought to settle down here in my old age. Must talk about it to Penny when she comes up.'

'When she comes up?'

'Yes, looking forward to seeing her.'

'Isn't she there yet?'

'Isn't she here? Damn it she isn't coming till Monday. I thought that's what you phoned about.'

'She left here this morning to come and see you because you've been ill.'

'Damn it, man, I haven't been ill. Just told you. Thoroughly enjoying myself watching some cricket.'

'So she isn't there?'

'No, she isn't here. Did you say she left this morning?'

'Yes, I took her to catch the train myself.'

'Good God, where can she be then? Never know what she'll do next.'

'Perhaps you'll ask her to phone me when she does arrive.'

'Yes, I'll do that. How is young Benjie?'

'He has a bit of a cold, but the doctor says he'll be all right in a day or two.'

'Jolly good.'

'And you'll ask Penny to phone me when she arrives?'

'Yes. I'll do that. Jolly good. Goodbye, old man.'

Eben put down the phone and looked across the room at Tilly.

'She isn't there,' he said. 'The old chap hasn't been ill and she had no intention of going there before Monday.'

Tilly said nothing.

Eben said, 'Where would you say she'd be and what would you say she'd been doing? I don't know where she is any more than you do, but I'll give two guesses what she's doing.'

There were tears in Tilly's eyes.

'And, Tilly,' said Eben, 'do me a favour will you, girl? Don't talk to me about forgiveness, there's a good soul.'

As Mark said, it was a small world.

On the Monday morning he called at Deerfield. Eben was always glad to see him and so was Tilly. They were having a cup of coffee, and Mark was lighting a cigarette, when Eben, thinking that perhaps some explanation was due, said, 'Penny's gone off for a few days.'

Mark said, 'Yes, I know.'

'Oh,' said Eben, 'I told you, did I?'

'No. I saw her.'

'When?'

'Saturday evening.'

'Where did you see her?'

'In Swansea.'

'Good God! Swansea? What was she doing?'

'Just going into the Mackworth Hotel.'

'Well, by damn!'

Mark could see the surprise on Eben's face.

Tilly said, 'Are you sure 'twas her? Did you speak to her?'

'No, I was just crossing the road, but it was her all right.'

'How d'you know, Mark?'

'Good God, Tilly, what's the matter with you, maid? D'you think I don't know my own sister-in-law?'

'What was she wearing?'

'Well, you wouldn't expect a man to notice something like that, but as it was Penny a bloody blind man couldn't help it. She had a red and black hat like a bit of a clown in a circus.'

'You saw her all right,' said Eben.

'Well, shouldn't I have seen her?'

'Not in Swansea.'

'Where then?'

'Bolton.'

'Oh hell, no. I wasn't in Bolton.'

'Nor Penny wasn't, and even poor old Tilly here's got to admit that.'

Mark said, 'I hope I haven't said the wrong thing.'

'No, no, boy. You needn't worry about that. I've tried to make a go of it, but I knew in my heart it wouldn't work. I've had my suspicions this long time and it'll be the end now. Things have never been the same since that affair with that damn little rat who was here during the war.'

Mark looked at him with his mouth open and clicked his fingers in front of him.

'That's it!' he said.

'That's what?'

'I knew I'd seen the bugger somewhere.'

'Who?'

'Damn it, that was him. In Swansea. He crossed the road after Penny. Followed her into the Mackworth. As I stepped on to the pavement I nearly bumped into'n. And I thought the shifty bugger looked at me a second time.'

'Well, I hope he recognized you and that it spoiled their week-end for them.'

When Mark had gone, Eben had an idea. He found the number in the directory and phoned the Mackworth Hotel. When they answered he asked for reception.

'I'm sorry to trouble you,' he said, 'but is Captain Smith-

Gilmour still staying with you?'

'Hold the line, please, sir.'

'Thank you.'

After a short interval the girl said, 'Hello.'

'Hello,' Eben replied.

'I'm very sorry, sir. Captain Smith-Gilmour booked out this morning.'

Eben put the phone down, pondered a while, and then picked it up again and asked for telegrams. Benjie was much better and keen to return to school. Even so, Eben addressed the telegram to Penelope Harter in Bolton. The message read, 'Phone immediately. Benjie very ill. Eben.'

It would certainly ensure that she would have to phone and that there would be no misunderstanding on that score. Then he made a point of being out all the evening, so that Tilly would take the call when it came.

Tilly, it seemed, keeping the peace, had told her Benjie was now much better and for her to stay on for a few days. By the time she returned, Benjie had gone back to school and Eben had moved his belongings into another bedroom.

When Penny came home Eben arranged for a hire car to meet her at Kilgetty station. At first she had tried to lie, but then she began to cry and, holding out her arms, said, 'Can't we make it up? You'll come to bed with me tonight, won't you?'

'Come to bed with you? Go away, you tramp, I wouldn't feel clean.'

The real disillusionment for Eben had come years earlier. At some times he felt he had done his best to make a success of the reconciliation, at others he would admit that finding his wife in bed with another man had not been the best background for making such a reconciliation possible. Maybe he was not big enough to forgive as he should. Then he would think that, for this reason, there could have been no real hope for reconciliation right from the start. Then he would follow his past back a little further and wonder whether, if it had not been for this, he could have been happy with Penny. And always he came back to where he started and recognized that he should never have married her, that it was his own fault, that he had been responsible for making a mess of his own life. Now, as then, when he thought he had to marry Penny, the only thing to do was to make the best of it – and, once again, he thought it could have been worse.

The farm was in good heart, well stocked and prosperous. The buildings had been improved and his sixteen years or so of hard work had much to show for them. If things went wrong completely, and he and Penny parted, his own share would be considerable. Just because it was the end of married life, it would not also be the end of the world. He was nearing forty now and he had Benjie to consider. The chances were that the boy would be turning to him more in the future than he had needed to in the past, and Eben was very happy at the thought of being able to help or guide him.

Taking stock of the situation on the farm he realized that he would have to make changes. Billy Seckerson kept wheezing on, seemingly indestructible, and Owen had developed into an experienced and capable young man. But Megan had never been replaced, and now Merry, too, was leaving. Eben knew that he would miss her for far more than the work she did and the responsibilities she had always been willing to take.

It was an afternoon in early October when they went together to move some young cattle home from the meadow at Heronsmill.

'They're a bit young,' said Eben, 'and it's time for them to be nearer the buildings in case we need to feed them a bit of hay.'

When they reached Heronsmill it almost seemed as if the cattle had anticipated their coming. They were near the gate and needed neither calling nor driving. Kicking their hind legs and cavorting with heads down, they galloped off in the direction of home.

'There's less grass here than I thought,' said Eben. ' 'Twas time for them to have a change.'

He looked round the field and towards the tumbled-down old house. Merry saw his far-away look and said, 'You love this place, don't you?'

'It was my home, Merry. It holds such memories for me.'

'All happy ones?'

'I think so. Most of them anyway. I think we always tend to remember the good things from when we were young.'

'I've never really seen the place properly.'

Eben seemed surprised. 'Well, look at that, and how long have you been here?'

'Three and a half years.'

'Is it as long as that?'

'It is indeed.'

'And now you will only be here for another three and a half days.'

'That's very exact.'

'I'm counting them carefully.'

Merry laughed lightly. 'Are you looking forward so much to being rid of me?'

'Don't say that, Merry. You know why I'm counting them.'

'Do I?'

'You know well enough, Merry, don't you?'

Merry looked at his serious face.

'Yes, I know,' she said quietly.

They stood in silence a while, looking at the remains of the old house with the great sycamore tree now overshadowing it. The same old tree which Hannah had remembered so fondly in her letter when she had written to tell Aunty Becca that Cecil had died. Up at the Gangrel, where Hannah had been born, the pine tree seemed higher than ever.

'Come on,' said Eben, 'I'll show you where old Gramfer Jenkyn had his blacksmith's shop and tell you about some of my relations. Have I ever told you about my relations?'

'Some of them. Gramfer Jenkyn, of course, and Aunty Becca. And you've told me a lot about Rebecca out in Canada.'

'Funny that, because she's the one I know least about. I've never even seen her. But her mother was beautiful. Odd how young Rebecca just disappeared like that and nobody's heard a word from her for years.'

'That's life though. You're all of you only names, thousands of miles apart.'

'Perhaps you're right. But I've never looked at it like that. I've always felt very close to her somehow. Especially sometimes when I've been up here.'

Eben walked with her to show her the remains of the other cottages, and told her of his boyhood and some of the characters who had gone away. Eventually they came back down the lane to the remains of the old mill itself, its foundations covered in ivy and sprouting young ash trees. Had Eben not known where it was they could have passed it without even seeing it. The leat was still there but it had silted up and was almost overgrown.

'Look,' said Eben, 'the gates are all open – the cattle will find their way home all right. Let's walk back through the wood.' One plank of the footbridge had rotted and broken away. Eben gave Merry his hand to help her across and they held hands for some way as they walked. The autumn tints had dressed the wood in its seasonal glory of gold and russet and brown, and already a carpet of leaves had been laid. Ford's Lake rippled and tinkled quietly, because it was the season of the year when these things should be so. Everywhere there was a great stillness. For some time neither Eben nor Merry spoke. At last Eben said, 'It's a lovely time of year, but give me the spring.'

'You prefer the spring?'

'Oh, yes. It gives you new hope somehow.'

'And don't you like the autumn?'

'I like it all right. I suppose I like all the seasons. But the autumn has something sad about it.'

'And you react to the seasons and so you feel sad.'

'I'm very sad just now, anyway.'

They had reached the old stile and Eben stopped. Merry leaned against the stile and waited for him to continue. He did not say anything more, however, and Merry smiled at him.

'All right,' she said, 'you tell me why you're sad.'

Eben took her hand. 'Just as if you didn't know, I'm sad because you're going.'

'I'm glad about that.'

'Glad you're going?'

'No, you silly man. Glad you're sad because I'm going.'

'I couldn't be anything else.'

'I'm sad about it too.'

'I suppose you're bound to go? Your mind is made up?'

Merry smiled her wistful smile and said, 'Yes, I'm bound to go.'

'Why?'

She tapped him gently on the nose with the finger of her free hand. 'Because I don't believe in fairy stories for one thing. And for another thing, what would happen if I stayed?'

'Well, it could . . .'

'No, don't say it, Eben. You don't mind if I call you Eben, do you?' It was the first time she had ever used his name.

'I've asked you often enough,' he said.

'Yes, but I didn't want you to think I was trying to put on you like.'

It was a relief to them to laugh, but Eben returned to the subject. 'What were you going to say?'

'I was only going to say, don't let's spoil things. I know

what you're going to say, and you ought to know by now that I'm very fond of you. I don't think I shall every marry and I hope that I shall always have you as a very special friend.'

'Will you keep in touch?'

'Yes, I'll keep in touch, and I'll be concerned for you and to know what happens.'

'What do you mean, what happens?'

'Well, you don't think things can go on as they are, do you?'

'On the farm, do you mean, or with my wife?'

'Both.'

'You don't like my wife, of course, do you?'

'Could anybody like such a creature?'

'What d'you really think of her, Merry?'

'She's a bitch. And I wouldn't trust her further than I could throw a bucket of dirty water.'

'I suppose that about sums it up.'

'And, Eben,' Merry suddenly said very earnestly, 'don't you trust her either.'

Eben looked at her wonderingly. 'What d'you suggest I should do?'

'I don't know, my dear, I just don't know. But one thing you can do is get your solicitor to draw up a proper tenancy agreement making Tilly the tenant of the Lodge.'

'By God,' said Eben, 'I think I will. But what do you think will happen to the farm?'

'I just don't know. All I'm saying is, watch the sly bitch.'

'You really do hate her, don't you?'

'What else do you expect me to do when I've seen the way that she's treated you?'

Merry turned her face towards him suddenly and, with never a sign of resistance on her part, Eben took her in his arms. He held her close but made no attempt to kiss her. When he pressed his cheek against hers he felt the tears which she was silently shedding.

'Goodbye, my dear,' she said at last.

Eben said nothing. He helped her over the stile and they walked home in silence. The following day Eben went to Heronsmill to dig up some lily-of-the-valley for Merry to plant in her garden at home, because she had said they were her favourite flower.

The final parting, which he was dreading, was made very much easier because Tilly came to the station with them and wept as she said goodbye. Merry shed a tear, too, and when

Tilly took her in her arms and kissed her fondly, there was nothing more natural than that she should offer her face to Eben, too.

As Eben kissed her on the cheek, Merry turned to Tilly and said, 'Only platonic, mind. None of this old messing about!'

'Aw, God love her little heart,' said Tilly fondly. 'I wonder how she's getting on.'

It helped to ease the tension until at last Eben and Tilly were standing together on the platform and the train was disappearing round the bend for Templeton. Merry leaned out of the window and gave a last little wave before her carriage, and then the guard's van, were lost to sight.

Merry wrote to Eben shortly after she left and thanked him for his many acts of kindness, saying how much she had enjoyed her time at Deerfield and that those years would always have a special place in her affections.

It was the early summer of the following year before she wrote again, when the country had scarcely recovered from the most awful winter Eben could remember. Snow had followed more snow, pipes were frozen for weeks on end, hay made black-market prices and the War Agriculture Committee sent their people round to see that no farmers tried to keep hay over for another year. The nation itself was in every bit as parlous a state and as near to starvation. Working conditions on the farms were intolerable.

Merry wrote:

> I have been thinking a great deal about you all lately for I know the winter must have been a wretched time for you watering the stock and trying to move about.
>
> I already despair of the present Government. They upbraid capitalism and then borrow from America. Having borrowed the money they proceed to squander it on importing tobacco and American films. I try not to become too much of an old maid in my outlook too early in life but when I see people going around puffing at their cigarettes I sometimes feel like asking them do they know what is it costing the country when so many people are so near starvation. If only the Government would get its priorities right there might be some hope of the people doing so too. Can you imagine anything more Quixotic and lunatic than this East African groundnut business when they have at the same time succeeded in rationing bread which had previously been beyond the wit of Government throughout two world wars? What a staggering achieve-

ment! I know I once made my wise statement about wars having to be paid for but even I, in all my great wisdom, couldn't foresee the advent of this breakaway movement from Fred Karno's army!

I don't know what you think about the new Agriculture Act. I'm sure you'll know much more about it than I do, but I must admit to having serious misgivings. It looks wonderful, but I have read it carefully and can see all sorts of problems. At the moment there is a terrible shortage of food, and everything that can be produced is desperately needed. But what happens when there is no longer a shortage, and I am sure that day will come? It took the farming industry a good deal of its time during the war years to recover from the betrayal of the previous twenty years, but now that it has done so I am sure that we shall see huge progress and increasing production as a result of new techniques. And, of course, the sinister bit in the Act, which nobody seems to have noticed, is that the reference to agreed prices is only for as much of the nation's food as it shall be in the national interest to produce. Ridiculous though it may sound now, what happens when we are producing too much to suit the Government and they insist on importing foods from countries where we wish to sell our industrial goods? Can't you just see the politicians twisting out of what everybody believed to be their commitment? See how your cynicism about politicians has rubbed off on me! Or is it that my years on the land have shown me how to sort the wheat from the chaff and given me a sense of values which enables me to distinguish between the gold and the dross? I am sure your farming leaders are honest men and able enough in many ways, but they cannot hope to be of any match for the 'city slickers' (of any political shade) and, like Esau, who was also a man of the fields, they have probably sold their birthright for a mess of pottage. You see, I know my Bible too! I'm not just a cold-minded economist. And I fear I weary you.

The letter then passed on to other things. Eben gave it to Tilly to read. It took Tilly quite a time to get through it, but when she had finished she said, 'My word she've got a long head on her.'

'Yes,' said Eben, 'she's no fool.'

It was not long after this that Algie Bromilow came. Ostensibly it was for a holiday, but, unknown to Penny, Eben had written to him and asked if it would be possible for him to come down to discuss certain things which were worrying him.

Penny insisted on meeting him at the station herself, and

they were back by the time Eben came in from the fields. He had been taking an evening walk round some of the crops and wondering whether to start mowing. The terrible winter had been followed by a late spring but, when it came, everything had grown at an unbelievable rate and now the glorious weather was making handsome compensation for so much that had gone before.

Bromilow greeted Eben warmly and sounded cheerful, but Eben could see that he was tired and ageing.

Supper was not a pleasant meal. Eben saw no point in trying to put a face on things any longer. As far as it was possible, he tried to keep friction out of it by talking sport with his father-in-law at the first possible opportunity.

'I suppose you haven't seen any cricket this year?' said Bromilow.

'No, I haven't,' said Eben.

'Neither have I. But I hope to see the South Africans. And I'd like to see Compton and Edrich in the form they're in this year. Jolly good cricketers. Getting a stack of runs.'

Before Eben had a chance to reply, Penny began to talk to Tilly. He thought it best to ignore her.

'Any hope of you coming to Swansea with me to see Glamorgan?'

'Not a hope,' Eben replied.

'Pity. I'd like to see J. C. Clay bowling once again before he packs up. I saw Glamorgan once last year. Makings of a good side. You mark my words.'

'So they say, but I just can't seem to make the time to go anywhere.'

'Well damn it, let's make the effort and go to Swansea.'

Eben couldn't resist the temptation. 'I suppose we could have a meal at the Mackworth.'

'Mackworth! Whatever for? Take some sandwiches and a flask with us.'

The innuendo had been lost on Bromilow, and he did not see the hatred in Penny's eyes. He had not yet heard the true story of where Penny had spent her week-end on her circuitous way to Bolton.

'No,' said Eben. 'I'm afraid it's hopeless for me to think about it. We're ready to mow and we're short-handed. We've been allocated a new tractor but there's no sign of it coming through. I hardly know which way to turn.'

'I know the problem,' said Bromilow. 'I saw some cricket last year, but, damn it all, this year I haven't had a minute.

Damned quack looked at my heart the other day and said take it easy. Gave me some tablets. Take it easy! Damn it, I'm sixty-five and tied up with the mill again. Thought I'd left it behind years ago. Machinery worn out and these damned Socialists are ruining the country.'

'Your brother-in-law reckoned the machinery in the cotton industry was obsolete years ago.'

'Was it? Well, he'd know. But I still don't trust this Socialist crowd. Communists really.'

Eben hoped it would be possible not to distress Bromilow, yet he knew he would take the story of Penny's behaviour very badly. He was not sure how to approach the subject but he was prepared to wait for a suitable opportunity. Surprisingly, Bromilow was the first to speak of the matter.

They were just finishing breakfast when Penny said, 'Now then, Daddy, what d'you want to do today? I have to go to Tenby this morning so you can come with me for a run. It will do you good.'

As usual, she had it all organized in her own mind.

'No, not this morning, my dear. I know Eben has things to discuss with me. Might as well get it over and done with.'

'Whatever can he want to discuss with you that we can't talk about all together?'

Eben said, 'There's no need to go into that. I asked your father to come down to talk over certain things with me and that's what we're going to do.'

'What things?'

'Things I want to talk over with him.'

'In that case I'll stay.'

'No, there's no need for you to stay.'

'But I insist. If it concerns me I have a right to be there.'

'Who said it concerned you?'

Penny coloured. She was plainly flustered.

'Well, of course . . . I mean, you said, didn't you? I mean, what can you possibly want to discuss with Daddy?'

Bromilow looked at her. He said, 'Penny, will you leave us, please?'

She flounced from the room without another word and slammed the door behind her.

Eben said, 'Let's go outside for a stroll.'

'Good idea. Never could stand these damned tantrums.'

The garden had not recovered its former air of being cared for, which originally Burridge had given it, and which Jimmy Cockles and the odd casuals had contrived to maintain until the war and requisitioning. Eben thought it probably never would. But they had managed to hook down the worst of the weeds in a very rough fashion, and at least it looked like a garden. Climbing roses had taken a hold on parts of the walls, and the white and dark purple lilacs were at their best. Aubretia, too, had spread everywhere and bees were busy amongst the shrubs.

The sea, way down at the end of the valley, shimmered in the early heat of another beautiful day, and the distant waves were but slender white ribbons trailing along the golden shore. It was a peaceful and lovely scene, and Eben was loath to spoil it. A flycatcher had taken up position on a solitary post from which it was making sporadic, darting sorties above the long grass.

Again it was Bromilow who came to the point.

'I see things are going very badly between you and Penny,' he said.

Eben looked at him and wondered whether, even now, he could spare his feelings. Merry's words, however, were in his ears and he knew there was too much at stake.

'Our marriage is finished,' he said.

'Finished? What d'you mean?'

'We're finished.'

'Is it mutual?'

'I'm not sure, but I've certainly finished with her. You may have noticed that I am sleeping in the Lodge. Tilly is sleeping at Deerfield as company for Penny. In fact it's only having Tilly here that has enabled us to carry on, and I don't know how long even she can go on acting as a buffer and keeping the peace.'

'Well, what's the trouble?'

Eben said, 'You no doubt remember that awful row, when she smashed my mother's jug?'

'I thought that was all patched up.'

As fairly as he could, Eben told Bromilow of further suspicions after Deerfield had been requisitioned, and of the eventual affair with Smith-Gilmour. Penny had never been good to her mother, and had generally acquired an unsavoury reputation. Eben also told him how they had contrived to keep the truth from him at the time, and of their attempt at a reconciliation which had only led to her assignation with Smith-Gilmour in Swansea.

After a long time Bromilow said, 'My dear boy, I can't tell you how distressed I am. It was shameful of me not to have seen exactly what was happening. But what can I do now to help put things right?'

'I don't want any more to do with Penny, if that's what you mean.'

'But surely you didn't ask me to come down here to tell me all this?'

'No,' said Eben, 'far from it. I've hated having to tell you, but I had no alternative because you had to know the background for us to be able to come to some sort of financial arrangement or understanding.'

Bromilow frowned. 'I can't think what you mean.'

'Can't you?' said Eben.

'No indeed. I'm completely puzzled.'

'Well, put yourself in my position. You enabled me to start, by putting the deeds of Deerfield at the bank. Your word was enough for the little money I borrowed at first, and I'll always be grateful for the way you accepted me, and all you ever did for me. But you've seen how this place has been built up.'

'Yes, indeed. Marvellous what you've done here. I admire you tremendously.'

'That's nothing. I've had the benefit of the war years. But what security do I have?'

'I really don't know. Never thought about it. Tell me, if you don't think I'm being impertinent, what *is* your financial position? Are things all right with you?'

'Oh, very much so. As things stand at present. You know, of course, that Penny and I farm in partnership. In theory. In practice, everything has fallen on me, and I wouldn't want it any other way.'

'Yes, of course.'

'But she can sign cheques. And now I've told you of her behaviour you'll appreciate what it could have meant. I couldn't afford to take chances, so as soon as things began to improve I insisted on transferring a certain amount of any profits there were each year.'

'Transferring?'

'Yes. Half to Penny and half to me. What she's done with hers I don't know, but I've saved mine and I've got a few thousand put by.'

'Jolly good.'

'Yes, as far as it goes. But it means that most of the time, particularly if we buy anything or improve the buildings, we're working on an overdraft. That's no problem as things stand. There's plenty of stock to cover it anyway.'

'And Deerfield itself, of course.'

'Which is yours, and which you've no doubt left to Penny.'

'Yes, of course.'

Eben fell silent and allowed Bromilow time for the implications to register. 'I see what you mean,' he said. 'Very funny position.'

Eben still said nothing, and Bromilow continued to frown. Eventually, he said, 'What do you want me to do?'

'First of all, I want you to know that I'm not all that concerned about myself – except that I don't want to lose what I've worked so hard for, so I'd like to think I had some security. For the rest, whatever you leave to Penny, I hope you'll do it in such a way that Benjie's interests will be protected.'

Bromilow looked sharply at him. He said, 'Damn it all, you're not suggesting on top of everything else that she wouldn't do the right thing by her own child, are you?'

'Apart from the fact that she's your daughter and that you've always idolized her, can you tell me one single thing she's ever done in her life that was for anybody other than herself?'

Bromilow fell silent again.

'I don't care who gets into bed with her from now on,' said Eben, 'but whoever it is, I don't want him to get his hands on what should be Benjie's. Would you want that to happen?'

Bromilow shook his head. 'No, by God. Splendid boy. But to think it should ever come to this.'

Eben said with a touch of kindness, 'I'm sure I can leave that to you. For my own part I'd like a proper tenancy agreement. If you leave the place to Penny in trust for Benjie I'm willing to pay a proper rent, even if she goes off with somebody else. But I don't want her bringing somebody else in here.'

Bromilow looked weary.

Eben said, 'I'm sorry it's had to come to this, and that I've had to distress you like I have.'

'That's all right, my boy. I've been a fool for too long. It's partly my own fault.'

'Of course, you've only heard my side of the story. You can ask Penny for her side of it, but I don't want to be involved, for I know how bitter it would be.'

'No, I shall say nothing to her. I don't like rows either. My mind is made up. As soon as I get back to Bolton I'll see my solicitors and change my will leaving everything in trust for Benjie.'

'And the tenancy?'

'Yes, that must be done too. They can arrange with you about the rent, and they'll draw up a proper agreement.'

'Thank you very much,' said Eben. It was a weight off his mind.

Bromilow made no further reference to the subject and obviously said nothing to Penny. Indeed he seemed to enjoy the rest of his short stay, and on the day he left he joked about his health.

'Have to get back to see the quack. I've run out of his pills. Once this Bevan chap gets his damned scheme through I expect we'll all have the same pills for everything and have to wear his damned spectacles whether we want to or not. None of these damned Socialists any good.'

Late in the evening on which he was due back in Bolton, Jerry Forsdyke phoned to say that Algie Bromilow had been found dead in the compartment when the train reached Manchester. At the inquest, the coroner said that had the deceased had the prescribed tablets with him he could well be still alive.

In the weeks which followed, Eben could see the pit opening beneath him as surely as when he had realized that his father was not going to allow him to go to County school.

Algie Bromilow had been buried in Bolton, and Jerry Forsdyke, who readily understood Eben's inability to make the journey, handled all the arrangements. Penny went, and stayed for a week. As a result of the uncertainty and the strained relationship which had followed her escapade at the end of the last season, she had not accepted bookings from any of those who had written to her concerning summer holidays. This much Tilly knew and Eben was glad to hear it. Time and again Merry's warning came back to him, but he could see no way, now that Algie Bromilow was gone, to do anything to safeguard his interests. Interviews with the bank manager and solicitor proved to be cold comfort.

Eben knew that Deerfield would have been left to Penny. Their farming business was something separate and he had no claim on Deerfield or the land. There was no tenancy agreement and no rent had been paid. The moment it suited Penny, he was out.

When she came back from Bolton, she was self-assured and well pleased with herself, and Eben knew the reason. Twice during the ensuing weeks she went off for a few days without saying where she was going, and letters, typed and in business envelopes, arrived for her from time to time. Eben knew nothing of their contents or their source.

Throughout these difficult weeks he was not idle. Whatever was in store for him he would have to face up to it. He was, however, concerned as to what would happen to Owen who had now been with him eight years and had become almost a part of the place. From his early days at Deerfield, Penny had made it plain to him that she did not regard him as one of the family. In return, he hated the sight of her and quickly settled into a routine which did not bring him into contact with the house. Even when Tilly came, Owen was happy to go his own way and bring his own food.

'Don't you worry about me now, Uncle Eben,' he said, 'I can stand on my own two feet.'

Eben had given him responsibility and shown that he had confidence in him. The boy had responded accordingly, and they had not had a cross word the whole time they had been together. He took after his mother, with the build and looks of the Harters, and had something of the reserved and quiet nature of his father.

They had started haymaking when Eben made his first tentative approach to him concerning the future, and Owen told him that he was thinking of getting married. Eben knew that for the last two years Owen had been keeping company with a girl from down Carew way. He had met her once with Owen one Saturday evening in Tenby, and once when he had called on Esther in Saundersfoot. A nice, sensible girl he had thought her, and he knew that Esther was very fond of her.

'Well, that's good news,' said Eben. 'Have you decided where you're going to live?'

Owen looked a little uneasy. 'Not yet,' he said.

Eben wondered whether Deerfield figured in his plans for the future and said, 'I don't know what's going to happen here.'

Owen said, almost eagerly Eben thought, 'You think you may be sellin' up then?'

'I'm afraid it's almost certain. Why?'

'Aw well, that would make it easier. I've been wonderin' how to break it to you, because it means I'll be going and I didn't want to leave you down.'

'That's good of you, boy. I won't forget it either. When d'you plan to get married?'

'There's nothin' definite yet, but Sarah's brother have been gave the tenancy of a hundred-acre farm, only nobody don't know yet and she've asked me not to say where 'tis. He've worked home all his life and their mother said he's to have all the stock and she'll help a bit as well.'

'And where do you come into it?'

'Sarah's father's dead but her mother owns their place. Forty acres. She said when Sarah's brother goes we can have it but we got to stock it.'

'And when is her brother going?'

'Next spring.'

Eben thought for a little while, then he said, 'Tell me, Owen. Will you be able to stock it?'

Owen said, 'It'll be tight linkin', but we're gwain to have a go.'

'Good for you.' Eben was relieved and well pleased.

'What will your mother do?'

'She'll be all right,' said Owen. 'Sarah's mother have offered to go and live with George when they moves in the spring, and his wife wants her to go. Then Mother could come and live with us.'

'Sarah's mother sounds a good sort.'

'Aw, drop dead, one of the best.'

'D'you think your mother *will* come to live with you?'

'Why no! She won't hear of it. She got more sewin' than she can manage and lodgers in the summer. And now she've took up the piano again, for their organist in chapel reckons she can't go on much longer. She've got rheumatics in her hands and she've asked Mother if she'll help her out.'

The following day Eben said to him, 'I've been thinking it wouldn't be a bad plan to mow the two meadows at Herons-mill this year.' An idea was already forming in his mind.

Owen looked at him. 'Well good God! What have come over you?'

With the increasing use of machinery there had been less activity at Heronsmill. The grazing on the banks had never been good, and for years it had been more convenient to graze the two little meadows than to mow them. The lower meadow which old man Wier had insisted on being ploughed had long since been re-seeded.

Eben thought it would be better not to give Owen his real reasons just yet. Instead, he said, 'Have you been up there lately?'

'Not this last week or two.'

'Well I took a walk up there yesterday evening, and I've never seen such a change. We should have put some cattle up there long before now. Another ten days and it'll be fit to mow.'

'Which way we gwain to get it from there?'

'We won't. Make a rick up there, and we can drive a few more loads up from here to make a decent rick out of it, and then we can feed it to some cattle next winter.'

'Up there at Heronsmill?'

'Yes, we'll do that.'

Owen shook his head as he walked away. Half laughing, he said, 'Good God, Uncle Eben, I should think your troubles have gone to your head at last.'

Eben laughed too. What could Owen know of his troubles?

Worst of all was the uncertainty. And then, at last, it was Penny who said, 'Have you thought about what we're going to do?'

'Do? What d'you want to do now?'

'You know very well what I mean. About the way we're living.'

'What's the matter with the way we're living? It suits me all right.' Eben was sleeping at the Lodge.

'It doesn't suit me anyway. We can't possibly go on like this.'

'Why not?'

'Well, it's not natural between man and wife.'

Eben shook his head and said, 'Tut, tut. Fancy you still thinking of that sort of thing at your time of life. *Ych-a-fi*, as Megan used to say.'

Penny blazed, 'What the hell d'you mean, my time of life? I'm only thirty-three!'

'Thirty-seven,' he said, 'thirty-eight next birthday.'

'Well, what's that?'

'Not far off forty.'

'And what's that got to do with it?'

'It's an age when you ought to be thinking of settling down.'

Her face brightened. 'That's what I wanted to talk to you about.'

'About what?'

'Settling down.'

Eben looked at her steadily. He knew what line she was going to take.

'I suppose you know,' she said, 'that this place is mine now and everything that's on it.'

219

'Not everything that's on it.'

'Well, don't let's argue about it.'

'Not unless you want to.'

'The place is mine anyway, to do what I like with. I can sell it if I like.'

'Yes, I know that.'

'And what would you do then?'

'I'd have to get out, wouldn't I?'

'Yes, you would. And you don't want that, do you?'

'Not particularly.'

'Well then, it's up to you.'

Eben looked at her thoughtfully. He said, 'In which way is it up to me?'

'All we have to do is start again, live together properly and that's all there is to it.'

'Is it really?'

'Of course it is.'

Eben did not speak for a moment. Then he said, 'You didn't know my Gramfer Jenkyn, of course.'

'You know I didn't. And what's that got to do with it?'

'Pity. There was so much wisdom about him and he had so many apt sayings. *Inter alia*, as the saying goes, he used to say – "If they haves thee once, shame on them. If they haves thee twice, shame on thee." '

'You poor fool. Can't you see what I'm offering you? And all I'm asking you to do is come to bed with me tonight.'

'Bed! I'd rather get into bed with a tarantula spider.'

Penny took a deep breath. 'All right, Mister Big Bloody Harter. We'll see. Just wait till I'm through with you.'

Still very cool, Eben said, 'There's one thing you haven't mentioned.'

Penny looked blank.

'What's that?'

'What is Tilly going to do?'

'Tilly?'

'Yes, Tilly. You know, my cousin. Cheerful woman with dark hair going grey. You must have seen her about the place. She's been here for about five years, doing work that you should have been doing, looking after your mother whilst you were whoring about the countryside, cooking for people who were putting money in your pocket. Remember her? You surely remember Tilly. Where's she going to go?'

'She'll go with you, I suppose.'

'Well that won't be much good because I'll be on the road.

220

And I wouldn't be able to afford to pay her. She only came here anyway because of all the housework there is to do on a farm and you weren't prepared to do it.'

'She has a house of her own in Tenby, doesn't she?'

'You're a woman of property. Don't you know about tenants' rights these days? It's impossible to get your hands on your own property. And Tilly, poor soft-hearted fool that she is, when she was here looking after our interests she took pity on a family and let house to them and they're out of the same lousy mould as you are. And now she's stuck with that and can't get them out.'

Becoming impatient, Penny said, 'Oh, well, she'll have to go and live with your sister in Saundersfoot.'

'I see. And you've asked my sister if that will be convenient, I suppose?'

'Me? Of course I haven't. What's it got to do with me? I've got myself to think about. If you want to bother about Tilly, that's your own business.'

'Yes, it's my business all right. And I'll take care of it. But I just wanted to give you a chance.'

Later in the day Eben found Tilly in the Lodge. He knew by her eyes she had been crying.

'What's the matter, maid?' he said.

'You knows what's the matter.'

'No, I don't.'

She sniffled and blew her nose. 'I don't want you to think I goes about listenin' to people, but I happened to hear your row with Penny. I couldn't help it.'

'Well, what about it?'

'To think anybody could be so ungrateful after all I've tried to do.'

'You knew what she was years ago,' said Eben. 'And as far as a house is concerned you can stop worrying about that as well.'

'I'm not worryin' about that. But where can you find a house these days?'

'What's wrong with this house?'

'But she's gwain to sell that as well.'

'Let her sell it, then.'

'And then we'll have to get out. She told me to start makin' plans as soon as I liked. That's what have upset me, her bein' so ungrateful.'

'Let's have a cup of tea, Tilly, and I'll tell you something.'

*

Benjie, fortunately, was not due to come home until near the end of the summer holidays. He had gone straight from school for an indefinite stay with a school-friend who lived near Mumbles, where his father had a boat.

Benjie had only been on holiday a week when Eben had a short, but very sensible, man-of-the-world letter from him:

Dear Father,

I have just had a long letter from Mother saying how badly you have treated her and that she is selling Deerfield. I have always thought she was rather unstable. What she does not know is that I know about the business with the officer bloke when the army was there. Don't ask me how I know about this because it was all rather embarrassing and I would rather forget it.

Mother says that you will be on the road but if it's all the same to you I would like to make my home with you wherever it may be. If I can be of help now and you want me to come home let me know and I'll come straightaway. Knowing what the atmosphere must be like I should think you would rather that I stay out of the way, so unless you send an urgent Save our Souls sort of message I'll stay put.

I hope you won't mind this short letter but Thunderguts and his old man can't wait to put to sea and time and tide, especially the tide, won't wait even for them. I was anxious to get this short letter to you for you to know where I stand. Give my best love to Aunty Tilly. What a brick she is.

In haste,   Benjie.

Eben read the letter a second time and there were tears in his eyes. He thought it best to send Benjie a post-card with a short message. It read, 'We've nailed our colours to the mast. Stay there and enjoy yourself. Father.'

Two days later, Eben had a letter on very ornate paper from the Pugsy Property Development Company:

We write to apprise you of the fact that we have purchased the property known as Deerfield together with the Lodge and all lands appertaining thereto at present in the joint occupation of Mrs Penelope Harter and yourself. We hereby inform you that we intend to take possession during the third week in September by which time we expect you to have vacated the premises.

At Mrs Harter's request we have instructed the Narberth auctioneers and valuers, Messrs Pearce and Glanville, to wind up whatever partnership may exist between Mrs Harter and yourself. They will notify you in due course of the date on which they propose to sell all the stock by auction.

The letter was signed 'Claud Pugsy'.

'Tilly,' said Eben, 'what is it they say in offices, d'you know? I think they call it opening a file. So if that's what it is then we'd better open a file. I reckon we're going to have some correspondence with Claud before we're finished.'

He had already reconciled himself to losing what he had worked so hard to establish. Half of the sale money would be his anyway. And he could not put a price on being rid of Penny at last. He had survived not being able to go to County school. He would survive this too. Spring would come again.

Penny must have been feeling really vicious to have sold to Pugsy. Eben doubted whether she would have had the top price from him, but she would have thought it was a move likely to cause him the most humiliation.

Having thought things over very carefully he replied to Pugsy. 'Dear Claud,' he wrote:

Nice to hear from you with apprisals of your intentions appertaining thereto. Looking forward to having you as a neighbour. It will be great fun for us all. Do you want me to demolish the concrete drinking-trough or may I leave it as a reminder of happier days? I've become attached to the old thing somehow and would miss seeing it from the bedroom window each morning as I rise so cheerfully to greet the new-born day.

Eben read the letter to Tilly.

She smiled and said, 'Like Megan would have said, you're a bugger, aren't you?'

'Tilly, Megan wouldn't have said any such thing.'

'No, she wouldn't, would she, God love her. I hopes she'll be all right.'

'Of course she'll be all right. You've got to have faith, see.'

'Yes, I knows, but she's such a bitty. Imagine a tiny thing like her havin' a baby.'

'And what did she say for the names? If it's a girl it'll be Merrial Matilda, and if it's a boy just plain Ebenezer. Good God, Tilly, those New Zealanders must think we're like something just come out of the Ark.'

Before Tilly had time to say anything the telephone rang. It was from Pearce and Glanville's office asking if it would be convenient for Mr Pearce to call that afternoon. Eben could not have been happier about the choice of auctioneers if he had chosen them himself.

Gaffer Pearce – a small man, whom no one had ever seen

wearing anything other than buckskin breeches, leggings and well-polished brown boots – arrived a few hours later with his bowler hat, as always, on the side of his head, and carrying a heavy, yellow cane.

When Eben had greeted him warmly he said, 'Tell me, Gaffer, what makes you think you'll be my choice of auctioneers for this job?'

Gaffer Pearce looked at him over the top of his gold-rimmed spectacles. He said, 'Can you think of anybody else who'd be brave enough to shove his nose into this hornets' nest?'

Eben slapped his knee and burst out laughing. 'No,' he said. 'You've got a funny job on your hands.'

'I expect we'll manage.'

'I'm sure we shall.'

'Before we start though,' said Gaffer, 'I'd like you to know that I'm very sorry to be here and if I can help you in any way I'll be only too glad.'

'Thank you very much, Gaffer, but do you know, it's a funny thing and you might find it hard to understand – I'm almost relieved about it.'

Gaffer looked at him shrewdly. 'If I had two medals I'd pin 'em both on you for what you've put up with. Now let's get down to work.'

He took a notebook and pencil from his pocket.

'How many head of cattle have you got?'

'How many altogether? Or for the sale?'

Gaffer looked at him. 'What d'you mean?'

'Well, I've sold some privately. But they haven't gone yet.'

'Who to?'

'To my nephew who works for me.'

'Oh, ho?'

'Yes,' said Eben. 'Oh.'

'How many have you sold to him?'

'If you're interested I don't mind telling you. I've sold him the whole of what I call the Blackie family. They're all descended from a cow I brought with me from Heronsmill when I came here seventeen years ago.'

'I know the strain. And never a bad 'un amongst 'em. How many?'

'Altogether,' said Eben, 'there are eight cows, eight in-calf heifers and five bulling heifers and yearlings.'

'And what's he going to do with 'em?'

'He's getting married next spring.'

'Wait a minute.' Gaffer smiled. 'I've got it. Carew?'

'That's it.'

'Lucky chap. Good family. Hard-working, tidy family.'

'So they say.'

'But what'll he do with 'em till then?'

'Keep 'em at Heronsmill over the winter.'

'Heronsmill?'

'Yes. I've got the tenancy of that land myself. I've told the agent I'll be giving it up next spring. It won't be worth me keeping it.'

'How will he feed 'em?'

'Oh, we've fixed that. There's a good rick of hay there. I've given him that as a wedding present. A couple of cows are due to calve in the winter, but he'll have to rig up a bit of zinc over the old buildings and put some calves on the cows. He'll manage.'

'Very good.' Gaffer put his pencil to the notebook and said, 'How much did you charge him for them?'

'Not meaning no disrespects, as the old lady used to say, what's that got to do with you, Gaffer?'

Gaffer lowered his notebook and put his pencil back in his pocket.

'Go on,' said Eben, 'tell me. What's it got to do with you?'

Gaffer pushed back his bowler hat, took his pencil out of his pocket again and scratched his head with it.

'D'you know something?' he said. 'That's a hell of a good question.'

'You think so?'

'It is. You always have run the entire business, haven't you?'

'Exactly.'

Gaffer smiled and looked over his glasses. He said, 'I'm up with you now and about a jump ahead. As a matter of interest, how much time have you given him to pay for them?'

It was Eben's turn to smile. He said, 'As long as he likes. I've sold 'em to him worth the money and I've given it to him in writing that he doesn't have to pay for them until it's convenient.'

'That could be a long time,' said Gaffer.

'It could, couldn't it. And it's all the same to me if I never have it.'

'What about your wife's share?'

225

'When Owen pays me, nobody's going to have a penny of it. I don't care what you say about it, I know I'm in the right morally.'

'That's as maybe. But what would the law say?'

'There's only one way to find that out, and that would be for them to take it to court.'

'I can't see 'em doing that.'

'They wouldn't know where to start, Gaffer.'

'I don't suppose they would,' Gaffer smiled. 'You're a hell of a man, Harter.'

'Like old Gramfer Jenkyn used to say – "If thee'rt wantin' a row an' a rumpus just tread on the tail of my coat." '

'How do I stand with you on winding up the partnership?'

'Just sell the lot and pay me half.'

'You're happy with that?'

'There's nothing else for it.'

'Well, that's fair enough and it'll make things easier.'

'There's only one thing.'

'What's that?'

'I don't know what my wife got for the place, but, whatever it was, a good part of what she was selling was unexhausted manurial value and tenant right for improvements.'

'But you weren't a tenant.'

'Jointly we were. Of her father. In partnership, although paying no rent.'

'Good point. Worth arguing.'

'So half of what my wife receives for tenant right will be mine. I'm willing for you to value it. You can keep my half of it back out of my wife's share of the sale money when you settle up and add it on to mine when you pay me.'

'I'll discuss it with her.'

'You do that. And when you have her agreement in writing, and not before, I'll agree in writing for you to conduct the sale and wind up the partnership.'

'This on top of the cattle gone to your nephew will drive hell into her.'

'That isn't difficult to do.'

Gaffer scratched his head with his pencil again. 'Tell me,' he said. 'I'm about two jumps ahead now. What have you cooked up to annoy Pugwash?'

'I'm not going to annoy Pugsy.'

'Aren't you?'

'No. Just drive him raving mad.'

*

In the weeks which followed, scarcely a day passed without somebody coming to Deerfield to measure and make notes, inspect walls and windows, and point down the valley towards the sea. Nobody came near the farm buildings or the Lodge.

Neighbours could not have done more with helping to get things ready for the sale, organizing the implements and numbering the cattle. Mark sent two men for a day. The sale, a considerable financial success, came and went, and Owen 'got his name on the book' by buying the tractor he had cared for so well. Even Billy Seckerson put in a few bids. He reckoned he had wheezed his way to an honourable retirement and would now 'only do a day here and there now and again if I feels like it'.

The sale over, cattle and implements all gone, apart from a few desultory odds and ends which their buyers seemed disinclined to collect, Eben awaited developments and did not go far from the house. Mark had told him what some of Pugsy's plans were, and reckoned that the new Town and Country Planning Act would not make things any easier for him when it came into force.

Two days after the sale, Pugsy arrived. Eben was sitting in a wooden armchair outside the front door, and blessed his good fortune. He could not have arranged the place and manner of the confrontation any better.

A new car pulled slowly into the front at Deerfield and stopped. It was not easy to get a new car. From the corner of his eye, Eben saw that Clarence was at the wheel, with his father in the passenger seat. At least, he thought, it looked as if it must be Clarence.

For a minute or two they seemed undecided as to what their next move should be. When they finally got out of the car there was no possible doubt as to the driver's identity. It was Clarence all right. He must now, thought Eben, be something like twenty-four years old. He was an inch or two taller than his father, but was still more Pugsy than Pugsy, and still wore large horn-rimmed spectacles. He was over-dressed, had a cigar in his mouth and a large ring on the little finger of his left hand. A huge watch, with an elaborate linkage system serving as a strap, adorned his wrist. The watch and the ring were only outdone by the size of the design of the ornate cuff-links which showed below the sleeve of his jacket.

As they approached, shoulder to shoulder, but with Clarence slightly to the rear, Eben looked up and feigned a smile.

'Well, bless my soul,' he said, 'if it isn't Claud at last. My dear old sport, how pleased I am to see you. And isn't that fair vision young Clarence? How the lad has grown. In girth of course. You must have fed him well during the recent lean years, Claud.'

Pugsy glared at him. 'Harter, what the bloody hell d'you think you're doing here?'

Eben screwed up his face. 'Oh, dear! Claud! Your language! But I knew you'd ask that. I was just waiting for it. D'you know what I'm doing? I'm reading poetry. About this Horatius chap. Very brave man you know. Just three of them held a bridge against a host. I see you don't know it. Let me read it to you. Here – "In yon straight path a thousand, may well be stopped by three." Look at that, Claud, and here I am but one. But then, you are only two, except that the door is narrow and you're such a fat pair of slobs, aren't you? And I sit here – reading poetry. An inoffensive occupation to be sure.'

'This won't get you anywhere, Harter. You're supposed to be out of here.'

'Why, Claud? Why?'

'Because I've bought the place with vacant possession.'

'Have you really?'

'You bloody well know I have. From your wife who owned it.'

'And didn't she tell you I was living here?'

Before Pugsy could answer, Eben held up his hand. 'Don't tell me. She didn't. But then, she's like that. It was very naughty of her. Oh, yes, I'm living here, Claud. And very comfortable too. The place needs some repairs, of course, but you haven't had a chance yet. Rome wasn't built in a day. And talking of the Romans, this Horatius chap . . .'

'Listen, Harter. This bloody rubbish won't get you anywhere. I tell you, I own this place.'

'Indeed you do, Claud, and I'm glad you admit it, for repairs will certainly be needed. I know you own it. I simply live here.'

'You're not going to bloody live here.'

'Oh, but I am, Claud, I am. Do let me read this bit to you about the Romans – "Then none was for a party; Then all were for the state; Then the great man helped the poor, And the poor man loved the great." There it is, Claud, in a nutshell. And now those days have come again, with this new Welfare State. I must admit I had doubts about that Socialist mob, but not any more. I'm all for them. I see years of indolence stretch before me. Now we're all for the state, and you're the great man being privileged to help the poor and provide me with a roof over my head. Not a good one, as I said, but you can do it in time. I won't rush you, but don't be too long about it.'

Clarence could stand it no more. 'Don't listen to this nonsense, Pop. I'm going in.'

He elbowed his father out of the way, but Claud caught him by the arm. He almost hissed at him, 'Don't be a fool, Clarrie. You know what Goldstein said. Leave this to me.'

'There you are,' said Eben, 'it's all here – "Was none who would be foremost to lead such dire attack; But those behind cried 'Forward!' And those before cried 'Back!'" – I'll tell you what, Claud. You be Sextus and I'll be Horatius, and then I can say this bit – "Now welcome, welcome, Sextus! Now welcome to thy home. Why dost thou stay and turn away? Here lies the road to Rome!"'

Eben looked up and, with the banter suddenly gone from his voice, put down his book and said very quietly, 'You're not setting foot through this door.'

As if inviting an attack upon his person he stared at Clarence and said, 'The old concrete drinking-trough is still there. I asked your old man if I should dig it down, but he didn't take me up on the offer. And I said, you're not setting foot through this door.'

Brushing Pugsy aside, Clarence said, 'I'll bloody show you whether I'll go in or not.'

As he came forward, Eben raised his foot and planted the sole of his boot on Clarence's ample stomach, straining to halt the impetus of his onward rush. Then, gripping the arms of the chair, with one heave he straightened his leg and pushed Clarence back into the path of the oncoming Claud. The impact was fearful. Pugsy staggered and raged at Clarence, 'You bloody young fool! Goldstein told you that's just what he wanted you to do!'

Eben had not even risen from his chair, which was hardly a position from which a man could be accused of assault.

'Shall I tell you about the Kilkenny cats as well?' he asked.

Pugsy, for answer, pushed Clarence roughly towards the car. As they went, he shouted over his shoulder, 'You'll bloody well be hearing about this.'

'Clarence has dropped his cigar,' called Eben. 'And, Claud, you won't forget about the roof, will you?'

Two days later Eben received a letter by registered post. It was from Bloggs, Goldburgh, Goldstein and Bloggs and he had expected it. He had had copies made of the two documents in which he felt sure they would be interested, and he had given much thought to his reply and to the points he would make. He had discussed the position with Mark who felt he was on safe ground and who was already keeping his eyes and ears open concerning any planning applications.

Pugsy's solicitors kept their letter short and to the point, merely calling on Eben to remove himself immediately from Deerfield Lodge where, they said, he was a trespasser, and informing him that they had already commenced legal proceedings to that end and would also be claiming damages and loss of profits. Rather to his disappointment they made no reference to any assault upon Clarence. When he had replied to them to his satisfaction, he took the draft copy to Narberth to show to his own solicitor who read it carefully, smiled, and suggested a few very small amendments. Eben came home and copied it out.

'Dear Sirs,' he wrote:

How very pleased I was to hear from you. I always think it is nice to renew old acquaintances and your letter brought back a few very happy memories.

Old Claud seems to be like the laws of the Medes and the Persians which altereth not. He hasn't changed a bit has he, unless it be for the worse? And that could hardly be possible. Once again he has failed to tell you the whole story and I rather suspect he has only given you some garbled version of the true facts. Who was it said that all we ever learn from history is that we never learn from history? You shouldn't have believed him, of course.

If the truth were to be told, and indeed why should we not tell it, you really have no business writing to me, and your doing so could have caused some offence. Fortunately, I am not like that. You told me to remove myself immediately from the above address. The only person who has a right to tell me to do this is Miss Matilda Perrot whose lodger I have the pleasure and privilege to be. She really is a most excellent cook and housekeeper in every way.

Why then, you may ask, do I bother to write to you? I will tell you. It is because I pride myself on being a fair-minded man and great peace-maker to boot, and I hope that my doing so will save a great deal of unpleasantness all round. If, having been acquainted with the facts, you still feel like taking legal action, then by all means go ahead. My solicitors, by the way, are Jones, Evans and Jones of Narberth, and I think you will find that they will also act for Miss Perrot. You may not think much of their name but I have every confidence in them.

Miss Perrot has been the tenant of Deerfield Lodge for some twelve months, paying a rent of ten shillings a week, with the landlord paying the rates. The rent is payable twice yearly, three months in arrears and three months in advance, the half-yearly rent being thirteen pounds. Her tenancy agreement gives her unimpeded access, without let or hindrance, by motor vehicle through the drive which crosses Deerfield front and I hope you will take particular note of this in view of planning proposals which, rumour has it, Claud has in mind. The agreement also specifically states that the landlord shall keep the place in proper repair, but more of that later.

I enclose a copy of this agreement. When you have perused it you may do with it as you wish, but I would suggest that if you would care to have it framed and presented to Claud he would appreciate it immensely.

You will also notice, I feel sure, that it was I who signed this agreement as the then landlord in partnership with my wife, and the thought occurs that you may therefore question its validity. This brings me to the second document of which I enclose a copy, and that is the most recent audited balance sheet of our farming partnership. You will see from this that the rent from Miss Perrot is shown as a receipt, and also that my wife drew a half share of the profits, so that she was obviously a willing party. If you say she was not consulted on this particular point I can only reply that neither was she consulted on any other decisions which I took and which were very much to her financial advantage. It had become imperative to the running of the business for Miss Perrot to remain, and I therefore took the course I did. You may argue it which way you like, but the sympathy of the Courts seems to be all with the tenant these days and, although I am not a betting man, I'll give you pretty good odds as to which way the verdict would go if you were so misguided as to attempt to obtain possession. Wouldn't old Claud make a good witness? I think Clarence would do even better, especially if he wore those cuff-links. Can't you just see them in the setting of a rural county court?

Now then, to the repairs. I had promised Miss Perrot that the roof would be stripped and a new roof put on as soon as a licence could be obtained and materials became available. She now requires this to be done and trusts that you can attend to the matter.

In due course I have no doubt you will be writing to Miss Perrot and, in due course, she will undoubtedly reply. You will read her letter and recall how Isaac said, 'The voice is Jacob's voice, but the hands are the hands of Esau'. It is Old Testament so you will no doubt know where to find it.

I did write to old Claud a little while ago to say that as we would be neighbours it would be good to live at peace, but obviously he didn't take me seriously. Even so, just assure him that I shall be his neighbour, if he comes to Deerfield, for as long as it suits me. I am sure Miss Perrot will allow me to remain.

A week later Tilly had a letter from Bloggs, Goldburgh, Goldstein and Bloggs giving her notice to quit. In a slow hand she copied out the letter which Eben had written for her with the proper counter-notice and, for good measure, saying that the housing authority's inspector had now seen the house and said it should have new windows as well. She would now be taking steps to see that the landlord was compelled to do this work.

Before Christmas Mark reported, with a twinkle in his eye, that Pugsy's planning proposals had run into trouble. The access to the Lodge was a particular problem. Early in the New Year, Deerfield was up for sale. With a sitting tenant in the Lodge, he lost money on the deal. Eben insisted on pouring Tilly a glass of sherry at supper-time.

'Let us drink to the health of Miss Merrial Singleton and give thanks for her far-seeing wisdom,' he said.

'That's jake,' said Tilly. Even she had found it difficult to love Pugsy.

Eben added, 'Or as the poet said, Tilly, "And even the ranks of Tuscany could scarce forbear to cheer." '

When Deerfield came on to the market, Eben considered buying it. Mark said he could help him to raise the money and, with his own half of the proceeds of the farm sale, plus what he had saved, he felt he was financially strong enough to be able to do it. There were, however, restraining factors.

He could not forget the country's betrayal of farming, the awful consequences of which he had seen when he was a boy at Heronsmill, in the years following what was now called 'the First War'. There was always the chance that the same thing could happen again following this Second War, and Merry had seen the possibility of this in her reading of the new Agriculture Act. It was anybody's guess. He was determined, too, that as much as possible of what he had should be available, if it should be needed, to help Benjie to complete his education.

Thinking of Benjie prompted him to think that to do what he was now contemplating was more a task for a married man than for a man on his own. He was neither widower nor bachelor and had given no thought of divorce, nor had he any thought of the possibility of marrying again. Normally, Tilly would no doubt have been willing to keep house for him, but it was here that the biggest problem of all arose.

In the previous summer Griff's wife had undergone an operation, and it had soon become apparent that it had not been successful. Deerfield had only been on the market a short time when Griff wrote to say that she was now very ill. Tilly went away to do what she could to help and stayed on for a short time after the funeral. Eben was more concerned about this than about his own affairs, and Deerfield was sold before he was able to make any decision. Life was like that, he thought. No doubt things would sort themselves out in time.

There was a further complication. Not long before his wife had had her operation, Griff had bought a house with some land not very far from Heronsmill ready for retirement to his beloved Pembrokeshire. Mark had obtained the licence for the building materials, and the builders had almost finished their work of improvement and decorations by the time Griff's wife died. Griff now began to have misgivings about the house being empty, fearing that it might be requisitioned because of the housing shortage, and he asked Tilly if she would go and live in it. He had a vague sort of idea that, when he was able to retire, Tilly could stay on and keep house for him.

The idea seemed to make sense, particularly when the young couple who had bought Deerfield called at the Lodge to make themselves known. When they realized that Eben had never had any intentions of continuing to live there, and had only made a stand in order to make life difficult for Pugsy, they made no attempt to conceal their relief. Eben was delighted that they had been able to buy the place, especially as they only wanted to farm it. Already there were signs of what the developers were going to do to the area. He arranged with them to be out by the spring but had no idea what he would do for a living. His mother, he thought, would have reminded him about the sparrows and the lilies of the field.

3

Heronslake

And notwithstanding all the sorrows they had seen before their eyes, and notwithstanding that they had themselves suffered, there came to them no remembrance either of that or of any sorrow in the world.

The Mabinogion

Eben had scarcely settled in with Tilly in Griff's house near Heronsmill when Penny wrote suggesting that they should be divorced. She explained that her solicitor could arrange for Eben to provide her with grounds to divorce him. He ignored the letter.

Even so, he was somewhat surprised when she phoned him a few weeks later.

'You haven't answered my letter,' she said.

'No, and I don't intend to.'

'Do you mean you won't even divorce me?'

Eben suddenly remembered her throwing the primroses into the stream and then trying to prove that it was his fault.

'You haven't changed a bit,' he said.

'What's that supposed to mean?'

'As devious as ever. Trying to imply now that I've refused to divorce you.'

'Well, haven't you?'

'No. But I'm not giving you grounds to divorce me, and I'm not wasting good money getting rid of you. So work it out for yourself.'

Eventually, Eben did divorce her, and Penny, in an undefended action, paid all the costs. He cared little about what some would have described as his freedom, but he was thankful to be rid of her at last. The sorrow and resentment had gone long since.

At least he had the satisfaction that Benjie was doing well. He had gone straight from school into industry in Birmingham. He made his home – if such a term could be applied to a place where he spent the occasional holiday – with Eben and Tilly, but he kept in touch with his mother and saw her occasionally too. It was from Benjie that Eben heard of Penny's remarriage, this time to a dashing Lothario younger than herself, whose every movement she watched with the eye of a hawk.

Tilly seemed to regard herself as settled in life, and looked forward to Griff's retirement. Eben meanwhile, in his hours at home, applied himself to improving the place, and eventually this became a consuming passion.

The house, now that it had been rebuilt, had three good bedrooms and another smaller room which could serve as an extra bedroom should the need arise. A downstairs wall had been knocked through to make two rooms into a very pleasant lounge, and Griff had insisted on the best equipment for the kitchen. Some solid, stone-built outhouses had been converted for use as a garage and large workshop.

But it was the land that Eben loved above all. The little place extended to about thirty acres, and through the summer months Eben grazed this with odd cattle or a few sheep which he had picked up cheap around the farms where his new business took him.

It was a business which he had started up at Mark's instigation, with Hugh Wogan, a former employee of Mark's who had just come out of the navy. They dealt in eggs, poultry and rabbits. Hughie ran the shop in Saundersfoot, and Eben did the buying around the farms.

Eben enjoyed the contact with other farming people, but it was his own land that he loved the most. Some of it was useless. A small field sloped away southwards from the front of the house to about three acres of rush and wilderness adjoining the boundary stream. The more he looked, the more he determined to do something about it.

When Eben wrote to tell Griff what he proposed, Griff wrote back and told him he must be made to consider shedding so much sweat to such little purpose. Eben wrote back to say that it was, on the contrary, to great purpose; by the time Griff retired it would be a place fit for an ex-city gentleman to live. In any case, he, Eben, would have the pleasure of visiting Griff and Tilly to look at his handiwork from time to time. Griff replied that he had hoped, with the way things were going, that Eben would stay on.

Whenever he could find the time, Eben, often stripped to the waist, would be found swinging axe or long-handled hook, felling gnarled trees and clearing matted brambles. When it was too dark to work he would read, as often as not these days about ponds and their construction, their plant and animal life and the birds they could attract. Once the way had been cleared, an earth-moving machine made short work of the rest, banking the sides in a few weak places and adding to what was already a small natural island in the middle of the pond. Here he planted a weeping willow and clumps of bamboos. Then, at last, he piped in water from the stream.

Soon after the lake had been completed Griff came home for a short visit and saw it for the first time. Eben thought he was looking very much older. Griff was delighted and said that, having done as much as he had, Eben might as well build a small landing stage and have a rowing boat.

The morning after his arrival, Griff looked through his bedroom window and to his great delight saw a heron standing statue-still on the island.

'It's prophetic,' he said. 'It's a sign. Like Moses and the cloud and things like that. You pair of heathens wouldn't understand. But they had things like that in the Bible. It's like a prophecy or something telling us to change the name of the place. I never did think much of the name, did you? Primrose Villa. Why didn't they call it Dunroamin'!'

'What d'you want to call it now?' asked Eben.

Tilly said, 'I thinks Primrose Villa's a lovely name.'

'I know it's pretty, Tilly, but here's this heron turned up to remind us of the old home, so we must act accordingly. This very minute. What about Heronspond?'

'That would be lovely,' said Tilly.

'Or Heronsflight. Or Heronsway.'

'Heronspond, I think,' said Eben.

'Wait a minute, what about Heronslake?' enthused Griff.

Eben considered. 'That would be good. Then it could refer to the pond or the stream. Sounds good too. Heronslake.'

'Heronslake,' said Griff. 'That's it. Heronslake.'

Griff indeed was greatly enthusiastic. He could now see the possibilities of what could easily become a lawn sloping down to this beautiful expanse of water. Eben had left the best trees, including some handsome oaks, which would provide acorns for the wild duck, and, even now, before anything had had a chance to start growing on the newly made banks, the place had assumed a new and distinctive character. Occasionally, after his return to London, Griff would send some shrubs or a few trees which he had bought somewhere.

'It's a great thing,' said Eben, 'to see old Griff taking such an interest. By the time he retires he'll have become a part of it.'

'I wonder,' said Tilly.

'What d'you mean, girl?'

'I don't know,' she said. 'Sometimes I just wonders, that's all.'

During the next five or six years, Eben prospered in business and found complete contentment at Heronslake. But there were one or two happenings which meant something special to him. One of the sadder of these was the sudden passing of Billy Seckerson.

Billy had reached his sixty-fifth birthday, the summer before Eben left Deerfield, and he had enjoyed the next couple of years at home pottering about on his little place. The years undeground had taken such a toll of him that it was remarkable that he had lasted as long as he had, yet his wiry, if not robust, frame had seemed so indestructible that he was somehow not the sort to be expected to die of a heart-attack in his own garden.

Whilst Billy was lying in his coffin in the front room, with the curtains keeping out the spring sunshine, they found Zulu dead in the field. As Billy would have said, 'That's how the world's made, I reckons.'

The day after Billy's death, Eben called to see if he could be of any help and found Mark already there on the same errand. Rachel was expected home from London later in the day. She had fulfilled her young ambition to become a nurse and apparently was doing well. Young Tommy was now about seven years old and had been 'brought up at his granny's'. To him, Billy and his wife were his father and mother, and Rachel his sister, but Billy had more than once told Eben that Rachel had never failed to send money home although they had tried to persuade her there was no need to.

On the day of the funeral a surprising number from the rural community turned out to pay their last respects, including some of those who had worked with Billy underground in his earlier years. Maybe he had done no mighty deeds in his time, but he had done no harm, and Thomas Gray had known enough men of his kind to pen the lines of his 'Elegy' in such a country churchyard as the one where they were now gathered.

Amongst the large family Rachel walked on her own as they returned slowly from the graveside. She wore a plain black coat with a white collar and cuffs, and a small black hat with white lace trimmings. She seemed self-possessed but, as she passed, she looked at Mark, and Eben saw in her eyes a sadness and a longing that had nothing to do with the loss of her father. He saw, too, the anguish in Mark's eyes as he returned her gaze.

Eben's business was prospering and he now employed a man and a boy and had put another van on the road. He was planting some young trees one afternoon well into the winter following the Coronation, when he heard Tilly calling. Looking up he saw her wave frantically and he hurried up to the house.

'Quick! Quick!' she called. 'In here! In here!'

Tilly was staring excitedly at the new television. With a sudden racing pulse Eben saw the face he remembered so well and which, for so long, he had been trying to forget.

'Well, thank you very much, Doctor Singleton, for joining us in our programme, and may we wish you every success in your new post.'

Merry smiled her lovely smile and, while the camera was still on her, Eben, as if someone had plunged a knife in his heart, noticed a dress ring on the third finger of her left hand, and suddenly realized how much she had always meant to him. He had not seen her since she had gone away, more than seven years ago, and now here she was on the screen, and all her fresh beauty and lovely nature were as alive for him as if she were in the room. She had written to him occasionally, and he had continued to write to her, but she had never made any reference to the possibility of a man in her life.

'Well, look at that,' said Tilly, as the camera swung away from her.

'What's it all about?'

'Oh, I don't know half all.' Tilly was almost breathless with excitement. 'But she've just been gave some wonderful job with some big firm and it's the first time for a woman to have the job. Well! Well! When I seen her I couldn't believe it. Fancy our Merry.'

'Did it say what sort of job it is?'

'Oh, Law, I don't know what they said, only I couldn't take my eyes off her. Fancy our Merry, and she looked lovely.'

'Let's have a cup of tea now I'm here.'

Tilly was making the tea when the phone rang. Eben answered and heard Mark's voice saying, 'Did you see the television?'

'Just the end of it. Tilly called me but I was down by the lake and I missed most of it.'

'By damn, boy, she's got her head screwed on.'

'What's the job she's got, then? I haven't been able to get much sense out of Tilly.'

'Senior economist with a big industrial firm, but I didn't catch their name.'

They exchanged a few pleasantries before Mark rang off. Scarcely had Eben replaced the phone when it rang again.

This time it was Owen, bubbling with excitement. And his wife had met Merry one day in Tenby when she was at Deerfield and she remembered her because she was lovely and so she was excited as well. But Owen was the really excited one, he said, because he had worked with Merry.

'But I wouldn't have saw her only Sarah called me because I was out in the cowshed and Sarah remembered her as soon as she seen her and she called me so I come running and gaw she looked good, didn't she!'

Eben thought how proud Megan would have been.

There were a few more phone calls and he began to wonder how many people must watch television.

Eventually Tilly said, 'What was that you was explainin' to me about them callin' her Doctor Singleton? I was so excited the first time I wasn't listenin' properly. You reckon she isn't a proper doctor?'

'No, no, girl. I didn't say that. I said she isn't a medical doctor. She's a doctor of philosophy.'

'How is that then?'

'It's a degree.'

'She must be clever.'

'Of course she's clever. But she was clever when she was with us milking cows.'

That evening as Eben sat reading by the fire he suddenly decided to phone her. It would be the most natural thing to do, yet his heart raced at the thought of hearing her voice again.

The number was engaged at first, but the operator said she would keep the call in hand. It was gone ten o'clock when the phone rang. Eben picked up the receiver with a hand that was trembling and heard the operator say, 'Your number is ringing now.'

A man's voice answered and Eben said, 'I wonder could I speak to Dr Merrial Singleton, please?'

'Who is speaking, please?'

'My name is Eben Harter.'

'Eben Harter?'

'That's right.'

There was a pause.

'Not Merry's Eben Harter? You mean where she was during the war?'

'Yes, that's right.'

'I say, how exciting! But look, old chap, Merry hasn't come home yet. Did you see her on television?'

'Yes indeed. That's why I phoned.'

'Well, how very kind of you. I'm her father, by the way. She's going to be terribly disappointed to have missed you. I tell you what, give me your number and Merry can ring you when she comes in. Let me get a pencil and I'll write it down. What's that? She has your number? Well, that's fine.'

'There's no need to bother her,' said Eben half-heartedly, 'I just wanted to congratulate her and tell her now nice it was to see her.'

'Oh, no, it's not the same. She'll want to speak to you. I know she will. What time do you go to bed?'

'Oh, any old time.'

'Well, I'll see she phones you, and thank you so much for ringing.'

When Tilly had gone to bed he recognized the futility of trying to read. He put a couple of logs on the fire and prepared to wait, just listening to the slow steady ticking of the old clock. When it struck midnight he knew not to expect a call now, but he still sat on and went over everything in his mind once again. How very friendly her father had seemed. How much had Merry told her family about him? And whose ring had she been wearing? Her letters had said nothing about any men friends.

The first ring of the bell shattered the silence and Eben was out of his chair and across the room and the receiver was in his hand before it could ring a second time. His mind was in a whirl as he said, 'Hello.' Then he heard her voice and said, 'Merry?'

'Of course it's Merry. Who else were you expecting to phone you at this time of night?'

'I'd given up all hope of hearing from you.'

'It was sweet of you to ring.'

'I'm afraid I missed most of your interview. What's the new job?'

'Well, mainly it will be to prepare a report on this European unity business.'

'Does that mean you'll be going abroad?'

'Yes, Paris.'

'How long for?'

'About a year.'

'Pity.'

'Tell me,' said Merry, 'how is dear Miss Perrot, Aunty Tilly?'

'Blooming. And she sends you her love.'

'And give her mine, won't you?'

'Why don't you come down and give it to her yourself?'

'Oh, Eben, I'd love to. You know I would.'

'Then why don't you? I've asked you often enough.'

Merry went quiet for a moment, then she said, 'I'm afraid to.'

'Afraid? What on earth are you afraid of?'

'Afraid I'd find out that I could believe in fairy stories after all. One reason I'm so late phoning is that there were some friends here when I came home and I wanted everybody out of the way before I phoned. So there's a confession for you.'

'Merry, why don't you come down for a holiday?'

'I'll think about it. I really will.'

'Tell me something. Who's the man?'

'Man? What man?'

'The man whose ring you're wearing.'

He heard Merry's lovely laugh.

'Good heavens, did you notice that?'

'Of course I did.'

'It was my grandmother's.'

'Well, why wear it on that finger?'

'It's just to keep the wolves away. The decent ones keep away and a girl knows exactly what line to take with the other ones.'

'Why keep them away?'

'I told you long ago. I'm not the marrying kind.'

'Pity.'

'Why?'

'Because I might ask you myself.'

Merry laughed again.

'Is there a man anywhere?'

'Don't be silly,' she said quietly. 'You know there's only ever been one man in my life.'

'And who was that?'

'If you don't know that, Mr Harter, you must be quite stupid. Now go to bed, and dream sweet dreams.'

But Eben did not go to bed. His heart was singing and he took some of Merry's letters, every one of which he had kept, and read them far into the night.

The next year dragged by for Eben, and it was a disappointment for both him and Tilly to hear from Benjie that he would not be home for Christmas.

In a previous letter he had said, 'We went out for a run

last week-end to the Lickey Hills, and it really was quite something.' The next letter said, 'Last week-end we went out to Clent, which is a beautiful spot.' When Eben wrote he asked Benjie when they might expect to hear something more explicit about 'we'.

Benjie replied in due course. He said:

> I take your point about the 'we'. 'We' is female and is quite a dish. She is a pathologist in one of the hospitals here. Her name is Jackie, which is short for Jacqueline, and she is a superb cook . . .

He then went on to say that Jackie, whose people lived near Esher, in Surrey, had invited him home for Christmas as her parents wanted to meet him.

> So it could be a case of getting my feet under the table as the saying goes. Maybe they're concerned in case she's cradle-snatching, for Jackie is three years older than I am. Nothing has been said, of course, and I don't think irate fathers these days demand of young men to know what their intentions are towards their daughters. I'll let you know if there's anything to report.

There was more to report and perhaps more quickly than Eben had expected.

On Christmas Eve, Benjie phoned. 'Father,' he said, 'I thought you'd like to know that Jackie and I have become engaged. Sorry you couldn't be here but all very sudden. Jolly good. Grandpa Bromilow's idea of life. No fuss. Over and done with. Jolly good.'

'And when can we expect to have the pleasure of meeting the young lady?'

'As soon as I can manage it, but I've got a big job on at the moment. One thing I must tell you. I had to go down to Cornwall a fortnight ago and I stayed a night with Mother. She calls her husband Tootsie. Need I say any more? But I'll have to ask them to the wedding I suppose.'

'It's your wedding, and she's your mother.'

'I have no doubt you'll be able to cope with the situation.'

'I'll do my best.'

'But, Father, there's something else you may be interested in. Or somebody, rather.'

'You're making it sound very mysterious.'

'Well it's not mysterious. Just one of these things about it being a small world and all that. There's been someone here this evening who knows you rather well. Talked about you

245

all evening. I think she's gone on you quite frankly.'

'She?'

'Yes, she.'

'What are you talking about, son?'

'Not what, Pops old bodykins. *Who.*'

'Well, who then?'

'Who Father? Well, who else but the divine Merrial Singleton?'

'Benjie. Talk sense, will you.'

'Sense? My dear honoured and esteemed old parent. Never talked more sense in my life. She's an absolute stunner. I only remember her in that ghastly Land Army uniform when I was too young to appreciate the female form divine anyway. But she's a raving beauty.'

'Well, what on earth is she doing at your future in-laws'?'

'Doing? Why, drinking to our future happiness, of course.'

'But why?'

'Oh, friend of the family. Very old friends. But I told you, didn't I? Small world and all that. By the way, Father, she's gone now but Merry said to tell you she'll ring you tomorrow evening.'

'Benjie,' Eben said, 'if she's an old friend of the family will you be asking her to the wedding?'

'I suppose so.'

'Don't suppose anything. Just make sure she's invited.'

'I say, Father, you haven't got ideas about her, have you?'

'Never you mind about ideas. Just make sure that she's at the wedding. And, come to think of it, the sooner you get married the better.'

The letters between Merry and himself had now become more frequent and affectionate and, although it was one of the quietest Christmas days he had ever spent, Eben could not remember one when he had been more excited as he watched the clock towards evening and waited for Merry's promised phone call.

She was bubbling with laughter when she rang. Eventually she said, 'What a character your Benjie has become. He came round this morning to warn me that he thought you had designs on me.'

'Of course I have. How long are you home for?'

'Only a few days.'

'And when will you be back?'

'In the spring maybe.'

'Merry,' said Eben, 'are you holding out hope for me?'

246

'Let's talk about things in the spring.'

'Don't you know your Tennyson?'

'Not like you do. What did he say?'

' "In the spring," said Tennyson, "a young man's fancy lightly turns to thoughts of love." The only thing is I'm no longer a young man.'

'How old are you now?'

'I'm forty-seven.'

'You poor old man. And have you gone completely white on top?'

'No, not yet. Just a few grey hairs around the temples.'

'And don't you know your country sayings? And you always telling me what your gramfer used to say.'

'What country saying do you mean?'

Merry laughed again. 'Don't they say it doesn't matter about a bit of snow on the roof as long as there's a fire in the hearth?'

'Yes, there's fire in the hearth, but . . .'

'Eben, there go those pips again.'

'All right.'

'Good night then, my dear. I'll write to you soon.'

'Good night. And take care of yourself.'

'I will. And God bless you.'

Spring still seemed very far away.

It was some weeks later that two letters arrived within days of each other.

The first, bearing a Canadian stamp, was addressed to Tilly and was from Rebecca. She had, she said, written twice following the death of her mother, but not having a reply on either occasion, somehow did not get round to writing again. Eben and Tilly talked about this and then recalled that, following the death of Billy Thank-you-Ta, a younger man had done the job for some time before it was discovered that he had a mental weakness and was known to have burned many letters. It later transpired that, shortly after Hannah's death, the family with whom Rebecca had been living had moved to another area, which seemed to account for the fact that Rebecca had never received the letters which Tilly and Eben had written to her at the time.

'And so you will be seeing your Canadian Rebecca at last,' she wrote. She was coming for a few weeks in May, and would write again when she had been able to make more definite arrangements.

Rebecca had addressed her letter to Heronsmill. Eben answered by return of post. Tilly cried and laughed alternately in her excitement and said they would have to write to Griff as well.

The other letter came two days later and was from Benjie to say that he and Jackie would be getting married in May.

An invitation will be coming in due course, enjoining you to R.S.V.P. and all that, but this is to give you as much warning as possible so that you can make all the necessary arrangements for ensuring that nobody will run off with your lake whilst you're away. And, of course, you will no doubt be wanting to set the wheels in motion for hiring the usual glad rags which seem to be the recognized attire for such occasions.

I have already written to the well-known lady economist to make sure, as far as it lies within my powers to arrange such a thing, that she will be there.

When Rebecca's next letter came she was able to give more details of her proposed trip, and Eben and Tilly were both delighted to know that she would be with them for Benjie's wedding.

The following week-end Benjie brought Jackie home to Heronslake. Tilly looked at her, put her arms round her and kissed her and said to Benjie, 'Isn't she lovely?'

She had honey-blonde hair and dark brown eyes with a generous mouth and open expression. She was of medium height and had a beautiful figure.

'I always knew that Benjie was no fool,' said Eben.

'Do you mean I've passed inspection?' Jackie laughed.

Tilly put her arms round her again and said, 'Oh, isn't she lovely?'

When Rebecca came, Griff met her at the airport and she stayed with him for a week. Her Uncle Griff, she told them when she came to Heronslake, had really 'given her a ball'.

Eben had told Griff to put her on the train for Swansea.

'It's a very slow journey from there on,' he said, 'even when the train doesn't break down. Why don't you come down with her? You haven't been for a long time.'

'Don't tempt me. I've got a lot on just now and I'd also due to go into hospital for a check-up.'

'Well, you know best. Will we know Rebecca when we see her?'

'Know her? Just look for Hannah, that's all.'

Eben had loved Hannah. Young as he had been when she went away, he remembered her well. Her leaving had been the most important thing in his life until his mother died. He wondered how he would feel towards this only child of Hannah, who had always had such a special place in his thoughts. Then he realized with a start that Rebecca must now be about forty. Yet when she stepped from the train he knew that he would have known her in the biggest crowd on earth.

Rebecca wore a light-weight costume of scarlet with a white blouse. A pale blue chiffon scarf was tied loosely at her throat, and Eben saw that she wore on her lapel the fine gold brooch of intertwined hearts which Cecil had given Hannah on their wedding day. She carried an expensive-looking case with expanding hinges which she put down as Tilly, in a flood of joyous tears, swept her into her embrace. Tilly had not seen Josh for more than forty years, and Griff she saw infrequently. Rebecca she had never seen, and she was her only sister's only child. What else could Tilly do but hold her close to her loving heart? Eben found himself wondering, with a pang of conscience almost, how much Tilly yearned for her family and how much she had missed in life through sacrificing for others.

'Aunt Tilly,' said Rebecca, ' 'tis mighty good to see you.'

'Oh, my honey, you're the livin' image of our Hannah. If only Mam could have saw you.' Then she hugged her again.

'I'm here too,' said Eben eventually.

'Sure,' said Rebecca, 'you were the one I always said I was going to marry.'

Eben took her hand and kissed her.

Eben had never thought of Hannah as being beautiful. Now he realized how beautiful she must have been, because Rebecca was about the most strikingly beautiful woman he had ever seen. The dark wavy hair had a grey streak, her perfect teeth flashed in her ready smile and the brown eyes danced with merriment. The Harter features were all there, but there also was somehow a serenity and composure about Rebecca which it would have been difficult to put into words. She was, Tilly said, a little bit smaller than Hannah, but she had a beautiful figure and attracted as many admiring glances from the women as from the men.

What they talked about as they drove home Eben could not afterwards remember, except that they talked all the way. At Tilly's insistence, Rebecca sat in the front with Eben. Every now and again she would break in to say, 'Now isn't that cute.' More than once she asked Eben to stop so that she could get out and take a picture of a farmhouse with the fresh whitewash bright in the sunshine, for the farm buildings intrigued her.

Rebecca asked a great deal about Gramfer Jenkyn. Her mother had talked so much about him and Eben, and young Hannah would be asking her so many questions when she got back, and that's why she wanted to take all these pictures.

Somewhere along the road it had struck Eben, as a result of a passing remark, that Rebecca might be religious. At supper time it was confirmed.

Eben said, 'Go on, Rebecca. Don't wait for anybody here.'

Slightly surprised, she said, 'Do you not say grace, then?'

'I'm afraid we don't.'

'Mother told me you always said grace.'

'We used to when Mam was alive, but I'm afraid we've slid back a long way since then. Do you say grace?'

'Always. At midday and at our evening meal.'

'Would you like to say grace for us now?'

'If you don't mind.'

'We'd love you to.'

Rebecca closed her eyes and said, 'Bless this food to our use, oh Lord, and ourselves to thy service. May we be thankful in our hearts for thy many blessings and ever mindful for the needs of others, for Jesus' sake. Amen.'

There were a few seconds' embarrassed silence before Eben said, 'You'll be thinking we're a right pair of heathens.'

'No, I wouldn't think that. It's easy to forget. But when you love the Lord you just want to give thanks. Do you not love the Lord?'

'What about you, Tilly?' said Eben.

'Yes, I loves the Lord. But we don't talk about it much, I suppose.'

'But, Aunt Tilly, we must be his witnesses. You go to chapel, of course?'

Eben remembered the letter she had written at the time of Hannah's death. Tilly had kept it, and Eben had read it again only recently, thinking that it was an oddly 'religious' way for a girl of her age to have written.

As soon as possible, Eben carried out his ambition of showing Rebecca Heronsmill. The gate had been replaced by a wire fence, the lane was overgrown with brambles and the old stone stile was hardly visible beneath them. They walked along the road and Eben found a place where they were able to climb over the hedge and walk down the bank above the Gangrel, where the old pine tree rose far above the growth and decay beneath.

Fern had now taken hold of the fields, and nettles and thistles were established where once cattle had grazed and Ben Harter had grown crops. Thorn hedges, untrimmed, had grown high and there were great gaps in the bottoms of them. Eben could scarcely believe that such a transformation was possible.

For all its air of decay, however, there was yet a great peace upon the place. There was blossom on some of the old fruit trees and a laburnum was drenched in its chains of gold alongside a riot of lilacs. And, joy of joys, in the blackthorn tree by what had once been Gramfer Jenkyn's blacksmith's shop, a blackbird still sang. As they walked down the bank, a heron rose on great wings, with its harsh croak rasping in its throat, and, with head drawn back and long legs trailing, soared above the trees and swept on down the valley to other reedy shallows. There were yellow flags down near Ford's Lake and the whole place was ablaze with primroses.

At the back of Heronsmill, in the shade, where the garden had once been, they found the bed of lily-of-the-valley in full bloom. Rebecca was thrilled and picked a bunch to make buttonholes for herself and Tilly for Benjie's wedding. 'And that will sure make us stand out,' she said. 'They'll just have to know we're on the bridegroom's side, and there won't be anybody else with a buttonhole quite like it.'

The houses, both at the Gangrel and Heronsmill, were a sorry sight and only the crumbling walls remained.

Rebecca asked many questions. Eventually, she said, 'Tell me, Eben, are you happy?'

'How d'you mean? Happy as distinct from unhappy, or in the sense of being contented?'

'You tell me.'

Eben said, 'I think I'm both.'

'You wouldn't want to go away from this area?'

'Oh, no.'

'But you're an educated man.'

'Indeed I'm not. I had to leave school when I was fourteen.'

'Yes, but you've got a good brain and you've educated yourself. You're very well-read.'

'And would that be any reason for not being happy to go on living as I am?'

'Have you not thought of marrying again to share all this

wonderful happiness?'

Eben smiled. 'I made one ghastly mistake and I'm not anxious to make another.'

'You're hedging.'

'What makes you say that?'

'Woman's intuition.'

Eben smiled again and she smiled back at him.

'When did you say you were here last?' she asked.

'Eight years ago next autumn.'

'Just look at that! "Eight years ago next autumn." Did any man ever have an answer so readily at his finger-tips? "Eight years ago next autumn." Just like that. And wasn't it eight years ago next autumn that Merry went away and left you in your happy misery?'

Eben looked at her blankly.

Rebecca was still smiling at him. She said, 'And isn't she still swanning around, footloose and fancy free?'

'What d'you know about Merry?'

'Mostly what you've told me. Or didn't you realize how much you've talked about her?'

Eben shook his head. He said, 'D'you know something? When I showed her round here and told her about the old place she said that I had talked a lot about you.'

'Then she must have been really jealous. That's a hopeful sign.'

'Oh no, not Merry. She has a beautiful nature.'

'Has she?' Rebecca laughed. Suddenly, spontaneously, she reached out and took his face in her hands and kissed him.

'Bless you,' she said, 'so have you. And I hope you'll be truly happy. And if you don't propose to her I'll do it for you. I just can't wait to meet her. But listen, there's something we still have to do.'

'What's that?'

'You can't think?'

Eben looked puzzled. Rebecca said, 'What's the first thing all the wanderers coming home here have to do? Mother said it was a tradition.'

'Well, well,' said Eben, 'fancy me forgetting that. Throw a stone down Lower Level pit! Did she tell you about that?'

'She sure did. Bless her heart, I sometimes wonder if she knew what was ahead for her, for not long before she died she said to me, "If you ever get back to Heronsmill, Becky" – that's what she always called me, Becky – "If you ever get back to Heronsmill, will you be sure to pile a stone down the

252

Lower Level pit for me?" Then she smiled, and I can see her now as she said, "And, Becky, you'll be sure to pile it, won't you? Don't just throw or even chuck it. You really will pile it?"'

There were tears in Rebecca's eyes, but suddenly she smiled again and said, 'Eben, why did Templeton Kilgetty?'

'The what?'

'Why did Templeton Kilgetty?'

Eben's face brightened and he laughed back at her. He said, 'Because it trod on Saundersfoot.'

'Why did it tread on Saundersfoot?'

'Because it wouldn't Stepaside.'

Rebecca laughed. 'You know it!'

'But I haven't heard it since I was a boy in school.'

When they arrived home, Tilly told them Mark had just been on the phone.

'He won't be able to come to the wedding. Jane have had another turn.'

It was no more than Eben had expected. All along he had doubted whether Mark would be able to leave her.

'What's the matter with her exactly?' asked Rebecca.

Eben said, 'It's the drink chiefly. She's been on it for years. Mark kept it quiet as long as he could, but you can't do that for ever. And now, of course, it's her heart. It's a miracle to me she's lasted as long as she has.'

Having Rebecca with them had taken their minds off the wedding for a while, but now there was a great bustle and opening of cupboards and pulling out of drawers and running up and down stairs. It was not a household attuned to the undertaking of long journeys or frequent excursions. This was an event.

They set off a good three hours later than they had intended. As they were leaving, they heard the first cuckoo.

'Hark at that,' said Tilly. 'Wish!'

'What are you wishing for, girl?' Eben asked.

'Oh, you mustn't tell nobody or it won't come true.'

The lake was throwing back shafts of morning sunlight and, in the warmth which was following a wet start to the summer, the young growth was green and fresh, trees were bursting into full leaf and a cloud of snowy bloom was upon the hawthorn. Out on the lake, wild duck floated near the busy, ever-darting moorhens, and the Canada geese stood, long-necked and watchful, upon the grassy bank. The cuckoo called again.

As they drove away, Eben turned to Tilly in the back and said, 'Now then, girl, you've been to Griff's and I haven't, so will you know the way?'

'Lord sowls no. I went by train.'

'But the train doesn't go all the way to Griff's. So will you know when we get there?'

'All I remember is there's a big pillar-box on the corner.'

'There you are then, Rebecca. You keep your eyes open and shout as soon as you see a pillar-box.'

It helped to break the tedium of the journey, with Eben and Rebecca vying with each other to be first to shout every time they saw a pillar-box.

They had breakfasted well just before they left, and pushed on beyond Monmouth to the Forest of Dean before stopping to eat the picnic lunch which Tilly had packed.

As the traffic became heavier and progress slower Eben began to think of Heronslake. 'Can you really see me living amongst this lot?' he said to Rebecca.

'Mother always told me that Grandma used to say, "The time and place do not count. It's the one who's there." '

'Aw! Did she tell you that?' said Tilly. 'I can remember her sayin' that well. God love her. She had some lovely sayin's.'

Griff's directions were so detailed that the last stage of the journey was very easy. Eben knew he was on the right road and he touched Rebecca's hand and winked. She smiled back. Seconds later, when he had already turned the corner, Tilly called out, 'There's the pillar-box! I knows that's the one. We're on the right road. There's the house – up there.'

As they drove up, Griff was standing by the gate. As Tilly tumbled out and flung her arms round him, he said, 'I was just wondering whether to send out a search party for you.'

For all his cheerfulness, Eben sensed that Griff was a sick man, and could see that he had lost weight. But he was very excited at having his family with him. Suddenly there was a furious ringing of the doorbell, voices were raised in hearty greetings and in came Benjie with his best man.

'You remember old Thunder?' said Benjie.

Eben had met him on the odd occasion when visiting Benjie at school, and it had always been one of his regrets that, because of the constant domestic strife, it had never been possible to ask the boy back in return for the number of times Benjie had spent holidays with Thunder and his family.

Benjie had filled out, and his horn-rimmed glasses gave him an air of maturity quite different from the owlishness of his earlier years. Yet he was still able to make himself look incredibly foolish and slow-witted whenever he wanted to. Thunder was dark of visage, brown of eye and black of hair. His rugged face wore an expression of constant merriment. He stood no more than five feet six and his shoulders were so broad that Eben half-expected him to turn sideways whenever he walked through a door.

There was no need for Eben to talk very much or make any great contribution to ensure the success of the evening, which gave him that much more chance to think about Merry. He realized that it was only hours now before he would see her again.

The next morning, Rebecca with her nimble fingers made two exquisite buttonholes for Tilly and herself from the lily-of-the-valley she had picked at Heronsmill two days earlier; they had packed it in damp moss and handled it with care ever since.

As Griff's car pulled into the wide frontage to the church, Eben saw only Merry's well-loved face. He tried to remain natural, and to still the hammer blows of his heart. He was vaguely conscious that Penny was standing across the way with a man hovering near her, but these things scarcely registered. Merry saw Eben as he got out of the car, and as they held each other's gaze Eben knew the answers to all the questions he had longed to ask her.

Smiling, Merry walked towards him, holding out both her hands. He drew her to him very gently and pressed his cheek to hers as he had done by the Lower Level stile when he thought he was losing her for ever. He felt the pressure of her gloved hands and was conscious of the gentle fragrance of her. Yet they had spoken no word when Tilly said, 'Merry, my love,' and flung her arms round Merry's neck.

'Miss Perrot, Aunty Tilly!' said Merry, and Eben could see that her eyes were swimming in tears of sheer happiness. As Tilly released her, Eben noticed that Merry wore a buttonhole of lily-of-the-valley surrounding a delicate rosebud of pale pink.

'Now then, Merry,' said Eben, 'I want you to meet Rebecca at last and Tilly's brother Griff, whom you may remember.'

Merry kissed Tilly again excitedly.

'Oh, my dear,' she said, 'it's so good to be with you again.'

Tilly had her handkerchief out and Griff said, 'Tilly was born when the tide was coming in. It's all the salt water overflowing.'

'I must go and speak to Penny,' said Tilly.

No one tried either to restrain her or make any attempt to go with her. Griff and Rebecca were far more interested in Merry.

'Now tell me about your lovely buttonhole,' said Rebecca.

Merry said, 'I made it myself. Do you like it?'

'Sure I do. But where did you get such lovely lily-of-the-valley?'

'Where did you get yours?' smiled Merry.

'Well now, these are by way of being just a little bit special because they came from the garden of Heronsmill.'

Rebecca's face was a study as Merry said, 'And so did these!'

Eben had guessed it as soon as he saw them.

She did not look at Eben now as she said, 'The flowers themselves didn't actually come from there, but the roots did. I brought them back with me when I left Deerfield, and planted them in our own garden. And I've looked after them myself and every year they've brought back happy memories and helped me to feel in touch. They're rather precious to me.'

'And what about the rose?' asked Rebecca.

Merry smiled. 'Well that's very special too. But in a different way. It's from a little tree grown from a cutting. And the cutting was sent to me right round the world by a very dear and special person.'

Merry's face lit, first with surprise, and then pleasure. 'Of course!' she added. 'She married your cousin Abel. It was my friend Megan who always saw to it "that nobody did put on me like".'

Griff looked at her. 'Do you know something?' he said. 'I love you.'

Merry made her mock curtsy. She said, 'Methinks sir ar't gentleman somewhat forward to speak thus boldly to lady of such chance acquaintance and met with scarce five minutes gone. But 'twas pretty speech and right noble sentiment.'

Taking her up in the spirit of her evident happiness, Griff offered her his arm and said, 'Wil't do me great honour, fair lady, and let me escort thee to yonder kirk to witness ceremony ancient and most sacred?'

'You can't do that, you silly man,' said Rebecca quickly.

'Oh, no, of course not,' he said.

People were already going into church, and had been doing so for some little time. Tilly, along with Penny, had moved further away and they were talking to someone else.

'Well, it's getting rather late,' said Rebecca, 'I think we ought to be going in. I'll walk with you, Uncle Griff, and Merry can walk with Eben.'

Eben allowed himself to be virtually shepherded along with Merry, in front of Griff and Rebecca, into the church. A young man, resplendent in morning suit with a fine carnation buttonhole, which had evidently come from the same source as those which some careful organizer had thoughtfully sent round for Griff and Eben earlier in the day, approached them to hand them the wedding service cards, raised a quizzical eyebrow and said, 'Friends of the bride or groom?'

'Bridegroom's father,' said Eben and, before he had time to think, he and Merry were following their young escort down the aisle.

Most of the two hundred guests were already in their places, and, as they went, Eben was conscious of heads turning and comments being whispered as the young man led them to the front seat. Almost immediately there was some shuffling of feet, and Eben sensed that Penny and Tilly were finding room for themselves in the seats behind them. Then a good-looking woman came in and sat in the front seat on the other side of the aisle. Merry leaned forward and smiled at her. She seemed surprised to see Merry in the front pew but she smiled back and waved a cheery greeting. Merry whispered to Eben, 'Nancy, Jackie's mother.'

Eben felt Merry's hand by the side of him on the seat. He took it in his own, and she returned the gentle pressure and made no attempt to take it away. He looked at her and saw that she was blushing.

'This is absolute madness,' she whispered. 'Whatever are people going to think?'

'Don't worry about it. I'm willing to make an honest woman of you.'

'Oh, Eben, we'll never live it down!'

'I know. I'm terribly upset, and deeply ashamed.'

'You're impossible,' she whispered. But she did not take her hand away until there was the sound of muffled voices at the back of the church, an air of hushed expectancy rustled through the congregation and the organ pealed forth the movingly beautiful chords of the wedding march from

257

Wagner's *Lohengrin*. The people rose, and Eben felt a lump come to his throat. Merry touched his hand reassuringly and, as he looked at her, she smiled back and he was oblivious to all else until Jackie, a breathtaking vision in white, moved slowly by on her father's arm to where Benjie and Thunder stood shoulder to shoulder as if they could and would face untold legions together. Then Benjie, very dignified, and not in the least stupid-looking, turned to meet her and to take her into partnership for life.

When the service was over and the time came for the signing of the register, Eben motioned to Merry, who gave him a despairing look. At the same time, Rebecca gave her a gentle nudge and Jackie's mother came across and said, 'You're coming into the vestry to sign the register, aren't you?' There was no way out.

In one last desperate effort, Merry turned deliberately and raised her eyebrows questioningly to Penny, in an attitude which plainly invited her to join them. Penny looked at her witheringly and turned her head away.

Afterwards, Eben realized that he had been vaguely conscious of Penny somewhere in the offing, yet at no time had he felt that he should speak to her, nor had he been conscious of ignoring her. He was completely indifferent.

As they emerged from the vestry, and the congregation rose, the full significance of what was happening dawned on Eben at last. He knew it was customary for the father of the groom and the mother of the bride to be followed by the father of the bride and the mother of the groom, or, as Griff tried to explain later, the wife of the groom's father. But Merry was on Jackie's father's arm, and did not this imply that she was there as Eben's lady?

As they came slowly down the carpeted steps to the accompaniment of Mendelssohn's Wedding March, Eben caught Rebecca's eye and Rebecca gave her mischievous wink and held her left hand in front of her with a blatant thumbs-up signal. What a great advocate for the Christians, thought Eben. If only there were a few more like her, preachers might be preaching to congregations instead of timber yards. Almost at the same moment he caught sight of Penny a little further back, and her expression was one of hatred and fury as she looked beyond Eben to Merry.

That evening Nancy and some friends were busy with sandwiches and coffee pots and everybody seemed to know everybody else. Griff had known several of the guests at the reception in the afternoon, and now he drew Eben to one side and introduced him to one of them. He was a man of about Griff's age, with bushy eyebrows and dark hair turning grey.

Griff said, 'This is a friend of mine, Jim Lewis. He's also my solicitor, which is a risky business.'

Jim Lewis shook hands with Eben and said, '*Siarad Cymraeg?*'

'I'm afraid not,' said Eben, 'we don't speak any Welsh in our corner of the world.'

'Oh, you're another of those foreigners from Little England Beyond Wales, as you love to call it.'

'Don't take any notice of him,' said Griff, 'he's a Cardi and has never learned to live with the shame of it. If you think it's such a big thing to be Welsh why did you come up here in the first place?'

'I've told you before. Because half the people who ever left Cardiganshire came up here to sell milk, and somebody had to make the sacrifice to come up and look after their interests.'

'And pick the bones clean,' said Griff.

Eben sensed the great bond of friendship between them. They were still arguing when Jack Robinson called for order.

Thunder was steering Merry towards the piano.

'Now then, chaps,' Jack Robinson said, 'at absolutely fantastic cost and enormous loss of life we have brought here tonight a great singer from a great land of singing. I say, is that right? It isn't? That's right, land of song.' Jack was slightly merry. 'I'm most fearfully sorry, old sport. Land of Song. Ladies and gentlemen, Mr Jim Lewis.'

There was some good-natured cheering before Jim said, 'Don't be daft, Jack. I can't sing tonight.'

'Go on,' said Griff. 'Like old Gramfer Jenkyn used to say, "Never let 'em say your mother bred a jibber".'

At mention of Gramfer Jenkyn's name, Merry smiled across at Eben, and, amidst the crowd, it was a moment shared.

Jim Lewis walked across to Merry at the piano and said, 'I'm terribly sorry about this. Can you play by ear?'

'No, indeed, and I'm not all that good with music.'

'What do you usually play?'

Merry smiled. 'Oh, "The Robin's Return", or something like that.'

'There's music in that cabinet,' Nancy said.

Thunder opened it and pulled out some sheets of music.

'What's this then?' Here we are. "Popular Songs from Many Lands".'

Jim looked through the song book and presently showed a page to Merry. She frowned, tapped out a few notes with one finger, and said, 'All right, let's try.'

Jim said, 'This is a little Welsh song called "*Y Bwthyn ar y Bryn*". You've heard the Welsh word "*hiraeth*", which means longing or yearning, but far more intense. Well this is what it's all about. It's a song someone is singing far away from his native land of Wales, seeing again the seashore and the streamlet, the woodland, and the churchyard where his people lie at rest, but above all, *Y Bwthyn ar y Bryn* – The Cottage on the Hill.'

Merry waited for complete silence before she played the introduction. And she played very well as Jim Lewis sang in a pure tenor voice that conveyed all the *hiraeth* of the exile, even to those who had only been told the sense of what he was singing.

Eben could see that Griff was deeply moved, and he wondered whether he was thinking of the Gangrel of the past or of Heronslake. Rebecca was enthralled.

Jim walked back to where Griff was sitting and Thunder now took charge and led some chorus singing. This, in turn, drew Jack Robinson into the act.

'I'll tell you what,' he said. 'Do you know "The Music Man"?'

'Of course I know it.'

'All right,' said Jack, loosening his tie and taking off his morning coat and throwing it on the back of a chair.

'By damn, it's his own,' said Thunder. 'Classy lot we've married into, mind. Can you sing?'

'Of course I can't sing. But you can. I'll do the actions for you.'

'Thank you, friend. I've told you before. There's something about you English. If only you didn't all have this fixation that you can play rugby!'

Thunder put his cigar carefully in an ashtray and drained his tankard before putting that out of the way as well. Then he turned to Merry for consultation.

'There's nothing to it,' he said.

'But I can't play by ear.'

'Don't bother to play. Just umpha, umpha. Anything like that.'

They tried it for pitch and Merry broke into an improvised vamp and looked enquiringly at Thunder who said, 'That's it. That's it. Now just keep it going.'

Through all the range of musical instruments they went, adding one each time, from violin to viola and triangle, and from trumpet to trombone. When they had exhausted that lot they added fish and chips and anything else they could think of or which anybody else could nominate. In the end the project was abandoned in helpless laughter.

Jack, however, was now thoroughly wound up. He put his arm round Thunder's shoulder and said, 'I say, partner, I'll tell you what. We'll give 'em "The Ball of Kerriemuir".'

Thunder winked a warning at Merry.

She got up and closed the lid of the piano. 'I don't know it,' she said, 'and even if I did I wouldn't play it for you.'

'I say, Merry, you're a communist. I'll tell you what. I've only just remembered. There's a party on at the hotel and I said we'd all go round there. Anybody coming?'

Merry exchanged a look with Jackie's mother who smiled and nodded. Merry said, 'All right, we'll take you round there. Come on.'

'I say, Merry, what a sport you are. Three cheers for the pianist. Where's my coat? I mean to say, I can't go like this. Bride's father and all that.'

Eben moved nearer to Merry and said quietly, 'Did I hear you say we'd take them round?'

'Yes, I said "we".'

'We?'

Merry whispered, 'Didn't you know I was a designing female?'

Eben squeezed her hand. He said, 'I was hoping you might be.'

In the noise of the general exodus Nancy managed to say to Eben, with a smile in which he saw a great deal of Jackie, 'Will you see Merry home safely?'

Eben looked at her. 'Good God,' he said, 'are you in on the act as well?'

She squeezed his arm. 'Of course I am. We all are. Benjie's told me all about it.'

'All about what?'

Nancy ignored his question. She said, 'I hope it works out. You see, I have a sort of vested interest. I want to be quite sure my daughter has the right sort of mother-in-law.'

Eben laughed, 'I'll do my best.'

261

Merry sat in the front and directed Eben. Thunder, in the back, managed to keep Jack Robinson away from 'The Ball of Kerriemuir' by singing Welsh hymns.

Darkness had fallen and the hotel was floodlit. Eben and Merry made no attempt to follow the others up the steps to the front door. Instead, he took her by the hand and they walked down the terracing towards the river.

Fairy lights were strung above them and, in places underfoot, fallen cherry blossom had begun to lay a thin carpet. The night was warm and clear and Eben knew an intoxication that had not come from any champagne glass. He leaned back against a balustrade in the shadow of one of the great willows. The water lapped quietly against a launch riding at anchor and the air was fragrant with the dewy scent of roses.

Eben took Merry's hands in his and held them to his chest. At last he said, 'I was terrified in case we couldn't have a little time on our own.'

'So was I.'

He bent his head and pressed his lips against her hands.

'We've wasted precious years,' he said.

'No, they haven't been wasted.'

Merry returned his gaze and in it there was never a doubt of her love for him.

'Why do you say that?'

'Please God it will make us appreciate each other all the more and make us less likely to waste any of the years that lie ahead.'

There was the sudden roar of a motor-cycle with an open exhaust, and then the traffic noise returned to its faint intermittent rumble.

'It's not quite as quiet as the Lower Level wood,' said Merry.

'Do you remember that day by the stile?'

'When you just held me close but didn't kiss me.'

'Did you want me to kiss you?'

'Yes, of course I did. But I was so glad you didn't. And so very proud of you.'

'There were tears on your cheeks that day.'

'I know. And a terrible longing in my heart.' She smiled her old wistful smile. 'And do you want to know something?'

'What's that?'

'It's been there ever since. Is it "*hiraeth*" you call it?'

'I don't know, *cariad*. It could be.'

Very gently he drew her to him and held her close and

pressed his cheek against hers. This time it was free from tears. And this time he sought her lips. He felt her tremble very slightly in his arms as he kissed her tenderly for the first time, and then she was clinging to him and he sensed the passion within her as waves of primeval longing roared over him and still she clung to him and he held her even closer. Her arms were round his neck and she kept them there when at last she turned her lips away from him and he kissed her neck and hair.

Somewhere far beyond the fairy lights the stars were twinkling in a clear sky and there was a great joy within him.

Very gradually, however, his mood began to change. Eventually he said, 'Merry, there's something that's troubling me about us.'

She smiled at him. 'All right. Now will the very serious Mr Harter, whose moods I once learned to know and understand and love so well, tell me what's worrying him about us.'

'Now you're making fun,' he said.

'Yes, I am.'

'Why?'

'Shall I tell you why? Because I think I can guess what you're worrying about.'

Eben said nothing.

Merry looked at him and said, 'You're wondering how you can ask me how much I'm earning and how much money I have and . . .'

'How on earth do you know that?'

Merry tapped him gently on the nose with her finger, as he so well remembered her doing that afternoon by the Lower Level stile.

'Because,' she said, 'you're such a stupid, independent, prideful, lovable man that you couldn't possibly ask me to marry you if you thought you couldn't keep me in the manner, as Benjie said earlier today, to which I have become accustomed. And I wouldn't think you're exactly a pauper anyway.'

'No, I'm not. But I'm not in your league by the time you reckon up that your people are no doubt much more than comfortable and that you must be earning a very good salary yourself.'

'Yes, that's all perfectly true.'

'Which makes it very difficult.'

'So?'

'Well, it's difficult.'

'Can I just tell you something?' she said. 'It might save us wasting a lot of valuable kissing time. I've given in my notice. But I've promised to stay on until about the end of June, which is only another month.'

'Why have you done that?'

'Because I'm beginning to believe in fairy stories again. I didn't believe in them that day by the Lower Level stile. I was twenty-six then and still not sure what I wanted out of life. But I know now. So I shall be home here very soon.'

'And what are you going to do then?'

'Well, I shall be out of a job, so I'm going to accept the long-standing, oft-repeated invitation of a very dear and special friend of mine – "only platonic, mind, none of this messing about" – to go and visit his home which he loves so much. And I'm hoping that if I play my cards right he might just ask me to marry him. And if he does I'll just keep him waiting a little while for the answer, but wild horses and roaring lions wouldn't stop me from saying yes. Because I love you, Eben – oh, dear God, I love you, and do I have to throw myself at you?'

'Merry, I'm afraid there's just one more thing.'

'And what is that, Mr Harter?'

'Heronslake isn't exactly my own home. You see, when Griff retires . . .'

'Don't you understand that home to me will be wherever you are? And do you think I'll care where it is as long as you're there? Kiss me.'

Breathless at last, he said, 'Are you insatiable?'

'That's a big word. What does it mean?'

'You're only thirty-five. Much too young to understand about these things.'

Merry held her wrist up to the light to look at her watch.

Eben said, 'Are you getting ready to give me the brush-off or something?'

She looked at him wide-eyed. 'Do you know what time it is?'

'About eleven o'clock? Quarter past?'

Merry said, 'Have a look at your own watch.'

It was a quarter to two.

'Well, you've really compromised me now. You'll simply have to marry me!'

When Eben and Tilly set off, Merry drove on ahead to pilot Eben until he could pick up the road for home. After an hour's driving they came to a roundabout and, beyond it, Merry pulled into a big lay-by and it was there that they said their farewells.

Parting with the others had been sad. Rebecca, after a few days with Griff, would be going back to Canada, and there was no knowing when they would see her again. Nor was Eben by any means sure about the prospects of seeing Griff. Not only could he see that he looked ill but, after breakfast, before they had gone round to Merry's, Griff had taken him into the garden where they could be alone and told Eben that he had appointed him as one of the two executors of his will and hoped he would not mind. The other, he said, was Jim Lewis, and Tilly was the chief beneficiary.

More than once Eben had noticed Tilly looking at Griff and he knew that she was worried. But he would not say anything unless Tilly chose to say something herself. Instead, he said now, 'What's all this about you going back to live in Tenby?'

'How not, then?'

'What's wrong with Heronslake?'

'It's too lonely for one thing.'

'Look at that now. And when did you make that discovery?'

'When you started listenin' for the phone and lookin' for the postman and starin' up at the moon like a body pisken-led and gwain about in a condrim.'

Eben laughed. 'I haven't heard those expressions since I can't remember when.'

'No, well, Merry said I ought to use 'em more oftener.'

'Why did she say that, I wonder?'

'Because I told her I was worried in case the way I talked might make her father and mother think you wasn't good enough for her.'

'And what did Merry say to that?'

Tilly looked a little flustered and coloured slightly. 'Never mind what she said. But she told me if I didn't talk ordinary she wouldn't marry you. She can't abide people puttin' it on and gettin' full of biggoty.'

'What did you think of her father and mother?'

'Oh, they was lovely. But Merry says her father is workin' too hard. These two days is the first days he've had off since last Christmas. Her mother wants'n to retire and settle down in Pembrokeshire.'

'And you want to go and live in Tenby?'

'Yes, I do.'

'What about when Griff retires?' He had tried to stop him-

265

self saying it, but the words were out of his mouth before he had realized.

'God love'n, poor old boy. Do you think he'll live to see it? Have you ever saw anybody lookin' so bad?'

'Aye, he looked in poor shape. But he'll come better yet.'

'I wish I could believe it. He've never been the same since that last time. I've knowed ever since then somehow that it's only a matter of time.'

'It's only a matter of time with all of us, girl.'

'Yes, I knows. But he've lost all the fun he used to have. And God knows he've been good. From the very first week he went away to work he sent somethin' home to Mam. He've always been wonderful about the family.'

Tilly had taken her handkerchief out of her bag and was dabbing her eyes.

'How old is Griff now?' said Eben.

'He won't be sixty till next year.'

'Is that all he is?'

'And he've always worked so hard, and that's all he've looked forward to all his life is comin' back to live at home.'

'Well, don't let's get upset about it yet. Let's hope he'll go on all right and he can come and live with Merry and me.'

The following morning, Eben called on Mark. Jane was very ill. Mark asked about the wedding, and Eben told him all the news in which he thought he would be interested.

'And have you fixed the wedding day?' asked Mark.

Eben smiled at him. 'I'm not in a position to propose to her as yet. And maybe she'll turn me down when I do.'

'Aye, that's quite right. So she might. Tilly phoned just before you arrived.'

Eben laughed. 'Ah, well, you've heard it all, then.'

Before the end of the week, Rebecca had flown back to Canada, and Merry had returned to Paris. Eben had spoken to both of them on the phone each evening, and they had obviously become friends.

Two days after Rebecca's departure, Griff was admitted to hospital. The following day, Jim Lewis phoned Eben and suggested that he should come to London. Eben went by train the same day, but Griff died before he arrived.

There was little that Eben could do to comfort Tilly from that distance and, whilst they were still working out plans for her to travel to London, she phoned Eben to tell him that Jane too had died. She felt she should stay, to be of some help to Mark, and Eben agreed with her.

266

Griff had left his affairs in meticulous order. His house and all its contents he had left to Tilly, and Heronslake and his motor-car he had left to Eben. He had left a thousand pounds each to Rebecca, Abel and Megan, and the residue to Tilly. Jim Lewis reckoned it would come to about ten thousand pounds. There was also a letter addressed to Eben. In it Griff said, 'I am leaving Heronslake to you because I know how you have come to love the place and also that you will always see that Tilly has a home. And you have made it what it is.'

He then went on to enumerate certain pieces of furniture, pictures and china which he knew some of his friends would like if Tilly did not want them, but he had left everything to her so that there should be as little complication as possible.

In a slightly less firm hand there was a postscript written following Benjie's wedding. It said:

It is so good to know that I have done the right thing in leaving Heronslake to you. Merry will lend the place an atmosphere of distinction, as well as love and serenity, which I could never do. I know she will help you to find great peace there and make up for the disappointments and bitterness you have put behind you. If you are ever blessed with a boy you could do worse than name him Griffith. After Gramfer Jenkyn of course! God bless you both.

Eben blinked away a tear as he read the postscript a second time, and thought how typical of Griff it all was, with that mixture of seriousness and fun, and as always so much thoughtfulness, right up to the end. Heronslake being his own meant little to him – it was so much a part of him now that for some time he had given no thought to the possibility of having to look for a new home.

Eben drove home in Griff's car, and Tilly was glad to see him back.

'Poor old Griff,' she said. 'Somehow I knowed as he'd never come back here to live. I always had a feelin' somehow. That's only me an' Josh left now.'

'And Abel and Megan, and Rebecca and her young Hannah, and Megan's pair of course. And Merry. Or don't you count her?'

Tilly blew her nose. 'Of course I counts her. When is she comin' down?'

'Soon, I hope,' said Eben.

'Well, then, we'd better see about gettin' the place a bit tidy.'

*

267

The great day arrived when Merry was to leave Paris and pay her long-heralded visit to Heronslake. Eben was ready to greet her, but she arrived earlier than he had expected. His pulse quickened as he swung in through the gate, for her car was already pulled up near the back door. As he got out of the car, Merry came from the house to greet him. She paused when she was still a yard or two away, and looked at him lovingly. Then he had swept her into his arms and was holding her close, conscious again of her sweet fragrance and kissing her hair and cheeks.

'Mr Harter,' she said at last, 'you're very strong and rough and you've messed up my hair.'

'And that's bad, is it?'

'Very bad. So kiss me properly.' She put her arms round his neck and gave her mouth to be kissed.

'Merry,' he gasped, 'have you been practising?'

'Not practising. Reading a book.'

'Then I'm not sure I approve of you reading such things. And tell me something. Where's Boyser?'

'Don't talk to me about the little tramp. Tilly and I have had a blazing row about him already. The minute we arrived she was actually cutting the best piece off the joint for him. And all she would say was, "God love the poor li'l sowl. He's bound to be hungry after he've travelled all that way and look at his li'l brown eyes. God love'n then." Just the same as if he was Dick Whittington's cat and had walked all the way. And there he is now sitting up looking at her as if he'd starved for a week.'

Hearing Merry's voice, Boyser came trotting through the door.

'Come and say how d'you do,' said Merry.

Eben bent to pat him on the head.

A black and tan Pembrokeshire corgi he was, stocky and fearless, with a friendly, intelligent face.

'How old is he?' said Eben.

'Three years old. My parents brought him back for me from Pembrokeshire as a puppy. It had to be a Pembrokeshire corgi from Pembrokeshire.'

'And why did you call him Boyser?'

'Didn't I tell you? After your old Boyser. I can remember the day you had to have him put down, and my heart went out to you and I longed to comfort you and didn't dare.'

Eben was glad to see that the amount of luggage indicated a long stay. Merry's room was the one Griff had always used, next to his own and with the same view, overlooking the lawn and the lake. It was looking at its best now and he knew she would like it. It has been hard work but he suddenly felt it had all been worthwhile. And Griff, when he had first bought the house and done so much work on it, had spared no expense.

Throughout supper, Merry and Tilly argued about Boyser who had, said Merry, recognized Tilly as 'a soft touch'.

'But, Tilly. You'll ruin him. If you feed him at table you'll only be making a rod for your own back and he'll become a perfect pest.'

'I always said you was hard. You wouldn't talk to me like that if our Megan was here to stop you puttin' on me.'

'All right then, Miss Perrot, Aunty Tilly, just give him a biscuit. Go on, give him a biscuit.'

'How?'

'Go on. Give him a biscuit.'

Tilly passed Boyser down a cheese biscuit from the table. He sniffed it, took it in his mouth very reluctantly, and then put it on the floor and ignored it.

'You see,' said Merry.

'Well, perhaps he don't like biscuits.'

'Oh no, not much he doesn't.'

Merry picked up the biscuit and put some butter on it. She offered it once more to Boyser and he ate it readily.

'Well, look at that,' said Tilly, 'he likes a bit o' butter on 'em.'

'That nonsense,' said Merry, 'has started since I've been away in Paris. I thought I was getting him away from his evil home influence. He is becoming, as Gramfer Jenkyn would have said, "nice-gutted".'

'That's quite right. But how do you know what Gramfer Jenkyn would have said?'

Merry looked from Tilly to Eben, smiled and said, 'How indeed?'

After supper, in spite of all Tilly's protestations, Merry put on an apron and washed up.

When at last they went out, Merry carried a cardigan on her arm and Boyser went with them.

'Do you feel cold?' said Tilly.

'Oh no. But I expect it will be getting chilly before we come back.'

'You're going to be late then?'

'Well, you see, my dear, Mr Harter and I have a lot of

important things to talk about.'

'Aw, that's a pity then. I thought perhaps you was gwain courtin'.'

'Tilly Perrot! You're putting all wrong ideas into a girl's head.'

'Well, that's all right, then. As long as we knows where we stands. I'm not gwain to mess about out here much longer for I got a house to go back to in Tenby. So now I've told the pair of you.'

'I told you,' said Eben, 'Tilly finds it very lonely here.'

Merry put her hand in Eben's as they walked round the fields and he showed her the few cattle and sheep he had. Boyser was like a spirit transported, home again to do the work for which long years ago his ancestors had been bred. He must have thought that he had really found his niche in life at last as a two-year-old steer came lumbering up to inspect this brazen intruder at close quarters. Horns menacing, white curly head down, he pawed the ground and breathed and blew his way inch by inch towards the unflinching Boyser.

Boyser stood four-square, ears cocked and brave brown eyes watchful. The hair along his back was bristling. Almost as the bullock lunged, Eben said, 'Get him, Boyser,' and Boyser, with all the deep instinct of his noble race, and a speed too fast to be believed, hurled himself round to the back of the bullock and had him by the tail in jaws that would hold on till death.

Enraged and kicking wildly, the bullock swung round to face his adversary who had so suddenly become his tormentor, but Boyser, like a bouncing cork, swung on his tail and would not let go. And then, with the heart gone out of him, the beast galloped away and his mates galloped with him, and Eben called, 'All right, Boyser.'

Boyser let go, stood watching the retreat of the vanquished foe, and then turned and trotted back, with the bounce of the boss-man who has just discovered himself, to a hero's welcome.

The light was failing and the sharp sliver of a new moon was already high in the dark velvet sky where the brightest stars were twinkling. Upon the water and all round them was a great stillness. There were doings afoot which Boyser did not understand, but he seemed to think they must be of some importance, and possibly confidential, for he withdrew to a discreet distance to wait patiently. And he had to wait a long time.

270

Merry's hair was tumbling round her shoulders, but only Eben was there to see when, very much later, they returned to the house. Tilly had long since gone to bed. On the table were two cups and saucers and drinking chocolate. There were also some finely chopped pieces of meat and buttered biscuits.

'Have you decided yet what you want to do for the next week or so?' Eben asked Merry next morning.

'Yes, lots of things. I'd like to walk down by Heronsmill and through the Lower Level wood, go to Morfa Bychan, go out to some of the islands where the seabirds are, and . . .'

'The birds will be gone by now.'

'Never mind, we'll go together.'

'Why d'you want to go to Morfa Bychan?'

'Because you spent one of the happiest days of your life there when you were a small boy and you've never been there since. And perhaps we can go to watch some cricket.'

'Cricket?'

'Yes, I used to love to dash to the Oval or Lord's at the end of the day in London.'

'The South Africans are in Swansea this week-end.'

'Playing Glamorgan?'

'Yes.'

Merry clapped her hands. 'Oh, Eben! Shall we go? On Monday?'

'Bank Holiday, mind. There'll be a big crowd there.'

'And that'll be more fun still. I've heard about the St Helen's crowd on a Bank Holiday. And I'd like to see Owen and Sarah.'

Sarah was a little shy at first, only having met Merry a couple of times, but it was impossible for anyone to be in Merry's company for long without responding to her. And Owen and Merry were old comrades from the days of the war. Eben knew that one thing they had always had in common was their loathing of Penny.

Merry looked at him and said, 'Lord sowls, what's't thee been doin' to thyself? Thou must 'a gone a real gorral guts an' proper scaddly.'

'There y'are, see,' said Owen, turning to Sarah, 'she haven't forgot.'

Merry said, 'And you haven't forgotten where your mouth is, by the look of you.'

Owen, in his early thirties, had already developed a fair stomach and a very definite double chin. His cheeks were red and cheerful.

Merry said, 'We'll have to raise the rack on'n, Sarah.'

'Oh, he loves his grub,' Sarah said, 'always first at the trow.'

'An' you always makes sure the trow is full too,' said Owen.

Merry sensed their happiness and was glad. The two children, a boy and a girl, six and five years old, were standing shyly behind their father and mother, chubby hands clasping skirt and trousers leg.

'Well, now then,' said Merry, 'are you going to show me your cows and tell me their names?'

The children took a hand each and they walked towards the field gate. As always when such things happened, Eben was conscious of his great love for her. But now he found himself thinking, too, what a beautiful mother she would be and wondering whether they would be blessed with children. It was something they had never discussed, but he suddenly felt a terrible physical longing for her.

Merry caught his eye, and it almost seemed as if she had read his thought, for she smiled, and coloured slightly.

Sarah had a homely face, and marriage had suited her. As Gaffer Pearce had said, 'hardworking, tidy family'. She was wearing shoes today, but a dark ring around the calf of each leg, where the tops of her wellingtons had left their marks, was clear evidence of what she more often wore, and Eben knew how many hours she spent every day helping with the milking and keeping the milking-plant and everything in the dairy so spotlessly clean.

The first animal to catch Eben's eye was a handsome black cow, standing slightly apart from the rest, eyes half-closed and contentedly chewing her cud. Owen had not bought a cow since he had started on his own, and every animal on the place had come from the Blackie family. Eben could have been back at Morfa Bychan that day all those years ago when they had seen his own Blackie's mother for the first time. He looked at the young cow admiringly and said, 'Who's this then?'

Owen said, 'You remember old Blackbird?'

Eben and Merry exchanged glances. Going to see Blackbird late on that frosty winter night had been one of the many happy memories they had both kept over the years. It was that night that Eben had told Merry all about the Blackie family and Morfa Bychan, and so much about himself. What a fool he had been to let her go away.

Merry's voice cut in on his thoughts. In her broadest Pembrokeshire she was saying, 'Proper owld skymer thicky tack was.'

'Aye,' said Owen, 'she was that. An' she stole the neighbour's bull not long after we come here. He got a good herd of Welsh Blacks. So this is owld Blackbird's daughter by a Welsh Black bull.'

'Well, look at that,' said Eben. 'Do you know, she's the spitting image of my first old Blackie. And her mother before that at Morfa Bychan for that matter. Is she as good as she looks?'

'Marvellous cow,' said Owen.

'And rich milk,' said Sarah. 'I keeps some of her milk back to make a bit of butter for ourselves.'

Sarah went back to make some tea. The others went on round the herd, and Merry was thrilled to find that a few of the cows were calves which she had reared when she was at Deerfield.

The buildings were trim and tidy, and everything was freshly painted and clean. Owen had bought another fifty acres of land and was doing very well. He had build up a good herd of cows and was growing a small acreage of early potatoes. There were three young heifer calves. And one of them was Blackie's.

'Well, would you believe it!' said Eben when he saw her. 'What bull is she by?'

'She's by a Welsh Black,' said Owen. 'When th'inseminator came round he happened to say he had a couple of shots of Welsh Black on, an' I don't know what come over me I just said go on then give her a Welsh Black. An' here's the calf.'

'Proper immoral, I call it,' laughed Merry. '*Ych-a-fi!*'

Eben looked at her. 'It's fate,' he said. 'Can't be anything else. It's meant to be.'

'How much do you want for her?' said Merry.

Owen said, 'What would you want with a calf?'

'She's been on to me about a cow for the house,' said Eben.

'Have you ever heard of such nonsense?' Merry said. 'They've got thirty acres and have to buy milk!'

'Cheaper than keeping a cow,' Eben said.

Merry smiled at Owen. 'But if you'd let us have Blackie's calf he couldn't resist that, could he?'

Owen knew what Eben felt about the Blackie family. He said, 'We'll have to ask Sarah. See what she says.'

When tea was over, Eben said, 'Now then, Sarah, and what

about Blackie's calf?'

'Who wants to buy'n?'

'I do,' said Merry.

'No, no,' said Eben, 'I'll buy the calf.'

'You can't both buy'n, can you?'

Owen and Sarah exchanged glances.

'What we better do then,' said Owen, 'is give her to you as part of our wedding present.'

'But, Owen,' Merry said, 'he hasn't asked me to marry him yet.'

'Haven't he?' said Sarah, looking flustered. 'We thought like as . . .'

'I'm going to ask her,' said Eben.

'And I think I'll say yes. And it's one of the nicest wedding presents anybody could give us.'

'We'll see she gets plenty to eat,' said Eben.

'I knows that,' said Sarah, looking at Merry. 'Owen have always told me about Merry with th'animals.'

'But there's no need for you to give her to us,' Eben said.

Sarah said, 'What's that compared to what you done for us?'

'That was different,' Eben said.

'How?'

Owen said he would deliver the calf the following evening.

When they reached Heronslake, they discovered that Mark, Rachel and Tommy had arrived.

After his wife's death, Mark had immediately made clear his intentions towards Rachel, and it seemed that she had come home the previous week intending to find a job in the area and stay. Merry took to Rachel instantly, and before long the pair of them had gone off together to walk by the lake. Tommy helped Eben make a place ready for the new young Blackie. Tommy had no interest in school, it seemed, apart from woodwork. His great delight was to be with the animals, but since his gramfer had died they had not had any at Light-a-Pipe, so would it be all right if he came up sometimes to feed Blackie and help a bit, perhaps at week-ends and that? And could he come up the following evening when the calf was due to arrive?

'Yes, of course, Tommy. Any time you like.'

They had been outside for quite a time, and getting on very well together, when Tommy said, 'Tell me, Uncle Eben, d'you think Uncle Mark will marry Rachel?'

The question took Eben by surprise. 'I don't know,' he

said. 'Why d'you ask?'

'I hope he will.'

'Why d'you hope that?'

Tommy looked at him very seriously.

'Don't you know?'

'Know what?' said Eben.

'Perhaps I'd better not tell you if you don't know. With him being your brother.'

'You can tell me anything you like, Tommy. It'll be safe with me.'

'Well, he's my father really.'

'Is he?'

'Who did you think my father was then?'

'I never thought much about it.'

'Well, everybody got to have a father haven't they?'

'And how d'you know that Mark is your father?'

'The kids in school started shoutin' after me. And then I started askin' questions.'

'And what else did you find out?'

'I expect you know the other bit. You know who my mother is don't you?'

'Rachel is it?'

'Of course it is.' Tommy smiled. 'Don't you think she's pretty?'

'Yes, very pretty. And very nice, too, which is more important.'

'So d'you think they'll get married?'

'Perhaps they will. Why are you so keen?'

'Well, if they was to get married the other boys couldn't shout bastard after me could they?'

Eben's heart went out to him. 'Do many of them do that?'

'No, not many. Only a couple.'

Eben could think of nothing to say. At last, he said, 'Let's wait and see. I expect it'll work out all right in the end.'

Tommy said, 'You won't say anything to anybody will you? Not for Uncle Mark and Rachel to know.'

'No, I won't say a word.'

Eben and Merry reached Swansea in good time on the Bank Holiday Monday morning, and Eben bought day-tickets for the members' enclosure. As they came up the steps on to the terrace at St Helen's, Merry said, 'Isn't this marvellous!'

All around them was a great stir and bustle. Down below, on the green out-field, cricketers were having a 'knock-up'.

Eben bought score-cards and hired two cushions before they found seats in front of the pavilion near the long flight of concrete steps leading down to the field. Eben pointed out the rugby stand opposite, and the playing area of the rugby ground.

'Did you ever play there?' Merry asked.

'Yes, twice.'

'And yet you never watch rugby now?'

'Very rarely. I feel as if I would want to be involved and can't be.'

'But you enjoy watching cricket?'

'Yes, I do.'

'Why don't you come oftener?'

'Perhaps because I've never had anybody to share the pleasure with me.'

Merry put her arm in his. She said, 'Shall we make a point of watching together?'

Eben smiled and nodded.

Merry took off her jacket and looked cool in an open-necked blouse. The sun shone and the ground became a mass of colour as the shirt-sleeved crowd spilled over on to the field. Small boys started up their own games behind the temporary seating on the rugby playing area.

Beyond the ground, the sea sparkled, people bathed and children ran about on the sands. Eben pointed out the English coast in the distance, and the electric train running back and fore to Mumbles. On the footbridge over the railway, a small crowd gathered for a free view, and a large cargo boat came up the channel, bound for the docks.

The Glamorgan fielding, like that of the South Africans, reached a high standard. When Wooller, the Glamorgan captain, chased after a ball with great lumbering strides the crowd cheered ironically.

'Why are they doing that?' asked Merry. 'I thought he was a national hero?'

'Yes, my love. But this is Swansea. And Wooller played rugby for Cardiff.'

'And Wales.'

'I know. But this crowd can only see a Cardiff man out there.'

'If Megan were here she'd tear them apart. She was a girl in school when Wales beat the All Blacks in 1935, and she's never forgotten it. She's so funny in her letters. Writes just as she used to speak. 'When the children are playing her up she says, "I do say to them I'll send for Wilf Wooller in a minute and you know what he done to your lot at Cardiff Arms Park so behave then will you?" And, of course, when the All Blacks were over here two years ago Wales beat them again. If they hadn't Megan said she would have had to come home. She said, "Abe do tease me something terrible until I do say what happened to the All Blacks at the Arms Park again then?" '

During the lunch interval he pointed out a number of well-known sporting personalities to her. J. C. Clay, the great 'father figure' of Glamorgan cricket, tall and dignified, was there chatting to Emrys Davies, the old Glamorgan opening bat, and now a first-class umpire.

' "The Rock" they used to call him,' Eben said. 'A wonderful servant to Glamorgan, and one of nature's gentlemen.'

'He looks it,' said Merry.

Across the crowd, Eben thought he caught sight of Ifor Jones, Welsh forward hero of his younger days, but before he could make sure, to point him out to Merry, the big bell had clanged and the players had started the long descent from the pavilion to the field.

When they had returned to their seats, Merry put her arm in his and said, 'Can I point somebody out to you now for a change? See the umpire like a little sparrow, standing at square leg? That's Harry Baldwin. Used to play for Surrey.'

Eben smiled. 'Who are they then? Do they play cricket?'

'They do happen to be the champion county at the moment and look like winning the championship again this year.'

'Is that all?'

'Isn't that enough?'

'I thought perhaps you'd tell me they also happened to give Glamorgan a hell of a caning on this very ground a week or so ago.'

'How could I do that when you keep telling me I'm a dear, kind soul? And there's something else. We're joining Glamorgan.' She opened her handbag. 'When I went to the ladies' room I also went to the office and got these forms. You can fill yours in now, but I'll keep mine for a little while, in case I do something silly like changing my name.'

They arrived home five minutes before Owen and Sarah and the two children arrived with the calf. When they arrived, Merry dashed upstairs and in a few minutes was down again wearing her old Land Army overalls.

'What shall I do next, Mr Harter?' she laughed.

As they went out, Mary and Rachel arrived with Tommy,

and Merry greeted Rachel with great affection. Sarah had not met Rachel before, but Owen knew her and had been a big friend of her father's, although so much younger.

'Do you think we're a big enough reception committee?' said Mark. 'This is a very important calf, mind. Could be founding a new dynasty.'

Eben's mind went back over the years to his mother's desperate struggle to get Blackie to take to the bucket. He wondered what she would have thought of the present gathering. He was sure she would have loved Merry. He hoped she would have loved Rachel too. He thought she would. And he knew she would have loved Sarah.

Very tired after their day in the sun, and planning to go to Morfa Bychan the next day, they went early to bed. Blackie was no trouble to feed in the morning, and Boyser, an interested spectator the previous evening, also came to help. Eben told Tilly how much feed the calf would need in the evening in case Tommy was uncertain. He was not sure what time they would be home.

Merry had packed a picnic basket. Given a choice, she said, she did not like either tea or coffee from a flask, and hot water from a flask was never quite hot enough to make a decent cup of tea.

'In that case, my love,' Eben said, 'you must have a choice.' They found a kettle and a teapot and put them with the basket.

It was another glorious day, and they packed bathing things and towels. When they were ready to put everything into the car Merry said, 'How on earth far shall we have to carry this lot?'

'No distance at all. And we'll be lighter coming back.'

'But I thought Morfa Bychan was a long way down from the road?'

'So it is, my dear. But we'll drive there across the sands. I'll explain to you on the way. We mustn't forget Boyser's ball.'

At mention of his ball, Boyser shot through the door, skidding on the tiled floor as he went, and came trotting back to Eben, as he came out of the house, to drop the ball at his feet. Eben picked it up and put it in his pocket. This was not part of the game, and Boyser sat and looked at him.

'All right, fellah,' said Eben, 'don't you worry now. We're

278

going in the car.'

Boyser hurled himself into a furious chase round the house. Car, if anything, was an even more magic word than ball, and for the two to have been mentioned together meant that great things must be afoot.

As they set off, Eben said, 'Do you know, Merry, I'm as excited as any child,' and he told her again something of the magic of that day when, as a small boy, he had gone to Morfa Bychan with his father and Mark.

'I've often wanted to go back there,' he said, 'but I've never got round to it. And now I'm glad.' He took her hand. 'It's a wonderful thought to me that now I'll be sharing it with you. Do you think I'm stupid?'

She squeezed his hand. 'Of course not. I've told you before that you're a sentimental fool, and it's one of the reasons I love you.'

'Well I hope you won't be disappointed, after all I've talked about it. But I can't help wondering how it will have changed after all these years.'

'You had a very happy childhood?'

'Early childhood, yes. Wonderful.'

'Which is perhaps why Morfa Bychan has always meant so much to you. It was the last big thing in your life before so much of the hardship and sorrow came. It's probably why you've always been attached to your Blackie family, because of the thread running back to Morfa Bychan and your mother struggling to feed her and all your other happy memories of her and family life. You loved your mother very much?'

'Oh yes. Wonderful woman.'

'Tell me,' said Merry, 'as a matter of interest. Is this the way you came that day when you were small?'

'Not quite. That day we went down Pleasant Valley first. Father called on Rachel's father on the way to have a look at a couple of cattle.'

'Poor old Billy.'

'Yes, of course, you were big pals. I forget these things. You're very much part of the scene really.'

'Of course I am.'

As they drove down the hill into Amroth, Eben said, 'We're back on the same road now as we came that day. But, my goodness, everything has changed.'

The cottages on the sea side of the road through the village had all been washed away and a sea wall had been built to replace them. Everywhere, it seemed, building was going on. The biggest difference of all, however, was in the numbers of the people.

That other day Dandy had trotted through the village with hardly anybody to be seen. Now, even before mid-morning, their progress was a crawl. Cars were parked everywhere, some with their windows open and radios blaring. Where there were no cars on the road, there were people.

Eventually they crawled to the New Inn, and from there they began to climb the hill and leave the crowd behind.

'Well, that's a relief,' Eben said, 'to be out of that lot!'

'Supposing Morfa Bychan is the same?'

'You can only reach Morfa Bychan on foot from the road and people don't like walking.'

'But you said we wouldn't have to walk.'

'What we'll do is drive to Morfa Bychan beach along the sands from Pendine at low water and dump our stuff. Then I'll drive back to the road and leave the car by the Green Bridge and walk down. But we'll have to walk back up this evening.'

'Do you think I'll be safe there, cut off by the tide and everything?'

'I wonder.'

Along the coast road there was a steady flow of traffic in both directions. They went on past Marros and dropped down the hill. At the bottom, Eben showed her where the track went down through the valley to Morfa Bychan. Then they drove on towards Pendine until they were going down the steep hill into the village with seemingly never-ending miles of golden sand stretching away in the distance and the sun dancing on the blue waters of Carmarthen Bay.

By the time they had driven a mile along the sands, beyond the crowds, they had the beach to themselves.

'Now we're here, we might as well drive further,' said Eben. 'The sands are quite something. Malcolm Campbell broke a couple of world records here back in the twenties and Parry Thomas was killed here. His car's buried up in the sand-dunes there somewhere.'

For a long way they drove in silence and complete solitude.

At high-water mark, bits of driftwood, plastic containers, tins and bottles had been scattered indiscriminately by the receding tide. A large, dead dogfish gaped vacantly at a couple of gulls which rose with some reluctance to drift further along the sands. Ahead of them, curlew rose and swept high over the sand-dunes, their long, curved beaks silhouetted against the sky. Small birds, which Eben took to be dunlin, hurried in close formation low above the surface towards the distant water's edge.

'It's fantastic,' Merry said.

At last Eben looked at his watch and turned the car in a wide circle. He said, 'Time to head back for Morfa Bychan, otherwise we'll miss the tide.'

'How far have we come?' Merry asked.

'About five miles.'

They could hardly see the cars and people now, even though they were driving back towards them. Eben pointed out the coastline to her, with Caldey Island away to the left.

'Have you ever been there?' Merry said.

'Oh, yes. Everybody's been to Caldey.'

'It's like that, is it?'

'Not really. It's different. It has an atmosphere all its own.' Eben told her something of its history, its monastery and its beaches.

'Can we go some time?'

'Any time you like.'

'Could we go tomorrow?'

'Well, of course. You're on holiday. Remember?'

As he drove back, Eben kept further out on the sands to avoid the crowd and drove on towards Gilman Point. On the fringe of the crowds, gulls waited for the day's leavings.

Approaching Gilman Point they came in under high cliffs, with caves beneath them and people settling down for a picnic or a day in the sun.

There was not much sand between the far rocks and the sea, but Eben drove on and up across the hard sand towards the high bank of pebbles and stopped the car. Boyser hurled himself out in an ecstasy of excitement and gave chase to a small flock of gulls. He seemed to know it was going to be one of those days. Eben unloaded the boot of the car and called to Boyser who came panting back to fetch the ball.

'Keep an eye on him, pet,' Eben said, 'in case he wonders what's happening and tries to follow the car.'

'What do I do then?'

'Just wait here and by-and-by you'll see me coming down over the pebbles there.'

Merry looked round. She said, 'Do you know something? There isn't a living soul in sight.'

Eben kissed her on the cheek. 'Sweetheart,' he said, 'time

281

is of the essence. I'll be as quick as I can.'

As he drove back round Gilman Point towards Pendine, Eben thought of George Wyrriot riding round on Pockets. He bought a flagon of cider at the Green Bridge Inn, and asked if he might leave his car in their car park. Then he went through the gate and followed the track along the bottom of the field and down the valley. He was conscious of little that was around him as he went, but he noticed that the cottage halfway down was now in ruins and that there were iron rods across the lane in places. He knew the beach had been used during the wartime invasion exercises.

Eben realized afterwards how foolish he was not to have expected Morfa Bychan to have disappeared. He remembered so well, on that other visit, getting his first glimpse of the small stone house, with the door and windows open, and a skein of smoke rising from the broad chimney. After all, Heronsmill and the Gangrel had tumbled to the ground, the same as the other houses and cottages before them. And he knew how the land at Heronsmill had changed its face, even though it had not lain abandoned and neglected nearly as long as this little piece of land at Morfa Bychan.

The fields now were overgrown with fern. Heather bloomed, and there was still bloom on the gorse, although it was not the riot of colour which it had been on that first visit which had taken place more than a couple of months earlier in the year.

Across the top of the pebbles was a thick concrete wall, wartime relic of the passing activity which had touched upon this lonely spot.

This was not the Morfa Bychan which he remembered, and yet it was a place of great peace.

Eben walked across to the stone mound which had once been the house, and put the flagon of cider upright in the cool water of the little stream. Then he covered it with fern. Already it was a very hot day. He came back then to where there was still a small area of grass, took off his jacket and walked to the top of the pebbles to look down on to the beach.

Merry had changed into a two-piece bathing costume and was throwing the ball to Boyser to pursue and return and pursue again. For a little while he stood gazing at the clean-limbed loveliness of her figure, and then she looked up and saw him and she spoke to Boyser and pointed up to where he was standing. As Eben came down across the pebbles Merry put on a wrap-over skirt made of towelling and stood looking up at him. As he jumped down on to the sands, she opened her arms to him and he swept her into his embrace.

She said, 'As I was saying when I was so rudely interrupted, there isn't a living soul in sight. But somebody said that time was of the essence.'

'It isn't any longer.'

'Oh! Does that mean you're going to start courting seriously fairly soon?'

'As of now. And there's a question I want to ask you.'

'Very important?'

'Yes, very. And it's serious.'

Merry looked at him. 'D'you know, I think you are.'

'I am.'

'What is it, my love?'

Eben said, 'It's something we've joked about a good bit. Between ourselves and in company. And now I want to ask you, Merry. Will you marry me?'

She looked at him wide-eyed. 'But, Mr Harter,' she said, 'this is so sudden!'

'I'm serious, Merry.'

'Why do you want to marry me?'

'Because I love you. I was a fool not to have known it long ago, but now that I've found you I can't bear the thought of life without you.'

'Well, that's one very good reason, and it's the sort of thing a girl likes to hear.'

'So what's your answer?'

She looked into his eyes for a long time.

'Can't you remember?' she said. 'Didn't I tell you that I hoped if I played my cards right I might be lucky enough to get such a proposal, and that I would, of course, wait just a little while before giving my answer?'

'How long?'

'I believe in former days it was customary to allow a period of some weeks to elapse. But, of course, we're living in changed and changing times. Would tomorrow do? By breakfast time, say?'

'As long as it's the right answer.'

'Don't you remember then, what I said about wild horses and roaring lions?'

He held her very close.

'Eben,' she said, 'there's still not a living soul in sight.' Then he kissed her.

They climbed the pebbles with the heavy basket and other

belongings and came out upon the grass sward.

'So this is Morfa Bychan,' she said.

'What d'you think of it?'

'It's out of this world.'

'Years ago there was a very famous old stonemason and sculptor lived here. He was a good musician, too. Played the bass viol and composed his own ballads. There's a picture of him and his wife, Jenny, somewhere. Spun her own wool. Made her own bread. Examples of his marvellous scroll-work are in the churchyards all round here. Tom Morris his name was. Gramfer Jenkyn knew him well.'

Eben had been prepared for the magic of his boyhood to be beyond recapture, but this day with Merry he was to know a joy and deep satisfaction he had never known before in all his life. He scarcely every thought of Penny now, but he was glad he had not followed his impulse, that disastrous day of the boating expedition, to sail on to this little paradise. For now it could be something that he had shared only with Merry, and it remained in his thoughts like Merry herself, as clean and unsullied, and marvellously tranquil.

But on this occasion he knew too that it was because of what Aunty Becca had said, about 'the one who is there', and the day had been so completely satisfying because he and Merry had been able to talk about ordinary things, and things which concerned them personally, and had all the time in the world in which to do it.

When Merry had been at Deerfield, they had had many long talks together so that they knew much about each other's attitudes and thoughts concerning many things. But their relationship had not been then what it was now.

When they had bathed, Eben dried himself and changed, and came in his shirt-sleeves to where Merry sat, looking down on the beach, combing her hair. He sat beside her and, picking up her hair-brush, began to brush her hair, which had tumbled down over her shoulders.

'That's nice,' she said.

Already it was beginning to dry in the warm sun and the waves were coming back into it. Presently he put down the brush and kissed her hair where it fell over her neck.

'You have beautiful hair,' he said.

'Eben. Methinks ar't gentleman very courteous and over gallant.'

'How so?'

'Dids't not see any grey hairs?'

'Just one or two.'

'Only one or two?'

'Perhaps three.'

'Or four. Or more. Yet said no word?'

'Why should I?'

'Thinkest not it is full time for maid to marry when she is thus old and has received proposal very honourable?'

'High time.'

'Then thinkest not 'twould perhaps be somewhat foolish venture at such far advanced age? 'Tis very old for maid has never loved before. Methinks such maid is maid no more but rather – old spinster?'

'Never spinster, my love. Say rather, unclaimed jewel.'

'But old. You would say old?'

'Not so old that she may not bear several children.'

Merry dropped her air of levity and looked at him. She said, 'Is that what you were thinking when you were looking at me with little Giles and Nel?'

'You know it was.'

She pressed her head close to him. 'Oh, please God,' she said, ' 'twould make me marvellously happy.'

For a long time, as she lay with her head against him, neither of them spoke until, at last, Merry looked at him and said, 'Eben. About this proposal of marriage you've made to me.'

'What about it?'

'Well supposing. Just supposing now. No more. Only supposing. Supposing I decided to accept it. What then?'

'You'd make me very happy.'

'Yes, but about the wedding, I mean. What sort of wedding would you want us to have?'

'Whatever sort of wedding you'd like yourself.'

'I love white weddings, of course. For younger people. But I can't really see that I have to advertise the fact that I've never been with a man or am pure or whatever it is it's supposed to mean.'

'Then what sort of wedding do you want?'

'Not too big. Just our own special friends. In my own church, of course.'

A thought seemed to come to her and she smiled. 'That will be nice, won't it? Benjie and you being married in the same church.'

Eben was looking at her.

She said, 'What's the matter, sweetheart?'

Eben said, 'Are you serious, Merry?'

'Of course I'm serious.'

He took her hand. Very gently, he said, 'We can't be married in your church.'

'Why ever not?'

'Nor any other church.'

'But why?'

He could see the puzzlement on her face. He said, 'Merry, my darling. Aren't you forgetting something?'

'But what?'

'I'm divorced.'

After long moments he could see the tears coming into her eyes.

'Don't take it so badly, my love,' he said.

Merry said, 'I'm thinking of you.'

'I know you are,' Eben said, and in that moment felt again the great fathomless depths of his love for her.

'But it's monstrous, Eben. I was christened there and confirmed there and I've always taken communion there. And I've led a decent life. You know that.'

'Sweetheart,' he said, 'you can be married in church. But I can't.'

'But what have you done that's so wrong?'

'I'm divorced.'

'But what's that to do with it? Everybody knows what a dreadful creature you were married to and what you had to put up with and how many times you forgave her and took her back.'

'But I didn't go on forgiving, did I? I divorced her.'

'And you were quite right. Morally right.'

'Indeed. And society allows this and accepts it. But the Church doesn't. Not for marrying in church anyway.'

'Then why not?'

'Well, can I try and put the Church's point-of-view?'

'How would you know that?'

'I won't say I know it properly. But I read a very interesting article about it some time ago. I meant to keep it but didn't. And I was interested because I'd already started living in hopes about us and could see this problem arising.'

'Before you go any further, Eben. It's no problem.'

'Isn't it?'

'No. If needs be, I'd live with you without any ceremony or bit of paper at all. It's just that I've always tried in life to do what I believe to be the right thing.'

'Do you mean the right thing as a Christian or as a member of society?'

'What's the difference?'

'All the difference in the world, my love. Because we're no longer a Christian society. Oh, yes, I know. Some people go to church and chapel, and some try to live what they believe to be Christian lives, and some don't bother at all. But it's when you come up against somebody like Rebecca that you begin to realize how far some of us are from what Christianity really is.'

Merry said, 'I loved Rebecca and she was dead keen for us to get married. Did you talk to her at all about this divorce business?'

Eben smiled. 'She sure knew her Bible. She quoted the Gospel according to Matthew, where Jesus said it was permissible for a man to divorce his wife when she had committed adultery.'

'So what about the Church?'

'They stand by the Gospels according to Mark and Luke. There's also another interesting bit in Paul's Letter to the Corinthians. The only thing is he keeps his options open and is about as ambiguous as a politician.'

'And what do Mark and Luke say?'

Eben thought for a while. Then he said, 'It's a big subject, Merry. And it isn't for me to say the Church is wrong. You see, marriage isn't a contract, like the bit of paper you mentioned just now. It's a sacrament. The Church's argument is that Christianity is about love, which it is. Love of people for one another. Love of mankind. A possessive love will die if it's not reciprocated, and in dying it turns to hatred. Which is why Penny grew to hate me. I had never loved her, and her so-called love for me was purely possessive. Probably because she hated the thought of somebody else having me. God knows why. But don't let's talk about that. Where love is creative, it isn't bartered or traded. It's concerned with the welfare of the one who is loved. And a vow of such love, as in the marriage service, can only be assured of fulfilment when it is an immortal love, on this sort of basis. Are you still with me?'

Merry was gazing out to sea. She said, 'I'm trying to follow it, sweetheart, but it sounds terribly deep to me.'

'You studied philosophy, didn't you?'

'Perhaps I wasn't very good at it. Which is why I've made up my mind to be a simple, country girl.'

'Well, there it is for what it's worth. Moses forbade adultery but permitted divorce. Jesus came along, however, and taught such love that adultery would not even be contemplated. And such love that where the partner committed adultery there would be forgiveness every time. Seven times seventy, I think it was. And he laid it right on the line that "those whom God had joined let no man put asunder".'

'Eben,' Merry said, 'it's just struck me. Mark and Rachel could get married in church, couldn't they?'

Eben thought for a few moments. 'I suppose they could.'

'Oh, yes. Mark's a widower and Rachel has never been married. But we know how they committed adultery.'

'Well, there's the Church's ruling for you. And if you're a member of a club you abide by the club's rules.'

'Stuff the club. I'm putting my money on Rebecca. We'll get married in chapel. If they'll have us.'

'They'll have us all right.'

Merry smiled wistfully. 'Shall we grow a patch of onions when we get married?'

Eben looked at her. 'Did you say onions?'

'Yes, onions.'

'I thought for a moment you said onions.'

'It was onions sorted out my thinking for me. As part of a report we were preparing when I was in Paris, I had to go to Brittany for a week or so, and I saw something of the Johnny Onion men. I suppose they used to call in this part of the world?'

Eben smiled. 'Oh, yes. The same little man used to call every year at Heronsmill, pushing his bike loaded with hanks of onions. We always had plenty of onions, but my mother always bought some from him just the same, and gave him a cup of tea and something to eat. He'd been calling at Herons-mill for more than forty years. When he called the year after she died I remember him taking off his funny little flat cap and holding it to his chest and the tears coming to his eyes. Aunty Becca bought a hank from him and fed him, the same as Mam had always done, but he never called again.'

'Yes, well, I saw how hard they had to work with their families growing these beautiful onions. Then the man would set off from Roscoff, the little port near where they were grown, and he'd be over here for four months of the year dragging around selling them. Straight from the grower to the housewife. Now, of course, my training as an economist told me that all this humping around by hand must be wrong. Yet, from what I knew of farming, I knew they couldn't hope to do any better if they were to let the trade do the selling. And then I saw the real lesson of it all, which wasn't the reason for which I'd gone there. Life isn't about onions or economics or markets or profit margins. It's about people.

'So where the economist in me said their way of life was nonsense, my love of the land and my interest in people told me they had something. And I'll tell you what they had. An appreciation of each other. My French was good enough for me to be able to talk to one of the wives, and I knew what she was trying to say when she said that, when her man came back at the end of four months, his family knew what he meant to them, and he knew what they meant to him. I'd known for so long what you meant to me and I suddenly wondered could I possibly mean as much to you. It was a pretty shattering thought.'

'Inspired by onions.'

'Inspired by onions. The day after I came back I handed in my notice. I was afraid, as I told you at Benjie's wedding, that you might have seen difficulties otherwise, and I couldn't take any chances.'

He took her to him and lowered her back on to the grass sward. It was very warm.

For a long time he kissed her. He kissed her eyes and hair and she clung to him, and he longed to possess her and to be one with all her yielding softness. The top button of her blouse was undone and he pressed his lips against her smooth white flesh.

At last she took his hair into her hands and pushed his head away.

'Eben, my darling,' she whispered, 'we must go.'

'Must we?'

He gazed into her eyes for a long time and was almost frightened at the intensity of what he saw there.

'You know we must, Eben.'

'Maybe so,' he said, and kissed her once again, very tenderly.

As she put up her hair it took her a little while to regain her composure. Eben was packing the basket and Boyser had his ball and was looking as though he would be willing to start another game.

'Eben,' Merry said at last. 'Are you hungry?'

'Very. What would you fancy?'

'What can you offer?'

'Ham and eggs. Ham, thick cut that is, and grilled. Two eggs maybe. A few mushrooms and fried tomatoes. Then gooseberry tart and custard. Or cream if you prefer. Then, as a finisher, home-baked bread, farm butter and strawberry jam.'

'Oh, Eben, don't! Just tell me where?'

'I said we'd be there about half-past seven.'

'But where?'

'Would you be any wiser if I told you?'

'No, I wouldn't. But is it a fact?'

'Irrefutable.'

They were ready to go. Merry put her arms round him and for a long time looked up at him.

'Eben,' she said. 'Thank you so very much.'

'What for?'

'For being strong when I was weak.'

He kissed her on the cheek and said, 'I'm still waiting for an answer to my question.'

'By tomorrow morning, my darling. In writing. So it will be quite official. All very proper and legally binding.'

She smiled mischievously. 'Supposing,' she said, 'just supposing, that's all. Supposing I decide to accept, and you're satisfied in the morning when I give you my written acceptance with certain clauses and safeguards written into it, I suppose you would buy me an engagement ring?'

'Of course, my love. And talking of rings, I notice you're not wearing your ring these days.'

'No. I told you that I was hoping some exciting sort of man would be buying me a proper engagement ring.'

'What d'you call exciting?'

'Oh, quiet sometimes. But very intelligent and well-read, immensely strong, handsome above a bit and completely trustworthy and reliable. And when he kisses a girl who's never been kissed in her life before, then – wham! Wouldn't you call that exciting?'

'And what sort of ring do you want me to buy you?'

'How much do you intend to pay?'

'I've no idea. What do you suggest?'

'You can get a very nice ring for about sixty pounds.'

'Would that be all right?'

'But I haven't finished yet. I was going to say I've seen a ring which I love but it's much too dear. And if you'd let me pay half it would be different.'

'How much is it?'

'Far too much.'

'Well how much is that?'

'Unless you'll let me pay half I wouldn't dream of it.'

'Oh, come on, Merry. Stop messing about and tell me.'

'Well, it's a lovely ring. But it's far too dear for what it is. It's a hundred and twenty pounds.'

'Then, seeing that you're the economist, can you explain to me why it's too much for what it is, unless you happen to be paying half, and in that case it would be perfect?'

'Oh, Eben, you make me feel like a cheap little gold-digger.'

'Tell me about the ring then.'

'No.'

'Look, Merry, If you're willing to tell me about it I'll be willing to look at it with you and discuss the financial side of it. Where is it?'

'In Tenby. In a rather nice shop called Simpson's.'

Eben laughed, 'Ha, ha. Old Theo.'

'He told me he knew you.'

'Years ago my father bought a piano off his grandfather in Narberth. Theo was named after him, I think. But Theo's father went over from music to jewellery and clocks and then moved down to Tenby and Theo carried on after him. He played a bit for Tenby the same time as I did.'

'So he told me. Then his wife and I got to talking and it came out I was staying with you and eventually he asked could he detect romance in the air and I said that would depend on how good a detective he was. So he said to tell you he hoped you would remember to support an old friend when it came time to buy an engagement ring and then he showed me some. And, of course, I went over the moon about the one I told you about.'

'You haven't told me about it yet.'

'It's an emerald. Odd, because I've always preferred diamonds. A nice single stone, you know. But this is a beautiful, square-cut emerald with baguette diamond shoulders. It's a little bit too small for me but we can have it altered. And you've promised to let me pay half.'

'No indeed I haven't. I said I'd be willing to discuss the financial side of it.'

'Well, what does that mean?'

'I thought that as an economist you could advise me whether I should pay for it out of current account, personal account, petty cash from the jug on the dresser, mortgage the house, realize on capital, draw it out of the post office, have it on the never-never . . .'

'Oh, Eben,' said Merry suddenly.

'What is it, pet?'

'We're so lucky. I was thinking about Mark and Rachel.'

Eben looked startled. 'What's the matter with them?'

'Rachel's told me she doesn't think she can marry him.'

'Why not?'

'She wants to do the right thing by Tommy, and she thinks she has hurt him enough already by bringing him into the world under such circumstances. She thinks it would only add to his problems if she married Mark, because one day he would find out that she is his mother after all.'

'Does that make any sense to you?'

'Of course not, but women are contrary creatures.' Merry smiled. 'Anyway, it is a bit difficult if Tommy really thinks she's his sister.'

'Heavens! I always thought the only question was whether or not Mark was his father!'

Never, said Merry afterwards, had she eaten such a meal or felt so at peace with the world. It was, however, anything but the end to a perfect day when they arrived back at Heronslake from the Inn to find a message waiting for Merry that her father had collapsed with an internal haemorrhage. Her love for him was such that she returned to London that night.

Eben drove Merry to Carmarthen. All too soon, the train was carrying her away into the darkness and he was alone, and lonelier than he had ever been in his life, on the station platform. He drove home slowly, with the window of the car turned down to let in the breeze as he went, for the night was warm. The headlights picked out a hedgehog searching the black-grey surface of the road for life infinitely smaller than itself, and Eben was careful to avoid it. A great moon hung in the sky, and Eben wondered whether Merry would see it from her window, as it shed its soft light across Carmarthen Bay to the Towy estuary, along the shore of which her train was rushing her away from him.

That night, for all his tiredness, Eben lay sleepless far into the small hours, until, with the pale moonlight streaming across his room, a faint sound disturbed him and he was aware of a presence. He reached out to switch on the light, and saw a pair of sad brown eyes looking up at him around the half-open door. Boyser had never come upstairs all the time he had been at Heronslake.

Eben put his hand down by the side of the bed and clicked his fingers. 'All right, boy, I know the feeling. I can't sleep either.'

He picked him up and put him on the bed. Boyser nestled in alongside him. Eventually Eben dozed off.

He called on Mark the next morning to give him the news.

'I'm in a bit of a hurry,' Eben said, 'so first things first and don't let's have any beating about the bush. What's the matter between you and Rachel?'

'I wish I knew, brother. All I know is that she says she can't marry me. I know she wouldn't want to live here, and you can understand that, so I've bought a house in Saundersfoot.'

'That's quick work.'

'Well, I've done it, and I can move in there a month next Saturday. So there 'tis.'

'And what does Rachel say?'

'She still won't marry me.'

'Perhaps I'll have a talk to her.'

'Are you a persuasive sort of bloke in these matters then?'

Eben smiled. 'I've had my moments. I've persuaded Merry to marry me.'

'Well, how blind can a man be! I reckon she'd have taken some persuading *not* to marry thee. But what she can see in thee, I don't know.'

'The other thing,' Eben said, 'is how much can I get for my car?'

'Which one?'

'The Austin.'

'She isn't very old, is she?'

'No, but the other car is newer still. And I don't want two cars.'

'How many miles has your car done?'

'Six thousand.'

'Let's have a look at her.'

Mark walked round Eben's car. He said, 'She's in spotless condition. I'm a bit out of touch at the moment but I reckon she ought to be worth five hundred.'

'Do you think so?'

'Well, I'll give you five hundred for her, and if she's worth more I won't do you.'

'What d'you want her for?'

'Rachel wants to learn to drive and she's willing for me to teach her.'

'So there's hope for us yet then?'

'I don't know, brother. But I'll do my best. Where you off now?'

'Tenby.'

'Well make sure you don't let anybody run into you, and when can I have her?'

'As soon as I come back.'

Eben found a place to park and walked through the town. The streets were not too crowded, but the beaches were packed with people.

That morning he had gone into Merry's bedroom and there, on the dressing-table, amidst so much which made him long for her, he had found her ring and wrapped it carefully in soft tissue-paper to take with him so that they would know the right size.

Theo Simpson and his wife had the shop to themselves when he walked in. This weather was not much good to their trade.

'Now then,' said Eben, 'I hear you've got a ring for me.'

Theo, tall but slightly built in his younger days, had developed something of a paunch. He was a cheerful man. His buxom wife was good-looking and homely. Theo, all smiles, put his hand under the counter and came up with the ring.

'Here we are,' he said, 'we put it to one side, for I said to Dolly there'd be one hell of a row with old Bone-crusher if he came in for it and we'd let it go. But where's the lady?'

'She's had to go home for a couple of weeks. Her father's ill. Oh, it's all right. Nothing too serious, and we'll be getting married as soon as she comes back.'

Dolly was leaning on the counter. 'Tell me, Eben,' she said, 'where did you find a smasher like that?'

'Ah, ha! I mustn't tell you everything.'

'My God, boy, she's for you!' said Theo.

'Caw! I should say. She came in here last week in the morning like this, when there was nobody in, and she was in a devil of a hurry, wasn't she, Theo? Bought two lovely figures and slapped the money on the counter, and no messing. Then, it happened to come out she was staying with you, and Theo said he'd played rugby with you and once she knew that, caw, there was no gettin' rid of her. Not as we wanted to mind. But I said to Theo after she'd gone, she've got it bad. I never seen nobody change their mind so sudden about being in a hurry.'

'And what about this ring, then?'

'Well, we started teasing her a bit see. And Theo said to tell you not to forget your old pals and she took it real serious.

I said to'n after, it was a bit of cheek like really, but she didn't mind a bit and she had a look at this tray of rings and oh, she said, isn't this lovely and we had her trying on rings here, and her and me was laughing like a pair of fools. Listen, Eben, you'll give us a' invite to the wedding, won't you?'

'Aye, aye. We'll do that.'

'The problem is, though,' Theo said, 'it isn't the right size for her.'

Eben took Mary's ring out of his pocket.

'Oh, that's fine. We'll measure him now. Here, have a look at this.' Theo passed Eben the ring.

'It looks very nice to me,' he said. 'Is this emerald flawless?'

Theo looked at Dolly in feigned disgust. Then he looked at Eben and said, 'What the hell are you talking about? Any time anybody shows you a flawless emerald you'll know the bugger's made of glass. The world has never seen a flawless emerald yet.'

'Well, I don't know much about these things.'

Theo laughed. 'You're not half the man your father was. He just said, "I'll have the best in the shop".'

Eben laughed. 'Well, aren't we having the best in the shop then?'

'Aye, aye,' Theo said. 'Unless you reckon the one in the window. There's a ring for you, mate. Have a look at that.'

Theo went to the window and came back with a large velvet tray with a diamond ring in the centre in splendid isolation.

'Here, have a look at it,' Theo said reverently.

It was a magnificent, single-stoned blue-white diamond and, even as he took it in his hands, Eben saw it throw out a thousand lights.

'If you want to talk about flawless,' Theo said, 'just look at that now.'

The diamond was beautifully cut, and mounted in a claw setting of exquisitely carved platinum. As he held it away from him he saw all the colours an artist's brush could ever paint dance out in brilliant hue, deep red and blues, greens and mauves and colours to which he knew he would be incapable of putting a name.

'My God,' he said, 'look at that for colours!'

'Aye,' said Theo, 'I can see you're learning fast. We'll make a connoisseur out of you yet. Have you ever seen a yellow quite that shade before?'

Eben turned the ring round in his fingers.

'Can't you see it? Hold it up to the light.'

Eben held the ring up to the light and went on turning it. 'I can't see a yellow,' he said.

'Take it over to the window then.'

He went over to the window and held up the ring and gazed into it for a long time. 'No,' he said, 'I can't see any yellow.'

Theo laughed. 'That's all right then. Any time you see yellow in a diamond you'll know it isn't good enough for the girl you've got.'

'Oh, I see,' Eben said, 'I am learning, aren't I? Did Merry see this?'

'Oh, aye,' said Dolly. 'I said to her to try it on and she said not on your life or she'd bolt through the door with it still on. But she tried'n on in the end and like I said to Theo after, you could tell there was real class about her the way she was looking at it. Where did you find her, boy? Come on, tell us now. She said she was a land girl with you but that's never right, is it? I said to Theo after, she was no land girl with hands like that.'

'Did this ring fit her?' Eben asked.

'Perfect,' said Dolly, 'like if it was made for her.'

'And did she ask how much it was?'

'No,' Theo said, 'she didn't seem to me to be the sort to waste time asking a lot of daft questions. I said to her, 'Don't you reckon this ring would suit you?'

'And what d'you think she said to'n? She's a case, isn't she . . . ! She said a girl would need a real sugar daddy to buy her a ring like that and Theo said couldn't she find a sugar daddy somewhere and she said, "Oh, no," she said, 'I'm far too long in the tooth for that".'

'How much is this ring?'

'You're joking,' said Theo.

'No, I'm not.'

'You're serious?'

'Yes, indeed I am.'

'Do you mean, how much to you, or how much it ought to be?'

'Both.'

'Well, look here,' Theo said. 'I'll tell you what this ring is. You know we had a special "do" here in the spring when we opened this new extension? We had this on display as an exhibition piece. And by God it's attracted some customers. You'd see 'em walk past and then they'd stop and come back and look at it, wouldn't they, Dolly?'

'But they didn't offer to buy it,' Eben said.

'Shall I tell you something?' Theo said. 'You're the first one to ask the price since we had it, apart from those who just wanted to know, and we'd say it wasn't for sale and tell 'em some daft bloody story according to how we felt and how daft they looked. But once they were in the shop it's surprising how many of 'em bought something before they went out.'

'And how much is it?' Eben said.

Theo took a gold propelling pencil from his pocket and did some figuring on a pad.

'It ought to be seven hundred and something,' he said, 'and if you bought it in London in Bond Street, God only knows what it would cost you.'

He looked at Dolly. Then he said, 'As it's you, and it's been worth it to us, I'll cut it right to the very limit and all we'll have had out of it is the prestige and interest it's created. You can have it for five hundred and eighty quid.'

Well, Eben thought, it was against the principles his father had instilled into him about breaking into savings or capital for such a purchase. But even a lady economist couldn't argue that his car was really capital, and even if she did he'd find an answer for her, like diamonds not depreciating like motor cars.

'I haven't got my cheque book with me,' he said, 'but there's a hundred and twenty in cash I brought with me to pay for this other trinket. You're sure she'll like this, are you?'

'If she doesn't, bring it back and have the emerald. And don't bother about the cheque for the balance until you know what her reaction is.'

Eben insured the ring that afternoon, and sent it straight off to Merry. With it there was a short note:

> With all my undying love to you, sweetheart. I'm afraid this isn't quite what you wanted, but the emerald ring wasn't the right size and there was a flaw in the stone anyway.

He called at Light-a-Pipe on his way back from the post office. Rachel was weeding the flower border in front of the house. Eben thought she looked less cheerful than usual.

'I've come to collect you,' he said.

'What for?'

'Tommy's rowing the boat now like a veteran, and he wants to take you for a trip around the lake.'

Eben saw the light come back into her eyes.

'All right, then. But I'll have to change.'

'No indeed. You're dressed just right.'

'Well, let me just tell Mother where I'm going and powder my nose.'

Eben took Rachel straight down to the lake and sat on the seat with her. Tommy was out in the boat.

'First of all,' said Eben, 'Tommy didn't even know I was going to fetch you. I've brought you here because I want to talk to you.'

Rachel dropped her eyes. 'About Mark, I suppose.'

'Of course. What's it all about?'

'It isn't about anything.'

'Merry's told me all the nonsense you'd been talking.'

'What d'you mean, nonsense? Did she say it was nonsense?'

'Of course she didn't. It's I'm saying it's nonsense. You know Mark has bought a house in Saundersfoot?'

'Yes, I know.'

'So that there'll be no unpleasant associations or memories for you. What else can he do?'

'There's nothing he can do.' She had put her hands over her face. 'Dear God,' she said, 'I wish I knew myself.'

'Wish you knew what?'

'What to do.'

'All you have to do is marry Mark.'

'I can't. And you know the reason, for Merry's told you.'

'About Tommy, you mean?'

'You do understand, don't you?'

'Of course I understand. It just so happens that it's a load of old rubbish.'

'What d'you mean?'

'I mean you're just being plain stupid. You say you have to think of Tommy. All right. Do you think he likes to have other kids shout "bastard" after him? Do you think he enjoys not having a father?'

'But you don't understand.'

'Don't I? How old were you when you first knew about the facts of life, as they say?'

'I don't know,' she said. 'About ten or eleven, I suppose.'

'And how did you find out?'

'Oh, picking a bit up here and there. Hearing older children talking.'

'Exactly. And that was before the war. Tommy is now gone twelve and children are even more knowledgeable these days than they were when you were in school. So I hope you won't be too shocked when I tell you that Tommy knows you're his mother and that Mark is his father.'

Rachel was looking at him wide-eyed. She said, 'You mean he really thinks . . .'

'He doesn't think anything, Rachel. He knows. He told me he knows. And if he ever should happen to come across the truth, the chances are he'll love you even more, the same as we do.'

Almost in a whisper, she said, 'What else did he tell you?'

'He asked me, didn't I think you were very pretty, and he said he hopes you'll marry Mark and then the other kids won't be able to shout "bastard" after him.'

Half-sobbing and half-laughing, she said, 'Did he really, Eben? Did he say that?'

'Don't ask me,' he said. 'Ask him yourself.'

Merry phoned Eben the day the ring arrived, and a long letter arrived a few days later:

> Diamonds are regarded as an investment, but that's not my idea. The only diamond I have, no money on earth could buy. I'm so happy at the moment that I'm like that story Griff told after Benjie's wedding – remember? Something about the Salvation Army man who has been accepted by the Lord Jesus Christ and was so happy he could jump up and kick a hole in the bloody drum. And Rebecca, bless her, so shocked and taking it in good part all the same . . .

The news of Merry's father was good, but on arrival Merry had found that her mother had broken her wrist. So she was going to have to stay up there a bit longer than they'd hoped.

Mark and Rachel had been married almost immediately, and they had come straight to Heronslake to stay with Eben while they waited to move to Saundersfoot. Tilly finally made her move back to Tenby.

Eben was in the process of selling his business to Hughie Wogan. Several times Merry had mentioned the possibility of starting farming again, and there was talk that Deerfield might be coming back on the market. It was not too far away. Eben did not really want to leave Heronslake, but there would be plenty of time to talk about all these plans with Merry when at last she came home.

Tommy was taking a great delight in coming to Heronslake although he still lived with Rachel's mother.

'We mustn't rush it,' said Mark. 'Once we start a family, she'll come to look after Rachel, and Rachel reckons that once her mother "claps eyes on the babbie", as Billy used to say, that'll be the end of it. She won't be willing to go home. There's a separate living unit in a wing of the house we've bought and that'll suit her down to the ground.'

'How is Tommy taking to it, d'you think?' –

'Oh, my dear man, he can't wait. If anything, it was his idea. And now he reckons that when he goes back to school next term and they have to start on a new woodwork project he's going to make an oak rocking cradle. So that's planning ahead if you like.'

Eben was not too sure that Tommy would be either with them or in school for very long. He was completely dedicated now to the animals, and Blackie was his pride and joy.

It was odd, he thought sometimes in his many lonely moments, how life had this way of still going on. Families came and went and somewhere, if people could find it, there was this thread running back through the years over countless ages since time began. Gramfer Jenkyn, now. Where had he come from, and his people in the north of the county, unknown at Heronsmill and long since forgotten. Griff had been named after him, yet had died and left no children. But Eben's own mother, Gramfer's daughter, had become the hub of a deep, religious faith which had held two families together. Right here, at the very root, they had allowed that faith to fade and languish. But, although Griff had left no children, his sister Hannah's Rebecca had come joyfully home from a far land, with her bright spiritual beliefs shining.

Apart from Mark, he had not seen so very much of his own family, yet it was his sister's boy, Owen, who had brought a Blackie back into his life – and that tied up again with Morfa Bychan, and with Rebecca's father, and now with Merry.

Then there was Griff's brother, Josh, who had gone even further away than Hannah had with Mam's written quotation from the book of Joshua in her Bible. And it was not only Rebecca who had kept the faith burning, for Josh's son, Abel, had come back to them from a much more distant land than Rebecca, right here to the very heart of where it had all started and, in his own quiet way, different perhaps from Rebecca's, but seemingly just as effectively, had touched upon a spiritual chord within Megan who meant a great deal to them, including Merry, whom he loved so deeply.

And Griff had hoped that if Eben and Merry were blessed with a boy they would perhaps name him Griffith. Then, of course, Merry would be part of the thread running through

Griff right back to Gramfer Jenkyn Griffiths, and you could go on and on thinking like this and still keep coming back to Merry. Oh, dear God, how he longed for her.

August gave way to September, warm and pleasant, but with a hint already of the autumn colours to come. All his life it had been spring that had filled him with new hope. Yet it was in the autumn he had walked with Merry in the Lower Level wood. And it was now, on the threshold of another autumn, that she was coming back to him, and no spring in all his life had ever held more promise than this.

Another long letter came from Merry at last. In with it was a short note which had obviously been put in at the last moment:

> My Dearest Love,
>   In terrible haste for you to get this at the earliest possible moment.
>   All being well I shall be leaving Paddington on Thursday morning on the nine o'clock train, and you can check what time that reaches Kilgetty.
>
> My undying love,
Merry.

Eben looked at the date on the letter again. What did she mean by next Thursday? He looked at the postmark, and saw that the envelope had been stamped on the back as well. Then he looked at the date. The letter had been posted the previous Thursday and he should have had it on the Friday, or certainly the Saturday.

'Good God, Rachel,' he shouted, 'she's coming tomorrow!'

'What's the matter, then? Don't you want her to come?

'But I should have had this letter *last week*! Damn it all, when Billy Thank-you-Ta was walking the round he had 'em here on time and could very nearly tell you what was in 'em. Now they've got this motorized delivery and nationalized railways and you're lucky if you get 'em at all.'

After a few hectic hours, Mark came home and said, 'I've never seen anyone like you in all my life. You've been dragging about here for weeks now, all come-day go-day God-send-Sunday, and then all of a sudden because you get a bit of a letter you're chasing about like a bloody blue-arsed fly!'

'Oh, Mark!' Rachel said, 'I'll write and tell Rebecca!'

'Aye, that's right.' He put his arm round her. 'And whilst you're at it, ask her what shall we call the baby?'

'Hush, Mark!' she said. She was blushing furiously. 'I've

told you it's too soon to be sure yet.'

Eben was staring at him.

'What are you looking at me like that for?' said Mark. 'We've been married nearly seven weeks, haven't we? What d'you think we've been doing since then? And why don't you give the girl a kiss, now that I've told you?'

As Eben waited on Kilgetty station, a life-time of thought went through his mind. By the time he had got everything done he was late getting there. As he thought. Well, looking at his watch, he was later than he had intended to be. But he still had an eternity stretching before him before the train was due.

Finally he persuaded the porter to phone Whitland. Yes, the train was on time and had left Whitland. Then he phoned again and yes, she had left Narberth. The porter was expecting a basket of homing pigeons down from Llanelly.

They heard two pings on the bell and the porter said, 'There she is, then. She've left Templeton.'

How long he waited after that in the warm September sun Eben did not know. It was bound to be only a few minutes but amongst so many other thoughts he had time to remember Hannah going off from here when she had been married, and it was a sad parting. It was sad, too, when Merry had gone away from Deerfield, but now she was coming back to be married.

Her luggage, how much of it he could not quite think, had come that morning addressed 'Merrial Singleton, c/o Mr Eben Harter, Heronslake.' Yes, he would take care of her. She wouldn't have sent her luggage if she hadn't been coming.

There was no smoke as the driver shut off steam and the engine came down round the bend and coasted down the slope. They reckoned they would all be replaced by diesels eventually. He was suddenly foolishly glad that Merry was coming in on the same sort of train that had taken Hannah away. The same sort that had taken Merry away too. And now she was coming back again. For ever. To be his. And his heart was beating wildly. And the great engine had rumbled by, and the carriages had clanked and rattled to a standstill, and there was no sign of Merry. Only the guard's van.

Then he turned, and there she was, down at the other end of the platform with just one case and some brown paper parcels. Probably presents for Owen's children or goodness knew what, because that was Merry.

302

For the rest of his life he would never know whether he had run down the platform or walked, or what had happened. But he knew that she was in his arms and, laughing, had tried to flash her ring at him before he had smothered her.

By the time they had become conscious of their surroundings the train had pulled out of the station and was rounding the bend for Saundersfoot. Along the platform the porter was loosening the fasteners of a wicker basket.

'We'd better watch this,' Eben said.

'What's he doing?'

Eben told her.

The porter was checking the time by a large pocket watch and entering something in a book with the stub of a carpenter's pencil.

As they watched, he lifted the lid and, with a flurry of feathers, the birds took to the air. Three times they circled the station, climbing to a great height as they went, to settle their sense of direction, and then the leader, with that instinct which had come down to him with all the certainty of his kind since Noah had sent them out over the floods, pointed the way that they should go. Like an arrow he pointed, straight and true, and, as one, they set off for the east.

Merry watched them go.

'That's how I feel,' she said. 'Released at last and going home.'

'You are home, my love,' said Eben and picked up her case.

Merry put her hand in his and they walked along the platform to where Boyser, going wild with impatience and excitement, was waiting in the car.

NEL BESTSELLERS

T045 528	THE STAND	*Stephen King*	£1.75
T046 133	HOW GREEN WAS MY VALLEY	*Richard Llewellyn*	£1.00
T039 560	I BOUGHT A MOUNTAIN	*Thomas Firbank*	95p
T033 988	IN THE TEETH OF THE EVIDENCE	*Dorothy L. Sayers*	90p
T038 149	THE CARPETBAGGERS	*Harold Robbins*	£1.50
T041 719	HOW TO LIVE WITH A NEUROTIC DOG	*Stephen Baker*	75p
T040 925	THE PRIZE	*Irving Wallace*	£1.65
T034 755	THE CITADEL	*A. J. Cronin*	£1.10
T042 189	STRANGER IN A STRANGE LAND	*Robert Heinlein*	£1.25
T037 053	79 PARK AVENUE	*Harold Robbins*	£1.25
T042 308	DUNE	*Frank Herbert*	£1.50
T045 137	THE MOON IS A HARSH MISTRESS	*Robert Heinlein*	£1.25
T040 933	THE SEVEN MINUTES	*Irving Wallace*	£1.50
T038 130	THE INHERITORS	*Harold Robbins*	£1.25
T035 689	RICH MAN, POOR MAN	*Irwin Shaw*	£1.50
T043 991	EDGE 34: A RIDE IN THE SUN	*George G. Gilman*	75p
T037 541	DEVIL'S GUARD	*Robert Elford*	£1.25
T042 774	THE RATS	*James Herbert*	80p
T042 340	CARRIE	*Stephen King*	80p
T042 782	THE FOG	*James Herbert*	90p
T033 740	THE MIXED BLESSING	*Helen Van Slyke*	£1.25
T038 629	THIN AIR	*Simpson & Burger*	95p
T038 602	THE APOCALYPSE	*Jeffrey Konvitz*	95p
T046 850	WEB OF EVERYWHERE	*John Brunner*	85p

NEL P.O. BOX 11, FALMOUTH TR10 9EN, CORNWALL

Postage charge:

U.K. Customers. Please allow 30p for the first book plus 15p per copy for each additional book ordered to a maximum charge of £1.29 to cover the cost of postage and packing, in addition to cover price.

B.F.P.O. & Eire. Please allow 30p for the first book plus 15p per copy for the next 8 books, thereafter 6p per book, in addition to cover price.

Overseas Customers. Please allow 50p for the first book plus 15p per copy for each additional book, in addition to cover price.

Please send cheque or postal order (no currency).

Name...

Address...

....

Title...

While every effort is made to keep prices steady, it is sometimes necessary to increase prices at short notice. New English Library reserve the right to show on covers and charge new retail prices which may differ from those advertised in the text or elsewhere. (3)